Praise for Sean Flannery— A Master of Intrigue and Suspense

MOSCOW CROSSING

"A satisfying number of twists, double deals, false leads and victims of untimely deaths . . . a blazing finale!"
—*New York Daily News*

"Authentic." —*The New York Times*

GULAG

"Highly reminiscent of *Gorky Park* yet the denouement of this novel is trickier and more exciting!" —*Rave Reviews*

"A whip-like story full of fascinating local color, clever—even deadly—political maneuverings and characters whose fate the reader cares about." —*Publishers Weekly*

"A fine spy yarn!" —*Chicago Sun-Times*

FALSE PROPHETS

"An elaborate . . . exciting spy novel!"
—*Publishers Weekly*

"A staple of that genre." —John D. MacDonald

BROKEN IDOLS

"A cracking good thriller!"
—Alfred Coppel, author of *The Apocalypse Brigade*

. non-stop suspense!"
—*The Denver Post*

CROSSED SWORDS

SEAN FLANNERY

JOVE BOOKS, NEW YORK

CROSSED SWORDS

A Jove Book / published by arrangement with
the author

PRINTING HISTORY
Jove edition / June 1989

ISBN: 0-515-10007-2

Jove Books are published by The Berkley Publishing Group,
200 Madison Avenue, New York, New York 10016.
The name "JOVE" and the "J" logo
are trademarks belonging to Jove Publications, Inc.

PRINTED IN THE UNITED STATES OF AMERICA

10 9 8 7 6 5 4 3 2 1

This novel is for Ray Peuchner;
somehow I think he knows why.

When to the sessions of sweet silent thought
I summon up remembrance of things past,
I sigh the lack of many a thing I sought,
And with old woes new wail my dear times' waste.
But if the while I think on thee, dear friend,
All losses are restored and sorrows end.

—Shakespeare
Sonnet 30

To life! To life!
After a summer of dreams and hopes,
All that remained were the winter songs
Of an old, old man.

—Anonymous

CROSSED SWORDS

1

Wallace Iver Mahoney was nearing seventy when on a chill winter's evening he arrived at West Berlin's Tegel Airport and took a cab to an old resort hotel on the Grosser Wannsee in the Grunewald Forest. The big pile of brick and wooden beams, which dated back from before the First World War, had variously housed royalty of the Prussian, Nazi, and American variety until it had been converted into a tourist hotel in the fifties. In stature Mahoney was an unremarkable man: five feet ten at 210 pounds. His hair was still thick, but absolutely white. Here is a man of great intelligence, one might have guessed by looking into his clear blue eyes. Here is a man who has been places, has seen things, a man who has suffered, as indeed he had. It had taken him a full forty-eight hours to reach Germany from his home in northern Minnesota, traveling under a number of different passports and taking extreme care with his tradecraft. He would be followed, of course. But all he wanted was another forty-eight hours. It was all he could hope for, given the extraordinary circumstances of his recall from retirement. A light snow was falling, wavelets lapped at the old dock just down the hill, and tall pine trees creaked in the slight wind. Mahoney supposed the hotel would be all but deserted because of the season. The downstairs was lit, but the upper floors were mostly in darkness. Only two automobiles and a dilapidated Volkswagen van were parked in front. He carried his single leather suitcase across the broad veranda and entered the hotel lobby, stopping just inside, a flood of memories coming back to him. It had been more than forty years since he'd last been here, but the place was exactly as he remembered it. An ornate chandelier hung over the grand staircase straight ahead. An archway led to a small bar to the right. A narrow registration desk was to the left. A big, open fireplace dominated the lobby, birch logs burning on the hearth. The outlines of a swastika that had been chiseled off the wall were clearly visible.

1

"Herr Greenleaf, is it?" a middle-aged man said, rising from behind the counter. He had a book in hand. "We've been expecting you, mein Herr."

"Good evening," Mahoney said, approaching the counter and putting down his bag. "My friend is already in residence?"

"Yes, of course. He arrived early this afternoon and asked for you. Shall I ring his room and inform him that you are here safe and sound at last?"

Mahoney might not have heard the question. He signed the registration book as Horace Greenleaf, which was a name out of his past. The only other guest to check in this day was C. A. Nostrand. In 204. "You have a front room for me as well?"

The clerk was tall, almost patrician, with flowing mustaches. Too young to have been an officer in the war, but his father might have been SS. A lot of otherwise good men in Germany had been held to menial jobs because of the taint of association.

"You will be in Two-oh-five. Adjoining rooms." He made a notation in the registration book, then turned and took a key from its pigeonhole. "No messages other than Herr Nostrand's."

"Any other guests here for the weekend, then?" Mahoney asked.

The clerk shrugged. "You know how it is at this time of the year. The Shumanns on the third floor. A second honeymoon. Albert Hauptman down the hall from them. He comes this time each year. We'll fill up for *Fasching* again, but then that's still weeks away." He smiled. "Not like the old days, Herr Green-leaf."

"No."

"So much tension," the clerk said. A name tag on his striped waistcoat read REUGER. "But then you are here for a rest, I think. Perhaps to relive some old times with a good friend. Herr Nostrand has spoken highly of you. Very highly indeed."

"That was very kind of him," Mahoney replied absently. He glanced toward the stairs, then across to the open doorway to the bar. "Actually we haven't laid eyes on each other for years. He seems fit?"

"Oh, yes, indeed, Herr Greenleaf. Very fit, as you say. A real gentleman, your Herr Nostrand. English now, is he? Perhaps an old émigré from the war?"

Mahoney was a burdened man. His past, which these days seemed clearer to him in memory than it ever had, was like a heavy weight on his shoulders. At times he felt a nearly over-

2

whelming urge to shrug it off, to run away, to hide his head in the sand. And yet he knew that was impossible.

"From Poland, I think, but I'm not sure. We knew each other from London. In the old days."

"The old days," Reuger repeated gently. "But then you have come to the correct place."

"Yes, I suppose we have," Mahoney said, taking off his overcoat. "Is dinner still being served?"

"Unfortunately not. But if you would wish for something . . . a sandwich, perhaps? To hold you until morning?"

"It's not necessary. But the bar is still open?"

"Yes, of course."

Mahoney stopped a moment to listen. But the hotel was quiet; the only sounds were the crackling of the fire and an occasional gust of wind in the chimney. "You might have my bag taken up, and then have Mr. Nostrand meet me in the bar for a drink."

"I'll see to it myself," the clerk said, coming around the counter. He took Mahoney's bag and coat and headed off toward the stairs, his words trailing after him. "Breakfast begins at six, lunch at noon, and dinner promptly at seven."

Mahoney looked at his watch. It was already ten. "The bar closes when?"

"At midnight, Herr Greenleaf," Reuger called over his shoulder as he started up the stairs, his voice suddenly hollow in the big room. "Unless you wish for later service."

"No," Mahoney said. He walked across the lobby, lingering in the warmth by the fireplace for a moment or two. It was much warmer here in Germany than it was in Minnesota, but as the years passed he was beginning to find that winters everywhere seemed colder than they used to be, and the summers much warmer and more humid. Marge would say that he was giving in to his *notion* of his age. Long before he had reached his fiftieth birthday she'd begun calling him "old man." Affectionately, but with a bit of chiding to the moniker. His father, until the very end, had never given in to his age. Not until the war, when he was too old for service and had to watch his only son go off to Europe. He'd been fond of saying that when there was snow—meaning white hair—on the roof, there must be a fire in the furnace. The fire was all but out, though, Mahoney mused. What was left? Cynicism? Regrets? Maybe a lingering fascination for the game?

The bartender came as a slight surprise. She was a youngish, heavyset woman with a mottled red complexion, big puffy cheeks, double chins, and a big bosom. He had expected a man here. Her

3

thick dark hair was done up severely in the back, but her eyes seemed nearly Irish in their brightness. No one else was present in the tiny dark room. Four stools were lined up against the thick, heavily scarred bar, three small tables against the opposite paneled wall. The only light came from behind the bottles.

"Ah, Herr Greenleaf?" she asked pleasantly. He nodded. "Reuger told me we were expecting a late arrival tonight. What would you like?"

"A cognac, please," Mahoney said. "I'm expecting my friend to join me."

"Yes, of course. You have had a pleasant journey, I hope?" She poured from a bottle of Asbach-Urhalt, and brought the drink around to where Mahoney had taken a seat at one of the tables.

"Danke," he said. "It was a long trip."

"Then take care not to remain up too late, Herr Greenleaf," she scolded. "We certainly wouldn't want you to fall ill while you are with us."

"No," Mahoney started to say, but then Chernov was standing in the doorway, and he suddenly lost his voice. He was glad that he was already seated because he hadn't counted on this sort of a reaction. Not this at all. And it frightened him just a little, the intensity of his hate. Chernov came the rest of the way in, ordered a cognac for himself, and then they were shaking hands as if they had parted only last week, as if it had not been years and years, as if nothing had ever happened between them. Two old spies, Mahoney thought, come together to do what? To say what to each other? To go over old ground or new?

"Hello, Wallace," Chernov said softly so that there was no chance of the bartender hearing him. "I assume you managed to make it this far without the tediousness of being followed." His English was British in pronunciation, but sometimes odd in its syntax. He was a large man, imposing in his bulk, with deep-set eyes and a thick, ponderous face. Mahoney thought he hadn't changed very much since they'd last seen each other.

"I've come alone. You?"

"Yes, naturally."

"But it won't last," Mahoney said.

Chernov had a confidence that he fairly exuded. "We have much to say to each other, Wallace. We will make the time." His drink came and he sat down across from Mahoney. Mahoney had brought a pistol. He thought that he should kill the Russian now, yet he wanted to hear what the man had to say. At least that.

4

Seven time zones to the west, John Mahoney, Wallace Mahoney's son, stood on the porch of his father's lake cabin in northern Minnesota watching the sun get lower in the sky, smoke curling lazily up from a chimney across the frozen lake. He had arrived from Washington around noon. The furnace had been turned down and the house closed up as if his father were planning on being gone for some time. Just coming into the cabin, he'd immediately known that their worst fears probably had some basis in reality. Yet watching the line of trees on the distant shore, he had the wild hope that his father would return, or at the very least telephone before it was too late. There had been no messages, nothing on the pad by the telephone, nothing in the trash, nothing in his father's bedroom. But his car was still parked in the garage. It meant he'd probably called a cab all the way out here. They'd find that out later in town, because they already knew that he had gone that way. They'd already found out that he'd taken a flight out of Duluth down to Minneapolis, but then his track had simply disappeared. "It's tradecraft, pure and simple, boyo," Farley Carlisle, the deputy director of Operations, had crowed. "He has no friends in Minneapolis. At least none that we know of. He didn't rent a car. We're assuming that he skipped out under a bogus name." For what reason? Why had he run? To whom had he run? The Russian, Chernov? His father had been the best, bar none, in the business. Even Carlisle would admit to that. Was this an old grudge? Was he out there settling old scores? "Like as not the old fool is running an operation," they'd said. But it would have to be a very special operation. The last time he and his father had talked he'd been saddened by how old his father had become. The years had suddenly caught up with him. John had seen it in his father's eyes, in the set of his shoulders. He'd been winding down. The long slide into darkness.

That was six months ago. This was now. Three days ago the extraordinary message had come through the American embassy in Moscow. Yuri Yevgennevich Chernov had asked for a meeting with Wallace Mahoney. Immediately. No place specified. They'd telephoned Mahoney, of course. "What the hell is going on? Who is Chernov? What is Chernov?" But Mahoney had denied any knowledge. Denied knowing the name. "I'm retired. Let's just keep it that way, Farley." His words. John had heard the tape. But what else had he heard? A quickening in his father's voice? A new purpose? A curiosity? How much could he read into a simple conversation?

A crow was cawing from over the lake, its call hollow in the distance. John spotted it, then watched as it made its way into the forest on the other side. His eyes strayed naturally to the water's edge just down from the cabin where the dock had been dismantled and lay beneath a pile of snow.

Ashes to ashes, dust to dust. In his mind's eye John could see himself standing on the end of the dock, smoking a cigarette. It had been night and he had been watching the stars. He had been trying to calm down, trying to think things out.

He half turned now as he remembered the sudden explosion lighting up the night sky, a huge fireball rising from the cabin, the pressure wave knocking him into the water. His wife and children had been in the cabin. Like now his father was gone. "Elizabeth!" he had cried, pulling himself out of the water, burning embers falling from the sky, the cabin roof collapsing inward, the entire building engulfed in flames. "Elizabeth!" he had cried. The memories came back, tumbling one over the other, as he thought they might if he were ever to come back here.

He went back up to the cabin, looking back once, then went inside where he turned up the heat, took off his coat, and poured himself a large bourbon, busywork to keep his mind occupied, because if he allowed himself he would once again sink into a deep, black pit of despair for everything that he had lost, and for everything that he had become.

John was very much like his father in the strong set of his jaw, in his no-nonsense attitude, in his intelligent eyes. He had started out as a chemical engineer for Monsanto in California what seemed like two lifetimes ago. But after the death of his wife and children he'd been recruited into the CIA. Like his father, then, he had become a spy. Hapless at first, they'd said, but he'd gotten better. He was motivated. He had developed a strong, abiding hatred for Russians that at times made him nearly paranoid. But even that tunnel vision had gradually lessened with his maturing years. Now at forty-three, a touch of gray at his temples, the first hints of a masculine thickening around the waist, he'd nearly become what his father had been at that age: a damned good analyst and sometime fieldman who could almost intuitively see patterns within patterns in any operation. His gift, like his father's, was one of spotting the anomalies, the glitches in the fabric of human relations. The oddities, no matter how subtle, seemed for John to stand out like lumps on an otherwise smooth bedsheet. In another way, too, he was a maverick like his father. But the Agency had put that character trait to good use as well.

They gave him field assignments when he simply could not take Washington any longer.

But now what? He'd been pulled off the Soviet desk to fly out here on a moment's notice. Find your father. Find out where he's gone. Find out what he's up to. You know him better than anyone alive. Not only is he your father, but you've worked with him, you know his methods, his thinking. But you couldn't know another man like that, could you? Not even if he was your own father. The inner recesses of a man's mind were his own; there were things inside of us, instinctive things, that we told no one. Not ever. Sometimes not even ourselves.

He lit a cigarette and leaning back against the counter in the kitchenette gazed across the great room toward the front screened porch. This was all new from the foundations up since the fire. But outwardly nothing had changed. His father had the place rebuilt exactly as it had been. But it was different. The stone in the fireplace might have been laid down on earth a billion years ago, but they were new stones to this place, new mortar, the hands of the masons new. The knotty pine in the walls and ceilings was new. As was the big braided area rug, and the rough, thickly upholstered country furniture. Nor were there any old mementos. All the photographs and dishes and his mother's silver—all that was gone. The physical structure was the same, but since the fire the soul had gone out of the place. Had the same thing happened to his father? Did it happen to all of us sooner or later? John mused.

The telephone rang in the living room by his father's chair. John put down his drink and hurried to it, catching it on the second ring. His father had traveled out to Missoula to the graveyard where three quarters of their family was buried. He had traveled incognito because he didn't want to be followed and bothered. But he knew that a fuss was being made on his account, so he had telephoned his cabin to see who had shown up. "Hello?" John said.

"We've just now arrived at the airport." It was Farley Carlisle himself. "Any word from him?"

"Nothing. What did you expect?"

"Easy now, John. I hope you didn't touch too much. I've brought along a team from Technical Services. They're concerned that you may have ruined something."

"There's nothing here. He's simply gone."

"He may have been seen by someone in New York. It's being checked now."

7

"Where, exactly?"

"JFK. The international terminal," Carlisle said. "Just hang on. We'll be out there in forty-five minutes."

It was nearly dark by the time the two cars came down the driveway. John had spent the last half hour erasing fingerprints, straightening out the cabin, putting it back the way he had found it. There was nothing to be found in any event, so it really didn't matter, his efforts. He merely wanted to avoid a big argument with whoever it was Carlisle had brought along.

He met them at the back door. Carlisle came up on the stoop first. There were three others behind him.

"He hasn't called?" Carlisle asked, his breath white in the frigid air.

"No."

"No messages? Little scraps left behind? Anything like that?"

"Nothing obvious."

"We'll soon see," Carlisle said, coming in, the others right behind him. They each carried a big leather case.

"Dick Cassidy, sir," the tall one said. "This is Bob Fortuna and Perry Nuhn. Technical Services. Sorry about this."

They went immediately into the great room where they looked around like bird dogs assessing a hunting field. They put their cases down.

Cassidy came back to where John and Carlisle were standing. He unbuttoned his overcoat. "Would you go over with me what you touched?"

"Liquor bottle, ashtray in the kitchen, a glass," John said. "I've kept it contained."

Cassidy was a skeptic. It was written all over his face. He also seemed just a little pained at that moment. "I appreciate that, sir." He looked over John's shoulder into the kitchen. "Liquor and glasses were in a cabinet?"

John nodded.

"And you did answer Mr. Carlisle's phone call?"

"Right," John said. "I also used the back door to come in, and I turned on the lights in the hall, the main room, and in the kitchen. Oh, and I turned up the heat."

Cassidy smiled just a little. "The bathroom, sir? Did you take a pee?"

"Not yet."

"Ice cubes out of the fridge for your drink?"

"Took it neat."

8

"Water from the tap?"

"I said neat," John snapped. He felt as if he were starting to unravel. Carlisle was paying close attention. He motioned for Cassidy to get on with it, and the Technical Services expert turned on his heel and went back into the great room where the others had taken off their coats and laid them in a neat pile in the middle of the floor so as not to disturb anything.

"The New York thing may have been a false alarm," Carlisle said. "I don't want us to go off half-cocked." His eyes were dark gray and very bright, but hooded. He took off his coat and hung it on one of the pegs in the back hall. "But you and I both know that he's run off to meet this Chernov for some ungodly reason or another."

"Where?"

"Who knows?" Carlisle said heavily. He took John by the arm and they went around the corner into the kitchenette. "I'll have one of those," he said, spotting the liquor bottle. "With a splash, if you please."

John took down another glass and poured Carlisle a drink, adding a little water from the tap. "Maybe it's nothing, Farley. Maybe it's just a coincidence."

"You turned up the furnace. Means he turned it down. He was planning on a long trip."

"Not a permanent move," John said, handing Carlisle his drink. "Otherwise he would have said the hell with this place."

"Or he wants us to think that. Would have given him a little more time. Does he keep any cash around here, John? Any little caches you know about?"

"I don't know."

"Passports? He must have a few he's not told us about. They all do. At least the good ones do. Gets in their blood."

"I suppose," John said, but he didn't really know for sure, except that he did know that in the old days his father had regularly maintained three or four complete identities—passports, driver's licenses, credit cards, checkbooks, country club memberships, letters, photographs, those sorts of things. But whether or not those papers had been turned in or destroyed when he retired, John had no way of knowing, though he could make a pretty accurate guess.

"You were with him six months ago, John. How'd he look to you then?"

"Tired."

9

"Did he say anything about taking a trip? Just closing up the cabin this winter and taking off, perhaps to warmer climes?"

"Not a word."

"Has he ever taken little trips like this before that you know of?"

"Come on, Farley, for Christ's sake. The man was a spy. He was gone all the time. As a kid I never remember my father at home for more than a few weeks at a time. Between assignments, I suppose."

"He never wanted the desk in those days," Carlisle sighed. He pulled at his drink, made a face, and put the glass down. "Filthy stuff," he mumbled. "Did he mention any friends he might have wanted to see?"

John shook his head. "But you might try Missoula. I thought he might have gone there."

"Where you mother and brother are buried?"

John nodded, his chest heavy. "And Elizabeth and the babies."

"Did he talk about them the last time you were here?" Carlisle asked gently.

"He's always talked about them. He missed my mother."

"A lot more these days?"

"I don't know. He might have. He's an old man. Getting older. They had a long life together."

"She was a good woman," Carlisle said as if from a distance. "In Moscow she was simply terrific."

"He might have gone to Missoula," John said lamely, filling the gap between them.

Carlisle looked up. "Right. Someone is checking it. We had much the same thought. What about this Yuri Chernov? Has your father ever mentioned the name?"

John started to say no, but something at the back of his head, some distant memory, some thought, something mentioned perhaps in passing, years ago, might have been there.

"Yes?" Carlisle asked.

"I don't know, Farley. The name rang a bell when I first heard it off the Moscow query. But I don't know. They're apparently contemporaries."

"Which is about all we're even guessing at," Carlisle said. "Donald thinks there is a Chernov on the KGB's Planning and Foresight Committee. Something of a liaison between the service and the Politburo. If he is the same one who called your father out, he'd be about the same age, and he'd be a hell of a catch. Enough of a catch for your father to go after him, wouldn't you agree?"

"There'd have to be more to it than that," John said, remembering how his father had looked and sounded last summer. There was another connection, he was sure of it. But for the life of him he had no idea what it might be.

He heard a noise from the bedroom. It sounded as if they were prying up the floorboards.

"There's nothing in your father's files about any previous contact with a Chernov," Carlisle said.

"No."

"Yet the message comes calling for a meeting with no designated meeting place. Just 'Come meet with me, Wallace,' and your father disappears. It was either prearranged, or there is a code word in the message. Something we've completely missed. No one can figure it, yet."

"Nothing from Moscow station?"

"Not a thing. They've no more of an idea who Chernov might be than we do."

"The message did originate inside the Soviet Union? They're sure about that?"

"No doubt about it."

"We're watching the Moscow airports?" John asked. He was thinking on four levels at the same time.

"And train depots. But he could be driving up from Leningrad. Chernov, if he is powerful enough, could have arranged something. No way of telling."

"My father is not a traitor," John flared. "I don't give a damn how this looks."

"We'll see, won't we," Carlisle said. "We'll just see."

Farley Carlisle had been his recruiter and then his boss, and still John did not know exactly how he felt about the man. His father hadn't thought much about him. Called him the "piss-ant." Given his time in service, by now he should have been deputy DCI, not simply head of Operations. He was an organization man, though. Never had an original thought in his life, the Agency wags said. And if he ever did, he'd send it around in memo for approval from half the Agency before he would dare to make the suggestion. He'd brought along a team of recruiters, including Tom Morris, the Agency's psychologist. "We'd like you to come work for us," Carlisle had said, stressing the *we*. "Your country needs you. We think you'd make a good agent. Every bit as good as your father."

He had had nothing to lose. His mother was dead, his brother was dead, and his wife and children had been burned to death in an explosion that had been set by the Russians, or someone just as bad, just as conscienceless. He remembered the Farm outside Williamsburg where he had learned everything from hand-to-hand combat, to weapons, to radio and cryptographic communications. He learned about letter drops, tailing—both front and back, passive and active—and he'd breezed through the short course in what they called Geopolitical Goals (the unofficial title of which was Justification for American Interventionism in Every Country in the World). Afterward they had put him on the Soviet desk analyzing reports translated from Russian newspapers and radio broadcasts. In those days he had been blinded by an absolute hatred because of what had happened to his family, so he had not immediately seen Carlisle's true measure. That came later when he worked with his father in Belgium and East Germany. Now, watching Carlisle impatiently follow the progress of Cassidy and the others, he knew that the man was running scared.

"What are you looking for?" he asked.

"We don't know, do we," Carlisle said. "Not until we find it, that is."

"We're going to look like fools when he comes back from Missoula and wants to know what the hell we were thinking of by coming here and tearing his house apart."

"I wouldn't mind turning out to be that sort of a fool, John," Carlisle said, looking him in the eye. "Believe me, I'm not the enemy here."

"Who is?" John snapped.

"Chernov."

"It may have nothing to do with his stupid message. Maybe he was looking for a way out. Maybe he thought my father could help him."

Cassidy and his team had finished in the bedroom. They'd pulled up some of the floorboards, had drilled holes in the walls, and had pulled down part of the ceiling. Carlisle looked in the closet. "Some of his clothing is missing. But not much."

"He never had many clothes."

"He had a black overnight bag, too, as I remember. It's missing."

John looked at him in amazement. "He took a trip, you know that."

"But his other suitcase is here."

"He won't be gone very long, then."

Carlisle closed the closet door. "Or he's traveling light and fast. That's a possibility, too, isn't it?"

"Anything is possible," John said in frustration.

Carlisle managed a tight little grin. "That's the point, isn't it?"

"The point is, he's no longer working for you, he doesn't have to answer to the Company, and he's done nothing illegal."

"So far . . ." Carlisle started to say, when Cassidy, his face flushed in triumph, appeared in the doorway.

"I think you'd better come take a look at this, sir," he said. "In the bathroom."

"What did you find?"

"His hidey-hole."

The toilet had been swiveled aside on its base, revealing a narrow little compartment in the floor. "The tiles around the toilet bowl were just too clean," Cassidy explained. "But we almost missed it."

They'd taken a green plastic fishing tackle box out of the hole. It sat open on the toilet lid. Two plastic bags and a soft cloth lay beside it.

"Gun oil on the rag," Cassidy said. "And I suspect the plastic bags contained his passports and cash. His little escape kit."

"Are you certain?" Carlisle asked, his eyes shining.

"About the gun oil, yes. We'll have to get the bags back to the lab to make certain what they might have contained."

"What kind of a gun does he have these days?" Carlisle asked, turning to John.

"A thirty-eight police special."

"Silencer?"

"I don't think so. He didn't much like guns."

"But he took this one with him," Carlisle said. He shook his head. "Goddamned old fool."

John couldn't tear his eyes away from the gun rag. "Maybe he threw it away. It doesn't mean he has it with him now." He was clutching at straws and he knew it.

"Let me tell you something," Carlisle said sternly. "Your father's tradecraft was, and I'm assuming still is, nothing short of brilliant. But he never in his life used it unless he considered what he was doing at that moment to be of vital importance—and I mean to stress this part most of all—and he felt that he was being followed or watched, or that his life was in danger."

John could see it just as Carlisle was seeing it, and he was sick at heart. The Russian had called and his father had run. With

13

a gun, money, and worknames. Plural. Goddamned old fool, Carlisle was saying again.

Tradecraft, that's what it's about.

John has come back to their Alexandria home on spring break. It is 1967, the war in Vietnam is beginning to turn ugly and John can't help but apologize for the fact that his father is in government service. The fiction is that his father works for the State Department, though in what capacity has always been left vague. Michael suspects nothing, but John thinks he knows the truth. It is evening, his last night home. His father has called him into the study for a nightcap and one of their little chats. John sits in front of the dead fireplace. He is filled with a secret indignation. All week he has been baiting his father about the escalating war to no avail. Mahoney hasn't risen to the bait. He never rises to such provocations. He is steadier than that. It's one of the character traits John so admires about his father. Until now. Under the gun like this he finds suddenly that he is of two minds. On the one hand he loves and respects his father, and in a small measure has a little fear of him. While on the other, John has some deep, very personally held convictions that what the U.S. is doing in Vietnam—and no doubt in Laos and Cambodia—is wrong: wrong morally, wrong politically, and wrong practically. Nothing can shake that conviction. Nothing at all. He means to stretch out college for as long as possible, but if need be he'll burn his draft card and emigrate to Canada. He's not a conscientious objector; he just hates this war. Yet his father is a part of the government. The State Department makes the policy, or at the very least they are the mouthpiece for government policy. Which means his father is one of *them*. . . . How in God's name to reconcile that notion with a four-year college education paid for by his father?

"It's been good having you back, son," Mahoney says. "Your mother especially enjoyed it this time." He pours two brandies and brings them over.

"I needed the break," John replies offhandedly. "There's been a lot of pressure."

"I expect there has been. And then there are your studies," Mahoney says with a little sad smile. He knows what the trouble is.

"It's not very easy at Stanford," John blurts, stupidly, he thinks, even as he says it. But he's a little flustered now that the head-to-head confrontation with his father—a confrontation that he's been angling for all week—is finally here.

"Nothing ever is, son," Mahoney says, sitting back in the big chair. He puts down his drink and goes through the deliberate ritual of lighting one of his big Cuban cigars. The fact that they came from Cuba is another point of irritation for John.

"I mean being the son of a *diplomat*. Someone who works for the *State Department*."

The sarcastic emphasis is not lost on Mahoney. "But I don't work for the State Department, John. Not actually. I thought you knew, or had guessed."

John doesn't quite understand. It's possible that his father is pulling his leg.

"What do you mean?" he says, his drink forgotten, even his college forgotten for just the moment.

"I'm a spy."

"What?" John is dumbfounded. His worst suspicions ever, have just—by his father's own admission—come true. Yet instinctively he feels that there must be something wrong here.

Mahoney has his cigar lit. "I'm a spy, John. My real employer is the Central Intelligence Agency. My State Department position is nothing more than cover. You can understand, of course, why such a fiction is necessary. Especially in this day and age. Actually, I've been with the Agency since the day it was formed—back in the late forties. Seemed like the thing to get into, and I suppose I have no regrets."

Still John is having trouble keeping his head straight.

"You can't be telling me this," he says, the words catching in his throat. "You work for the State Department."

"That's my cover."

"Cover?" John shouts. It's what he's suspected, yet now that his father is making the big admission of guilt, John isn't so sure. It's reverse psychology.

"It's called tradecraft. And I'm going to have to ask you to keep it from your friends at college. Even your closest friends. Wouldn't do either of us much good these days, I suspect."

No, it would not, John thinks then and now as he watches Carlisle and the others in their frenzied search. His father's tradecraft is still the best in the business, bar none.

Mahoney got to his feet and stretched while Chernov paid for their drinks and had a word with the bartender. He was coming down, finally, from his hurried trip. He was tired, and though the hate was still there, its edge had been dulled by actually being here like this. Walking out into the lobby, he once again sought the comforting warmth of the fire. The hotel was very quiet, unlike the other time when he and Chernov had faced each other across a table, just the two of them though the place was packed. But they had eyes only for each other. They were both going places. They knew it of themselves, they could see it in each other, and they both understood that their knowledge was dangerous. They were natural enemies, like the fox and the hare, and they were destined for battle. This place was where the opening salvos had been fired— no, that wasn't right. This was the place where it had all begun, but this was neutral ground. From here they had been able to see the starting gate, but at that point, until they lined up and heard the starter's pistol, they were not in competition. In fact at that time they were still allies, though the Russians had been spying in the U.S., especially on American atomic bomb research, for a number of years. It had seemed only natural to Mahoney to come here to this place when Chernov's message had arrived. It had been summer then; their lives and careers were just getting started. Now it was winter; their lives were nearly over. Yet he did not think Chernov had come back, at some risk, he supposed, merely to reminisce. There was something else. Something he'd seen in the Russian's eyes, in the set of his shoulders, in the timbre of his voice. Chernov was troubled. Perhaps even frightened. There was little doubt of it in Mahoney's mind.

During the long cab ride down from his lake house to the Duluth airport he'd tried to find his justification for coming in response to Chernov's call. His internal traveling orders. His price of admission back into a world he'd spent a lifetime trying to extricate himself from. Chernov was an old man—they both were—and he'd been to and seen a lot of places in his long career. He'd be highly respected now in the Soviet Union for his successes. He'd be privy to things. Old men in the Soviet Union were venerated in a way unknown in America. Chernov would definitely have heard things. Would have seen things. Would know things. And now he was coming out to talk. In Minneapolis, Mahoney had changed identities and had flown immediately to Chicago's O'Hare Airport where under still another identity he had gotten lucky with an Air France flight to Montreal booked nearly solid, so his would simply be another face among several hundred. Anonymous.

A log fell on the hearth, sending a cloud of sparks rising up the chimney. Mahoney felt an urge to lie down and sleep there and then. An old man's plight. There'll be plenty of time for sleeping in just a few years. No need to rush it. Had he come purely with revenge in his heart, revenge disguised by simple curiosity, or some more complex patriotic duty? "We went back a long time together. I knew that he was important, that what he would have to say to me would be worth the risks." A restless night in an airport hotel outside Montreal and the morning flight to Paris under still another identity—his last other than Greenleaf, which he had saved until Germany. The train to Brussels, a flight down to Munich, and finally the short hop to West Berlin's Tegel Airport. His track was clean. He wouldn't be found, or at least they'd never find him by trying to pick up his trail out of the background noise. If they were to reach this point—and Mahoney had no real doubt someone would—they would have to come to it along another route, one of deductive logic.

"Old woes or new," Chernov said, emerging from the bar.

Mahoney turned with a start, just a little guilty that he had been caught drifting. What sort of a silly old man am I, coming here like this? What's done is done. We can't ever bring back the dead.

"I was thinking about the first time we met here."

Chernov smiled indulgently. "Just after the war. We were going to conquer the world, you and I, each in our own way. I don't think either of us realized just how big a place it was."

"Or how ugly."

Chernov shrugged. "That too." He seemed impatient in an odd way. He wanted to get on with it, and yet he did not want to disturb the pace they'd already seemed to set for themselves.

"Have our lives made any difference?"

"Don't become maudlin," Chernov replied. He flicked his right hand as if dismissing a servant.

"But you were a very bad man, Yuri Yevgennevich."

Chernov laughed out loud. Mahoney wanted to reach out and slap him across the face. His own cheeks were suddenly flushed and warm. Chernov was watching him closely.

"Is that why you came here, Wallace? To settle old scores—real or imagined? Did you bring a gun? Do you mean to shoot me? Perhaps you will sneak into my room while I am asleep, place the barrel of your pistol against my temple, and then pull the trigger. A few ounces of pressure, no more, and my life would be ended, your revenge complete."

"There is some comfort in the thought," Mahoney said steadily.

"Save it for later, Wallace. Save your anger, too. We've work to do, you and I—together. Important work. More important than anything we've ever done. Afterward, maybe the bullet wouldn't be such a bad way. I might even be canonized as a hero. My family would benefit. It's Russian life insurance."

17

"What do you want? Why did you come here like this?"

"Why did *you* come here, Wallace? Perhaps that's more to the point."

"To kill you."

Chernov nodded. He'd known it. "It's one of the reasons I asked for you specifically. I knew that you could not help coming here. Nothing would have held you back. But now that we are together I ask only that you hold your bullet until you hear me out."

"I'm listening."

"In the morning we will begin."

"Now," Mahoney insisted, though he didn't know why other than the fact that his anger was beginning to burn brightly again.

Chernov sagged a little, as if the load he was carrying had suddenly gotten too heavy. "Something big is about to happen, Wallace. Very big. Something you and I will have to prevent. But you will have to trust me, and I will have to trust you."

"That's not likely," Mahoney said dryly.

"But very necessary. You say I am a bad man. Well, it is true. But what about you? Is your past so clean? Are you so free of sin? You're going to have to find the answers in your own heart, Wallace. Because without your trust we will have failed. Both of us. Our entire lives."

"Tell me now," Mahoney insisted stubbornly, though already the fight was going out of him.

"You have questions, and I can answer them. All of them."

"With the truth."

Chernov nodded. "In all her splendor, the truth. And in the end you will understand what we must do."

Alone in his room Mahoney tried to stop his hands from shaking. Everything he had done, everything he had worked for in his life seemed to be coming into some kind of focus now. All the heartaches and anguish, all the deaths, all the lies and all the people whose lives had been ruined, the nights in foreign cities, the loneliness, the ugliness, all of it was coming back as a solid whole.

He went to the window and looked down across the snow-covered clearing through the trees toward the lake. Berlin glowed in the night sky to the north. They were surrounded here. A tiny enclave in the middle of East Germany. How had the world changed in the last forty years or so? From the simple to the complex? From the relatively safe to the infinitely more danger-

18

ous? From warm to cold? Is your past so clean? Chernov had asked. He took out a cigar and went through the ritual of lighting it, the flare of the match reflecting back at him from the dark window glass. Either his life had been successful and therefore worthwhile, or it had been an extraordinary waste of time. Did he want to know? Did any of us?

2

The past isn't such an easy thing to reconcile with the present.
What had Chernov come looking for down their separate pasts?
Remembering is a selective process. We tend most easily to forget
the pain, and yet it is through pain that we learn our most valuable
lessons. What lessons here?

It was said that intelligence services tend to attract religious and
altruistic people of high ability. So be it. At least on the Western
side. And the description fit Mahoney. But in the beginning there
were only two people in Mahoney's life who mattered: his father,
Conrad Iver, and his uncle, Fredrick Dean, and both of them were
dead long before he had ever made his mark in the shadow world
of the spy. What was significant was that both of them had caused
him pain. Both had fought bitterly for his devotion if not his love,
for his soul if not his goodwill. It was a contest between two
brothers who, Mahoney had come to understand in the end, had
loved the same woman. It was from this upbringing that he had
found the strength of purpose to put himself through school, join
the Army and finally the OSS. And when he looked back it had
always been, until this moment, through half-closed eyes for fear
he would see something, would remember just what it had really
been like. No lies now, no half truths, hidden meanings. The
atmosphere was correct, and this evening he was sixteen again for
just a moment or two, could look through the eyes of such a young
man, could catch a realistic if fleeting glimpse at what his world
had been. He could remember a summer day in particular, how the
heat seemed to lay over the city of Duluth in great awful sheets
that barely seemed to shift with the blast-furnace wind that came
down from the pine forests. He could hear it starting in a valley a
long way off, coming closer so that he wanted to run away and
cringe and hide someplace dark and tight and safe. It was the kind
of a summer's day—and he experienced others just like it later in
his life, so that he'd developed a phobia about hot summer
days—in which he just knew that something very bad was on the

verge of happening. And it did. Someone had telephoned from the cabin on Shultz Lake that Uncle Fred was dead, and Mahoney rode up with his mother and father in their old Pontiac. That was just the week after his father had come home from work at the U.S. Steel Company's wire mill in Morgan Park with the story about Tom Granville. The day had been another scorcher and working around the open-hearth furnaces was grueling at best. One of the guys had called Granville down from the loading gantry for a drink of cool water. When he got down someone handed him a big stone jug. But it was supposed to be a joke. The jug hadn't contained water. It had been filled with a powerful lye solution. Before anyone could stop him, Granville—whom Mahoney had always remembered as a huge, powerful man—took a deep drink. Immediately the lye burned his throat. He dropped the jug and stepped backward in absolute agony. Already it was too late for him. He knew it, all of them did. It took six men to control him so that he could be carried down to the infirmary where for hours his screams could be heard all over the plant as the lye slowly ate away his body from the inside out. "It was just a joke," Conrad said. And Mahoney had seen in his father's eyes, in the fear there, that it was he who had perpetrated the hoax. Conrad had been the cause of Granville's death. And although it frightened him, he didn't seem to have any remorse for it. "What's done is done, Wallace," he was fond of saying. "Don't ever look back. Forge ahead with a strong will."

Mahoney remembered driving up over the hill from West Duluth, along the Miller Trunk Highway and then on the country road through the trees back to the lake where his uncle had built the cabin with his own two hands years before. It was Uncle Fred's retreat from life in the city. He was a bachelor. The lake was his retreat from his brother's wife. A lonely life, Mahoney had always thought, though on the many weekends he had spent with his uncle, fishing and swimming in the summer, hunting in the fall, skiing in the winter, the lake hadn't seemed lonely, it had seemed a haven. He remembered long hikes through the woods, nights sitting talking on the screened porch watching the stars, weekends of cold rain when they sat by the fire playing checkers and listening to the radio. Now he was going up the hill for a far different purpose, his father grim-lipped, his mother crying softly.

Fred's body was in the changing room in the boathouse behind the cabin. He was lying sideways on the narrow cot, his legs draped loosely over the edge, his bare feet splayed out as if he had lost his balance and fallen backward. The old double-barreled twelve-gauge shotgun lay on the floor, both barrels discharged. The stench of gunpowder and blood was thick in the tiny space. The back of Fred's skull was splattered across the cot, up on the pasteboard wall, dripping from the small window, and even hanging in strings from the bare roof rafters.

It was the first dead body he had ever seen, and although he wanted to be sick, his father had insisted, over his mother's ineffectual protestations, that he was old enough to share in what he called "the responsibility of family." He was one of the pallbearers from Bell Brothers Funeral Parlor, and carrying the coffin up from the hearse to the gravesite at Calvary Cemetery, he kept seeing his uncle's lifeless form on the cot. He kept hearing the coroner's initial assessment that it had taken a great deal of ingenuity to hold the shotgun up to his mouth like that and actually pull both triggers at the same time. He must have used his toes for it because no one's arms were long enough to do something like that with such a big gun. The trouble was that Mahoney could not, for the life of him, imagine his uncle sitting on the edge of the cot, the barrels of the big twelve-gauge in his mouth, groping with his feet for the triggers. The idea was at once ludicrous and macabre. It would have taken a man of great will and courage to do such a thing, the coroner said, to which his mother finally did object not only strenuously but violently and loudly. She was Catholic. The act of suicide was not an act of courage, it was an act of cowardice, and it was a mortal sin. He had been cleaning his gun and it accidentally discharged. A tragic accident. The coroner had finally, if reluctantly, agreed, and so it was listed on the death certificate in order that Uncle Fred could be given a proper Catholic burial.

What Mahoney had to do after that was get on with his life. Forget. Put it all behind him. Forge ahead with a strong will. But of course he could not. He could forget selectively, but he could not forget everything. The act was a part of the baggage he would carry with him for the remainder of his life. That act, plus his father's behavior afterward. He had managed until this moment— fairly successfully, too—to bury that particular set of memories behind the good ones. The fishing and the hunting and the talking.

To see at all one must have eyes. To see deeply one must have compassion and understanding for all sides of an issue. It was a lesson he had struggled to learn from his Uncle Fred, but one that his father taught him during a single afternoon, so that at the boat-house and afterward at the funeral when his father was drunk and distant from everyone, even his wife, Mahoney could understand and see—truly see. Nick Blotti, Len Sampson, Lazlo Shumatz, and all his father's cronies from the North Pole Bar on Raleigh Street dreamed endlessly about careers in sports in those days. Especially a career in major league baseball. They all played on local softball teams. And they were good in a small industrial town, in their boozy way. But only Conrad had been good enough to have a real shot at the majors. The farm team for the Chicago White Sox in the days before the Second World War was in Duluth, and Conrad had tried out, as a young man, for the team as a catcher. And he'd done well. So well in fact that the manager had taken him aside and told him he could very probably make the team if only he were a couple of inches taller. Five feet three, even then, no matter the talent, was just too short. "They'd razz you, kid. Razz you to death." Of course it was nothing more than a test. If Conrad had had the heart for it, nothing could have stopped him, and at least he would have been given a shot on the farm team. Instead, he went back to work at the wire mill, got married, had a child, and like ascending to a seat on the New York Stock Exchange got his permanent stool at the North Pole, where his friends could understand and sympathize with him.

But they hadn't understood, of course. They could not. Nor could Mahoney, growing up with little or no interest in sports, understand his father's increasing bouts with the bottle, with a moroseness that turned each year a little farther toward a distance and a meanness that was exacerbated by Mahoney's growing closeness to his Uncle Fred.

Years later Mahoney had tried to look up some of his father's old friends, to ask them about it, but the few who were left could only remember their softball days together, and the feeling that Conrad could have made one hell of a major league ball player. He'd tried down in Chicago, too, with the White Sox management, but no records had been kept. "If he was any good we wouldn't have let him go, believe me." The story was a dime a dozen.

All this was beyond the ken of a thirteen-year-old boy who in junior high school was on the chess team, in the glee club, on the debating team (at which he was nothing short of brilliant), and a library assistant. Not a bookworm, but a quiet, studious boy who had the ability, partially innate, partially learned, to figure things out. Math and science were easy, as was tinkering with an old radio receiver, with a Gilbert chemistry set in a tin box, and a bicycle that was apart in the backyard as much as it was on the run, not because it was broken but because he wanted to see exactly how it worked and derive the pleasure of taking something apart and successfully putting it back together again.

They were, for the most part, bad times. His father was drinking heavily by then, and knocking his son around for the slightest infraction. Yet he clearly remembered other times in which he could sit down and talk with his father. Really talk with him. During baseball games on the radio, they would talk between innings. About baseball, of course, but also about college, about the happenings in Europe, and about how his father wished the coming war would have happened sooner so that he could have had a chance to do something about it. He remembered going with his father down to the North Pole and drinking Nesbitt's orange pop out of tall glass bottles, eating salted peanuts, and playing the bowling machine in the back. He remembered going grocery shopping with his father (his mother never shopped) and was amazed at how the man could mentally add up the prices for everything they bought, so that at the checkout counter he was always exactly right, to the penny. He remembered once being trusted to take the bus out to the steel plant on a Friday to pick up his father's pay envelope because their house payment was due on that day, and riding all the way back home clutching the envelope tightly in his pocket.

The good times were the exception and served only to confuse and hurt Mahoney who was increasingly driven to compare his father to his Uncle Fred. He remembered his father in those days as a powerfully built man with a big chest and arms that seemed too long for his body, bulging with muscles. Conrad had always longed for a son to follow in his footsteps. Someone who would make the majors. During the spring he would pull Mahoney out of the house, give him a glove and a ball, and they would go to the backyard to practice. Mahoney didn't really mind, but his heart wasn't in it, and his father kept egging him on to throw harder, to put more into it, to hustle, to catch the skipping grounders thrown at him. One afternoon Mahoney obliged his father, pitching the ball with every ounce of his strength, and fielding the imagined hits. It was a dangerous game. At first his father was surprised and enjoyed the competition, but he had been drinking most of the day and his reflexes weren't what they normally were. Mahoney threw a wild ball that hit the grass a few inches ahead of his father's glove, bouncing up and catching him in the chin, knocking him over backward, startling him more than hurting him. "Father," Mahoney cried, throwing down his glove and rushing over to him.

24

"You son of a bitch," his father swore, his eyes narrowed in hate and rage. Mahoney tried to step back to avoid the fist coming directly at him, but he was too late. His father's roundhouse connected solidly with his face, breaking his nose, loosening several of his teeth, blood gushing everywhere, his head snapping back. He remembered that it didn't hurt very much until afterward, when his father explained that young Wallace had been hit in the face by a ball. Mahoney did not counter the lie. But he understood his father for the very first time; he understood what a lost dream can do to a man. How it can change him, make him sour, make him bitter, powerless, so that he would lash out at the slightest provocation.

It was Mahoney's watershed, and their secret. A few years later, after Uncle Fred's death, after Mahoney had graduated from college and was about to go away to the army, his father took him aside and apologized. By then Mahoney's mother was dead, so it didn't really matter any longer, but on that day Mahoney had begun to forget the hurt, remembering only the lesson he had learned because of it. And he had come to love his father then, as he did now, despite that hurt. Because he understood.

There were always relatives in those days. At Thanksgiving and Christmas, of course, but especially during the summer for picnics at Pike Lake, or Wheaton's Resort on Big Lake, or Jay Cooke Park, or down on Park Point. When Uncle Fred was twenty-five he developed cancer of the larynx, so the surgeons cut out his voice box and some of his throat, leaving him with a small round hole at the base of his throat, just above his breastbone, through which he could breathe. He always carried several small tablets and a pocketful of pencils with him wherever he went, because he loved to talk. In fact Mahoney's earliest remembrances of learning to read and write were on his uncle's knee. It was an early summer, Mahoney was ten or eleven, and there was a great picnic at Cloquet up over the hill for the fourth of July. There was a Ferris wheel, a merry-go-round, bumper cars, giant swings, games, swimming, canoeing, softball, beer tents, cotton candy, then at darkness the fireworks which in those days seemed to go on forever. There were children everywhere, and Mahoney played hard, though throughout the day he would spot his father and Uncle Fred together in the beer tent talking furiously, his father gesturing wildly, his uncle shoving his note pad in his father's face, and he would stop and watch them from a respectful distance, wishing he were a little bird in the rafters so that he could see and hear what they were arguing about. But he knew better than to go over there, especially when his father was like that.

The afternoon seemed to switch on and off like an electric light. One of the local kids nearly drowned in the pond, a softball game ended in a fight, the fire department this year wouldn't let any of the kids near where the fireworks had been set up, and a bunch of the older boys had gone up over the bowl toward the St. Louis River where they were smoking cigarettes. Mahoney hadn't been included, so he swung back past the beer tent again. His father was still there, but Uncle Fred had left and Mahoney suddenly got very worried about him, imagining all sorts of terrible things. He ran across the midway down to the pond thinking about the kid who had nearly drowned, and thinking that his uncle could not call out for help if his life depended on it. All the earlier excitement had died down and no one payed much attention to him. But surely, he thought, someone would have noticed a drowning man. Even a speechless one, so he turned and hurried back over toward the fireworks, and beyond to the picnic grounds where his mother and some of the other women had set up.

"I can't find Uncle Fred. He was at the beer tent and now he's gone," Mahoney told his mother, out of breath.

She looked up and smiled. "He's playing horseshoes," she said. And it was at that exact moment that Mahoney spotted his uncle's coat lying on one of the blankets, the coat in which he kept his note pads and pencils, and he instantly knew what he was going to have to do.

"I meant I'm supposed to fetch his coat, and I've looked all over for it, even in the beer tent," he blurted.

"Silly boy," his mother said. She nodded toward the blanket. "Lunch is in an hour. Have you seen your father?"

Mahoney picked up the coat, then looked guiltily up at his mother. "The beer tent."

Her lips compressed a little and she nodded. "We'll eat in an hour."

The horseshoe pits were on the opposite side of the park from the pond, behind the softball diamonds. Mahoney retraced his steps through the midway and on the far side, beyond the Ferris wheel, slipped into the woods that bordered the park. He sat down behind a tree so that he couldn't be easily seen from below, but if he wanted to see anyone coming he merely had to look over his shoulder. He had a Camel cigarette and one wooden match that he had snitched from his father early that morning before they had set out, and he lit it, pulling the smoke into his lungs and coughing only once before he settled down. Careful not to get any ash or dirt on the coat, he took the tablets out of the pockets, and laid the coat aside. He didn't feel too guilty about this because he figured the argument in the beer tent had probably been because of him. His father was pushing him toward baseball and his uncle was pulling him toward hunting and fishing. The first tablet was blank, the second contained a grocery list on the first page and nothing after, but the other two tablets were filled with writing, some of it barely legible scribbles.

He studied the two in an effort to make some sense out of which might have come first, but gave it up immediately. It didn't matter, he thought, so long as he could figure out what had been said about him.

"You started it. I just came for a beer," his uncle had written, the pencil marks smudged from repeated handling.

Started what? Mahoney wondered. And what had his father said to elicit such a response?

"Old history. Old history," Uncle Fred wrote. "No use to bring *that* up now. Won't do any good. Not you, not Katy"—Mahoney's mother—"and certainly not the boy."

Mahoney took a deep drag on his cigarette, excited now. What was the *old history* his father and uncle were arguing about? The dialogue was tantalizingly close and yet distant. He could almost hear his father's voice raised in anger, and almost hear the strange whistling noise Uncle Fred made in his throat when he was upset.

"Bullshit! Bullshit! Bullshit!" The angry words were scrawled across the next page. And on the third page: "Don't be a prick." "It was never that way and you know it."

Mahoney leaned back against the tree, a sadness and even a strange fear rising up in his gut, making him just a little sick. His uncle and his father had been best friends from his earliest memories. But lately, over the past couple of years, they had seemed to drift apart. Or rather they'd seemed to be engaged in some sort of competition. But for what or whom Mahoney couldn't guess. At least not then.

"I'm telling you exactly that," Uncle Fred wrote on the next page. "If you don't believe me, tough shit. Just don't ruin it for your family."

A shadow loomed over Mahoney and he turned with a start and looked straight up into his uncle's face. He hadn't heard anyone coming, he'd been so engrossed.

"You were having a fight about me and Mom," he blurted to cover his guilt now that he was caught.

Fred had a wonderfully expressive face that was weatherbeaten from years of outdoor living in all seasons. But it was a kindly face, caring and knowing. He was huffing through the hole in his throat as he reached down and took the tablets from Mahoney. He picked up his coat, brushed it off, and turned to leave. Mahoney jumped up.

"Uncle Fred," he cried. "I'm sorry." He felt just awful, as if he had betrayed the trust of his very best and only friend, which in a very large sense, he knew, he had.

Fred turned back, his eyes a little moist, and he shook his head. He wanted to talk so badly that his lips moved a little. Mahoney felt very sorry for him at that moment. He would have given anything, absolutely anything, to have the power to heal.

"I saw you with my dad," he said. "In the beer tent."

Fred took out a pencil and a tablet from his pants pocket. He quickly wrote something and held it out for Mahoney to see. "Nothing to worry about, Wallace."

"What's 'old history,' then?" Mahoney asked. "You said it wouldn't do my mother or me any good. What, Uncle Fred? What won't do us any good?"

Fred smiled. "*Snoopiness*," he wrote, underlining the word.

Mahoney tried to protest, but Fred held him off and wrote again. When he was finished he looked at what he had written as if he wasn't at all certain he should show it to his nephew, but then he finally held it out.

"Trust, forgiveness, and love," he'd written in a neat script. "You and I have to trust each other, even after today. We have to forgive, too. For everything. And we have to love, no matter what."

Mahoney didn't know what to say. There were more questions in his mind than before. He felt that it was vitally important that he know what was going on. Yet he knew that he had already caused too much hurt as it was.

Fred smiled again and nodded toward the picnic grounds. "Lunch is almost ready," he wrote. "And put out that cig before I tell your mother." He pocketed the tablet and he and Mahoney left the woods.

Mahoney took off his shoes and his tie and laid down on the soft bed, but although he was tired, sleep would not come. He was being a silly old man, he told himself, dredging up such old memories to absolutely no purpose. There were a few summers, though, like those in which he had learned so much: pragmatism from his uncle and a certain cynicism from his father. Both of them had been lost souls almost from the beginning, and his sometime sadness in those days was nothing compared to the regrets he felt now for the lives that were permanently out of his reach.

"At least I didn't kill myself," his father had told him cruelly months after the funeral when Fred's name had come up.

The wolves were gathering, Mahoney thought, closing his eyes. He could feel their presence as strongly as he could feel his own sense of building urgency.

3

The early evening hours seemed to go on forever in John's mind, although the tempo continued to pick up with a number of new arrivals including a vanload of "friends" from the FBI's field office in Minneapolis, along with a couple more of Cassidy's admirers from Technical Services. Carlisle continued to be the man of the hour, of course. "After all, it is my man who has gone walkabout," he cried at one point. He was closeted in one corner of the living room with Brooke West, the AIC from Minneapolis, and his communications man who had set up a portable telephone system so that they could leave the cabin's main land line open in case Mahoney did telephone in. John watched the proceedings from a position he'd taken up just within the kitchenette. Cassidy and his hound dogs had attacked the cabin with a renewed vigor because of the one prize they'd already unearthed, and because the Company men were the experts and the Bureau only the poor cousins. A third Bureau agent was speaking on one of the cellular telephones to someone in Washington, and the two others who had come up were outside with one of Cassidy's new arrivals, presumably checking Mahoney's old Chevrolet, the boathouse, the dilapidated greenhouse, and the grounds. "He's to be detained without charges," Carlisle said. "As far as your people are concerned this is to be treated as a simple missing person." In John's mind they were making a great deal of fuss about nothing in the sense that if his father had merely gone on vacation, say to Missoula, a lot of energy was being wasted here, but in another sense, if he really had taken off, finding him would be far more difficult than looking for the proverbial needle in the haystack. His father had the facility of blending into his surroundings. He could be five miles away or five thousand, and they might never know it, at least not the way they were going about it.

Every operation began like this, he thought. The busload of experts brought in to uncover the first bits and pieces, and in so doing trampling the ground, missing sometimes the most obvious or significant, and certainly announcing to their quarry that the hunt was definitely on, like dogs baying in the distance while the fox puts miles and miles between them.

Except this was his father they were hunting, and it gave him a secret little thrill knowing that if the old man wanted to lose himself, there wouldn't be a damn thing they or an entire army of Carlisles could do about it.

He turned and stepped back into the kitchenette where he poured himself another cup of coffee from the pot he'd brewed earlier when company started arriving. They'd been pretty thorough up to this point, he had to admit. Partially because of the fresh impetus of expertise that West's people had brought with them, but in a large part, of course, due to Carlisle's exhortations. The man was mad with barely controlled rage. "How in God's name could he have done this . . . just dropping off the face . . . why the hell . . ." Nothing personal, Farley, but you're an unmitigated ass. They were checking with the local cab companies to make sure that Mahoney hadn't been picked up out here by a private car. By a person or persons unknown. They had a man at the phone company checking every call that had been received by or placed from this number over the past few months. Ditto with the post office where his father maintained a box, and with the grocery and liquor stores where he got his provisions. "Hasn't been drinking too much lately that you know, John?" Carlisle had asked. They were trying to find out who his physician might be these days, to make certain there wasn't a health problem they should know about. Drugs perhaps. Other than an almost full bottle of aspirin and a completely full bottle of sleeping pills, there were absolutely no pharmaceuticals (as Carlisle called them) in the house. "Odd, wouldn't you say, for a man of his advanced years?" West had asked. "Not odd," John had replied rather snappishly. "Bloody heroic, if you ask me."

Cassidy, who had been out on the screened-in front porch, came inside the cabin, stamping his feet against the cold. He came around to John in the kitchenette.

"Your father smokes cigars, doesn't he, sir? Big Cubans, if I remember rightly."

"Half a dozen a day," John said. "He has a friend in the State Department who gets them for him. Probably through Guantánamo Bay."

Carlisle had looked up. He and West were watching.

Cassidy was troubled. "Didn't quit recently, perhaps?"

"Not that I know of."

31

"What is it, Dick?" Carlisle asked, coming over, West right behind him.

"It's Mr. Mahoney's cigars, sir."

"What about them?"

"None here. Not one. An empty box, a couple of empty humidors, plenty of matches and ashtrays, but not one cigar in the house."

It was another nail in the coffin. "Maybe he ran out," John suggested lamely.

"Maybe he was planning on a long trip and needed enough to last him," Carlisle countered. "Could have made a fuss, though, through U.S. customs."

"Enough so that they might have missed his gun," Cassidy suggested.

"I see your point."

"Did you check the freezer?" John asked.

"First place I looked once I found the empty boxes," Cassidy said. "I'll keep looking."

"Do that," John said sharply.

"Steady now," Carlisle cautioned.

West had paid very close attention to the entire exchange. He was a tall, thin, hawk-faced man with dark eyebrows, penetrating eyes, and an irritating manner. "We'll need a list of your father's relatives," he said after Cassidy left. "He was born and raised here in Duluth, from what I understand."

"There's no one left," John said.

"Friends, then. He did come back here to retire. There must be someone."

"He outlived them all."

"No cousins, maiden aunts? Brothers-in-law?"

"They were all dead before I was born," John said. Which was a pretty sad commentary on the state of a family. He was the last of the Mahoneys. He and his father. No tedious family reunions for them. Not now, not ever. He missed his brother, especially at this moment. Michael had been the clown. Michael the Lighthearted, they'd called him.

"Then why'd he come back?" West insisted. "What was here for him?"

John focused on him. "This place belonged to a favorite uncle. He used to come up here weekends all through the year, when he was a kid."

"Your father inherited the place, is that it?"

"It came up for sale when he retired, so he bought it. He and my mother came here after Moscow."

"Where's your mother these days?"

"Dead."

"Well, then, what about her relatives?" West asked without sympathy. "Is there anyone on that side of the family who your father might have jogged off to see?"

"There's no one."

"Frankly, I find that hard to believe, Mr. Mahoney."

Carlisle turned on him. "Believe it," he said.

"I'm merely trying to do my job," West said. "Which is impossible in this case unless I get more information."

"Then I suggest you get on your people downtown. They'll come up with something. The man didn't live in a vacuum, after all."

"No, I suppose not," West said. He turned and went back to his communications man.

Carlisle turned his attention back to John. It was just the two of them now. The agent and his runner. The operative and his operator. He pursed his lips. "They can cover the domestic ground much faster than we can," he said. "It wasn't my idea to bring the Bureau in on it, but Donald wants fast action on this. If your father is still in the States, they'll close the holes. If he moves, they'll spot him. If he's gone foreign on us, our stations will cover the obvious."

Which leaves me, John thought. Send a ferret to catch a ferret, a spy to catch a spy. A son to catch a father. Only this father wasn't going to be so easy.

They'd unlocked the old boathouse beside the cabin, fifty feet up from the edge of the frozen lake. It and the greenhouse on the other side of the driveway were all that was left from the old days. On one side Mahoney's aluminum fishing boat and motor were stored for the winter on an old, rusted trailer. A workbench cluttered with cans of paint, rags, bits of wire and scrap metal, a few tools and some old fishing gear ran along one wall. A riding mower was parked beside it. Leaning against the wall were an old double-edged ax, a couple of shovels, a spade, a hoe, and some other rusted garden tools. A half-dozen fishing poles were hung neatly on a rack beside the window. A cabinet beneath it contained two large fishing tackle boxes filled with jigs and lures, hooks, leaders, weights, bobbers, plastic worms, pliers, knives, and spools of monofilament fishing line. At one time the boathouse had been divided into two rooms, the smaller of which had been used as a changing house for swimmers. The well head and water pump were in a far corner. Cassidy was tinkering with it.

"Any idea how this works, sir?"

"It's automatic when the pressure gets too low," John said from the doorway. Carlisle had gone over to the workbench where he was looking through some of the junk Cassidy's people had already examined. They left labels indicating what was already cleared and therefore safe to touch. The boathouse looked like a decorated Christmas tree, inside out.

"I meant the hose," Cassidy said, stepping aside. A long green garden hose was coiled up on the floor. It was connected to an outlet on the pump. John had never seen it before.

"I don't know," John said, coming over.

"Odd, it being out like this."

"He uses it to water the lawn, I suppose."

"Begging your pardon, sir, but not in the winter."

"So he left it there since fall."

Cassidy picked up the end of the hose and water dribbled out of it. "My guess is that it's been used in the last day or so."

"Maybe he washed the car."

"Car's dirty. We checked."

"Maybe the pipes from here to the house froze up. That's possible in this weather. He could have run the hose over for fresh water."

Cassidy turned a valve at the back of the pump. The motor came on and the hose stiffened as it began to fill with water. He turned it off.

"There would have been water damage over there. When water freezes it expands. Bursts the pipes. Then when it thaws out again, the pipes leak. We checked that, too."

"Then I don't know what you're getting at," John said, but he did. It was an anomaly. Something out of the ordinary that might mean something.

Carlisle had taken an interest. He came over. "What's this about the hose?"

"Someone's used it in the past couple of days, but I can't imagine why. Can you?"

One of the Bureau's men had come to the door. "Telephone for you, sir," he said to Carlisle.

"Right," Carlisle said, glancing up. He shook his head. "Are you sure it was used so recently?"

"Reasonably. The floor is wet under it, and there's still water in the coils. He'd have drained it for the winter, I'd have thought."

"A skating rink," the FBI agent said.

They all looked at him.

"I do it for my kids in the winter. Flood our backyard. When it freezes they've got their own rink."

"My father has never skated in his adult life, that I know of," John said, but suddenly he knew what his father had done.

"No, I suppose he hasn't," Carlisle said. He smiled. "I'll be back in a jiff."

When he was gone, John looked at Cassidy and he could see that the Technical Services expert had a pretty fair idea what the hose had been used for as well.

"Not a skating rink," Cassidy said. The pump was nearly equidistant from the front door and the back window facing the lake. "We'll try the front door first."

"He's hidden something," John said.

Cassidy nodded. "Dropped it in a hole, filled it with water, and when the water froze covered it over with snow."

"It'd only work until spring. Which means he plans on coming back before then."

"Or by spring he figures it wouldn't matter what we found," Cassidy said, uncoiling the hose. "Sorry, sir, but it's my job."

John held the door for him as he backed out the door pulling the hose after him. When it was fully extended he was about seventy-five feet away from the boathouse, at the edge of the driveway just beyond the cabin and slightly beyond the green-house. He started left, back toward the cabin, keeping the hose taut, his steps describing a large arc in the snow. At the cabin he turned and walked the other way toward the greenhouse, coming again to the limit the hose could be stretched. He left it there and came back to the driveway.

"Somewhere here," he said. "We'll need lights. Tools." He looked up. "Send my people out, would you, sir?"

To try to hold on to the sanity of the present while being violently propelled toward some future action that was distasteful was an exercise in futility, John decided. The past was all that mattered for the moment. The immediate past, the distant past, the far distant past. All of it was like a river of calms and rapids and even waterfalls, the source of which was all but lost ten million years ago. An ice age. Another, alien time. He could clearly remember being three and a half when his mother had to admit herself to the

35

hospital in New York where she had Michael. Alone because her husband was off somewhere on government work and could not be reached, no matter the emergency. "Be a big boy now, you're the man of the family," she'd told him. He remembered that it was the very first time that he hated his father for being gone. He wanted to marry his mother and take care of her and his new baby brother, so that his father would never be able to find them, or leave them again.

In another violent wrench of time, he saw himself greeting his father and mother at the airport when they'd returned from Moscow after Michael's death in Montana. They'd brought three Russian children with them, children whose father had been killed in Moscow. He remembered how his parents had held on to each other, had actually leaned on each other for support in their grief. But his father had turned out to be strong enough for them all. For his wife, for John, for the Russian children. And he remembered how much he truly loved the old man then. And that how nothing on this earth could shake that love one iota.

Now he realized how much he was frightened for his father as he watched Carlisle put down the telephone, hesitate for just a moment, then turn around. It was bad news.

"Have they found him?" John asked. "Is that what the call was about?"

Carlisle shook his head. "No." He glanced toward the back door. "What's going on out there?"

"Cassidy thinks he's on to another hiding spot." They'd already begun digging in the backyard. "The mother lode."

"We'd better find it, John. Something. Anything. Soon." Carlisle went into the kitchenette where he dumped his cold coffee into the sink, poured himself a stiff measure of bourbon in his cup, and downed it neat. He shuddered, then put the cup down carefully on the counter. "That was Alex just now."

"Hayes?" John asked.

"Right. The Russians, it seems, are on the move."

Alex Hayes was Carlisle's chief of Operations. The pope of the third floor who sat on the right hand of God, and knew everything that was to be known, and then some. He was one of the bright young ones who had worked under the elder Mahoney in the sixties and seventies.

"They're looking for Chernov?"

"Presumably," Carlisle said, turning around to face John. "We've got a man out at Frunze, the military airfield in Moscow.

A Major Trusov and a contingent of a dozen staff officers and legmen just flew out in one hell of a big hurry. Toward the west."

The name wasn't familiar to John. "KGB?"

"Decidedly. Major Antonina Filipovna Trusov is deputy chief of their Special Investigations department."

It was as if a load had suddenly been taken off John's shoulders. "They chase after defectors. The KGB thinks Chernov has skipped out."

Carlisle held up a hand. "Not so fast. On the surface I might tend to agree with you. But Alex has some other thoughts. Special Investigations also watches for penetration agents."

"Either way it doesn't point to my father being a traitor."

"But it is another very strong indication that your father is out there meeting with Chernov."

"I'll give you that."

"That's good of you," Carlisle hooted. "So the two of them are out there doing what, for God's sake? Exchanging information? Talking like a couple of old magpies just let out of the zoo?"

"My father's not that way."

"What way?" Carlisle asked sharply.

"He never opened his mouth."

"Unless there was a trade involved. He was a tradesman, after all."

"He was a loyal American."

"Your use of the past tense doesn't exactly fill me with confidence."

"He was a spy, goddamnit. Don't play word games with me. The CIA created him, used him."

"Oh, no, I beg to differ. He came to us in the old days a full-blown operative."

"What the hell would you know?" John said sarcastically.

"I know everything, mister. What the hell do you think a spy is? You're one, just like your old man. What the hell are you?"

John was at a loss for words. Something was clicking inside of him. He kept seeing explosions, flames and sparks shooting up into a night sky. He could feel the heat on his face, against his body. Pressing him backward. Down. Down.

"It's love of the game, John. That and motivation." Carlisle started to turn away, but then changed his mind. "I'll tell you what you are. You're a pissed-off little boy whose family was wiped out by the Russians. So you're out there getting your revenge."

"My father isn't seeking revenge!" John shouted. Carlisle's words were like hot pokers in his gut.

37

"No? What about your brother, Michael? It was because of the Russians that he was killed."

"That came later."

"Your father had an unhappy, fucked-up childhood, or didn't he tell you that? Your uncle—who was really his father, by the way—shot himself right here. Out in the boathouse when your father was only sixteen. Your grandfather, Conrad, who as it turns out was really your great-uncle, drank himself to death after causing his wife to die of a broken heart."

"Christ!" John murmured, stepping back from the sheer weight of the words. A thousand memories were spinning around in his head at the speed of light. Old photographs, old stories that his father used to tell him. Lies?

"And if that's not enough motivation for you, John, then how about your mother?"

John was having trouble catching his breath. He was seeing Carlisle through some sort of a red haze. The words boomed and echoed in the room, shot from a cannon.

"The Russians killed her."

John closed his eyes. "She died of cancer," he heard himself saying as if from a great distance.

"An ingested carcinogen. Long-term. Probably in Moscow. It was the big thing in those days. Ruins the effectiveness of the opposition's operatives if they don't know."

"Why . . . ?"

"It's the Russians," Carlisle said bitterly. "Don't ask me why . . ."

"Not that, you son of a bitch. Why now? Why tell me this now? My father never knew."

"Maybe not. But then again maybe he's guessed. Maybe someone told him." Carlisle shook his head again in disgust. "It's time you opened your eyes to the real world. This isn't the Sunday supplement. There are bad people out there. And your father is mixed up with them right now. We either find him, or the Russians find him. And God help him—God help us all—if the Russians get to him before we do."

"Why wasn't it stopped?" John asked. "If you knew it in Moscow, why didn't you stop it?"

"We knew what they were doing, but not to whom specifically, and not exactly when or where. There was no way of stopping it."

"Christ, you could have gone public."

"With what? We had no proof. Still don't, for that matter. And they eventually stopped."

"You don't really know. You can't be sure."

"We're sure, John."

"You can't be, goddamnit!"

Carlisle turned and poured himself another drink. "All right, John," he said heavily. "We can't be sure."

"No," John said, understanding that Carlisle was just holding him off, and hating him for it. But he didn't want to go any further with it. Not now. Not about his mother, nor about his grandfather and great-uncle.

Carlisle had gone to the back door and was looking out the window. The backyard looked as if it had been bombed. Craters pockmarked the snow where Cassidy's people had dug in the frozen ground. The hose had been pulled back into the boathouse and had been led out the window into the front yard.

"Look, I'm sorry I brought it up," he said. "Bad timing on my part."

"But you were going to tell me eventually?"

Carlisle shrugged. "We all make mistakes in this business. We simply try to keep away from the fatal ones. Not always with much success, I'm afraid. Do you understand?"

"I understand," John said. It's just that my world has been turned upside down. My past has been rendered totally useless to me in a single blow, yet nothing's changed, I'm still the operative and you the operator.

"It's just that Alex is worried. And when he's worried I get worried. If we don't get to your father before the Russians, he's a dead man. Or worse."

John wondered what could be worse than death. Everyone was outside now. He and Carlisle were alone.

"Before they kill him they'll take him apart piece by piece, date by date. Places, names—including yours—simply everything."

"It can't be allowed to happen," John said woodenly. Again he felt a sense of detachment, as if he existed on more than one plane at the same time.

Carlisle turned around. "No, it can't, John. You'll have to go after him. We'll keep everything sealed for you, but you're going to have to dig him out."

"It's a big world, Farley." John felt as if he were treading water. "Lots of places for a determined, able man to hide."

"Don't let's play games here. The Russians aren't. They've sent the best. We have to assume they know about the message

39

and that they know Chernov at least as well as we know your father."

"They've only sent a woman and her admirers . . ."

"They've sent the *best*, John. Tonia Trusov is a killer. Alex knows all about her. When you get back to Washington he'll brief you. They call her the Black Widow or Scorpion, or some such nonsense like that."

"Bullshit."

John was starting to come down from his earlier emotion, and he was swinging now too far toward cynicism. He knew it and so did Carlisle.

"She received her training in helicopter commando school and from there spent three years with the KGB's Department Viktor murder squad before transferring over to Special Investigations. She's beautiful, Alex says, well connected with the Soviet brass, and at barely thirty she runs one of the most important departments in the entire Komitet. Not a woman to be taken lightly, by Alex's reckoning."

John knew that he should be paying attention to what he was being told. It wasn't going to end here at the cabin. It wasn't going to turn out so neatly. The telephone wasn't going to ring with his father on the other end, apologizing for putting them through so much trouble. But he was confused now, and tired, and just a little battered.

"We're assuming she and her people are heading into Europe, which means your father probably did not enter the Soviet Union. At least that part is good news."

"I told you he wasn't a traitor."

"I never said he was. He and Chernov are probably meeting in Europe, though."

"East or West?"

"Good question. Trusov and her people left Moscow aboard a military jet transport, which means they'll almost certainly be landing behind the Iron Curtain."

"Which doesn't tell us a thing."

"We've got AWACS aircraft patrolling the borders, and Alex thinks we'll get lucky with one of our KH-11 satellites. In any event he thinks we have a fair chance of pinpointing exactly where they do land. If it's well within the Eastern bloc, let's say Czechoslovakia, then it's a safe bet your father and Chernov are meeting across the border. But if they set down in East Berlin, it's possible, just possible, that Chernov crossed the border and they're meeting in the West."

"Or East Berlin itself," John said.

"That too is a possibility, but Chernov will have to know that his people are looking for him. He'll want some safety."

"Which would put us back to square one."

"What do you mean?"

"They could be anywhere, even here in the States."

"Not if Trusov and her people are flying into Europe."

"If they were in the States, she wouldn't fly from Moscow to New York, Farley. She'd first come out to Europe, probably with some fanfare."

"Such as getting herself spotted at Frunze."

John nodded. "Something like that. Once in Europe she'd get herself lost so that she could take an ordinary commercial flight across the Atlantic. Just another tourist. We're watching her, and she knows it. It's called insulation."

Carlisle's lips compressed. He nodded. "Alex said the same thing." He sighed. "What the hell was he thinking about, running off like that? Why the hell didn't he talk to us?"

Just then John could have named a dozen reasons, but Cassidy had come to the door with the same proud, hunting-dog look on his face that he'd seen when they'd discovered the plastic box beneath the toilet.

The search had been abandoned in the backyard, which was now dark. The lights had been moved to the front where the hose snaked out of the boathouse window and down to the edge of the frozen lake. Two of Cassidy's people were chopping a big hole in the ice, thirty feet from shore, while the others, along with West and his Bureau people, stood around watching. John and Carlisle had put on their overcoats and stood with Cassidy a little apart from the others. The night was extremely cold, well below zero, John figured. A light wind had sprung up and they could see their breath in the work lights.

"What have we got down there?" Carlisle asked impatiently.

"Don't know for sure just yet, sir. But it looks like a box or a suitcase of some sort. We were just able to make out its outlines through the ice."

"A bait box left from this fall?" John suggested.

Cassidy looked at him. "If that's what it is, your father went through an awful lot of trouble hiding it. We found where he partially melted the ice, and then chopped the rest of the way through it down to the open water. A good ten, twelve inches of it. We figure he dropped the box through the hole, let the hole

41

freeze up overnight, then ran water over the entire area to cover what he'd done. Damned clever if you ask me, sir."

The flat sound of the ax chopping the ice echoed across the lake. With all the lights and activity out here tonight, John wondered what the people in the cabins across the lake must be thinking. His father knew some of them. He was about to mention it to Carlisle when another thought suddenly struck him. He took a step forward, then stopped, his stomach sinking.

"What is it?" Carlisle asked.

"He knew," John mumbled. "Christ!"

"He knew what? What are you talking about?"

The others were watching him. Cassidy was nodding. He had had the same thought. "It would appear so, sir," he said. "This would have taken him a couple of days. A lot of work."

"Unless whatever is down there has nothing to do with his disappearance."

"I'll give you that, sir. Just. But the timing would have been tight. And just a little on the coincidental side to my way of thinking."

"Would someone mind explaining to me what's going on?" Carlisle demanded.

"Let's get the box out of there first, Farley. Then we'll see," John said.

The hole in the ice was about four feet in diameter now. The dark, slush-filled water rose and fell as if the lake were breathing. Steam rose into the much colder air. They'd brought a garden rake down from the boathouse. Bob Fortuna, one of Cassidy's people, knelt down on the ice and lowered the rake through the hole.

"There it is," he said almost immediately.

"You've got it?" Cassidy asked.

"I can feel it," Fortuna said, fishing around with the rake. The water was at least three feet deep. "No handles that I can tell. Ridges on the surface. Maybe as big as a small suitcase. It's moving. I can move it around. But it's heavy. Probably weighted."

"Maybe we can slip a rope around it," Cassidy said.

"How about a net?" one of the others suggested.

"I'll get it," John said. He took off his overcoat and laid it out on the ice next to the hole. Fortuna pulled the rake out of the hole, the water freezing almost instantly on the handle and the tines.

"What do you think you're doing?" Carlisle asked.

"We could be here all night trying to get it out of there," John said, taking off his suit jacket. He handed it to one of the Bureau men, then took off his tie and unbuttoned his shirt.

"Water's pretty cold, sir," Cassidy said.

"Just hang on to my legs. I don't want to go under."

John knelt down on his overcoat and looked down into the water. Despite the work lights he couldn't see anything beneath the surface. Cassidy and Fortuna got behind him, each of them grabbing one of his ankles.

"It's just a little to the left," Fortuna said.

When he was a kid they used to go swimming sometimes in the spring just after the ice had gone out. But that was in upstate New York, and it wasn't below zero. He took a deep breath and then plunged headfirst into the hole, the water surprisingly warm at first after the much colder air temperature, but pitch-black and claustrophobic. He forced his way deeper, the water rising above the waistband of his trousers and up to his scrotum which instantly tightened, nearly taking his breath away. His fingers brushed the top of the case, and then he was touching the sand of the lake bottom, his head already beginning to pound because of the numbing cold. For a panicky moment he became disoriented, but then he felt the case again and there was a handle. He had it suddenly in both hands and they were pulling him back up through the hole to the surface and the lights and the incredibly cold wind against his torso.

Someone took the case from him, and they helped him to his feet. He was blinded by the strong lights. Cassidy threw a coat over his shoulders. "Up to the house with you, sir," he said. Someone was on the other side of him and together they hustled him off the frozen lake, up the front yard, and around the side to the back door. By the time they hit the stoop John found that he could barely move his legs, and had to be helped into the house.

In the bathroom they ran the shower, and helped him strip and get up into the tub, the lukewarm water hitting his body like streams of molten lava at first. But then the feeling slowly began to come back to his body, and they left him alone so that he could think again how much he hoped he was wrong out there. He and Cassidy. But knowing in his heart of hearts that they were not wrong.

They'd brought him one of his father's old sweaters and a pair of baggy trousers. When he came out into the living room they had gathered around the open aluminum case which turned out to be the waterproof kind that photographers use to carry their equipment. The contents were laid out on the big table. His father had used four bricks to weight the case. The rest of the material was packaged in a dozen big clear plastic bags. John knew what it was, and what it all meant.

Carlisle looked up, a genuinely pained expression on his face. He shook his head. "The goddamned old fool."

"It's his passport factory, sir," Cassidy said. "It's all here. Blank passports for a half-dozen countries—ours as well as theirs. Photographs. Inks. Stamps. Pens. Watermarking equipment. Even a small plastic laminating kit and press."

"He's used that kind of stuff before," John said lamely, wondering even as he said it why he was still fighting the inevitable.

"He was a fucking expert at it," Carlisle swore. "Among other things."

Cassidy held up one of the passports. "Your father's," he said. "The legitimate one, that is. So, wherever he's traveled, it wasn't under his own name." He looked back at the bags. "No telling how many he manufactured and took with him."

"More to the point," Carlisle said evenly, "this wasn't done up overnight. He knew that he was going to be leaving the country, days—maybe weeks—ago. Chernov's call was a ruse. A bloody ruse that took us all in. Some sort of a signal which I, like a complete fool, obligingly passed along to your father."

Either that, John thought, or a lever to pry his father away from here. Insurance. An extra enticement for him to actually do it.

One of the telephones had rung again. "It's for you, sir," the Bureau technician said. "Washington."

"Bloody hell," Carlisle snapped.

4

Mahoney awoke in a cold sweat, his heart racing, his kidneys aching, and his bladder full. It was three in the morning. The wind had increased; he could hear it moaning through the eaves and rattling a loose window shutter somewhere.

He lay for a long time in the darkness resisting the urge to reach over for Marge lying beside him. She wasn't there. He knew it intellectually, and yet old habits died hardest. She'd been beside him in spirit, if not always in physical fact, for the majority of his adult life. His rock of Gibraltar. The anchor around which his ship had ranged the world. He knew all there was to know about loneliness and living alone. He'd learned those lessons well over the past couple of years since her death. But he figured he could also write the book on leave-taking and on returning, he'd done it so often. That, and on heartache—hers as well as his. She had saved his life, or rather had literally made a life for him out of his aimless wanderings. Whereas he had dragged her down, had subjected her to an existence of waiting and wondering and worrying that in the end had been the cause of her death. Too late, too late to make amends now, he thought. The guilt was his burden that he would carry with him to his grave. Christ, but it hurt. "I had something to do with it along the way, old man," she would have said. He could hear her speak sometimes as if she were actually right next to him. More than forty years of marriage was like a powerful narcotic to the system. When it was finished the withdrawal symptoms were no less painful or debilitating. When he watched her die in the hospital in Duluth he would have gladly exchanged places with her, and once again it was her strength, not his, that sustained them. Now she was gone. Forever.

He threw the covers back and got out of bed. His legs were stiff and for a moment or two he remained standing at the side of the bed enduring his pain. But then he moved slowly over to the window and looked outside. It was like being in prison here, except that outside lay danger, while inside the hotel lay his salvation. His freedom. His revenge, at last. The Volkswagen van was gone, but a new Mercedes sedan was parked halfway up the driveway. It had come sometime within the past few hours. Another guest, he supposed. Not the police. There was no short-wave antenna on the car. They would not have come so soon in any event. Not this soon.

Turning away from the window he went to his leather bag open on the stand next to the tall, oak *Schrank* in which the desk clerk had hung his overcoat. By feel he released the false bottom and removed his pistol and packet of ammunition. The narrow compartment was lead-lined to foil airport security systems. It was an idea that had been around for a lot of years. He carefully loaded the snub-nosed .38, replacing the remainder of the shells in his suitcase, then went back to the window. Nothing human moved below. Only the dark tree branches waved in the night wind. Cold and lonely sentinels.

Chernov's first call had been like manna from heaven. His second was not only unnecessary but foolish. There was nothing that could have held Mahoney back from coming here. No force on earth could have stopped him. Revenge was going to be his. But the extraordinary lengths to which Chernov had gone had bothered him all the way over. And still did. Yet the Russian's concerns, real or imagined, were nothing by comparison to the fact of Marge's death.

He slipped the gun in his trousers pocket, and in stocking feet let himself out of his room. He stood in the corridor for a long moment, listening to the sounds of the hotel. A dim yellow light from the lobby filtered up the grand staircase, and he could smell the odor of woodsmoke from the fireplace. But the hotel was mostly quiet, only a few vagrant sounds penetrating the silence: the wind from outside, a pump running somewhere, briefly, a toilet flushing above. In the old days he often got up at this hour. His quiet time, to think, to be alone. Marge always knew the moment he got out of bed, but she would leave him alone for an hour before she would get up, fix him a drink, and then sit on the floor at his knees, or in the chair next to his, just to be with him. To provide comfort, to signal him that no matter his worry, he was not alone, nor would he ever be as long as she lived.

In the early days they read poetry to each other. It was a holdover from their college years. Later, though, they'd stopped it, not because the romance had gone out of their marriage—it had never died—but because they no longer needed poetry to let each other know how deep their love ran. They knew simply by looking at each other, by being in the same room. They understood even from a distance what the other was feeling, if not thinking.

He walked down the hall to Chernov's door and tried the handle, but it was locked. No sounds came from within. He's sleeping now, waiting until morning when he would start his apologia. Some old men wrote memoirs while others tried to make amends for the wrongs they had committed. Only it wasn't going to be that easy. Not this time.

At the head of the stairs, he once again stopped to listen. But nothing moved below, and he started down, his right hand trailing on the ornate banister. The stairs switched back beneath a tall stained-glass window and from there he could look down into the lobby past the fireplace toward the registration desk. Besides the flickering fire on the grate only one light had been left on, leaving most of the lobby in shadow. He went the rest of the way down and at the bottom walked directly across to the desk where he took down the spare key for Chernov's room.

This was for Marge. An act that ironically she would not approve of. But he'd run out of options, and certainly he was running out of time. Chernov's call to arms had been a gift, the answer to an old man's final request. Standing in the darkness with the ability and the willingness to do this thing was the culmination of a life that had had its beginnings in college and its real ending at the hospital in Duluth.

It had always been difficult to think of Marge as ever being a young, foolish girl, though he supposed she must have been. But when he met her at the university she was fully grown, a woman whose head was on straight in a world that was on the verge of going crazy. It was early 1938 and Europe was busy rearming itself. Two years earlier Hitler had reoccupied the demilitarized zone of the Rhineland and the Spanish Civil War had begun. The following March Germany and Russia had sent troops to the Iberian peninsula, and in July the Sino-Japanese War had begun in earnest with the Marco Polo Bridge incident. Mahoney had come down from Duluth in the fall of 1937 to enroll in the college of business at the University of Wisconsin in Madison. The Shultz Lake cabin had been sold after Fred's suicide and most of the money had gone into a trust fund for Mahoney's education—a fact his father bitterly resented. "Here we've got bills and Wallace is running off to play with the rich men's children at college. It just doesn't make sense." But Uncle Fred had been very specific in his will, a document that came as a complete surprise to Mahoney as well as to the rest of the family. Who could have suspected that quiet Fred would have thought so far ahead, the comment was made after the funeral. The money from the sale of his estate was to go to Wallace for his education and for nothing else. There wasn't much money, of course. The Great Depression was still a fact of life; the National Recovery Administration had only been dismantled a couple of years earlier. But costs were low, and the result of the sale of Fred's property and personal belongings was enough to guarantee Mahoney four years of school at Madison. Along with his father—but for completely different reasons— Mahoney, too, resented Uncle Fred's will because it meant giving up the cabin. "It should have remained in the family," he told his mother, or anyone who would listen. A good portion of his youth, the happiest part had been spent there. He vowed that someday he would buy it back, an act that took him nearly forty years to realize. In the meantime he was in school using Uncle Fred's money, and he was damn well going to do the right thing. He was going to make a mark for himself, and for the family. The only way out of the blue - collar cycle of birth - marriage-factory work-retirement and finally death with little or nothing to show for a lifetime of toil, he figured, was business. With the coming war the shrewd businessman was going to make a killing. The right young man, educated properly, would go a long way toward making his own fortune. Mahoney was a cynic beyond his years in those days. That and a worrier. Leaving home on the train, he'd looked into his mother's eyes and he could see the fear for herself there, mingled with a hope for her only son. Years later he'd come to realize that he and Uncle Fred had been her only real hope for salvation from a life that had somehow gone terribly sour for her. Fred was dead and gone, so her son was her very last link to sanity. In a few years she would be dead, but at the time, though Mahoney had seen and recognized her fear, there was nothing he could do about it in the immediate sense. He was wrapped up in his own world, his own troubles, which began for him in his very first semester. He simply was not cut out for business. For the "accountant mentality," as he would come to call it.

On their twenty-fifth anniversary Mahoney had bought Marge a diamond ring. It was her first, and she cried when she opened the little box and he'd put it on her finger. They had not been able to afford it when they got married, and they really couldn't afford it then. "If I had stuck to my guns and gone into business, we wouldn't have had such a difficult life," he said. By then they had had several embassy assignments, his cover as an undersecretary in the economics section requiring them to socialize with foreign government ministers whose wives' fingers always seemed to be adorned with half their country's wealth. He had seen the looks on their faces, and how sometimes Marge would try to hide her left hand, bare except for a cheap gold wedding band. She had tried to refuse the ring, of course, but Mahoney wouldn't hear of it. In the end she agreed only if they would consider the ring their little nest egg: their money in savings, as she called it. "I wouldn't have you any other way, old man," she told him. "You're working for your country and I'm proud of you."

Marcus Overholt was his academic adviser in his freshman year. His office was across from the observatory, facing Lake Mendota. First-semester grades had been posted while Mahoney was home on winter break, and Overholt called him in when he got back to campus. It was the final few days of registration before the second semester began, and the campus was a madhouse of returning students and faculty.

"You are a people person, Wallace," Overholt had begun. He was a dapper little man who always wore three-piece wool suits, wire-rimmed glasses perched precariously on his thin nose, and old-fashioned shoes with pointed toes. Most of the students didn't like him. He was a tough, uncompromising man who'd managed to survive the depression intact by dint of his economic genius. Mahoney liked him because of his forthrightness.

"Ordinarily," he said, "such a quality is requisite for a successful career in the business world." He had Mahoney's transcript in front of him. "To understand people, of course, is to understand honesty and integrity—or the lack thereof—all important factors for success. But that simply is as far as it goes within you, Wallace. You have somehow managed to fail nearly every course you took. Dismally so, I might add, in your business and economics classes. Marginally so even in English. But you did shine, for some reason inexplicable to me, in psychology." He pushed the transcript across his desk. "In fact, in psychology you somehow managed an A."

Mahoney had known, of course, that he had done poorly. But he had never suspected this. He was at a loss for words. Returning home, a failure, the steel plant loomed in front of him.

"Ordinarily I would advise you to drop out of school, get yourself a job somewhere, or perhaps travel the country before it's too late, and then in a year or so return to your studies," Overholt said. He got up from behind his desk and looked out the window across the lake, now frozen for the winter. "In your case, however, I don't think that is either necessary or wise."

Mahoney was miserable. He'd wasted Uncle Fred's money. "No, sir," he mumbled.

Overholt turned back. "No, indeed. I spoke with Dr. Robie about you. He heads our psychology department. He thinks you have promise."

"Sir?" Mahoney asked, looking up. This was coming out of left field as far as he was concerned. The psychology class he had taken had been nothing but a lark. A filler for three credits because an economics class he'd wanted to take had been filled. He had barely studied and had skipped half his classes because he figured what the instructor was telling them had been nothing more than common sense, mixed with a little technical jargon. Much ado about nothing.

"I've taken the liberty of making an appointment for you, Wallace," Overholt said. He took out his pocket watch and looked at the time. "You've got only a few minutes to make it, as a matter of fact. And Norman Robie is not a man to be kept waiting."

Mahoney jumped up, they shook hands, and at the door Overholt called to him.

"By the way, find yourself an English tutor, Wallace. You're not going to get anywhere unless you learn how to write a decent report. Even Freud managed somehow."

Mahoney had been devastated. But thinking about it now, he understood that Overholt had in fact been very kind. Dr. Robie had become his friend and mentor, a relationship that was to last well into the sixties when the old man, then a professor emeritus living still in Madison, finally died. And even more importantly, because of Overholt's last bit of advice, he met Marge.

The first time he saw her he knew that she was going to be his wife. In many respects she was very much like his mother; she had a calmness about her, a gentle beauty, and soft eyes that looked out onto the world with a trust and a hope that no matter how bad things might seem at the moment, they were bound to get better. But there was a bit of humor to her as well; that was plain in the slight upturning of her lips at the corners of her mouth. She could laugh. It was one of her many endearing qualities. Her hair was short and light brown, her complexion fair. In those days women of breeding did not expose themselves to the sun. She came from Winnepeg, Canada, where her father owned a huge lumber mill. He'd sent his daughter south for a proper education, and to meet the "right" young man. (He wasn't too happy that Mahoney was a failed business major.) Her accent was barely noticeable except in words such as *about* or *out*, and the soft British *a* in words such as after. She was short, barely five feet four, but she had a lovely figure and wonderful legs that even when she got older retained their shapeliness. He was forever trying to get a glimpse of them when she sat down or got up, and after a while she began to tease him coyly. It was at that point he began to realize that she had actually noticed him.

She was a year younger than he, but a year ahead of him in school. She had enrolled when she was only sixteen, and as an English major she stayed at one of the sorority houses. He remembered going there for his tutoring sessions and afterward in the dark he would stand across the street in the shadows and watch the house, hoping to catch a glimpse of her through the windows. "I always knew that you were out there," she told him later. "I used to tell the other girls about it, and they'd giggle that I was falling in love with a voyeur."

School seemed to go by in a blur for him. His English grades began to climb, but he worked very hard for the improvement, if for no other reason than to impress Marge. But psychology continued to be nothing more than common sense to him, so he seldom studied for more than an hour or two an evening yet came out with mostly A's. He and Dr. Robie, who perhaps saw in the young Mahoney another Freud or Carl Jung, became fast friends. In the first year when Marge was often too busy with her own studies to see him, Mahoney would go over to the professor's house where his wife would serve them coffee and schnapps and they would listen to classical music and discuss the psychology of the madmen in Europe. "Look to a man's youth for his motivations," Dr. Robie said. "If you hope to understand his present actions, you will have to first know his past." It was the beginning of motivational analysis, which would become so critical in the Agency. Years later it was a brand-new thing all over again that some whiz kid on the Soviet desk at Langley tried to pass off as his own invention. But by then Mahoney had been a lot of places and had seen a lot of things, so he wasn't put off by the kid's misplaced enthusiasm.

He remembered how in the next years, however, he and Marge began to spend nearly all of their free time together, so that their studies began to suffer, and Dr. Robie got worried. "If you're going to continue with your studies and go on to graduate school, you will have to give up this girl," he said. "If you get married you will never become a psychologist." It was true. He knew it and Marge knew it, but neither of them wanted to look beyond the next week, certainly not to the next semester. In the meantime they juggled their study time as best they could, knocking out sleep because it wasn't important, so that they could be together. Nothing else mattered to them.

Because of his disastrous first semester, Mahoney could not graduate with his class. Instead he had to wait until the end of the fall semester in 1941. Marge had finished eighth in her class of 325, and earned her teaching certificate, and went to work as a teaching assistant at the university. Her father by then was agitating for her to return to Winnepeg, despairing that she was ever going to meet anyone in the States who would amount to anything. He and Mahoney had come face-to-face on Marge's graduation day, and the old man had offered him five thousand dollars, U.S., to turn his back on his daughter and walk away. He never told Marge that, but he had always thought she'd guessed. It was never mentioned between them. And he supposed her father, who died in the late fifties, never said anything about it either.

The university was gearing up for finals week when the Japanese attacked Pearl Harbor. Mahoney was studying in the dorm when the news came over the radio. Someone down the corridor came running, shouting something about the Japs, and within the hour the entire campus was listening to the horrible news. Marge had stayed on at the sorority as a housemother. Mahoney ran across campus and without knocking burst in. He raced across the living room and bounded up the stairs to the second floor, girls everywhere screaming: "There's a man in the house!" Marge came to the door of her room dressed in an old housecoat, her hair up in curlers, tears in her eyes. She had heard the news. "What does it mean, Wallace?" she asked.

"I'm enlisting in the Army as soon as finals are over," he shouted over the pandemonium. "I think I can get a commission. Dr. Robie said he would help. Maybe even in G-2. They need psychologists."

She nodded, in her serious way. "I understand."

"I don't know how long this thing is going to last. But I think it'll be years. Maybe five years."

"I'll wait for you."

"Will you marry me?"

"Yes, Wallace. I'll wait for you. I promise."

He remembered that the corridor was filled with half-clothed girls who were hanging on every word. Marge said that everyone of them thought that the scene that night was the most romantic thing they'd ever witnessed. Their stoic heroine promising to wait for her warrior-lover who was about to go off into mortal combat.

"Now," Mahoney shouted. "Will you marry me now? This week? Before I leave?"

She seemed to think about it for only a fraction of a second, then solemnly nodded. "Yes, I will, Wallace," she said.

And then they were in each other's arms, kissing deeply, the sorority girls laughing and shouting and clapping and crying.

For Mahoney the entire war seemed to pass in darkness. Whenever he thought back to those four years in his life, he remembered only nighttime. At Fort Benning, Georgia, where he took his initial training after boot camp, he studied around the clock, putting in many more hours than he ever had in college. His mother had died in his second year of college, and his father died early in 1942, for which he was given a few days' compassionate leave. Marge, who had gone back to Winnepeg to be with her father for the duration, came down to Duluth to be with her husband. They had slept together only twice: once on their wedding night in Madison at the Fess Hotel and once on the night before he had left for the Army in her sorority house bedroom. After the funeral they went back to his parents' house in West Duluth where Marge arranged a huge lunch for the mourners, who didn't leave until nearly midnight. Mahoney's train left for Fort Dix, New Jersey, at eight in the morning. From there he had orders to ship out to England.

It struck him that this was the very first time he had ever been in the house when his parents had not been around. He was the last of the Mahoneys, he reflected bitterly. There were no aunts or uncles left, certainly no one here in Duluth other than friends. In southern Minnesota he thought there might be some cousins on his mother's side, but he had never met them and they hadn't been at the funeral. At least he didn't think they had, although he'd seen a lot of people at the cemetery whom he hadn't recognized. There had never been anyone on his father's side except for Uncle Fred. So the end of the family was nearly complete. He went out into the backyard to have a smoke before going up. The light in the bathroom was on. Marge was getting ready for him. She'd even managed to clean up the spare bedroom, and he found suddenly that he was a little nervous about being here like this with her. Partly because her background was so much richer than his, and

53

he was ashamed of his position. But also because it felt odd being with a woman, even if she was his wife, in his parents' home. He could feel his mother's presence everywhere.

When he finished his cigarette he went inside, locked up as he had seen his father do a thousand times in the past, turned off the lights, and trudged up the stairs. At the top he hesitated a moment.

"Marge?" he called softly.

"I'm here, Wallace," she said from the back bedroom.

"Be just a moment," he mumbled, and he went into the bathroom, closing and for some reason he couldn't understand, locking the door. He leaned with his back against it and closed his eyes. He was frightened of death, he decided. His uncle's, his mother's, his father's, and in the morning he would be off to Europe where the possibility of his own death was great. Once again he saw his Uncle Fred's body slumped on the cot in the boathouse. When he dreamed about that moment it was always in color. He hung on every gruesome detail until he thought he had gone crazy. Somehow he had become morbid. The war was going badly and it was going to change him for the worse. He just knew it. It was the beginning of a classic psychotic neurosis. Soon he would begin hearing voices. He'd begin doing things that later he would not be able to recall. Return of the repressions was the technical term for dreams. Well, brother, he had plenty of repressions just lately, and seeing his father's body in the coffin at the church this afternoon hadn't helped a whole hell of a lot. He raised his hands in front of his face and opened his eyes. They were shaking. Christ on a cross, my war hasn't even started and I'm going to pieces. He'd been told stories at Fort Benning about young second louies showing up at the front all full of spit and polish. "At least you're not West Point," Captain DeSanio, his company commander, had told him. "The OCS guys seem to have a better chance of it with the men in the first few months. Of course, after that it doesn't make any difference. If you've survived that long you're a combat veteran and no one will screw with you. It's up to you to hang on that long." Mahoney closed his eyes again. "Keep your ass down and your mouth shut and you'll come out okay," the captain had said.

"Wallace?" Marge called from the other side of the door.

He straightened up guiltily and turned around. His heart was pounding. "Just a moment," he said. He flushed the toilet.

"Are you all right?" Marge asked.

"Just fine," Mahoney said, unlocking the door and opening it. Marge looked up at him in concern. She was wearing nothing but a silk negligée. Her hair, which had grown longer in the last year, was down framing her sweet, innocent face. He thought how much like a desirable angel she looked at that moment, and he felt like such a heel.

"What is it?" she asked. "Are you thinking about your father?"

There was a lump in his throat. He nodded, not trusting himself to speak. She reached up and took him in her arms, holding him close as she whispered in his ear. "It's all right," she said. "I understand."

"I'm frightened," Mahoney blurted, surprised even as he said it.

"I know. And so am I. So is everybody."

She didn't understand. How could she? She hadn't heard the horror stories coming back from Africa and from England and the Pacific. She hadn't seen the bodies coming back in boxes, row after row of them, or the men on stretchers or in wheelchairs, parts of their faces blown away, limbs missing, barely human figures hobbling into the convalescent care hospitals. "The poor bastards," his friend Frazier had said. "The lucky ones are pushing up daisies on the other side of the ditch. I, for one, sure as hell don't want to come home like that." The mission was intelligence training. They'd been sent down to the hospital in Atlanta to interview returning casualties from the battles in the Pacific, and in Huntsville the first of the German and Italian POWs. The sights and the sounds and especially the smells had not been pretty.

"Don't ever worry about me, Wallace," Marge was saying.

"Maybe we should have waited," he said.

She pulled away from him and looked up into his eyes, her lips compressed. It was the very first time he'd ever seen her angry. "Don't ever say that. Never again, not unless you're sorry you married me. In that case we'll end it here and now and I'll never bother you again."

"I didn't mean that," he said. He felt miserable.

"Then don't be stupid. I love you. We're husband and wife. You have a job to do and so do I. Let's get on with it so that our lives can someday return to normal."

He didn't know what to say. He felt terrible and yet he was bubbling over with love and admiration for her.

"We're going to have children and a very long life together. I never want to hear you talk like that again. Do you understand me?"

Mahoney nodded. "I love you, Mrs. Mahoney."

"And I love you, Mr. Mahoney," she said. Her face softened

55

and she took his hand. "Now I want you to make love to me. Afterward you'll still have time for a few hours of sleep before you have to catch your train."

Their lovemaking was slow and very gentle, and unlike the first two times—which had been the first two times for either of them—not hesitant. Her breasts were small and firm, and although her waist was tiny, her hips was fairly broad. Perfect for having children, Mahoney thought as he lay with her in the darkness, her wonderfully soft body against his.

"Are you sleeping?" he asked much later.

"No," she said. "But you should be."

"I can't."

She propped herself up on one elbow, her other hand lying on his chest, and looked at him in the dim light from outside. "Is it your father? The funeral?" She'd been waiting for it to hit him.

"I don't know. I don't think so. Not yet, anyway. It's just that I don't want to waste these last few hours."

"We have the rest of our lives."

"I'll come back."

"You'd better," she said.

But he had been thinking about his father, and about his Uncle Fred and about the North Pole Bar, and the baseball games, and about fishing and hunting, and the cabin. In death they all seemed much larger and more real than they had in life. It was, he supposed, because he had been with them as a child. Their deaths had come when he was a man. All that was left, then, were memories. In the end that's all any of us were ever left with.

In terms of his life with Marge, the war was over almost before it had begun. He'd had only one leave since his father's funeral, in the spring of 1944, just before the invasion of Normandy. He and Marge managed to rent the Shultz Lake cabin from the kindly couple who had bought it from the estate, and there in the tiny bedroom, shivering under the blankets because it was a particularly cold weekend, they conceived John, their first child, who was born the next January when Mahoney was on the Eastern Front working with his Soviet counterparts in military intelligence. Officially he was demobilized in August 1945, but Bill Donovan—Wild Bill to his friends and detractors alike—who had headed the wartime OSS had created what he called the VSS, Veterans of Strategic Services, which was to be the interim intelligence agency until the CIA was officially formed in 1947. Mahoney remained in Europe until the week before Christmas, working with General Rheinhard Gehlen, the Nazi anti-Communist spy master who would eventually be used to create the *Bundesnachrichtendienst*—the BND, West Germany's new secret service. Suddenly he was home.

The war had changed him. Drastically so. He'd gone away a young man trained in psychology but unsure of himself, unsure of his heritage and even of who he was and where he was going. He returned a man, convinced that he had found his calling, an expert at what he did, but not at all sure how his wife would take to it. It was to be the very last time he ever made that mistake about her. He hadn't counted on her mettle.

Donovan was having a tough go of it in Washington. Truman, with a stroke of his pen in September, had abolished the OSS, and the only thing holding the new VSS together was Wild Bill's charisma. The bulk of the new, loosely knit organization had been reassigned to the U.S. State Department in research and analysis, a job that was promised to Mahoney if he would only agree to one more year in the field.

The charade wasn't going to last very long, according to Wild Bill. Sooner or later Truman would have to see the light and a proper secret service would be authorized. In the meantime their job was to not only hold on to the wartime-trained personnel they already had in place, but to begin recruiting new blood. Especially from academia. We need bright young people, Donovan preached. Well-schooled, highly motivated men and women who will be willing to serve their country. The war may be over, but the real battle is just beginning.

Mahoney was sent back to the University of Wisconsin ostensibly to enroll in graduate school, under Dr. Robie, picking up his studies where he left off. In actuality he was to open a VSS Office of Enlistment, which was to be his first peacetime clandestine operation, the first time he had to lead a double life among his own people, and the beginning of a long life of the unspoken lie between him and his wife. He simply did not know how she was going to take it, and the changes within him. He didn't know if he could give up either.

Marge came down on the train from Winnepeg with the baby. Mahoney had traveled directly to Madison where he had arranged for an apartment off campus (Donovan was paying him fifty dollars a week, plus a small budget for the office and the money for his tuition and books), reestablished his ties with Dr. Robie, and enrolled for the spring semester beginning in January. It had all happened within five days of his return from Europe, and he hadn't had any real time to worry about Marge until he picked her up at the train depot.

It was snowing lightly and it was bitterly cold when he drove up in a taxi and saw her standing out front with John bundled up in her arms, two suitcases at her feet. His first thought was that she looked like one of the refugees he had seen all over Europe. And his second thought was that she hadn't changed at all.

"Hello, Marge," he said rather formally, stopping two feet away from her. There were a lot of people bustling around them.

She looked up into his face. He always remembered that he had gotten the impression at that moment that she was studying his face to make sure she really knew him, that he indeed was her husband. At last she smiled, stepped forward, and handed him the baby.

"Mr. Mahoney, meet young Mr. Mahoney. John Conrad."

Mahoney held his son in his arms. It was the first time he'd ever seen him. The pictures Marge had taken had never reached him. And then she was in his arms, and they were kissing, and John was wailing at the top of his lungs because he had no idea what was happening.

When they parted, Marge was crying. "I dreamed of this moment every night for the past four years, Wallace. And now that it's here, I can hardly believe it."

"Neither can I," Mahoney said stupidly.

"I love you."

"And I love you."

"That's all I wanted to hear," she said. "You take your son—he weighs a ton. I'll get the suitcases."

"I've changed, Margery," Mahoney blurted.

She picked up the bags. "I should hope so."

"I mean really changed. I'm not the same kid who went to war." He wanted it out in the open here and now, so that they could deal with it.

She smiled too. "I've changed too. I'm a mother."

"Maybe you won't like me so much now . . ."

She laughed out loud this time, the sound musical. "It's for sure I'm not going to like you, Mr. Mahoney, if you make me stand here all afternoon so that I freeze to death."

Late that night, after John had settled down, and after they had eaten their dinner and were lying in each other's arms in the big fold-out bed in the living room, she studied him again as she had at the train station. He watched her watch him, noticing how her nostrils flared sometimes when she was thinking, how an artery throbbed delicately at the side of her neck, and how her left eyebrow would rise just before she was about to speak. Something was troubling her, and he thought it was him after all. She was seeing the change in him, and he braced for it. A lot of couples who were married before the war were not going to make it. And he was frightened of losing her. But what she said came as a total surprise to him. He never questioned their marriage again.

"My father lost his business," she began. "But it's all right. He has a small house now, he had a good job, and he has his friends. He'll survive."

"Christ, I'm sorry," Mahoney said. He had been worried about himself while all the while she had been carrying that burden.

"Don't swear."

"Sorry."

She nodded. "After graduate school, then what?"

"But what about your father?"

"After graduate school, what?" she said evenly.

"I have a job with the State Department. Research and analysis."

"Guaranteed?"

"It looks that way. But it might mean we'll have to live overseas."

"I like to travel," she said. "But I want you to understand, Wallace, that my father will never be able to help us. When he dies there will be no inheritance."

Mahoney sat up in bed. "You think that's why I married you?"

"No," she said, smiling slightly as if she had won her point. "Nor did I marry you for any preconceived notion of some sort of life you were going to provide for me. I married you because I love you." She smiled again. "Now, let's never talk about this again, Wallace. Never."

Dr. Robie shed a tear when Mahoney received his master's degree in December 1946 and announced that he would not be continuing with his studies. Marge shed a tear when they moved out of their little apartment. Madison had become their home. And John wailed at the top of his lungs, because that's what he always did when he sensed something was wrong. But Mahoney returned to Washington to a quiet hero's welcome, the first of many such homecomings in the years to come. All told he had recruited twenty-three prospective agents for Donovan. Many of them were disaffected students who had missed the war and were enthralled

59

by Mahoney's stories, a few of them were returning veterans on the G.I. Bill, but a third of them were instructors who felt they were in dead-end jobs and could be of more use to themselves as well as their country in Washington. It was always a point of pride with Mahoney that not a single one of his recruits washed out. All of them went to work for the CIA when it was formed, and in later years became the backbone for Mahoney's support group: his fan club, as they became known. One of them was later sent back to Madison to act as a permanent recruiting agent, and retired a full professor of mathematics in 1980.

Their time in Madison also marked the solidification of Marge's quiet stoicism and absolute trust in her husband. Mahoney's cover story to her and to the university at large was that he was a specialized tutor. It was how he said he earned his money. He would carefully select the students he thought he could recruit and would begin his courtship. He would talk with them, sometimes through an entire night, often at their dorm rooms or apartments. Some of them were young women. Sometimes he took them to dinner, or to ball games. Once he even took a prospective recruit fishing for a weekend in northern Wisconsin. Marge never said a word. He always suspected that she'd known, or at least guessed in some vague way, that his work at the university was not what it appeared to be on the surface. Not entirely, though he did graduate with honors. But she loved him, and trusted him implicitly. When he said everything would be all right, she believed him. "Stupidity, not trust, if you ask me," his chief of station in Germany told him ten years later. After the man had picked himself up off the floor, he apologized and never said a thing about it again, either directly to Mahoney's face or behind his back. Marge was anything but stupid.

Washington seemed just as hectic in those days as it had during the height of the war. For a time, however, there didn't seem to be any purpose or real focus to the hubbub. People were busy, but doing what, no one seemed to know, exactly. Mahoney went to work for the State Department, his desk in a tiny cubicle that he shared with two other ex-OSS officers. Down the hall the translators were manufacturing reports in English from newspapers flown in daily from Europe and the Soviet Union. It was the job of Mahoney and his crew of "oddballs" to make some sense out of the reports. They used to hang huge charts out in the corridor—there was no room in their cramped office—with lists of Soviet government appointees and their promotions. Over a year's time they could and did chart the progress of dozens of men, among them Nikita Sergeyevich Khrushchev and Vyacheslav Mikhailovich Molotov. The notion was that, given enough time, the oddballs would be able to predict with some reasonable expectation of accuracy just who was on the ascendancy and would someday assume power.

Incredibly boring stuff most of the time, but it was giving him the background that would stand him in good stead in later years. Often, though, on weekends he and Marge would attend diplomatic gatherings, more often than not at the Soviet embassy on 16th Street just down the block from the University Club and within sight of Lafayette Square and the White House. In that case his cover was as special assistant to the Deputy Undersecretary for Economic Affairs. Mahoney always thought that Overholt, his former academic adviser at the university, would have been proud of him in that role. Keep your eyes and ears open, he was told. But they weren't getting a clothing allowance in those days, and sometimes he supposed they looked a little underdressed. They'd leave early because they were ashamed of their appearance. Afterward they would stop back at the State Department and Marge would wait in the lobby while he ran upstairs to type his report. Never once did she complain, even one autumn when he was upstairs nearly five hours. When he came back down, Marge was asleep on one of the couches. "Some party," she mumbled when he woke her and led her home.

Everyone was collecting intelligence data in those days—the military services, the State Department, Donovan's VSS—but no one really knew what was going on. That year, under prodding from Peter Vischer, who was the secretary of the Joint Chiefs of Staff Intelligence Committee, Truman gave in and created an office called the Central Intelligence Group—the CIG—which was supposed to receive and collate all intelligence data gathered by the other services, and report directly to a National Intelligence Authority composed of the secretaries of State, War and Navy, and the president's chief of staff. In less than two years the CIG had absorbed most of Donovan's former OSS people, all of the FBI's foreign intelligence networks, the individual military units, and in the process tripled its intended size.

Donovan sent Mahoney to New York to set up an office near the East River, not far from where the United Nations would put up its headquarters in 1952. No one was quite certain where the CIG would eventually wind up, and no one wanted to put all their eggs in one basket. Not just yet.

Marge took this move with her usual aplomb, and they set up housekeeping in a small loft apartment in Greenwich Village, which was about the only place they could afford at the time.

But it didn't last long. The CIG continued to grow, and since a majority of its staff were former OSS officers, Wild Bill's people literally took over, lock, stock, and barrel. The CIG became huge, with its own budget line, its own banks, its own policies, and even its own airline. "Bigger than State by '48" was the new motto, and the Mahoneys were called back to Washington in 1947 when the National Security Act was signed creating the Central Intelligence Agency.

From that moment on they never looked back. Michael was born in 1948, so now they had two children to cart around, but Marge never complained, not once, not even when they bounced around the world, sometimes on a moment's notice as when they left Spain in the middle of the night having just arrived there four months earlier. Or the first stint in West Germany when they lived in a rat-infested railroad flat in Bonn. That assignment lasted three years. It was always cold in the winter and hot in the summer, Mahoney remembered. Austria had been a plum. Their apartment along the Schuller Strasse downtown was large, bright, and airy. They had been able to afford a maid and a cook then, but it only lasted two years before they were posted back to Germany, and then back to New York in 1953, the year after the United Nations moved into its new headquarters.

Nor did she complain each time they returned to Washington only to find that everything had changed: the city, the people, even the politics. They always seemed to be on the outside looking in during their sojourns in Washington. "Their bad luck city," she came to call it, even though she would have willingly stayed there for the rest of her life if her husband's job had required it.

Then came more overseas postings, finally ending in Moscow for the second time in the late seventies during which their youngest son Michael was killed in an operation that had somehow gone bad. Marge was devastated. The wind was finally out of her sails. They'd bought the Shultz Lake cabin and settled in for a long, healing retirement. He watched her die there, his hopes and aspirations and purpose for living fading and dying with her.

"Don't be bitter, old man," she'd told him as she lay dying.

John's wife Elizabeth had come up to be with her. She did her hair, fixed her makeup, and bought her a new housecoat. She had wasted away to nothing by then, the cancer had spread throughout

62

her body, but Mahoney thought she was the most beautiful woman he had ever known. She was interred that winter in Missoula, Montana. Their son Michael had lived and worked in Montana and had fallen in love with the mountains and the high plains. He was buried out there, and Marge had wanted to be with him. In the spring when the ground had thawed she was buried next to him.

"It was a good life," she told him. "Don't ever think otherwise."

An induced carcinoma. It had been his secret now these last four years. He had no proof, of course, but the timing was right (the Russians had been doing a lot of it in those days), the cancer was correct (no explanation for it, Mr. Mahoney, it's just there and it shouldn't be), and he bided his time until now.

Vengeance is mine, the Lord said. But He'd not been dealing with the Russians when He said that.

He crossed the lobby and started up the stairs. At the end he had wished for only one thing, and that was peace. Not peace for the world, or any such grand notion, but simply peace for himself. Peace of mind, peace in his heart. Forgiveness, even. Of course that had been an irrational thought, then and now. As it was irrational to believe that Chernov personally had had a direct hand in Marge's death. But it was possible, a little voice whispered at the back of his head. Such an operation would have been consistent with Chernov's style. In 1956 more than two hundred Hungarians, many of them in the wings waiting to form an opposition government to Communist rule, had been poisoned, not shot, during a secret conciliation conference the Soviets had conducted. Chernov had been on the negotiation team. Shortly afterward he'd been promoted. In Mexico in the sixties and in Poland in the early seventies, similar events—though admittedly on a much smaller scale—had happened at the same time Chernov had been posted nearby. Coincidence or design?

For a time Mahoney had made it a point to keep loose track of the man. He would surface here and there, always a wave of destruction and death in his path. Shattered lives. Ruined ambitions. He was the grim reaper. But then the Russian had faded from view and his name had been all but forgotten, slipping off the actives list, presumed either killed or demoted or both. But Mahoney had known in a visceral way that he was still there, in the shadows perhaps, but there nevertheless. He had expected to run across Chernov in Moscow, but had not. His absence had been troublesome at first, but then there had been other considerations, other projects, other distractions.

"It was a war we were in, you and I, Wallace," he'd said a few hours earlier in the bar. "Do you think that I love my country any less than you do America? Do you think I am any less of a patriot than you?"

"You have murdered hundreds of people in the name of patriotism. Innocent people."

"By whose standards?" Chernov had flared. "You kidnapped three innocent Soviet children, brought them to the United States, and had them brainwashed. Is that any less monstrous?"

"After my son had been kidnapped and killed."

"It was an accident, his death."

Any doubts Mahoney had had, though, were dispelled almost from the moment Chernov had strode through the doorway. He had seen the guilt in the Russian's eyes. That and the knowledge that Mahoney knew or had guessed about Marge's death.

At the head of the stairs he stopped again to listen. But the hotel remained quiet. He unscrewed the small light bulb in the stained-glass sconce above a hall table, plunging this part of the corridor into darkness. The only light now came from beside the bathroom door fifty feet away.

He had never actually shot a defenseless man in cold blood. In fact he didn't like guns; he distrusted them. He had seen enough death in his career to last ten lifetimes. He had witnessed with his own eyes the results of a gunshot wound his Uncle Fred had inflicted on himself. He had seen and smelled the senseless destruction so that just the thought of it turned his stomach inside out. But he'd also been witness to the horrifying antics of madmen such as Chernov.

He moved slowly down the corridor to Chernov's door and listened. As before no sounds came from within. He had thought about waiting until tomorrow, or even the next day before doing this. But that had been the simple vanity of an old man who thought that no matter what happened he would be able to control the situation. He wasn't so sure now. There was no real guarantee that they wouldn't be traced here sooner than he expected. He'd wanted forty-eight hours, in a small way so that he could have the time to savor his final victory, but in another way because he had actually wanted to hear what Chernov would say for himself. Curiosity about why Chernov had made contact after all these years. Why he had come out of hiding. Why me, of all people?

Why now? What has he brought with him that is so important he is willing to risk his life?

Something big is about to happen, Wallace. Something very big. Something you and I will have to prevent.

Carefully, so as to make absolutely no noise, Mahoney slipped the key in the lock and slowly turned it. For a moment it seemed as if the mechanism were jammed. He increased the pressure. Suddenly the lock turned with a loud snap, and he froze.

He remembered standing before another door just like this one, flatfooted and frightened at what he might find on the other side, yet determined to go through with it. How his heart pounded, how he strained with every sense to pick up a sound, a light, a movement, anything. But then as now, he heard nothing.

Stepping back, he took the .38 out of his pocket, pulled the hammer back, and careful to keep the gun away from his body and out ahead of him, he eased the door all the way open.

Chernov stood in front of the window, his body framed in silhouette by the dim light from outside. "Hello, Wallace," he said.

Mahoney raised the pistol.

"Please don't," Chernov said sharply. "Not yet."

The weapon was heavy and unnatural in Mahoney's hand. He began to squeeze the trigger.

"I beg of you, wait! Hear me out! You cannot begin to imagine how terribly important this is to me. To you. To all of us."

"My wife was important to me," Mahoney said through clenched teeth.

"I know who killed her. And why. And how."

Mahoney's hand shook. "Tell me."

"Afterward. First listen to what I have to say."

"You're the great destroyer."

"I was. For God's sake, man, now we can become the saviors."

"No," Mahoney mumbled, shaking his head.

Chernov sagged a little. He turned to look out the window. "I knew you were coming tonight," he said resignedly.

"You should have run."

Chernov turned back. "There's no place left to run. Didn't you know?" He lowered his head. "I beg of you, Wallace. On my hands and knees, gladly. Hear me out."

"Goddamn you," Mahoney said, a heaviness coming into his chest. "Goddamn you to hell," he said. He lowered the gun, then turned and very slowly walked back to his room.

* * *

Lying again in his bed, Mahoney remembered a bit of poetry from out of his past.

> To life! To life!
> After a summer of dreams and hopes,
> All that remained were the winter songs
> Of an old, old man.

He cried for everything he had lost, because he finally understood that there was no way of bringing any of it back.

5

The holy zeal had come upon Cassidy since his two significant discoveries. He and his people along with several of West's FBI technicians had started at the beginning. This time it was their aim to miss absolutely nothing. In the very foreseeable future, John figured there would be nothing left to the cabin, the boathouse, or the greenhouse except for piles of carefully tagged rubble. They were literally dismantling the place, board by board, stone by stone.

Carlisle had been on the telephone for a long time. He had switched to the cabin's line for more privacy despite the risk of possibly missing an incoming call, although by now the line was being monitored here and down at the main telephone exchange in Duluth.

West was dividing his time between the other telephones and a constant stream of his people coming up from the city for hasty little conferences after which his people would race away again, presumably with fresh instructions, and West would make another call. The Bureau was making an all-out effort. It wasn't often they got to work in such close concert with the glamour boys over at the CIA, and for the right man who could pull it off with élan, there would almost certainly be a promotion. It was evident in the almost theatrical concentration in West's stern mannerisms.

John had kept himself apart from most of this, but his time was coming. He felt as if he were a hunting dog being held back on a leash. At one point Carlisle had put his hand over the telephone's mouthpiece and called across to him, "Don't you go anywhere, mister. There's something you're just going to have to hear."

"Nowhere to go yet," John had mumbled, but Carlisle had already turned back to the telephone and couldn't have heard.

The most damning evidence so far had been his father's passport factory, and the fact that it had been so carefully hidden. Not just locked up, stored in a closet somewhere. But also, significantly, not destroyed.

"If he wasn't planning on coming back here, he would have burned the stuff," John had argued.

"I'm afraid I can't quite agree with that either, sir," Cassidy had replied doggedly. "It could also mean that your father doesn't give a damn."

"Then why did he go through such lengths to hide it in the first place?"

"It's a matter of time. He wants some, that's all."

John could hear his father speaking. Keep them guessing, son. The man who is off-balance can't think straight. And when he finally does figure the one thing out, throw him another curve. Tradecraft, after all, is nothing more than one man's plan for confusing another man's thought processes. But to what end, and where in the world had he gone?

It had been drizzling when John had been out at the lake last. They'd worn rain suits and big plastic hats and had taken the aluminum fishing boat out in the middle of the lake. There had been some trouble up in New York with the Cuban delegation. No one seemed able to keep the names and faces straight. At one count there were sixteen of them, including secretaries, and in the next there were seventeen of them. The U.N. security people thought there were a half-dozen new faces among the second batch. But in the following week everything had gone back to normal. The shifts seemed to come every eight or ten days. The few they had stopped for identification checks had valid papers, and because they had diplomatic immunity it was hard to get close to them.

"They're probably running half a dozen floaters up there," his father said, baiting his hook. "Twins or close enough alike to use the same passports over and over again. Take the whole list down to Miami and circulate it. My guess is you'll pick them up there. Probably running couriers out of Havana, too."

They'd found three of them in the first week, and everyone but Castro was happy. But it had been so damned simple.

Carlisle had been writing something in his notebook. He glanced over at John who was perched on the big table, shook his head, said something into the telephone, and put the instrument down. West looked up.

"I'm taking John with me for a little ride," Carlisle said, his thoughts obviously elsewhere. "You can hold the fort here for us."

"Wesley is bringing the telephone logs up. I think you'd better be here."

"Did they find something?"

"I think so," West said. "But he wouldn't say on an open line."

"It'll keep for a half hour," Carlisle said, making his decision.

"You're the boss," West conceded.

"Yes," Carlisle said. He motioned for John.

Outside, before they climbed into his rental car, Carlisle looked back at the cabin. "Damn," he said softly.

"What is it, Farley?" John asked. The night was very still now, the stars brilliant against the velvet black background.

"Trouble. Goddamned big trouble for all of us, I think."

The dirt road led three miles around the lake, past a small country church and then out to the paved county highway that led back down to Duluth past the airport. It was late, and there was no traffic or lights anywhere. Carlisle turned south and almost immediately pulled off the main road, onto another dirt track, proceeding until they were out of sight of the highway. He turned off the car's lights so that there was no chance of being seen by a passerby.

"That was Alex again on the phone. He's been down in Archives turning the place inside out."

And making a big row in the process, John thought. But it wasn't his place to make comment. Not yet. He was here to listen.

"It was none of their business," Carlisle said. He closed his eyes momentarily. "Christ," he said softly. "This will have to be kept from West, you know that, don't you?"

"What is it? What did Alex find?"

"He's got a handle on Chernov, finally. Name of Yuri Yevgennevich. A captain-general in the KGB, but retired now. He's been acting as a liaison to the Politburo, apparently on a quasi-official basis. Sort of the Soviet version of the old boy network."

"It's why his name didn't show up on our actives list," John said.

"Right," Carlisle said heavily. "My policy. My mistake. And I'll suffer in hell for it, I'm sure. But at least we know who he is, and it isn't good no matter which way you look at it, John. In fact it couldn't be much worse."

"Does my father know him?"

"I don't see how he could help but know him. But there isn't a single reference to Chernov in your father's reports. Not one."

"That's a big stack of paper to go through in such a short time, Farley."

"As soon as Alex picked up the first hints he called everyone in. They dropped everything else."

"Quite a big piece for him to bite off, wouldn't you say?" John said. He was trying to envision the headquarters at Langley. He'd seen the place on emergency footing only once before, and that was when they thought Andropov had been assassinated and a possible coup d'état was in progress in Moscow.

"Donald is involved now. He's going to the president first thing in the morning."

Donald McLean had been appointed Director of Central Intelligence nine months ago. He was young, aggressive, and a close personal friend of the president. He was anything but an alarmist.

"You have to understand that this has gone beyond a simple missing person," Carlisle was saying. "I expect the president will be calling Gorbachev as soon as Donald finishes with him."

"Why, in God's name? What the hell is Chernov?"

"Your father's twin, if such a thing could exist. His counterpart in the KGB."

"An old retired spy."

"Yes, but an old man who knows as much about the KGB as your father knows about us. Organizational charts, operations, budgets—everything from A to Z."

"Old information, Farley. My father hasn't been operational since Brussels."

Carlisle looked at him. "Do you think you're the only person who comes out here to confer with the master? Christ, they're calling him the guru of the mount. He has half the Agency eating out of his hand. He knows what we're up to, all right, just as Chernov knows about his people." Carlisle leaned a little closer. "Let me tell you something. You talked about insurance before? Well, your father invented the game."

"He's just an old man."

Carlisle sat back. "I'll be surprised if the president doesn't order him shot on the spot, no questions asked. Him and Chernov. I'm sure the Russians have already been given the same orders. If they've had a chance to talk, then neither of them can be let back into the stable alive."

"That was an incredibly stupid thing to say to me," John said. He felt dangerously at the edge of his control.

"And what you just said wasn't terribly bright either," Carlisle countered. "I told you before, I am not the enemy here."

"And I asked you who was."

"Chernov. Nothing has changed, only now the stakes have just gone up. He has a hold on your father."

"What are you talking about? You said there was nothing about him on any of my father's contact sheets."

"They probably first met in Austria near the end of the war. Your father worked with a bunch from the GRU. Chernov was there, according to our files."

"So were a few million other Russians."

"Chernov was stationed in New York when the U.N. opened in 1952. He was in Spain a few years later, then Berlin, then Athens, then back to KGB headquarters. He had been transferred out of the military by then. Alex has it all, John. Chernov's postings file reads like your father's. Even to the extent that each time your father was rotated back to the States, Chernov was assigned embassy duty in Washington."

"They were after my father. They always have been. Trying to neutralize him. But they weren't very effective."

"The Russians may have a different explanation," Carlisle said softly.

"What?"

"They might rightly suspect that your father was shadowing Chernov, not the other way around. Look at it from their perspective."

"My father had no control over his assignments."

"Not at first, I grant you that. But after a while he did."

It was coming now. John could feel it.

"Who was working whom. It's come down to that, I'm afraid."

"My father is not a traitor."

Carlisle looked away. "There are some who don't know him like we do. Kim Philby was well loved among his own people."

"You can't be saying that."

"Others will be considering the possibility. We can't keep a lid on it much longer."

It was crazy, but John found that he no longer had the strength to protest. A case of circumstantial evidence was building up against his father, and he had no defense against it. Everything his father had accomplished in his career, every place he'd been, every person he'd had contact with over forty years, every report he had written could be construed either as brilliant work, or as the work of an even more brilliant double. A traitor. A mole.

"There is a second possibility here, too, John," Carlisle said. "One that's not much better."

"What's that?"

"That this Chernov was probably either involved with or at the very least knows the details of your mother's death."

John shivered. Someone had just walked over his grave. "My father will kill him if he finds out."

"He loved her very much," Carlisle was saying from a distance. "You can't possibly imagine how much."

"More than his own life?"

"Yes, that much."

"More than his own country?" Carlisle said. "So much more, in fact, that he would be willing to trade everything he knew for one single scrap of information? Who killed his wife."

"I'll find him," John said. "I'll find them both."

"And then what?" Carlisle asked.

"I won't kill my own father."

"No one is asking you— "

"I'll bring them back."

Wesley wasn't back yet with the telephone logs. West was on the radio trying to track him down. Apparently he had left the telephone exchange nearly two hours earlier, and he had simply disappeared. He wasn't answering his car radio. Cassidy's people were in the attic now, and already half the ceiling boards in the back of the cabin had been removed and stacked outside.

"The first flight out of here leaves a few minutes after seven," John said, looking at his watch. It was half past one. Lack of sleep and worry were starting to catch up with him.

"See Alex as soon as you get back, but I'd stay clear of Donald for the moment," Carlisle said. "He'll have his headhunters out."

"Aren't you coming back?"

"Not right away. I want to see if anything else turns up here."

It was a measure of how important they all considered his father's disappearance to be. Normally DDOs did not go out into the bush, especially not DDOs like Carlisle. Yet here he was grubbing with the common field hands, as he called them.

"What about afterward?" Carlisle asked.

"Afterward?"

"After you see Alex. What then?"

"I don't have a single idea," John said. And he didn't. At least not yet. He figured his father could literally be anywhere by now, including right next door, though it was more likely that he and Chernov were meeting somewhere in Europe. It narrowed things down a bit, even more so considering that Europe was chopped in half east and west. Still it was a damn big place. Where to begin?

"Well, I think we'd better start coming up with ideas, and damn soon. This situation won't remain stable for very long."

John looked at him carefully. "What if we don't find him, Farley? Neither us nor the Russians, I mean. What if he and Chernov just don't want to be found, and aren't?"

"Don't say that," Carlisle groaned. "We're in enough trouble without—"

"What if he just shows up back here next week, or next month, and demands to know what the hell happened to his cabin?"

"It's not going to happen that way."

"But if it did, Farley, what then?"

"We'd have some hard questions for him, I can tell you that much. Like where the hell have you been, my old friend? And just what the hell have you and Chernov been chatting about now?"

"What if he denied everything?"

A slight smile crossed Carlisle's face. "He would have to be pretty convincing to me to believe that."

Oh, yes, John thought, his father was convincing when he wanted to be. He had lived the life of a spy. He knew the game and all of its nuances. He also would have to know by now that his cabin would be crawling with "experts," uncovering his little secrets. He would know that by now they had found his passport factory under the ice in the lake. He'd know that they had found his hiding place beneath the toilet, and that his gun was missing. So maybe Cassidy had been correct when he suggested that his father hadn't destroyed the evidence of his tradecraft because he was merely buying himself some time. Sowing a little uncertainty in the minds of his pursuers. It meant that he was coming back, or at the very least that he expected to be found sooner or later. How much later was the question. If he had gone to kill Chernov, it could have already happened. But if he had gone to talk, to trade information as Carlisle had suggested, it would take longer. Twenty-four hours? Forty-eight? Seventy-two? How long to sum up an entire secret service? How long to name names, pinpoint places, settle on dates? How long to spell out the intent of the Agency? A lifetime, he suspected, to do a proper job of it. But certainly in forty-eight hours they could cover the high points. He'd been gone at least that long already. If he had traveled out of the country, though, say to Europe, he would have covered his tracks, which took time. Perhaps even two full days and nights. Which meant he might not have arrived at his destination until last night. Perhaps only hours ago. Maybe he and Chernov hadn't even come face-to-face yet. They'd have to test the waters first, he supposed. Make absolutely certain that their meeting spot was clean, that neither of them had planted anything, or that neither of them had allowed himself to be followed. Tradecraft took time if it was done right.

"Yes?" Carlisle prompted.

John focused on him. "I was thinking that if he went to Europe, he's only just arrived." Another thought struck him. He turned and looked toward the bedroom.

"What is it?" Carlisle asked.

"His clothes," John mumbled, crossing the living room and stopping at the bedroom doorway. The room was a shambles. Everything had been taken out of the closets and drawers. The bed had been stripped, the mattress completely taken apart. Half the floorboards had been pulled up, revealing the insulation between the floor joists.

Carlisle had followed him. "Talk to me, John."

"Get Cassidy in here, would you?"

"Right," Carlisle said, and he left.

John went into the bedroom, careful not to slip and fall through to the insulation batting. The chest of drawers had been dismantled. His father's clothes had been stacked in neat piles in the corner, each item tagged. Shirts, socks, underwear in one pile. Slacks, shorts, ties, belts in another. In what was left of the closet, his suits and sports jackets had been gone through, tagged, and then rehung on the wire hangers. Nothing there. So what was he missing?

Cassidy appeared in the doorway, Carlisle right behind him. "Yes, sir, what is it you wanted to ask?"

"My father's clothes."

"Yes, sir."

"Did you have any sense of what was missing? I mean what he might have taken with him?"

"Underwear, socks, a couple of shirts and maybe a pair of trousers or two. Hard to be certain."

"Warm clothes, or cool clothes?" John asked.

"Sir . . . ?" Cassidy started to say, but then he caught up with John's thinking, and his face lit up. "Right," he said. "Winter clothes. He took a sweater with him. We're fairly sure of it. A dark sweater. It was stacked on top of a white one. Second drawer from the top, right-hand side. His light linen jacket is still hanging in the closet. Definitely winter clothes."

"Which means?" Carlisle asked.

"Which means, Farley, that he didn't go south. If it's Europe, he's not on the Riviera. Wherever he is, it's chilly there, just like here."

"That's not much."

"But it's something," John said.

"I've found him," West called from the living room.

Carlisle turned around. "Who have you found?"

"Wesley. With the phone logs. He's downtown at the city jail. Seems they arrested themselves a Russian spy."

"When?"

"Not more than an hour ago, apparently. They picked him up for speeding. He was claiming diplomatic immunity. He showed his passport to the arresting officer who was sharp enough to call his desk sergeant who in turn called his shift supervisor who realized that Duluth is off limits for Soviet nationals because of its shipping, so they arrested him."

"They're holding him now?" Carlisle demanded.

West spoke into the telephone. A moment later he turned back. "Yes, they are. But they want to know if he can telephone his embassy in Washington."

"Absolutely not!" Carlisle roared. "And tell them we're on our way."

"It couldn't be one of Trusov's people," John said. "Not this soon."

"No," Carlisle said. "He was probably sent out from Washington to take a quick peek. They don't think Chernov or your father are here. They're just covering all the bases."

"I want to talk to him."

"You'd better change your clothes. I'll go on ahead with West."

"I'll be right behind you," John said, his muscles bunching up. "And, Farley?"

Carlisle had started out the door. He turned back. "Yes?"

"I'll want to talk to this one alone. Someplace quiet."

Carlisle looked at him for a long moment, and West, who was pulling on his coat, stopped, his eyes growing wide.

"I don't want him killed, John."

"Someplace real quiet, Farley.

John kept his anger intact all the way down the hill. It was like a hot, sharp flame in his gut that threatened to flare up out of control at any moment. But not now, he told himself, not this time. At least not here.

Duluth was like a ghost town at this hour. He parked his car on First Street in front of the courthouse, across the street from the newspaper, and went inside. They were waiting for him in the shift supervisor's office. The sign on his desk read Lieutenant Burwick. He wasn't happy, but between West and Carlisle they had gotten him settled down.

"We have him in one of the interrogation rooms down the hall," Lieutenant Burwick said. He was a very large, well-built man in his early thirties. He had a bulldog face. "But I'd just as soon you fellas would get him out of here."

"As soon as he's fit to move we'll be taking him to Washington," Carlisle said smoothly. He glanced at John.

"He's just fine . . ." the cop started to say, but he saw the expression on John's face, and the words died in his throat. "Jesus," he said softly.

"I'd like to see him now," John said.

West had distanced himself from John and Carlisle. The lieutenant appealed to him, but West shook his head. "This one's out of my hands," he said. "It's their show."

"I don't want any trouble."

"No trouble," Carlisle said. "Why don't you just call an ambulance. Have them standing by out back. Just in case. No siren, please."

"If I say no?"

"Then you *will* have trouble, Lieutenant. I don't think that Russian in there is worth it, do you?"

Again he made a mute appeal to West, who was clearly uncomfortable, but he said nothing. John felt sorry for the cop, but he was thinking about Major Trusov and her people who had a head start on them. The clock was running and they needed answers now.

"Last door at the end," the lieutenant said. He picked up the telephone. "I'll call the ambulance."

Wesley was waiting for them outside. "I've got those telephone logs," he said. "There's something you should see."

"Not now," John growled. He and Carlisle walked down the corridor together, stopping at the last door in which a small wire-reinforced window was set at eye level.

"Go easy in there," Carlisle said.

"I won't touch him if he gives me the answers I want."

"It won't do us any good if you kill him, damnit."

"I wonder if they'll be giving my father the same consideration," John said bitterly. He looked through the window. The Russian was seated at a small table. He was smoking an American cigarette. He looked up, his eyes meeting John's, and he flinched.

"His name is Sergei Dmitrevich Sebryakov," Carlisle said.

"Do you know him? Is he on any of our lists?"

"No. And it's possible, John, that he knows nothing."

"Was he armed?"

"A Makarov. Nine-millimeter."

"We'll just see then, won't we," John said. "I don't want anybody in there until I'm done."

"Easy," Carlisle warned again.

"Yeah," John said. He opened the door and went inside. The Russian stubbed out his cigarette and jumped up. The tiny room smelled of smoke and sweat.

"I demand my rights. I am allowed a telephone call," the Russian said. His accent was thick but his English was good. He was short and very stocky, his hair and eyebrows thick and jet black, his features Slavic.

"You have no rights here, Sergei. In fact it's likely that you might not leave this little shithole of a room alive. Unless, of course, you wish to cooperate with me."

"I wish to call my embassy."

"I am not a policeman," John said. "I am CIA."

"Fuck your mother," the Russian spat, and John smashed his fist into the man's chest just above his left breast, shoving him back against the wall, the color instantly leaving his face.

"I will ask questions, and you will answer them or I will kill you, Sergei," John said evenly. "Do we understand each other?"

Sebryakov was trying to catch his breath. His eyes were wide with pain and with the understanding that he was in serious trouble here. John could see it.

"Do we understand each other?" John repeated his question.

The Russian nodded warily.

"What were you doing here in Duluth?"

"Spying on ships—"

John hit him again, this time in the solar plexus, the breath coming out of him all at once, along with a spray of spittle. He sat down on the floor so hard that when his mouth snapped shut he chipped a tooth. He gagged a moment later and threw up in his lap, the stench instantly filling the small room. John pulled the table aside and got down on his haunches in front of the Russian. It was everything he could do not to kill the man here and now. Little flashes and explosions were going off in his brain.

"What were you doing here in Duluth?" he asked, keeping his voice even.

The Russian dragged his head up, flinching again when he saw the intensity in John's eyes. He tried to speak, but he couldn't. He leaned forward and threw up in his lap again.

John grabbed him by the hair and raised his head. "What were you doing here, Sergei?"

The Russian closed his eyes. "I came to see a man," he whispered, his Adam's apple bobbing up and down as he tried to control his stomach.

"What man?"

"Wallace Mahoney."

"Were you to speak with him?"

"No, only to see if he was home. There is a dacha . . . a lake cabin."

"You weren't bringing him a message?"

"No, I swear to you, no message."

"Who sent you to see Wallace Mahoney?"

Sebryakov hesitated just a moment too long before he spoke. "The ambassador," he blurted.

"I don't believe you," John said. He could see in his mind's eye the explosion lighting up the night sky behind him.

"I swear . . ."

John yanked the Russian's head against the wall with his left hand, and smashed his right fist into the man's face, breaking his nose, splitting his lips, and breaking at least three teeth. The Russian was suddenly choking. He was thrashing around wildly, tearing at his throat. John pulled him forward and pounded his back. A second later he coughed up a large piece of one of his teeth.

"I don't think you can take much more of this," John said reasonably. He straightened the Russian up. "I simply need a few more answers, and then your injuries will be tended to and we'll take you back to Washington."

Blood was flowing freely from Sebryakov's battered nose, and he seemed to be having some trouble focusing his eyes. "Moscow," he blubbered like an old grandmother who has taken out her false teeth.

"Your orders came from Moscow? Is that what you're trying to say to me?"

"Yes, yes."

"When?"

The Russian looked at John uncomprehendingly.

"When did you receive those orders from Moscow, Sergei?"

"Yesterday."

"Who were you to report to once you had finished at the cabin?"

"I don't know," Sebryakov said, tears coming to his eyes. "I swear to you. It is only a line number on my teletype. A message code. Nothing more."

John stared at him for a very long time, and finally got to his feet. This was nothing more than a legman, a grunt, sent out here to nail down a possibility that was remote at best. But he had been armed.

The Russian looked up at John.

"Tell me, Sergei, what if Wallace Mahoney had been home at his lake cabin? What were your orders?"

"To report back."

He was lying again. John could see it in his eyes, and in the way he was holding his body, girding himself for another blow.

"But you were carrying a gun. I think your orders were to kill him if he was there. Kill him, and perhaps someone else. What was the second name they gave you, Sergei?"

"There was no other name."

"Tell me," John said, towering over the man.

"I can't tell you what I don't know."

"Oh, I think you'll tell me," John said. He glanced over at the door. Carlisle's face was framed in the window. His expression was flat and cold. After a long moment he turned away and was gone.

John looked back down at the Russian who had started to cry again. For a moment he realized what he was doing, what he had become, and he almost gave it up. His stomach was churning. But this was the real world, wasn't it? The real world in which the innocent suffered right along with the guilty. He had not made the rules, in fact he had not even been a player in the game when his family had suffered.

"A name, Sergei, that's all I'm asking."

The Russian said nothing; he just watched John. He seemed like a wounded animal now who had given up the fight and was cowering in a corner just waiting to die.

John got down on his haunches again and touched the man on the cheek. "The hell of it is that I already know the name of the other man you were sent here to kill. But I want to hear it from you."

Still the Russian held his silence.

John thought that years ago when he had wanted to run away to Canada to avoid the draft, it was partly because he had hated the

79

war in Vietnam. But mostly it was because he hated violence of any kind. He had come such a terribly long distance since then. All of it downhill, he reflected bitterly.

"I'm going to kill you now," he said in a reasonable voice. "But it won't be a hero's death, because no one cares."

Sebryakov mumbled something in Russian.

John reached out and gently wrapped his fingers around the man's throat. Sebryakov reared back and grabbed at John's wrists, trying to pull them away. But John was too strong. He increased the pressure. The Russian's eyes began to bulge out of their sockets and he defecated in his pants, the smell almost overpowering.

"One name, Sergei," John said through clenched teeth, easing the pressure just a little.

"Chernov," the Russian gasped. "It is Chernov."

John released his grip. "Who is he?"

"A traitor," the Russian croaked.

"You were sent here to kill him?"

"Yes."

"And Wallace Mahoney?"

"Yes!" the Russian screamed. "Yes! Yes!"

John stood up very slowly and then stepped back. His knees were weak, his hands were shaking, and he wanted to throw up. Nothing made any sense to him anymore except for revenge. It was an empty salvation, though, and he knew it. He could almost sense his mother's disapproval all the way from her grave, yet he could not help himself. He could not stop. Not now.

At the door he knocked once without bothering to look back. Carlisle let him out immediately, the stench wafting out into the corridor.

"Jesus Christ," Carlisle gagged, stepping back.

"It isn't as bad as it looks," John said, closing the door. West and Wesley were waiting just down the hall outside Lieutenant Burwick's door. They didn't look as if they wanted to come any closer.

"Did he tell you anything?"

"He came here to see if my father and Chernov were at the cabin. He had orders out of Moscow to kill them."

Carlisle glanced down the corridor. "Your father took a call three days ago from Helsinki, Finland."

John looked at him sharply. "Chernov?"

"No way of knowing," Carlisle said. "But they talked for

80

twenty-eight minutes. If it was him, he must have returned to Moscow and called the second time from there."

"Why?" John asked, his mind racing.

"Maybe your father refused to meet with him, so Chernov called us to force his hand. I don't know, John. Nobody can figure it. But it does explain how your father had the time to hide the aluminum case in the lake."

"He was already planning to leave before Chernov called us."

"Apparently Chernov wasn't sure. So he made the second call."

"He was taking a big risk."

"Yes, he was. It means that whatever he wanted to talk to your father about was big business."

"I'll find them," John said. "You can count on it." He stepped around Carlisle and strode down the corridor and out into the night. He needed a bath and a drink. In the morning he would begin.

Carlisle made two telephone calls from a pay phone in the lobby of the Radisson Hotel on Superior Street. The first was to the lake cabin. He spoke with Cassidy.

"He's taking the seven-ten back to Washington. Make sure he's on the plane."

"Yes, sir," Cassidy said.

His second call was to a Washington number. "The hunt has begun," he said.

"We'll tail him from this end."

"Whatever you do, don't let him spot your people. God only knows what he's capable of doing now."

6

To relive a life in memory was in some ways more painful than experiencing it in the first place. For Mahoney, going back like this served to remind him of the mistakes he had made, and since it was done, he could no longer alter the facts. He stood at the water's edge looking toward the British sector of Berlin to the northwest, the hotel behind him. It was seven. Sometime while he slept the weather had deteriorated. Snow blew down from a gray, overcast sky in long ragged plumes that were already building up snowbanks against the boles of the thicker trees. He had slept for only a couple of hours, no more, and the cold air on his skin felt somehow unnatural. The lake was mostly frozen except for a long narrow patch of black water in the middle.

Coming down from his room he had smelled breakfast odors from the dining room, but none of the guests had been up yet and the morning desk clerk had either not arrived or was off somewhere attending to other duties. Someone had put fresh logs on the fire, however, because it had been burning cheerily on the hearth when he crossed the lobby and let himself out. Last night seemed as if it had happened in another century. He had come outside to clear his head. Curious, he thought now, how distant memories seemed so much clearer these days than those closer to hand.

He felt in his pocket for the gun, his fingers curling around the grip for just a moment before he let go. He would have to keep it with him at all times now. Chernov had known in his heart what to expect, but Mahoney had shown his hand last night, dispelling any doubts either of them might have had. In the dim morning light, however, he still had no real idea what had finally stopped him. It certainly had not been Chernov's pleading like an old woman, though it had touched Mahoney more than he wanted to admit. Nor had it been a weakness on his part to go through with what he had come here for. He had the means and the willingness still.

Smoke was coming from the chimney, and when he turned

around he could smell the clean birch odor, inviting, timeless, even innocent, like sea smells on the beach, or a stand of pine in the fall, or even a maple forest in the spring when the sap was running and was being collected in little buckets. But there was no innocence here, was there? Not on Chernov's part, not on his. There were no innocents, after all. Certainly none in his life since Marge had died.

He started back up toward the hotel. The Mercedes was still parked in front, its plates West German, a big *D* plastered on the trunk lid. Last night he had been a little concerned that someone had already come for them. But after a while when there was no knock at his door he'd realized his fears were groundless. Some- one would be coming, but not yet. Not so soon. The Mercedes belonged to a late-arriving guest, nothing more, he told himself as he came up the road and crossed to the front veranda.

A much younger man was behind the desk writing something on small white cards from the registration book when Mahoney came in stamping the snow from his feet on the big rug in the vestibule. He looked up as Mahoney crossed the lobby.

"Greenleaf. Any messages for me this morning?"

The young man, whose name tag read SCHEMMERHORN, glanced over his shoulder at the pigeonholes and shook his head. "No, sir."

"I was expecting another friend," Mahoney said. "I saw the Mercedes outside and I just wondered."

"Herr Langenfeld," the clerk said. "He arrived very early this morning."

"No, it is not he," Mahoney said regretfully. "My friend is an American, and he might not be alone."

"No, sir, no one like that has arrived. Would these friends have made reservations?"

"I think not."

"Is it possible they might have changed their plans?"

"Oh, no," Mahoney said, and smiled. "They will be here today or perhaps tomorrow. You might inform me as soon as they come in."

"Of course," the clerk said. "Will you be having breakfast with us this morning?"

"Yes," Mahoney said. He started away, but then turned back almost immediately. "Has Herr Nostrand come down yet, by chance?"

"I haven't seen him, sir."

"You might call his room and ask him to join me in the dining room."

"Yes, sir," Schemmerhorn said. "Enjoy your breakfast."

"Thank you, I will," Mahoney said.

The dining room was located on the far side of the hotel, down three broad steps from the level of the lobby. Large windows looked down through the trees toward the Wannsee and the blowing snow. A fire was burning in a large fireplace at the far end of the room. Only one table was occupied by an old gentleman in a light green wool suit with the darker green velvet collar of the *Jagdaufseher,* which was equivalent to an American gamekeeper. He looked up when Mahoney came in, nodded, and went back to his newspaper and coffee.

"Will you be one this morning, mein Herr?" the maître d' asked.

"Herr Nostrand may be joining me."

"Very good, sir." He led Mahoney to a small table between the fireplace and the windows. "Coffee?"

"Please. And the *Berliner Zeitung,*" Mahoney said, removing his overcoat. The maître d' took it and Mahoney sat down.

His coffee and newspaper came. The Soviet leader, Mikhail Gorbachev, was coming to West Berlin next month.

He had been to Washington, to Ottawa, to London, and to Paris in the last six months. Something is afoot, the editorial warned in a boxed section on the front page.

Europe was all but disarmed of nuclear missiles, so what was left for the Soviet government to gain here? What new concessions was Gorbachev looking for?

There would be no Kennedyesque *"Ich bin ein Berliner"* speech for him here. The German peoples, East or West, would not stand for it.

Rapprochement, yes. Friendship, no.

Nothing had changed; nothing would ever change. He sat staring beyond the words on the front page of the newspaper, wondering where the real story was here. To successfully read a German newspaper, or fathom a German mind, for that matter, was to have the ability to read between the lines. Now as then. The Russians had known it instinctively. It had taken him years to learn it.

They were worried about the so-called "National Redoubt," in which Hitler and his SS were supposedly setting up an impregnable fortress in the mountains of the Ober-Salzburg. It would take years and countless hundreds of thousands of lives to dig them out. Eisenhower wanted to split Germany into two parts, meeting with the Russian army on the Elbe River between Magdeberg and Dresden. The Americans were barely sixty miles from Berlin, but they were held up because of what turned out to be the phantom fortress to the south. It had been nothing but a propaganda campaign waged by Goebbels—the last of the war—but American and British intelligence estimates gave it high marks for plausibility. The Russians, however, hadn't been taken in. They were driving west with everything they had. Mahoney, who was a captain by then, was sent to Vienna to talk some sense into General Gregori Zhukov's general staff. Of course it was a thinly disguised effort on the Americans' part to slow the Russians down. No one wanted them first in Berlin, least of all Churchill who was bitterly criticizing Eisenhower for the slowdown. Of course no one thought Mahoney's mission would succeed, but they were desperate times, and no effort was to be spared if a few lives could be saved. In this case it would have amounted to tens of thousands of lives had the National Redoubt been actual fact.

The Russians had taken up headquarters in a huge mansion on the north side of Vienna's Donau Kanal. The place was in absolute bedlam twenty-four hours a day. Staffed largely with a contingent of Polish "volunteers," no one really knew at any given time just what was going on. Most of the Poles couldn't speak Russian, most of the Russians couldn't speak Polish or English, and Mahoney and his staff between them spoke only a smattering of French, a lot of German, of course, and American Apache Indian, which they sometimes used for secret communications on open field telephones or radios. His secondary mission, which Donovan had personally spoken to him about, was to find out what the Soviet military intelligence estimates were for afterward. For when the war was finally finished. No one expected the Russians to turn around and march back home. But no one knew for sure what they were planning. It was no small task, considering the language barrier. He and his crew were billeted in a small brick building behind the main house. The Russians wanted them isolated, compounding their problems even further. In the first six hours they had found a half-dozen bugs in the old coachhouse, so they had to confine their real talks to the outside, though he had always wondered if the grounds hadn't been bugged as well.

On their first afternoon Mahoney gave his briefing to a full house in the staff dining room. It had been a carefully rehearsed speech that told the Russians nothing more than they already knew. Mahoney had felt uncomfortable at the time, because absolutely everyone knew the actual reason he had been sent out, but no one held it against him personally. Zhukov hadn't been there himself, but one of his generals, a name Mahoney could not recall, had asked him point-blank if he wanted to help win the war, or merely talk about it.

"Of course I want to help, General. We all do," the young Mahoney had replied.

"Then we will help you chase down this terrible rumor once and for all."

"How is that, sir?"

"I propose to send you and one of my intelligence officers across enemy lines to find out firsthand. Rumor or fact."

Mahoney remembered the deathly silence that followed this suggestion. He'd been told later that no one had really expected him to take up the offer. Everyone had been certain that he would ask for time to confer with his commander, and then quietly slink away into the night, allowing the real soldiers—the Russians—to get on with ending the war. But his brief had been as simple as it had been direct. "Find out what you can over there, Mahoney. No matter what it takes."

"We'll leave tonight," Mahoney said. "I trust that you will supply me with the necessary equipment, General."

The general had turned and shot a hard glance at one of his officers, who as it turned out was a young Captain Chernov, and then thumped the flat of his massive paw on the table. "So be it," he said, rising.

Everyone got up. "Thank you, sir," Mahoney said.

The general smiled not unkindly. "I think, Captain, that perhaps your balls are bigger than your brain. But good luck."

"We might come back with something interesting."

"Oh, I'm sure you will," the general said, laughing, and he turned and left the room, most of his staff following after him.

Chernov came around the table and without introducing himself, which Mahoney found a little odd at the time, shook his hand. "I have a young lieutenant who is anxious for action. His name is Yuri Zamyatin."

"And yours, Captain?"

"It is of no consequence," Chernov had said. "Though if you actually do come back alive, I promise to buy you a drink."

"Anything but vodka," Mahoney said evenly.

Chernov threw his head back and laughed. "I think I can manage to find some American whiskey."

"That would be just fine," Mahoney said, though to that point in his life he had never so much as tasted whiskey, good or bad. But he'd made his point.

Of course there had been no National Redoubt, Hitler had been stuck in Berlin at the end, and when his assignment with Zamyatin was finished, Chernov had been gone, and Mahoney had been sent back to his own unit on the other side of the Western Front. It wasn't until months later, when they all met in Berlin at the conclusion of the war, that he ran into Chernov again. This time the Russian introduced himself and handed Mahoney a bottle of Kentucky blended whiskey.

"I am sincerely happy to see that you made it back alive," Chernov said. "Yuri was very impressed with you."

"He is a good man," Mahoney said. Hard, he thought, and cruel as only a Russian can be, but the Nazis deserved it, didn't they?

"But you see there was nothing to the rumors."

"You knew it."

Chernov shrugged. "No one faulted you for trying, Captain. In any event, you got what you came looking for."

Mahoney said nothing, and Chernov smiled in his patronizing way, patting him on the arm.

"We are not going to march home after all."

"Neither are we," Mahoney said.

"Well, then, you and I will probably be seeing a lot of each other," Chernov said. "But not always as friends, I suspect."

Berlin in that spring and summer had constituted the very end of the beginning of Mahoney's training. He'd thought, to that point, that he knew people. He'd gone through much of the war smug in the belief that he was at least as much of a psychologist as he was an intelligence officer. And with the Germans he had been mildly successful. But with the Russians all bets had been off, and he had gone back to the States seriously rethinking his views. The Russian had three principles, or so the old proverb went. Perhaps, somehow, and never mind. Or, the Russian is clever, but it comes slowly, all the way from the back of his head. In the end, they said, life is unbearable, but then death is not so pleasant either.

Before the end of the war, however, the Russians were America's allies. The real enemy was the Germany and, to hear some of Donovan's people talking at the time, in some measure the British as well.

Officially the OSS had not been formed as a military entity until October 1942. Before that time Donovan's crowd were all civilians working under a rather loose charter. Mahoney had been stationed in the south of England for several months, where he was interrogating German POWs, when Donovan's call came for bright young men and he took the train up to London. Donovan was staying at the Connaught Hotel in those days, and Mahoney remembered him standing in the middle of his expansive suite surrounded by dozens of men, a big .45 military automatic strapped to his hip. A young captain who had just returned from an operation behind enemy lines stood before him. "Well, son, what mischief have you been up to this time?" Donovan asked. Everyone laughed and the young man went on to give his report. Mahoney remembered thinking how unmilitary everyone seemed even though the OSS was now officially under the purview of the Joint Chiefs. Almost everyone was dressed in civilian clothes, and even the ones who were in uniform never bothered to salute. They seemed like a big happy boys club out on a great lark.

Donovan's adjutant, who had looked over Mahoney's papers, brought him in and introduced him to the man. Donovan turned around, his eyes bright, penetrating, his gaze steady. "Who've we got here, Barney?"

"Lieutenant Wallace Mahoney up from Lewes."

Donovan looked at him a moment longer. "So you want to be a spy, is that it, son?"

"I'm a psychologist, sir," Mahoney said.

"Can you shoot a gun?"

"Not very well."

"Do you speak a foreign language?"

"Not yet."

A few men snickered, but Donovan waved them off. "Hand-to-hand combat?"

"Never been in a fight."

Even Donovan had to smile. "Well, son, we're certainly in a big fight now." He looked away for a moment. When he turned back it seemed as if another thought had occurred to him. "By the way, Mahoney, who do you hate?"

"Stupid people," Mahoney said without hesitation.

Donovan nodded. It was the answer he wanted to hear. "You're hired, son. I think it's time we got ourselves a good psychologist." He stopped. "You are good at that, aren't you?"

"The best."

"Good," Donovan said. "Good. It's St. Albans for you."

St. Albans was a small town to the north of London, outside of which the British Secret Intelligence Service had set up a training camp. Donovan had worked a deal with the British to train his OSS men in exchange for a lot of American money and material. The British were looking forward to creating a super multinational intelligence-gathering agency, and at first they treated their American cousins as somewhat naïve country bumpkins. After all, the Brits had been at this game for a very long time, since before the First World War, and they were in their own words, "Pros who work at a frowsty old brothel." It was an in joke. The cousins had a lot to learn and the British were just the ones to teach them.

At first, Mahoney remembered, their training went reasonably well. They were up at the crack of dawn for five-mile runs and calisthenics (though none of them really understood why in heaven's name an intelligence officer had to be in such good shape), after which they would spend the morning on one of the firing ranges, on the confidence course, or in hand-to-hand combat drill in a big old barn of a building that had once been used as an opera house though no one could explain what it was doing out in the middle of the countryside. In the late afternoons and evenings they were given intensive language training; Mahoney studied German. One of the running jokes at that time had to do with G. B. Shaw's quip that America and Britain were two great nations separated by a common language. "How can we teach the bloody sods German if they can't understand English?" an instructor quipped. They also learned letter and number codes, simple substitutions, one-time pads and magical cipher wheels, along with radio communications, forgery and the production of secret documents and identification papers, and all the other skills so basic to the trade at which the fledgling OSS were all tyros. In later years it was this very background that served as the starting point for new trainees at the CIA's Farm outside of Williamsburg. The lessons hadn't been forgotten, though later, of course, they'd been greatly expanded.

Looking back, however, it was sometimes hard to believe that they accomplished as much as they did in such a short time. The British were all heavy drinkers who'd break at one for lunches that would often last most of the afternoon. Yet, at first until the honeymoon was over and the British realized that they, and not the Americans, were going to be playing second fiddle in the game, they did learn. But it was a one-way street. The Americans were getting everything and giving nothing in return. Every hard-won lesson learned from an action behind enemy lines was kept within the OSS and not shared with the SIS. After a while some resentments began to build up.

But in the beginning it was all new, and Mahoney was soaking up his tradecraft like a sponge under the guidance of his mentor, Colonel Sir Rupert Brookes-Waite, who himself was a psychologist and had spent an entire year in Europe in the twenties studying under Freud. "In order to understand an individual, you must first understand his national consciousness," Brookes-Waite told him. It was a variation on Dr. Robie's old theme about looking to a man's youth if you wanted to understand what motivated him as an adult. "Take the Germans, for instance," he said. "In order to understand what makes the buggers tick, you must understand the simple fact that the Germans have never really taken Christianity into their hearts." It was his favorite theme. The Germans believed fully in the Nordic concept that the soldier-hero who has fallen in battle is the only creature worthy of ascending into heaven. It was a national mania that Hitler had used to whip Germany into a frenzy. But it also was a principle by which every German consciously or unconsciously lived his or her life. "Worse than Irish fatalism or even the Brit's God, King, and Country. The German will fall in battle, all right, but not because he believes it is kismet, and certainly not simply for Der Führer, but because he sees himself as a tragic and nobel hero, which makes him the most dangerous soldier on the face of the earth."

Of course Brookes-Waite had studied German philosophy and psychology, not Russian, otherwise Mahoney supposed his view would have been radically different. Everyone knew, that when it was over, they were going to have to deal with the Russians, but no one had any real idea just how difficult and dangerous a task that was going to be. Not then.

And then there was graduation. Mahoney had been promoted to first lieutenant and after the big weekend party at St. Albans he went down to London to see Donovan for his assignment. Nothing seemed changed in the several months Mahoney had been gone. Donovan was holding court in the same hotel suite, he had the same people around him, the same gun at his hip, and possibly even the same suit of clothes on his back. Mahoney was the first of the graduates and Donovan wanted to know how everything had gone up there. He told him straight that there already was a lot of resentment building up among the British. "They think we mean to take over the entire war without consulting them." Donovan had smiled. "Well, so, we are," he'd said. "What do you think about that?"

"We'd better get on with it, sir," Mahoney replied. "They've got a twenty-five-year head start on us."

"How would you like to go to Lisbon?"

"What's there?" Mahoney asked, startled. He thought he would be dropped behind enemy lines somewhere on the Continent.

"German spies," Donovan said. "It's time we put your psychological theories to the test."

Neutral Portugal was literally a nest of spies all through the war. German spies, British spies, Free French spies, and American spies. Mahoney had been sent to Lisbon as a free agent. He would not be working out of the American embassy, nor was he to make contact with any of the other OSS or SIS already in place, except for a courier if he got himself into trouble and needed to call for help. His cover was as an expatriate Canadian who held a Portuguese passport, who had a bad leg, and who had preferred to sit the war out someplace safe. But a man had to live, didn't he? The Americans and especially the British hated him and his kind. He was a war profiteer. But they knew that he could be a valuable source, because it was expected he would be dealing with the Germans. In effect his own people were providing him with the credibility he needed to infiltrate at least on a small level German Abwehr operations.

Donovan had sent him over with three specific tasks in mind. The first was the business of American and British newspapers. The OSS was fairly certain that someone in Lisbon was supplying the Nazis with Allied periodicals on a regular basis. Copies of *The New York Times,* for instance, were showing up in Berlin within a couple of weeks of their publication. Such newspapers were an important source of raw intelligence data for the Germans. In addition, they provided the German High Command with a "feel" for the public's sympathy with the war, and by checking the Help Wanted ads gave them an understanding of the industrial strengths and weaknesses of their enemy. Mahoney's job was to find out if in fact the Germans' source for these newspapers was indeed someone in Lisbon, and if so who it was, and finally, if possible, to put a stop to it.

Mahoney had a small apartment in Santa Cruz, a picturesque section of the city located between the inner and outer walls of the sprawling Castelo de São Jorge. Narrow little side streets all led to a charming little square bounded on one side by a parish church, on two sides by houses, and on the fourth by shops and a very good French restaurant. It was just a short walk to the downtown area and the region of the docks and wharves. He missed Marge in those days, and always thought that after the war he would bring her back to the city. He did, but it wasn't the same. Perhaps, he had thought then, it was the danger and his sense of mission that had made the city seem so special for him. When he came back it wasn't there, and he had been disappointed.

Within a week of his arrival he found out that the newspapers were coming through Lisbon, all right. They were being brought in by Portuguese fishermen who begged, stole, or bought them from incoming British and American cargo ships. The fishermen were very poor, and the newspapers brought very big money. A *New York Times* no more than two weeks old would bring an immediate one hundred Reichsmarks, which was worth about forty dollars U.S. His conclusion was that stopping the traffic would be next to impossible. It would be easier, he reported to Donovan, to make sure that no departing U.S. ships carried such newspapers—which would be impossible—or that *The New York Times* did not run stories that would be of benefit to the Nazis—even more impossible.

Mahoney's reports were written down in longhand on plain white paper that he then photographed and reduced to microdots. He had been sent over with the equipment and after a while he got pretty good at it. The microdots were inserted in letters to his uncle William back in London. It was a system that worked for him throughout much of the war.

His second task was to discover if Lisbon was somehow connected with the pipeline of spies entering the United States. A number of Germans had been intercepted crossing the Rio Grande River into Texas. Under interrogation one of them had admitted coming up from Mexico City. Beyond that, he wouldn't say a thing. Within a month Mahoney had found out about the so-called *Schleusung*, or "sluice network," in which German spies were brought into Portugal and put on boats bound for South America. From there they made their way north to Mexico and then across to the States. It was an open secret around the docks that Mahoney had easily been able to piece together.

There was nothing they could do about it in Lisbon, or on the high seas. There simply weren't enough naval vessels free from other duties to check every single merchant marine vessel out of Lisbon. But Mexico City became a major focal point for American efforts, and of course patrols along the Rio Grande were stepped up.

His biggest job, though, was in running down the Yugoslav Dusko Popov, who was one of the key German agents in all of Lisbon. The British first got wind of him through an industrial draftsman by the name of Hans Hansen. He was a Dane, his mother German, and he had supposedly fled the Nazi advances and wound up in England. He was living in Barnet, a northern borough of London at the time, and Scotland Yard was following him around, watching him spy on British airfields, factories that had been hit in German bombing raids, and on the placement and types of weapons in the antiaircraft posts spotted in and around London. Their plan was to neutralize him by feeding him false information that he would radio back to the Abwehr listening post in Hamburg. They wanted to know first, however, where he was getting his money. He always seemed to have plenty. If they could find that out, they figured they would have identified the paymaster for a lot of other German spies operating in England whom they didn't know about yet. The one thing they did know was that his money apparently came from an agent in Lisbon. Possibly a man named Popov.

Mahoney had built up a network of underground contacts in Lisbon. Men who were making money any way they could. It didn't matter to them which side ultimately benefited as long as they were paid in hard Western currencies. Mahoney set himself up as a Jewish theatrical agent who had a lot of money in British pounds sterling.

"Britain is going to lose the war," he told anyone who would listen. He wanted to change his money for some other currency. American perhaps. It was an irresistible bait for the Germans. Eventually he was put in direct contact with Popov himself and a deal was struck. Popov was to give Mahoney dollars, and Mahoney in turn through his agents was to dispense pounds sterling to half a dozen designees in London. All of them of course were Abwehr agents. They'd fallen right into the laps of Scotland Yard. The Abwehr was happy too: they were killing three birds with one stone. In the first place they were funneling money to their agents through a seemingly legitimate avenue. Secondly, they were taking a big rake-off from the deal, so they were actually turning a profit on each transaction. And finally they were sticking it to a Jew.

Donovan's next letter was congratulatory, but ordered him back to London immediately. His sojourn in Portugal was at an end. It had been brief but very interesting. But it was time now to get on with the real war. His skills were needed in North Africa, then Sicily, and eventually, of course, on the European continent itself as the fighting was brought into Hitler's backyard. But Mahoney always remembered Portugal as his very first assignment, the place where he had met the enemy and had found him wanting.

Waiting for Chernov to show up, watching the falling snow, drinking his coffee and thinking of his own frailties, his own uncertainties now, Mahoney was brought back to a strange interlude in the war. It was London, the spring of 1943. The British had just about driven Rommel back to Tunisia and Mahoney was getting ready to ship out with an OSS/SIS team. They'd intercepted a number of Rommel's transmissions back to Berlin, and they wanted someone in Africa to make sense out of what he was telling the Führer.

"Exactly what is it that you do in here all night, alone," Tom Corbett asked, coming into Mahoney's Connaught Hotel room without knocking. Corbett, who was a couple of years older than Mahoney, was going across with the team tomorrow.

"Sleep?" Mahoney suggested hopefully, looking up. He'd not been sleeping well lately. He had just written a letter to Marge and was feeling a little guilty for some reason.

"Wrong answer, recruit," Corbett said, waving his finger. "Your date, along with mine, awaits downstairs in the lobby at this very moment. The bastards wouldn't let me bring them up here."

"I don't think so, Tommy," Mahoney said. "Not tonight." But Corbett had gone to the closet and was pulling out Mahoney's dress uniform. He laid it out on the bed.

"We're not shipping out until noon, they're suckers for an American uniform, and they are certifiably horny. An unbeatable combination, pal."

"Doesn't matter to you that we're married?" Mahoney asked, and he felt like three kinds of naïve fool.

Corbett laughed. "I must have been drunk that night. Did you propose, or did I?" He hauled Mahoney out of the chair, his eyes falling on the letter to Marge and he stopped. "That's how it is," he said. "You're afraid of getting a case of the guilts. Or maybe bringing home the crabs."

"Something like that."

"You may be dead tomorrow, my lad," Corbett said, recovering nicely. "Besides, as long as you don't fall in love with them, who cares?"

Mahoney hesitated. Corbett leaned in a little closer. He had been drinking; Mahoney could smell the raw booze on his breath. But he wasn't drunk.

"We need it, my friend, you and I. Tomorrow is another day. Maybe the last."

"The spooks?" Mahoney asked. It came to all of them at one time or another.

"Yeah," Corbett said. "Pretty bad this time."

"Do you want to sit and talk? Have a couple of drinks?"

"I need life, my boy. Life! Do you understand?"

"Sure," Mahoney said thoughtfully. "Sure, I understand." He got dressed.

God help him, but he still remembered his girl's name, both of them as a matter of fact, because Tom Corbett was killed two days later when he stepped on a land mine in the African desert. Lyla Ingram and Sunny Margot. They were nurses somewhere, though that part was never made quite clear, nor did Mahoney ever discover how Tom met them. He had the knack. They were just there, the three of them, and Tommy had thought about good old Mahoney, so they had come back to the Connaught. Corbett had wanted to sneak them up, but he couldn't get them past the MPs at the elevators.

"If you can't take the man to the mountain, then take the mountain to the man, or something like that," Corbett had explained on the way down.

They were both young and not very good-looking, but they were sincere. Corbett kept prattling on all night about how "sincere" they were. "Such a rare commodity these days, you know."

They wound up at the girls' apartment. Corbett and Lyla took the bedroom, leaving the pull-out cot to Mahoney and Sunny. They listened to music on the radio and finished the last of the wine.

"Your friend Tom is quite the kidder," she said.

"He's frightened," Mahoney answered, though he didn't know why he was being so open. It just seemed natural with her.

"I understand," she said. "How about you? Are you frightened too?"

"Just now, scared to death."

"Of me?"

He nodded.

"You're not a pansy, then, are you? You don't look like one. Married?"

"Very," Mahoney said. He felt like a heel for leading her on all night. And he tried to apologize, but she shrugged him off.

"Me too," she said. "But I haven't heard a thing from him since Christmas." And then she was crying and he was holding her, conscious of her body against his, of her faintly musky, feminine odor.

"I understand," he said soothingly.

After a while she looked up into his eyes and kissed him lightly on the lips. "I think you do," she said. "And I appreciate it. I mean, I really do."

Mahoney started to move back, but she held him closer.

"Just hold me for a little while longer," she said. "Maybe just for tonight. I won't put the move on you, I swear to God. But I just can't sleep alone for another night. I think I'll blow my brains out if I have to, you know."

Mahoney was feeling wretched because at that moment he wanted nothing more than to make love to the girl. It would be so easy, she was so vulnerable, Marge was so far away. No one would ever know, and no one would ever be hurt.

They held each other for a long time until finally she stopped crying and she pulled back, a thin smile on her face. "You can't, and I understand."

Mahoney didn't move.

"Go on with you," she said. "Your wife is a lucky woman."

"I don't want to sleep alone tonight either," he said, reaching for her.

She started to cry again. "Oh, shit," she said.

All of a sudden the war was over. A lot of people were heading home. Everywhere there was happiness and light and the promise of a coming summer. The long night had ended. Mahoney flew up to Bern, Switzerland, where Allen Dulles, who had headed the wartime OSS office at the Reich's back door, was closing down the bank and getting ready to head back to Washington.

"Big things are in the wind," Donovan had told him in London. "This war might be over and done with, but the real battle is just starting."

It was the Russians, and from what Mahoney had seen so far, he tended to agree with the man. He'd just returned from his meeting in Berlin with Chernov and his GRU staff under General Zhukov. Still fresh in his mind was their superior attitude. They were well staffed, well armed, and in a perfect position to take over all of Europe. They weren't afraid to let the Americans know that once the dust settled, the map of Europe would forever be changed.

"I would have thought that the Swiss operation would be closed down by now," Mahoney said.

"It is, but Allen wants a word with you about a German general I want you to find."

"There are a lot of them around," Mahoney said. "Perhaps G-2 or CIC would be more qualified to deal with this. If he's still alive."

"He's alive, you can bet your bottom dollar on it. Trouble is the Army might not know what to do with him."

"But we do?"

"Indeed," Donovan had said. "But Allen will explain it all to you. We have to find him before the Russians do. At all costs."

"And then what, sir?"

"Why, make a deal with him, of course. Ship him back to the States, out of harm's way until the situation in Germany can stabilize."

"A deal, sir? With a Nazi?"

"He hates Communists, son. And at this point that's all that matters, don't you see?"

Mahoney hadn't seen at the time, not completely, although he could see at least the surface wisdom of using what the German secret services had learned about the Russians. But making a deal with a German general? He thought it a little farfetched at the time. A view that Allen Dulles did not share.

During the war Dulles and his staff had been lodged in a big house at Herrengasse 23, in an old section of Bern, from where he had run as many as a hundred agents at any one time. It was early afternoon when Mahoney arrived. Two canvas-covered Army trucks were parked out front. Soldiers were coming and going in a steady stream, loading file cabinets, big wooden crates, dozens of cardboard boxes, and office furniture aboard the trucks. The OSS was definitely closing down here.

"Where can I find Mr. Dulles?" Mahoney asked one of the GIs bringing out a four-drawer file cabinet on a hand truck.

"Upstairs, Captain. Last door down the hall."

Mahoney went in, ducking another GI rolling a file cabinet out the door, took the stairs two at a time, and walked down the corridor to a big office. Dulles was a few years younger than Donovan, but his hair was thinning and gray, he sported a trim mustache, wore wire-rimmed glasses, and looked ten years older than he really was. He reminded Mahoney of a preacher (in fact he was the son of a Presbyterian parson), soft-spoken and very charming. He was quite a contrast to Donovan. At that moment he was talking with a good-looking dark-haired woman.

"What can I do for you, Captain?" he said, looking up.

"Bill Donovan asked me to come see you," Mahoney said.

"You're Mahoney?"

"Yes, sir."

"Glad you could make it on such short notice. I was just leaving myself, but I wanted to have the chance to brief you beforehand."

The woman was staring at him. Dulles suddenly remembered his manners. "Mary Bancroft, Captain Wallace Mahoney, one of Wild Bill's boys."

"So very pleased to meet you, Captain," she said, shaking Mahoney's hand.

He'd heard of her, of course. She was the daughter of the publisher of *The Wall Street Journal*, and was an expatriate American who had been living and studying in Switzerland under the psychiatrist Carl Jung. When Dulles showed up she had gone to work for him, analyzing press reports at first, and then people Dulles wanted to recruit. Someone once said that dealing with her was "like wrestling with a boa constrictor." Mahoney remembered her as a charming if extremely astute woman.

"Have you heard the name Rheinhard Gehlen?" Dulles asked.

"He headed an Abwehr office, I think," Mahoney replied. The name was vaguely familiar to him.

"FHO, actually," Dulles said, "*Fremde Heere Ost*, under the German High Command. He spied on the Russians. Mary has actually met him, before the war of course."

"A very bright, capable man," she said. "Prussian, but not so pig-headed. He has style."

"I'm supposed to find him before the Russians do?" Mahoney asked. They'd closed the door and the moving sounds were distant.

"I think it's important, Captain," Dulles said. He looked out the window. "We're going to be rebuilding Germany, putting some sort of a government into effect so that we can eventually ease our way out gracefully. In the meanwhile the Russians won't be sitting still. They have big plans for Eastern Europe."

"They have long memories, all of them very bad, against the Germans," Mary Bancroft said.

"And the means now to do something about them," Dulles

added. "Once the situation is stabilized, Germany will have to have its own secret intelligence service."

Mahoney shivered a little. The notion struck him as callous in the extreme. They had just defeated one of the greatest armies in the world, and now Dulles was calmly talking about starting it all over again.

"The good captain doesn't share your enthusiasm," Mary Bancroft said.

"Someone will have to watch the Russians from this side," Dulles said. "We're going to have our hands full."

"We need someone who understands the Russian mentality," Mary Bancroft said. "A commodity we are short of at this moment, from what I've seen."

Mahoney had to agree with her. He was himself fresh from meeting with Chernov and his staff. They were coming from another planet by comparison to the Nazis he had interviewed.

"Gehlen is just the man for the job. If he'll take it. If he isn't already dead. And if the Russians don't get to him first. They'll want to try him for war crimes."

"Why just one man looking for him?" Mahoney asked. "Why me?"

"It wouldn't do to alert the Russians to what we're up to," Dulles said. "And Bill gives you high marks. The very highest."

"What about G-2 or CIC?" Mahoney asked, ignoring the compliment. "Anything from General Bradley's people?" He didn't think he was going to like this assignment.

"Nothing yet, but everything is still so fragmented up there that it'll be months, perhaps even a year before everything gets straightened out. Right now everyone is worried about winter. It's going to be awfully tough on a lot of people."

"He may have headed south," Mary Bancroft said.

It was the Ober-Salzburg all over again. But there was no National Redoubt, and he'd heard that Hitler's Eagle's Nest at Berchtesgaden had been found completely deserted. It was a large mountainous region. A lot of territory to cover, a lot of hiding places, and he said as much.

Dulles plucked a fat file folder off his nearly bare desk and handed it to Mahoney. "This is everything we know about him. I'd suggest that you begin with Twelfth Army Group—they're up in Wiesbaden now. Talk to Ed Sibert. He heads up their G-2. Tell him I sent you. If he has nothing, you can work your way down the chain of command. It's my guess that Gehlen is sitting it out somewhere in a holding cage because nobody knows just what they've got on their hands."

"Have you tried calling Twelfth Army?"

"Too dangerous. The Russians have got intercepts on half our phone lines, and spies right in headquarters. This has to be done in person, and very quietly. Do you understand?"

"Yes, sir," Mahoney said.

"And when you find him, tell him what we want."

"What if he refuses?"

Mary Bancroft smiled. "Tell him that you'll turn him over to the Russians," she said. "I think he'll cooperate."

The assignment was over practically before it began. Which was just as well because Mahoney always looked back upon it as one of the most personally distasteful things he'd ever done, though Gehlen did go on to create and head the West German *Bundesnachrichtendienst*—the BND—one of the most effective anti-Communist secret intelligence services in the world. It also marked the beginning of Mahoney's understanding that he did not understand the Russian mind, and that he had a long way to go if he were ever to become an effective operative.

"We've got him right here," 12th Army Group's G-2 chief, Major General Edwin Sibert, told him in Wiesbaden. "In fact he's been here ten days now. What's your interest in him?"

"Mr. Dulles sent me down to talk to him, sir," Mahoney said, hardly believing his good fortune. He had flown directly from Bern and hadn't even bothered to check into the BOQ before presenting himself to Sibert.

"Is he still in Bern?"

"On his way back to Washington by now, sir. He asked me to offer the general a deal."

"What sort of a deal?" General Sibert asked.

"Mr. Dulles would like him to come to Washington, where it would be a little safer for him. It's my understanding the Russians would like to get hold of him."

"What would happen in Washington?"

"They want to offer him a job, sir. They're planning on setting up a German intelligence service. They'd like him to run it."

Mahoney had waited for the explosion. Sibert was a frontline officer, and he had seen firsthand what the Nazis were capable of. But it never came.

"My thoughts exactly," Sibert said. "But we've been talking

ourselves blue in the face with him to no avail. He is one stubborn son of a bitch."

"Yes, sir," Mahoney said. "Mind if I give it a try?"

General Sibert looked at him for a long moment. "You're one of Donovan's boys?"

"Yes, sir."

Sibert nodded. "We're holding him at the Villa Pagenstecher, just outside of town. Good luck."

"Thank you, sir. But Mr. Dulles instructed me to tell him that if he didn't want to work for us, we would send him over to the Russians."

Sibert grinned. "That ought to rattle his cage."

Mahoney clearly remembered driving out to the villa the next morning. Security was tight and he had to show his papers, including General Sibert's personal authorization for the visit, three times before he was finally admitted into the sprawling house itself. They met in a rear garden where Gehlen was having his coffee. He was alone, though there were guards all around the place.

"I've come to offer you a proposition, General," Mahoney said without preamble.

Gehlen was a slightly built, dapper man in his early forties. He was dressed in civilian clothes, his shirt collar open. He'd been out in the sun recently; his face showed the beginnings of a tan. "Have you read my report?"

Sibert had mentioned that Gehlen had written a 129-page report detailing his work with the FHO, and his assessment about the continuing threat from the Soviet Union, but Mahoney hadn't seen it.

"No, I have not."

"I suggest you do so, Captain."

"We'd like you to come to Washington to meet with Bill Donovan, Allen Dulles, and some others."

"Yes?" Gehlen said, the first glimmerings of interest showing in his eyes. "To what end?"

"The establishment of a German secret intelligence service, whose purpose would be to monitor Soviet activities in Europe."

Gehlen smiled. He nodded. "Now we are finally getting somewhere," he said. "But I have four basic conditions—"

"Either that or you will be handed over to the Soviet authorities within the next twenty-four hours," Mahoney interrupted.

"As I was saying, Captain, four basic conditions, which I trust you will relay to your superiors."

Mahoney didn't like the man, didn't like being there, but he stifled his emotions. He was learning. He nodded stiffly.

"My organization will be autonomous, and under my exclusive management. My organization will be used only to procure intelligence on the Soviet Union and Communist bloc countries. Once a German government is established, complete control of my people will be transferred to it. And finally, my organization will never be called upon to spy on my own people."

"May I remind you, General, that at this moment you are a prisoner of war?" Mahoney flared.

"You may, Captain, but believe me, I do not need reminding," Gehlen said. "But on your way out, take this thought with you. Adolph Hitler was a monster, we all knew it, but he was nothing by comparison with Joseph Stalin. The Russian bear has awakened, Captain. Take care it doesn't bite you."

"The police are here," Chernov said, suddenly looming in front of Mahoney. He sat down.

"Where?" Mahoney asked.

"In the lobby. Checking the registration. I think it is nothing more than a routine passport check, though. Yours will hold up to such scrutiny?"

"For the moment," Mahoney said. "But I think it is time now for us to make our preparations. Someone will be coming."

"Yes, I think you are right."

7

Lakewood Nursing Care Home was located along Lake Barcroft in Fairfax County, southwest of Washington, D.C. On this late afternoon, driving down from the city, John Mahoney again got the impression that he was being followed. This morning when he had left Duluth he had spotted Cassidy hanging around across the terminal, pretending to read a newspaper. After what had happened in the police station Carlisle had wanted to make sure his star pupil wasn't running amok. Cassidy was an amateur legman. It didn't really matter that he had been spotted; in a fashion it was Carlisle's way of telling John that they were looking out for his welfare, that they truly cared, and that although they wanted his complete cooperation, if he faltered, they would be there to help him back to his feet. But this was different. He was certain that he had picked up a tail at Dulles Airport around noon when his flight had come in and he had taken a cab back to his Georgetown apartment. Inside he had waited by the window, watching traffic below on P Street. He'd seen no one out there, no suspicious cars parked up the block with a couple of men inside waiting, watching; no glint off the lenses of binoculars in the windows of the apartment buildings across the street; no vans with silvered one-way windows hesitating at the traffic light; no odd-looking people walking too casually down the street. And yet he had *felt* a presence watching him, waiting for him to make his move, expecting him to do something. Just as he had felt the same presence on the way across the river to CIA headquarters earlier. "You're probably imagining things—you're keyed up," Alex Hayes had told him. "But we'll check it out."

If it was Carlisle again, they might back off, or then again they might be a little more careful. It's paranoia, his father used to say. It comes to us all sooner or later. The good ones know how to live with it, how to use it to their best advantage. The bad ones, however, allow the feeling to consume them so that they become afraid to lay their head on a pillow and go to sleep at night for fear that someone is taking aim at them through the window.

Coming up the long sweeping drive to the nursing home, the lowering sun was directly in his eyes and he had to pull down the sun visor in order to see. He checked his rearview mirror, but the road was absolutely empty behind him. Traffic flowed along highway 244, but no one had turned off behind him. There was no one there, he kept telling himself, and yet he *knew* there was. It was a sixth sense that all good spies developed sooner or later, not simple paranoia. Not now, not after last night. If the Russians had sent someone out to Minnesota to look for his father and Chernov, wasn't it also likely that they would have put two and two together and realized that the Agency would be sending the man's son after him? Who better to go after the best than the prodigal son? Follow him and see where he leads. Or, if they had their own leads, follow him until he is alone and vulnerable, and kill him. He settled back in his seat a little so that he could feel the pressure of the Beretta automatic in its holster at the small of his back. Irritating at times, but comforting now.

Hayes had been waiting for him in his third-floor office, his desk a mass of photographs, files with diagonal red stripes signifying secret material, computer printouts, and the remains of at least three partially eaten meals.

"Farley is on his way in," Hayes said. "He'll be back tonight."

"Did they find anything else out there?"

"Not a thing. And by the way, that Russian you mussed up is raising holy hell. They had to sedate him. He'll be coming in sometime tonight as well."

"I didn't hurt him that bad."

"A few broken ribs, a cracked sternum, half a dozen teeth knocked out or loosened, seven stitches in his tongue where he bit it half through, a hairline fracture of his jaw, a small bone chip floating loose in his left cheek, a left eye that won't focus, the odd stitch here and there on both his lips, and some possible heart damage, not to mention a lot of bruising and one bent ego."

"He came gunning for my father," John protested.

"I know," Hayes said, holding up a hand like a traffic cop at a busy corner. "He's in deep shit and he knows it. That's why he was making such a fuss."

"Right," John said. His stomach felt sour and although he'd taken a long, hot shower he still felt a little soiled around the edges, as if he had stuck his hand in a toilet and couldn't get the tap water hot enough to get himself clean.

"East Berlin is the place," Hayes was saying. He passed a couple of satellite photographs across the desk to John. "That's Trusov and her people landing at the military side of Schönefeld Airport. Same tail numbers."

John studied the photographs for a moment though he couldn't make much from them. The photo analysis people knew their job, however. He trusted their judgment. "Anything from our people over there?"

"If she's left the city, it wasn't by any routes we know about. Of course that doesn't mean a damn thing in itself."

"What else?"

Hayes was a big burly man with thick dark eyebrows, big beefy arms, and a barrel chest. His voice was surprisingly soft for his size. He sat back, the chair groaning under his weight. "We got the final word on Chernov, and it's not very good."

"I know. Farley told me."

"He's big potatoes, John. The biggest short of the KGB director himself. And they'll be wanting him badly. They'll be pulling out all the stops now."

John was thinking about his mother. Carlisle had been guessing. There was no way for them to know for certain that Chernov had been directly involved, or for that matter that his mother had been one of the victims of some Russian plot. The doctors had turned up nothing unusual. It was cancer, plain and horribly simple. She was an old woman and she had finally succumbed. But if his father had thought that the Russians were responsible, if his father even suspected that Chernov was remotely involved, blood would definitely be spilled.

"Why did he call for a meeting with my father?" John asked.

"That's the sixty-four-dollar question," Hayes said. "Take a stab at it, and you'll probably be as close to the mark as any of us. Who knows, he might even be coming over, and your father is the only one he trusts."

"There's no actual proof that they worked together."

"No. But they are contemporaries."

Again Chernov's name triggered some distant memory at the back of John's head. Something from a long time ago, something mentioned perhaps casually, or something overheard in the night. He couldn't quite put his finger on it, but he knew it would come to him if he just left it alone for a little while longer.

"Your biggest problem, short of actually finding them, of course, will be this Major Trusov," Hayes continued. "One tough broad, from what I've been able to dig up."

"Have you got something on her for me?"

Hayes handed over a thick file and John opened it. Her wide, dark eyes stared up at him from a black-and-white eight-by-ten glossy photograph that seemed to have been taken at a beach somewhere. It was daytime, and there were other people around her. She had evidently just looked up, directly toward the camera, almost as if the shot had been carefully posed. He thought she was a beautiful woman. Her dark hair was long, her eyebrows delicately arched and finely drawn, her cheekbones high, her nose tiny, and her lips full and beautifully formed. There didn't seem to be any harshness to her. If anything she seemed almost amused in the photo.

John looked up. "How'd we get this?"

"Odessa, a couple of years ago. She was apparently there on vacation. One of our people happened to spot her and managed the shot. There are others of her, but that's the best."

"She's beautiful."

"Yes, she is, but believe me when I tell you that she is a killer and very, very good at her work."

"What about her background, her history?"

"It's all in there, John, what little we know. Apparently she was recruited out of Moscow State University. That's the very first reference we have on her."

"And now she's been sent after my father and Chernov," John said, staring at the photograph.

"Yes. And she's not a snatch-and-run artist, John. She's leading no rescue team. She's come out to kill them. Plain and simple."

"Your dad always did like the water, but he sure as hell wouldn't like it here," the old man grumbled.

John stood next to him at the water's edge wondering if he should reach out and take his arm. Stan Kopinski, who at one time had been the majordomo of Archives first in the OSS in the early days, then later with the CIA, had been one of his father's best friends. He was nearing ninety now. His mind was still reasonably sharp, however. John had seriously doubted he would get anything from the man, but now his hopes had risen a little.

"He grew up around it," John said. The wind was cool off the lake.

"Always gabbed about that lake cabin in Minnesota. He and Marge were going to retire there. And did."

"Did you ever go out there?"

"Once, before your mother died. A bit rustic for my tastes," Kopinski said, laughing a little.

John remembered him as a short, roly-poly man with a thick head of jet-black hair. He was incredibly frail now, and what little hair he had left was snow-white, his pink scalp showing through. His face was wrinkled, leathery, and marked with liver spots. But his eyes were bright.

"She was a good woman," Kopinski said. "The very best, bar none. Christ, your father was devoted to her. Never once cheated that I know about, though he had the opportunity."

No, John silently agreed. But he was never at home. It was a different kind of cheating. In its way every bit as hurtful as the other. "There's a bit of trouble, Stan."

Kopinski glanced back up at the sprawling complex of the nursing home, then into John's eyes. He nodded. "That piss-ant Carlisle telephoned and asked if I'd heard from your father lately."

"What did you tell him?"

"I told him to mind his own business, that I had troubles of my own. I told him that I'd just shit my pants." Kopinski laughed, his voice high, thin. "He thinks I'm senile."

"Did you hear from my father?"

"I figured if something was going on, you'd be showing up sooner or later," Kopinski said. "Not since last summer, kid. What's going on?"

"Does the name Yuri Yevgennevich Chernov mean anything to you?"

"Your father's nemesis," Kopinski said so softly that at first John wasn't sure he'd heard him correctly. "But that goes way back."

"Nemesis?"

"His opposite number. The grim reaper. The destroyer."

"We've looked down his track, Stan, and his postings sheet reads like a dead ringer for my father's."

"I know that," Kopinski said sharply. "In fact I helped your father set up his assignments so that he could chase after his Russian."

"His name isn't mentioned on any of my father's contact sheets."

Kopinski laughed. "Come on, kid. No contact, no entry. Is your daybook so complete? Do you jot down a little note every time you happen to be at the same urinal trough with someone who might be the opposition?"

"What was he after? My father, I mean."

"With this Chernov?"

"Yes."

"Why, the grand prize, kid, what else? The fucking gold seam. They were like two toughs flexing their muscles in front of each other from the first time they met. It was during the war. Your dad was working for Donovan, and Chernov was GRU." He shook his head. "Came and asked me if I had anything on him."

"Did you?"

"Just that he was GRU on General Zhukov's staff. Your dad thought Chernov was going places. Figured he was going to end up being a dangerous man. Wanted to know all there was to know about him. 'We'll come across that bastard's path again,' he told me."

Kopinski had been one of the lucky ones who got out of Poland in 1940 and made his way to England. His wife and children hadn't been so fortunate, however. After the war he had gone back to search for them, but they were all dead. He worked at first for British intelligence, until he'd been recruited by Donovan first as a translator—he spoke half a dozen languages—and then later as chief of Archives setting up the CIA's memory. He never forgot a name, a face, or an incident. A lot of good spies came to rely on his abilities.

"He's gone after him," John said.

"Where?"

"I don't know. I was hoping you might help me."

Kopinski was staring out across the lake again. It was hard for John to gauge what he was thinking. His father had always said that he would make a great poker player. *Inscrutable* was the word he'd used.

"Carlisle has sent you chasing after him, is that it?" he said as if he found the notion particularly distasteful. "They're all sons of bitches over there. But then they always were." He looked up. "It's a sorry goddamned way to make a living, John."

John lit a cigarette after first offering one to Kopinski, but the old man declined.

"He's after Chernov finally," Kopinski said.

"Three days ago Chernov called our embassy in Moscow and said he wanted to meet with my father," John said. "No time mentioned, no place specified. Our people relayed the message to Langley, and we called my father."

"Who denied even knowing Chernov," Kopinski said with relish.

"Now he's missing."

"How many passports has he got with him?"

"We don't know. Several at least, but he left his own behind."

"Of course. Is he armed?"

"Possibly."

"Money?"

"Unknown. We tracked him by cab from the cabin to the Duluth airport and from there down to Minneapolis where he disappeared."

Kopinski was grinning, perhaps remembering other evenings when he was young and himself on the hunt. "What do Carlisle and his crowd think is going on?"

"Farley is worried that my father is sharing secrets."

Kopinski laughed out loud. "That's rich," he hooted. "Of all the people in the world, Yuri Chernov is definitely one man your father would never, repeat *never* share anything with, much less a secret. Carlisle must have his head up his ass."

"I think my father plans on killing him."

"I might have believed that a few years ago, but time has a way of softening our worst hurts."

"Farley told me a nasty little story, Stan," John plunged ahead. He hadn't intended telling this to Kopinski; it was just coming out. "Something about my mother's death. That Chernov may have been involved with it somehow. Do you know anything about it?"

Kopinski might not have heard him. "I'll have one of those cigarettes now, John."

John lit one for the old man who held it in the Eastern European way, between his thumb and forefinger, the filter cupped in his palm.

"If my father knows or even suspects such a thing, he would have gone to Chernov with passports and money to cover his tracks, and a gun to kill him with."

"Yes, he would."

"He wouldn't tell any of us for fear we'd try to stop him."

"I agree," Kopinski said wearily. "He'd go it alone."

"The problem is that Chernov is also missing and his own people are out looking for him. Special Investigations. If they find them first, they'll kill my father. Last night one of their Washington people showed up at the cabin."

"They're after Chernov. You're after your father. So, it's a race."

"To where?" John asked.

"Before you can answer that, kid, you're going to have to figure out why."

"Revenge."

"That may be why your father went off," Kopinski said. "But it doesn't explain why Chernov made the call in the first place. If your father is truly driven by revenge, then what is driving Chernov?"

"Maybe he wants to defect."

Again Kopinski laughed. "Oh, no," he said between gasps. "Anything, and I do mean *anything* but that."

Kopinski was off and running.

The sun had set across the lake. Behind them lights had come on in the nursing home, and the few people who had been out on the lawn had finally gone inside. John could smell dinner odors wafting down to them on the light breeze and he felt a little guilty that he was keeping the old man from his meal, but Kopinski was in the glory days now, in the late forties and early fifties when the CIA seemed to be doubling in size every few months or so, and a lot of good men were carving out very big careers for themselves. It was all practice for Korea, which in turn was still more practice for the cold war of the fifties and early sixties. The real enemy was and always would be the Soviet Union, according to their way of thinking at the time. The problem was that no one understood them. According to Kopinski there weren't a dozen men in the United States in those days who knew what the hell was going on behind the Iron Curtain, let alone what sort of people they were really dealing with. "Everyone talks about the inscrutable Oriental mind, well, let me tell you, the Russians are just as distant to our way of thinking."

Mahoney came back to London at the end of the war, before everyone had packed up and gone home, raving quietly about this GRU captain he'd met and spent a few days with. The son of a bitch is going places, he kept saying, and I don't have the slightest notion of what's behind those eyes of his. Chernov became his test case. Mahoney figured that if he could understand one Russian, any Russian, Chernov for instance, he would be well on his way toward understanding all Russians. A dangerous generality in most instances, but in this case he figured he had something. He'd watched Chernov operate among his own people and he thought that it was a pretty safe assumption that if ever there was a John Doe of the Soviet Union, Chernov was it. The peasant had to be discounted from the equation, of course. As did the average farmer-soldier or the average factory worker or even the average bureaucrat. What Mahoney was looking for was a handle on the ones who either ran the military-industrial complex, or who would someday take over the reins of government. The decision makers, the ones who would have the influence. He wasn't at all convinced at that point that the Russians would necessarily turn out to be such a terrible threat. It wasn't that he was discounting the warnings, it was simply because as far as he was concerned all the facts weren't in yet. He was reserving his judgment at least for the moment. He was going to watch Chernov until he had the man figured out, and then he would make his decision.

But that didn't happen until 1961 when the Russians began putting up the wall dividing Berlin, and in a flash of sudden insight Mahoney finally understood what it was he had been looking for all those years.

John was brought back to that period in his own life. He was sixteen, and in his last year of high school. They had just returned from a very brief posting in Madrid, and he remembered that his father and mother were upset because they'd had to leave on such short notice, but excited by the prospect of possibly being sent next to Moscow. In those days, as through most of Mahoney's career, his cover was usually as an undersecretary for economic aid or development at whatever embassy he was stationed at. They were always entertaining in those days, foreign officials coming and going from their home at all hours of the day and night. No one knew much about Vietnam then; that would come a few years later. For the moment all eyes had been turned toward Europe where Soviet troops and tanks had put down one bloody revolution after another. When the news came that they were constructing a wall completely around West Berlin—around the entire city, the American, British, and French sectors, around the lakes, the streams, and even the forests—no one could believe it. John had taken out an atlas and had stared in disbelief at what had to be patent nonsense. The Chinese had built a great bloody wall across an entire country, but that had been years and years ago, had involved the labors of literally hundreds of thousands of people and had taken decades to complete. What could the Russians be doing? Certainly nothing by comparison. Walls and pyramids and Babylonian hanging gardens were all magnificent oddities of a far distant time, not present-day political statements. No one in America could believe it either, despite what they were seeing on television. At school in Alexandria, in fact, it wasn't even mentioned. Everyone went about his business as usual. No one cared because it seemed so ludicrously impossible. And even if the Russians were throwing up some barbed wire to stop the defections across the border, Washington would not stand for it. Within a week whatever had been put up would certainly be torn down. That's what the war had been fought for, hadn't it? So that despots and their crazy schemes would no longer be allowed to flourish?

Mahoney was one of the believers, however, Kopinski said. He wasn't as surprised as everyone else was. He had known that something crazy was going to happen over there. Ever since Hungary a few years earlier, he knew that the Russians would never be satisfied until they had complete control over all of eastern Europe. Berlin was the final holdout. An island city surrounded by East Germany. It had to be isolated.

The CIA went on emergency footing. Messages were flying back and forth between headquarters and its station at the embassy in Bonn as well as the Agency's West Berlin operation at the consulate. It simply could not be true—even though the British had earlier shared intelligence that such a thing was indeed going to be built—but it was.

Everyone was asking what this latest move by the Soviets could possibly portend. Another revolt that would be put down by tanks? Were there already tanks in place? Were the Russians planning on starting a shooting war over this thing?

The French were furious, as were the British, but they were looking to Kennedy to do something. But do what, short of a showdown with guns, no one knew.

A few early reports coming in painted a pretty grim picture. Hundreds of East Berliners fearing, and rightly so as it turned out, that they were going to be stuck in the eastern zone tried to get out. There was a lot of gunfire, but still the White House was silent for the most part.

For months there had been tickles about increasing KGB activities in East Berlin. Chernov, who had been stationed in Madrid, had been recalled to Moscow, and when he emerged it was as head of what in those days was called the Thirteenth Department, or sometimes Line F of Department Viktor. It was the First Chief Directorate's killing and sabotage section. In the early '70s it was finally renamed the Department #8, but then, as in 1961, its aims were the same: the development of the ability to sabotage foreign transportation and communications networks, to wreck foreign public utilities, and to assassinate anyone who got in their way. *Mokrie dela*, such actions were called: "wet affairs,"

112

because blood would be spilled. A wall around West Berlin certainly fit the bill, and Mahoney figured Chernov would be there.

Then as now, John found himself thinking that Chernov had been more than his father's nemesis. The man had been a virtual one-man Lorelei. A siren on the rocks: "Come to me. Come to me." His song irresistible.

"He flew out that night as part of a special assessments team," Kopinski said. "We needed the hard facts before we could do anything, anything at all. They were shitting in their pants over at the White House. It couldn't be as bad as all that, they were telling us. But of course it was."

"Did my father actually see Chernov? Did he get to talk to him?" John asked.

"He saw him, all right, but of course by then Chernov was enough of a bigwig that such a meeting was impossible. Although I think if your father could have arranged it he would have gone over for a chat."

"Are you sure he didn't?"

Kopinski shrugged. "I'm not sure of anything, John. None of us should be, but I think if he had actually done it he would have said something to me about it." He shook his head. "No, they didn't get together that time. At least not to have words with each other. In any event it would have been extremely dangerous. Everyone was trigger-happy. The entire city was like a powder keg ready to blow sky-high at any moment."

"But you said my father finally figured Chernov out then?"

"That's right."

"How, if they didn't meet?"

Kopinski smiled a little sadly. "Understand, John, that for the previous fifteen years or so your father had made it his avocation to study the Russian mentality. He was becoming something of an expert. Hell, *the* expert. Langley didn't know whether to shit or go blind over him. When he was in Washington they'd put him on the Soviet desk where he was a virtual genius. But his talents were simply too valuable to be wasted behind a desk stateside, so they'd send him out into the field wherever they felt the situation might heat up."

"I'm surprised he wasn't stationed in Berlin."

"He was before and later, but at that moment he was between assignments, back on the Soviet desk. When he got over there he

113

only had to stay a couple of days to find out what he wanted to know, and he came back."

"What did he tell you?"

"His report predicted that the wall would go up and that it would be permanent unless we stopped it now. Not just a few miles of barbed wire and some fencing, but an honest-to-God concrete and brick wall with a no-man's killing zone around the entire city." Again Kopinski was lost in the memories. The rest of the team had remained in Berlin. Mahoney had returned alone, ostensibly to collate and analyze the field reports that were streaming in to headquarters twenty-four hours a day. "Five bells on the teletype signified an incoming Flash designator, a message of extreme importance. The comm center sounded like a Christmas concert around the clock."

No one wanted to believe him, Kopinski remembered. But his report was forwarded to the White House all the same where it was either lost or ignored, because nothing, absolutely nothing was done about the wall. "And the hell of it was that the Russians would have backed down had we objected. They were not willing to start an all-out shooting war over it. The wall just wasn't that important to them. There were other considerations."

Kopinski was a Republican because, in his own words, every Democratic administration to come down the pike had been soft on the Russians. "Too busy trying to institute their great domestic social welfare programs to look east" was how he put it.

"My father must have been angry," John said.

"Sure he was, but he wasn't surprised, and neither was I," Kopinski said. "His reports on the wall and the Russian presence in Eastern Europe were brilliant. The very best he had ever written. There wasn't one of them up on the seventh floor who could dispute it. He knew the Russian mind, finally. He knew what made the bastards tick."

"You said my father returned early to *ostensibly* work the desk," John said. "What did you mean?"

"The sooner he finished his reports, the sooner he would be sent back out into the field. Europe. He wanted to try out his new theories in practice."

"What new theories?"

"About the Russians—what the hell do you think we've been talking about, kid? Your father chased after Chernov for fifteen years without making any real progress, and then he goes to Berlin, stands on a big tower, sees the man across the border, and all of a sudden he knows. He was like a kid at Christmas opening his presents."

"Knows what?" John nearly shouted in his frustration.

"What makes Chernov tick."

"What's that?"

"The man is afraid of making a fool of himself. He's afraid of being seen as an uncultured, uncouth barbarian. It is the great Russian fear, and it's as simple as that. Scratch a Russian and you'll find a spirit that practically wallows in tragedy but is afraid to admit it to anyone on the outside. It's the national mania. It's why the little old *babushka* walking down the street will stop and scold a mother if she thinks the younger woman is mistreating a child. 'They think we breed mothers in the Soviet Union who do not know how to raise their children,' she might say. It's why Gorbachev fired his minister of defense after a young kid flew his airplane from Germany to Moscow. It had nothing to do with air defense—hell, you can't load an atomic bomb aboard a Cessna 172—it had to do with saving face. The Russians were embarrassed."

"They were embarrassed in Berlin," John said, beginning to understand.

"Exactly. Here they had their great state, and people were deserting it in droves for the Western sectors. The Russians wanted to stop it because they were being made to look like fools. But they would also have backed down had we forced their hand, because that would have made them look like even bigger fools."

"What did Chernov's being there have to do with my father's sudden understanding?"

"We'd put up a big observation tower on the Friedrichstrasse, fifty yards away from Checkpoint Charlie. The first thing your father did when he got there was to climb to the top and look across the border. He wasn't watching them construct the wall; he wanted to know who was on the other side watching us."

"He couldn't have expected to see Chernov. Not just like that. I mean the chances of the man actually being there had to be ten thousand to one."

"But he was there. On the other side, up in his own tower, watching to see what the West was going to do."

"He was head of their assassination bureau—what the hell was he doing there?"

"I don't know, but your father knew that he would be there, and he wanted to see how Chernov would react once he knew that your father was there as well."

"And?"

"He was there, and embarrassed."

"What?"

"Your father watched through the binoculars, and the moment Chernov spotted your father he climbed down the tower, got into his car, and drove away. He didn't come back."

"And from that my father understood the Russian spirit?"

"As easy as that," Kopinski said. "*Kulturny*—it's everything to the Russian. Ever since the Revolution in 1917 they've been trying to make a go of their great experiment. Whenever it seems to be falling apart around the edges they do something stupid and usually dangerous. All to save face."

A small child's embarrassment when he's caught with his hand in the cookie jar, John thought. In the field the Russian was tough, but the one back in Duluth had folded almost too easily.

Kopinski looked up toward the nursing home. He had finished his cigarette some time ago, and he asked John for another.

"Your father was pretty good up to that point. He had had quite a few successes under his belt. Plenty of respect upstairs. But it wasn't enough for him. And thank God for it. Because after 1961 he was nothing short of brilliant. Inspired, they used to say. It was true."

"So where is he now, Stan?" John asked, lighting both their cigarettes.

The night had become quite chilly. The old man seemed pale. His hand shook when he raised the cigarette to his lips.

"Where did those two old men get themselves? What are they talking about? You know that Chernov now is a special adviser to the Politburo. Evidently some sort of a liaison from the KGB. He'd have a lot of secrets running around in his head."

Somewhere across the lake John heard a motorboat, its high-pitched whine grating, intrusive just now. He thought it odd that somebody would be out on the lake at this time of night, and especially in this season. He looked for its running lights, but he couldn't pick them out from the backdrop of lights from houses on the other shore.

"He was involved in the operation," Kopinski said, not looking at John. "In the late seventies. The rumor was that they were poisoning embassy staff in Moscow. At first we thought it was with microwaves. Later we figured that they had poisoned some of our people with a chemical, though exactly how, we never found out. The operation stopped as abruptly as it began."

116

John's stomach was tied in knots. So it was true about his mother's death after all. Carlisle hadn't been lying. He wished just now with all his heart that he didn't know.

"If my father knows, he will kill Chernov," he said.

"Without a doubt. And I'm sure Chernov knows it."

"Then why did he call my father, of all people?"

Kopinski finally turned to face him. "Because he knew that nothing would stop your father from meeting with him. Alone. No force on this earth could have kept your father back. It's why he took his workname passports, and it's why he took his gun. He went to Chernov to kill him. To settle the one big score between them."

"Chernov wants to commit suicide, Stan, is that what you're telling me? Or what? I don't understand."

"Chernov trusts your father. He knows your father presumably at least as well as your father knows him. He also knows that your father has the respect of the Agency and of the government as well. He called for your father to tell him something that is so important he is willing to risk his life for it."

A cold wind suddenly wrapped itself around John, holding his heart as if in a deep freeze. "What could it be?" he asked.

Kopinski shook his head. "Only Chernov knows that. But whatever he brought with him, it's the most important thing in his entire life. He's ashamed. He wants to be absolved, and your father is the only man on earth who can grant him absolution."

"Where are they, Stan?"

"Berlin, of course," the old man said. "East or West I couldn't say, but definitely Berlin. It's where it began in the forties just after the war, and it's where their battle solidified in 1961 with the building of the wall."

The sound of the motorboat was much louder now, though it was impossible to pinpoint the direction because of the effect of the water on sounds.

"It's a big city, Stan. What else can you give me? Anything. I've got to find them."

"There might be one man still left over there who knew both your father and Chernov from the early days. Bernhard Heiser. He was a general in the West German BND. One of Gehlen's right-hand men. He was there that day in 1961, and afterward."

"Where does he live?"

"Bonn, the last I heard. He's retired by now, of course. And I don't even know if he's still alive. But he might be able to help."

"We can't get the Germans involved in this."

"I'm not saying that," Kopinski countered impatiently. "Heiser had the respect of your father. He is a good man, or at least he was. Tell him what you know, and if he can help you he will. He has no love for Chernov, or for any Russian, for that matter."

"What if he can't or won't help?" John asked. It was too loose and yet he knew he had nothing else. Not really.

Kopinski shrugged. "Then your guess is as good as mine, John. Like you said, it's a big city and if your father wants to stay truly lost, there won't be much you or all of Carlisle's horses can do about it." He laughed bitterly. "Chernov's tradecraft isn't so shabby either."

The motorboat was practically on top of them. All of a sudden it was throttled back. John looked up in time to see the dull glint of a low dark hull barely fifty feet offshore.

"Down!" he shouted, pushing Kopinski to one side as he tossed his cigarette, rolled left, and clawed for his gun. A half-dozen shots were fired from the boat. Kopinski grunted something and was thrown backward. John was down on one knee and he started firing. The motorboat's engine roared to life again, waves washing up on the pebbled beach as it started away. "No!" John shouted, jumping up. He fired three more shots in rapid succession, and suddenly a big fireball rose from a spot a hundred feet offshore, a heavy *crump* rolling across the lake, echoing off the bulk of the nursing home behind him.

Someone was shouting something from up the hill and people were coming on the run as John turned to Kopinski lying in a bloody heap on the brown grass. He had been hit three times, twice in the chest and once below his left eye, half the side of his face gone. They'd probably used night spotter scopes. He was dead, and probably hadn't known what hit him.

John knelt down beside the old man, gently touched the pale skin of his forehead, and then carefully closed his eyes. It can happen to any of us at any time, his father told him a few years ago. But even if you understand this fact, you're never quite prepared for the death of a friend, and you certainly will never be prepared for your own. So don't go out there trying to be a hero, son. Stay alive.

"He's dead," he said, looking up as the first of the people from the nursing home arrived. And then one of the big attendants in a white uniform was lifting him off his feet and shaking him like a rag doll, but he didn't care.

* * *

The only light in John's apartment came from the kitchen. It was late and he wanted to sleep, but he knew that he could not. The military jet that would take him to Ramstein Air Force Base was waiting out at Andrews, if he was going to be allowed to go after all. Carlisle had been beside himself with rage. "Right here in my city!" he cried. "To one of my own people!" Through it all a part of John's brain wondered about the performance. There had been something studied, almost fake about it. As if Carlisle were more interested in impressing those gathered around him that he had "people" whom he could call his own, than he was grief-stricken about the assassination of a very good man. He stood by the window in his darkened living room looking down at P Street. This time there were two men waiting in a car below. Carlisle had insisted they be on hand. "We don't want any more nonsense happening on our home turf," he'd said. John thought that the car below was the same one he might have seen several times in the city. But he couldn't be sure. In any event it no longer mattered. He would either go or he wouldn't.

"You'd better get away from that window," Alex Hayes said, coming from the kitchen.

John turned around. "They weren't after me," he said. Though how he knew that he wasn't quite sure.

Hayes had mixed them drinks. He handed John one of them. "How could they have known about Kopinski?"

"He was one of my father's friends. He knew a lot. Apparently they thought too much."

"But he didn't tell you anything useful."

John shook his head. He hadn't told them about Heiser. Not yet. That was his own little secret for the moment. Keep secrets and live; share them and die. Cynical but true sometimes. "They couldn't know that. Any word on the boat?"

"Not yet. Technical Services is still out there, but we're having a hell of a time keeping the media away from Stan's true identity, along with yours, of course. They're screaming bloody murder."

John stirred the ice around in his glass and took a deep drink. It was mostly bourbon. He was following in his father's footsteps in more ways than one, he told himself. Hayes was watching him carefully, as somebody might watch an epileptic for signs of an impending fit.

"Farley wants you to stay put until we can get some sort of a handle on this thing," Hayes said. "Why don't you come away from that window?"

John sat on the edge of the couch, willing himself not to lie back

119

lest he close his eyes and drift off. He was very tired, but the clock was definitely running now. The trouble was, he had no idea how long the countdown would last before the big bomb went off. If and when it happened, though, he suspected the fallout would be deadly.

"Kopinski thought they might be in Germany somewhere," Hayes said into the breach. They'd already gone over this ground, but he wanted to make sure of everything before Carlisle swept in with his own questions.

"That's where my father apparently first met Chernov."

"Just after the war?"

"Right."

"And then again when the wall was going up?"

"That's what Stan told me."

Hayes sighed. "Not a goddamned thing in any of your father's reports. Of course the first encounter would have been listed in the old OSS files. Paper records. So far we've had no luck. It could be weeks or even a year before we'll ever run it down."

"This situation won't last that long," John said.

"No," Hayes agreed. "But I think it's a safe bet that wherever your father and Chernov met for the first time is where they're meeting now. Unless something else was set up during the Helsinki call."

Berlin, John thought. Just at the end of the war. There had been a lot of meetings between the American, British, Free French, and Soviet forces. Meetings that Heiser could not possibly know about. He assumed the German would have been sweating it out in an Allied POW camp somewhere in Germany at the time. But it was his country, after all. And his was the only name he had to go on now. If he could get to the man without being followed. If the man was still alive. If he knew anything. The lack of possibilities was endless.

The telephone rang. Hayes answered it. "Yes," he said softly. He looked up at John a moment later. "He's all right. We're just waiting for the green light here."

The trouble was, John thought, he should have known better than to drag the old man out into the open. He had felt he was being watched, only he had assumed it was Carlisle's people. Duluth should have told him otherwise. If they had sent a man out there, they certainly wouldn't be missing any bets here in Washington. If they had remained inside, Kopinski would still be alive.

Hayes was holding out the telephone for him. "Farley would like to have a word with you," he said.

John got up and went to the phone. "Yes?" he said.

"John? How are you, really?"

"I'm all right," he said. "But it was my fault, completely. I shouldn't have taken him outside."

"You couldn't have known."

"Someone has been following me around Washington since I flew in today, Farley."

"Did you spot them?" Carlisle asked sharply.

"No. But there's been someone there, all right. No doubt about it now."

"I'm not convinced," Carlisle said stubbornly. "They're simply following down the same tracks as you are. Looking to your father's old friends for clues. You beat them to it. Is there anyone else we should know about? Anyone else you want to talk to? If there is, for God's sake, John, just give me the word and I'll bring them into protective custody and you can have a go at it in safety."

"No one else, Farley. It's time now for me to go to Germany. They're there someplace."

"Any ideas?" Carlisle asked cautiously.

"I'm going to start with the BND," he said, tempering his lie of omission with a small truth. "They met someplace in Germany at the end of the war."

"You've got the green light, John. But be careful, please. Just find those old fools and bring them home."

"I will."

"If you need any help, any help whatsoever, Berlin station is yours."

"Thanks, Farley," John said, and hanging up he wondered for just the moment why Carlisle had mentioned Berlin specifically, and not simply Germany.

8

Mahoney arrived in Hannover a little after six in the evening under his Greenleaf workname. He took a cab from the airport to the Inter-Continental Hotel on Friedrichswall where he checked in, booking the room for three days. His entry to West Berlin had been by air, which meant he had no East German transit visa in his passport, so he had to fly out the same way. At the airport he had made a great show of selecting his destination. He was on a leisurely tour of Germany, he explained to the Pan Am clerk. Although he had an elderly aunt in Munich, he also had very close friends in Frankfurt am Main whom he desperately wanted to see. Settling, however, finally on Hannover he engaged the clerk in a lengthy discussion about air fares, holding up a long line behind him. He turned several times to give his apologies, thus fixing his face and description to at least a dozen more people. He did the same at the Inter-Continental Hotel, tipping a little too well so that he would be remembered, and expressing a good deal of concern that he would have to give up his passport for the time being. "Purely routine, Herr Greenleaf," the impatient clerk had assured him. Once he was in his room he mussed up his bed as if he had slept in it, left a few pieces of clothing on hangers, and by eight slipped unobserved out the back way where he disappeared into the city. Five blocks from his hotel he took a cab to the train depot, where without fanfare he purchased a round-trip ticket to West Berlin and boarded the train a few minutes before its scheduled departure time of 9:00 P.M., this time traveling under his work-name of Fredrick Oliver, an anonymous little man obviously on holiday, and obviously without a care in the world.

Sitting alone by the window in his compartment, he watched the last of Hannover's suburbs slide away into the night and had the oddest sensation that he had done this all before. The feeling was almost one of déjà vu, except that he found he was thinking he was coming back into himself. Two halves separated that were finally coming together after a very long and arduous journey. Only he didn't know if he wanted to be joined.

Chernov was somewhere on the same train as Wilhelm Fassbender, a West German workname. The game they were playing was a dangerous one that at best would buy them only a day or two more at the Grunewald Hotel. They had both laid a track from West Berlin that had probably already attracted some attention. The hounds would be converging on Hannover. It would keep them busy, but only for a little while.

At Grunewald their passports had already been examined and recorded by the police, and since they had not checked out— they'd only gone for a day trip to see old friends elsewhere in Berlin—they wouldn't have to show them on their return. Chernov had rented a car in Berlin that he had parked at the train depot. "Their back door," he'd explained. They would not have to take a cab back out to the hotel, and should the need arise, they would have a possible way out.

Back in the field like this, on the run, Mahoney thought how ridiculously fast his life had passed. During the living of it he had often been impatient for an hour to be gone, or for the next week to be here so that he would be finished with whatever disagreeable task he was involved with, or that it would be two years hence so that he could leave some particularly offensive assignment for another more interesting place. It was ironic, he thought now, that he had gotten his wish. Time had passed.

There was one very brief interlude, he thought riding through the night, in which he could have done something about Chernov. One moment out of his past that would have taken care of at least one set of problems in his future. But of course he had been too shortsighted to take the opportunity when it had presented itself. He had been too filled with pride, with his own sense of purpose, with a youthful zeal that perhaps glorified the struggle more than it venerated a long-term purpose. And now he was truly sorry for it, though he finally had the old man's understanding that exchanging one set of decisions for another was no guarantee of a better life.

It was nearing Christmas of 1948. The Berlin airlift, known officially as Operation Vittles but known irreverently in Washington as Operation Rathole because everyone figured America was tossing its money down a bottomless pit, was in its fifth month. The couple of million or so Berliners along with the garrisoned troops were surviving after a fashion, and in fact among a certain class of Berliners profits were even being made, but the situation was simply intolerable. The stalemate had to be broken. To that end Washington was sending over a team of negotiators to speak with the Russians, to see if anything could be done. With the constant overflights of Allied aircraft through East German airspace, there was a lot of concern that a trigger-happy Russian pilot might take it into his head to open fire one night, and then all hell would truly break loose. No one wanted that, least of all—so Washington figured—the Russians. What did we have to lose, after all? Talk is cheap. Give a little, take a little. Although in March President Truman had spoken to Congress about the "cold war" against totalitarianism, compromise was still the best game in town, and at least worth a shot.

"You speak German and you know your way around over there," Dulles told Mahoney. "I'm sending you with the negotiating team. You'll hold the rank of major for the operation. G-2. They'll expect at least that much, so your presence won't be questioned. Just keep your eyes and ears open."

"What are we looking for?" Mahoney asked. He was thinking about how he was going to explain to Marge why he would be missing Christmas with them.

"We want to know how long the bastards are going to keep up the blockade."

"You think the negotiations are going to fail?"

"Almost assuredly."

"Maybe the Russians don't even know themselves how long they'll stick with it. That's up to Stalin."

"But you should be able to get a sense of their resolve, Wallace. A sense of their iron. We're operating in the dark here. If we had some idea, any idea, it would help."

Berlin had changed drastically since the war. Everywhere were signs of reconstruction in the western sectors, mostly halted now, however, for lack of material because of the Soviet blockade. The signs were all there, nevertheless, that the Germans, given half a chance, would prosper. A smoke pall hung over the city. The only coal the West Berliners were getting these days was of the soft variety. Downtown smelled like a sulphur works, and automobiles left outside overnight would in the morning be covered with a thick layer of black soot. From any spot in Berlin, day or night, you could hear the big transport aircraft pounding in from the west. At first Mahoney had looked up when they'd come in, but he soon noticed that everyone else in the city had gone deaf. If the planes stopped, he supposed, they would look up. The noise was their heartbeat. Their lifeline.

The American delegation was billeted on the third floor of a relatively undamaged apartment building on the Potsdamer Strasse a few blocks from the Tiergarten and not far from Checkpoint Charlie, the main entry into East Berlin. On the first morning they were driven in three staff cars into the eastern zone where they met their Soviet counterparts in the old Berlin city hall on Rathaus Strasse (how appropriate it was thought). There were no East Germans present. No pretenses here, Mahoney remembered thinking. This was something strictly between the Americans and the Soviets. The big two postwar powers. Even this far from the airfields in the western zone the incoming aircraft rattled windows, and an occasional bit of plaster dust would settle from the ceiling onto the long, green conference table. The place smelled like urine and wet dog. Outside it had begun to snow.

After the formally polite introductions the Russians offered coffee or tea, which the Americans declined, offering in return cigarettes, which the Russians declined and the meeting began. The Americans wanted the blockade stopped, of course. And the Russians demanded that the violations of their airspace immediately cease. For humanitarian reasons, if nothing else, the West Berliners had to be fed; surely their Soviet cousins could understand the simple logic in that. "We cannot simply allow them to starve," General Holister said. "Then we will feed them," General Bazhanov replied. "But we cannot abandon our sector of Berlin. Nor can we permit ground corridors through sovereign territory of the German Democratic Republic."

In the afternoon the talks shifted to war reparations. The Soviet peoples had suffered terribly at the hands of the Nazis. They were, in retaliation, stripping most of Eastern Europe of its industrial capacity. The Nazis were expunged, the Americans argued. Let the German peoples rebuild. "Not at our expense," General Bazhanov flared in a very thinly veiled reference to the Marshall Plan. In the first two years since the war the U.S. had sent over more than twelve billion dollars in aid to Western Europe. The Marshall Plan authorized by Congress had put another six billion-plus into the war-ravaged economies. In the eastern zone, however, the Soviet government hadn't spent a single ruble, and already there was a lot of unrest and dissension against Soviet rule, especially among the people of Hungary. It was the real reason Stalin had closed Berlin to all non-Russian traffic.

Nothing had been accomplished on that first day—nor would

anything be accomplished, formally, over the next four days—and at five in the evening the American delegation rose as one and prepared to leave, stiffly declining the Soviet offer of a meal and drinks. Mahoney was pulling on his overcoat in the broad corridor outside the second-floor meeting room when a door down the hall opened and Chernov, dressed in a Soviet Intelligence Service uniform, lieutenant colonel's insignia on his shoulder boards, stepped out. He was speaking to someone inside the office he was just leaving, his back momentarily turned to Mahoney who had stiffened in recognition. He remembered the hum of conversations around him, but suddenly all the air had left the building, and he was in a soundless vacuum. Chernov said something else and turned, closing the door behind him. His eyes met Mahoney's and he hesitated for only a split second before he turned and walked the opposite way down the corridor, disappearing around the corner, not a hint in his expression that he had recognized Mahoney.

"Major?" Holister called from the head of the stairs. "Are you coming?"

Mahoney looked up, startled. "Yes, sir," he said, and he crossed to the stairs. With Chernov anything was possible, he thought. But with Chernov he would have to be careful. He found at that moment that he was almost afraid of the man.

The Potsdamer Strasse apartment building was bedlam. The negotiating team had taken over an entire floor. A long corridor ran the length of the building. The rooms in front overlooked the street; those in back looked down on a rubble-strewn courtyard in which old ladies were picking through the bricks, tossing the good ones into wheelbarrows, and throwing the others into big bins. Several of the rooms had been set up as offices. They had brought a total of thirty people out from Washington. Eight, including Mahoney, were on the actual negotiating team. The others worked as typists, analysts, and translators. They had worked steadily through the late afternoon and early evening typing up a rough transcript of the meeting. The real G-2 on Holister's staff was Stewart Bryce, a rat-faced little captain who'd been graduated from Harvard magna cum laude, and was making the Army his career. He wanted someday to become a full general and he made no bones about it. Nor did he hide his outright distrust and dislike of Mahoney. Although most of the staff understood that Mahoney wasn't who he was presented as, no one knew for certain exactly what he was, or why he had been included on the team. During the sessions with the Russians he had made no contributions, and during the evening debriefing he merely sat and listened. But Bryce thought he knew what Mahoney was. "You're from the State Department, Mahoney," he said, his East Coast accent thick. "Here to spy on us, to make sure we don't give away the kitchen sink. Well, I can tell you that I do not like spies." Which was a curious statement for a G-2 to make. But Mahoney did not challenge him. Bryce fussed around the general day and night, handing him reports, passing him little notes, even going so far as whispering little confidences into Holister's ear at the odd moment. The general had been told by his boss, the Army Chief of Staff, that a civilian masquerading as an Army G-2 major would be included, and that no questions were to be asked of him. Holister was West Point and he knew how to follow orders, but after the first day he began talking around Mahoney, ignoring him for the most part, even forgetting at times that the mysterious G-2 major was even in the room.

It was what Mahoney had wanted from the start. Nothing was going to be produced from the actual meetings in East Berlin except for rhetoric and some carefully staged acrimony. The Russians had no intention of honoring the Americans' naïve good-faith proposals to end the blockade, nor were the Americans prepared to give up their airlift. The entire world was watching to see what would happen. No one was going to back down. The fact that Chernov was in East Berlin, however, changed everything. Mahoney was going to suggest to General Holister that he be excused from the team so that he could fly home and report to Dulles that the Russians were stonewalling it. That nothing would be gained by his continued presence. And in fact they had everything to lose. If the Russians suspected that one of the negotiators, even a silent partner as it were, was CIA, the meetings would be immediately terminated. It wasn't a message that Mahoney wanted to bring home, but one he had figured he would have to leave with nonetheless. Until he had spotted Chernov. The only thing he needed now, he figured, was a lever with which to dig the Russian out of East Berlin.

Rheinhard Gehlen, who had spent a brief sojourn in the States, had been given his four demands and had been sent back in 1946 to establish a German secret service. His first operational headquarters had been set up at Oberursel near Frankfurt, but the next year he moved everything down to a big compound at Pullach just eight miles outside of Munich. From there he had built an impressive network of experts, analysts, translators, communications and codes people, as well as his spies who were doing quite a good job all across Eastern Europe. His people worked under the cover of commercial enterprises all across Germany. Often they went under the name *Jalousie Vertrieb Zimmerle & Co.*, manufacturers of venetian blinds (and some venetian blinds were actually made by his companies). The branch in Berlin was code-named simply 9592, and was run by Bernhard Heiser, a former Abwehr lieutenant colonel, whose offices were out by Templehof Airport. General Holister had been more than happy to excuse Mahoney from the second day's session with the Russians. "Wish I could skip out myself," he said.

After the team had left for the eastern zone, Mahoney borrowed a Jeep and drove over to the airport. Traffic on the highway was thick with trucks bringing supplies into the city proper. It was still snowing, the morning gray and overcast. None of the flights had been canceled, however. The BND office was located in a section of old factory buildings that had not yet been rebuilt. Wooden bulkheads had been erected, blocking off the lower floor. Heiser was on the second floor.

"Good morning, sir," a young, plain woman said when Mahoney came in. The reception room was small. Fake windows over which venetian blinds were hung lined all four walls.

"Good morning," Mahoney said pleasantly. He had changed into civilian clothes before coming over. "I am a friend of Herr Heiser."

"Have you an appointment, sir?"

"No, I'm afraid I don't. I've just flown in from the United States. My name is Mahoney."

"I am sorry, sir, but Herr Heiser is not here at the moment. Perhaps if you left a message?"

"It is very important," Mahoney said. "Perhaps if you could telephone him. Tell him that I am here, and that we have mutual friends in Washington as well as at Pullach."

"Very well, sir," the girl said, rising. "If you will just wait for a moment I will see if Herr Heiser can be reached." She turned and disappeared through a door, giving Mahoney a brief, tantalizing glimpse of a much larger office beyond.

She was gone for several minutes, during which time Mahoney got the distinct impression that he was being watched. Perhaps through one of the fake windows, he supposed. When she returned it was with two burly men, their shirt sleeves rolled above their elbows. She stepped aside.

128

"If you will just place your hands away from your body," one of them said pleasantly.

Mahoney did as he was told, and the one expertly patted him down while the other stood back and impassively watched. They found his wallet, and his military .45 automatic in his shoulder holster.

"This way, sir," the other one said, holding the door open.

Heiser was a man of medium build with deep-set very dark eyes, thick black eyebrows, and shiny black hair that was slicked down and so severely parted that his scalp showed stark white by contrast. He accepted Mahoney's gun and his wallet, then rose from behind his desk and held out his hand. Mahoney crossed the big room to him and shook hands.

"You come as something of a surprise, Mr. Mahoney," Heiser said, his English very good.

"Have you verified who I am?" Mahoney asked.

Heiser nodded. He motioned for Mahoney to have a seat. The other two men remained standing by the door.

"I need your help in a small matter," Mahoney began.

"I thought you would have been at the Rathaus in the eastern zone this morning."

"Nothing is being accomplished over there."

"Nothing will ever be accomplished with the Russians, Mr. Mahoney. It's why you and I are in the business." He smiled sadly, opened Mahoney's wallet to his G-2 identification, and studied the photograph for a moment. "What can we do for you?" he said, looking up.

"Do you know the name Yuri Chernov?"

Heiser thought a moment, looked toward his two men, then shook his head. "This is a significant name?"

"I met him during and just after the war. At the time he was GRU on General Zhukov's staff."

Heiser's eyebrows rose. "An important man."

"I saw him yesterday. In East Berlin. He was dressed in the uniform of a KI lieutenant colonel."

Heiser sat forward. "This one was on the negotiating team?"

"No. When we were leaving I spotted him coming out of an office."

"Did he see you?"

"Yes."

"Did he recognize you?"

"I'm almost certain of it. It's possible he believes I am still with Army Intelligence."

"But not likely, I would suspect. The KI would have you spotted. They have taken over not only the GRU, but also the foreign sections of the MGB. A powerful man, your Lieutenant Colonel Chernov. We will add his name to our rogue's gallery. Thank you for giving us this."

"I would like to arrange a meeting with him."

Heiser's eyes narrowed. "Yes? And for what purpose, Mr. Mahoney?"

"To talk."

"On what subject?"

"The blockade."

Heiser smiled. "I think there is more to it than that," he said. "You have the authorization for such an unprecedented meeting? You have come here with orders?"

"No, nor will there be time to get them," Mahoney said.

"I see. And what makes you think that this Russian would agree to such a meeting?"

"He knows me from the war, as I have already said."

"During the war you were allies. That is not the case at the moment. Perhaps he would try to kill you, and perhaps he would believe it was a trap on your part."

"The meeting would take place somewhere very public. Just the two of us. He would have diplomatic immunity in any event. As far as I know he has committed no crimes against the Federal Republic."

"His presence here is a crime," Heiser flared. "You are playing a dangerous game, I think. A personal game of matching wits."

"He is my enemy as much as he is yours," Mahoney argued. "And the fact that the Russians are here will not change very soon. You know it and I know it."

"Then why do you wish to meet this man?"

"I want to know him."

Heiser's eyebrows rose.

"He's not going to go away either. In time he will become a very important man, I think. Much more important than a simple KI lieutenant colonel."

"I will repeat, Mr. Mahoney, that you are playing a dangerous game."

"Aren't we all?" Mahoney said, sitting back. "Will you help me?"

Heiser looked up at his two men again. Whatever passed between them Mahoney wasn't sure, but Heiser seemed to come

130

to a decision. "You would have us pass a message to him, if that were possible?"

"Yes, sometime today. Preferably before this evening."

"And where would this meeting take place?"

"Here in the western zone, of course. I thought about the Ballhaus Resi. Is it still in operation?"

"On Hasenheide," Heiser said. "Yes." The Ballhaus was a huge nightclub that featured telephones and message chutes on each table. Before the war it had been a pickup joint. If you spotted someone at another table who caught your fancy, you could either telephone or send a written message by pneumatic chute. It was a place, Mahoney thought, in which a totally private meeting could be held in public, with little or no danger for either party.

Heiser thought about it for a moment, then nodded. "Yes, if he would come across he would come to a place like that. He would bring his own people with him."

"He would come alone."

"I don't think so, Mr. Mahoney. No, I don't think your Russian would come alone. And neither will you. In this I must insist."

"For protection only. I will not want him approached under any circumstance short of an act of violence on his part."

Heiser nodded. "You will share the product with us?"

"As far as possible," Mahoney said.

"You wish the meeting this evening?"

"Yes."

"We will try, Mr. Mahoney. Shall we say eight o'clock?"

"Make it ten," Mahoney said, thinking about the staff meeting tonight. He wanted to know if Chernov had been at today's session looking for him.

"Ten it will be," Heiser said.

"Yes, as a matter of fact there was a new face at this morning's meeting, but not at this afternoon's," General Holister answered Mahoney's question just before the eight o'clock staff briefing. Bryce was hanging just off the general's left shoulder as if he were a guardian angel.

"A large man? Deep eyes? Big face? A lieutenant colonel?" Mahoney asked, describing Chernov.

"A captain's uniform," the general said. "But it sounds like the same one."

"Is he someone we should know about?" Bryce asked.

"How was he introduced?"

"He wasn't."

"And he wasn't there at the afternoon session?"

"No," the general said. "Who is he?"

"If he is the man I'm thinking of, he's a Soviet intelligence officer. Watch out for him."

"Do you have a name?" Bryce asked.

"Not yet," Mahoney said.

At nine-thirty Mahoney took a cab over to the Ballhaus. Once inside he was required to pay a stiff cover charge after which he was led to table 58, several rows back from the stage on which a young woman was singing American torch songs from the thirties. She was quite good. The place was about three-quarters filled at this hour, mostly with American and British men and groups of young and not so young German girls. Already the place was in full swing. Messages were popping back and forth with curious little sucking sounds, and a lot of the guests were speaking softly into their telephones. Mahoney hadn't seen Chernov on his way in, though it was still a little early. Nor had he spotted Heiser's people. He suspected they were here, however. The telephones were probably being monitored as well. Only the message chutes would be safe.

The waiter came and Mahoney ordered a bourbon and water. The nightclub was very large. He estimated that there were at least five hundred people here. On each table was a light that illuminated the lower halves of the patrons' faces, lending an eerie and yet even more intimate air to the big room. The dance floor was half filled with couples, in some cases two men, Mahoney realized. In Berlin, he thought, anything was possible.

When the waiter returned with the drink, he laid the bill on the table. Written on the back was a note: *Outside. When I think it is safe I'll catch up with you.* Mahoney looked up.

"The gentleman wishes to remain anonymous for the moment, mein Herr," the waiter said.

Mahoney paid him. "A large man, was he?"

"Yes, sir," the waiter said, and he turned and left.

Mahoney scanned the crowd. If Chernov was here and wanted to remain anonymous, it wouldn't be so hard. He casually pocketed the check and took a deep pull at his drink. The message opened all sorts of possibilities. If Chernov wanted to eliminate him, it would be relatively easy to do at night in Berlin. On the other hand if he'd wanted to talk, to seriously talk, the Ballhaus wasn't such a good idea after all. At least it wasn't from his standpoint. It was likely, then, that he had spotted Heiser's people here. It also was likely that Chernov had not come alone after all.

His telephone rang. He answered it. "Yes?"

"What was the note?" Heiser said.

"He wants me out of here. When he thinks it is clear he'll make his approach. But if he sees your people he won't make the contact."

"What do you want to do?"

"I'll walk to the Tiergarten. Don't follow me. Station your people in the park."

"I have a bad feeling about this, Mr. Mahoney."

"So do I," Mahoney said, and he hung up. He shook his head, smiled to himself for the benefit of anyone watching, then finished his drink.

Outside, the snow was falling in big gentle flakes. There was little or no wind. Traffic sounds seemed muffled and far away in the night; even the constant drone of the incoming aircraft seemed distant now. At the corner he turned up his coat collar and headed toward Kleist Strasse, aware in a big way of his own vulnerability just now. He kept his eyes open for anyone who looked suspicious, but in Berlin everybody looked suspicious. It was a city of strange characters. It was a long walk up to the Tiergarten, which was a big park right in the heart of the city, and he had time to think about what he was doing here like this. Dulles would approve, and he was sure that Donovan would too. The risks were well worth the possible gain if Chernov could be brought in of his own free will. And that was the entire point, wasn't it? There was a certain amount of conceit to the idea, but if Chernov could be turned, or at the very least compromised this evening, it would be counted as a victory.

Chernov stepped out of the doorway of an apartment building three blocks from the Ballhaus, startling Mahoney nearly out of his shoes.

"Hello, Wallace," he said, smiling. He wore the uniform of a U.S. Air Force pilot, his cap pulled over at a jaunty angle.

"Yuri," Mahoney said, his breath coming out white in the cold. His heart was thumping. He was conscious of the pressure of the gun beneath his left armpit.

"Really quite clever of you to choose the Ballhaus to meet. But I'm afraid your BND friends were a little too obvious." Chernov glanced up the street. "Where were you heading?"

"The Tiergarten."

"Of course." Chernov smiled again. "They would have gone

133

ahead. For your own protection, I suppose. But believe me when I tell you that I wish you no harm. You wanted to talk, I want to talk."

Mahoney felt outclassed, and very probably at this moment, outgunned. An old Mercedes staff car pulled around the corner and stopped at the end of the block.

"I missed you this morning at the meeting," Chernov was saying. "But then you would have needed the time to get the message to me. And Captain Bryce was there. If he was my subordinate, I think I would fire him. He is not very good, do you think?"

Chernov was either playing games with him, or he thought Mahoney was still in the Army. It was an opening, however slight. They started to walk toward the corner. Very close, two old friends out for an evening stroll.

"I won't give up without a fight, you know," Mahoney said, indicating the waiting staff car. He could see two men in the front seat and a third in the back.

Chernov looked up. "They are friends here only for our protection, Wallace. Nothing more. But if you don't want to ride, it is perfectly fine with me; we shall walk. You must know, however, that Berlin these days is a city filled with hooligans."

"I prefer the fresh air."

"Then what in heaven's name are you doing in Berlin?" Chernov asked wryly.

"Wondering when this stupid blockade of yours will come to an end," Mahoney shot back.

"That is only for Uncle Joseph to say."

"But you would have a good idea. It's why you are here in Germany, isn't it? To assess our strengths, our weaknesses?"

"Intent," Chernov said. His eyes were bright. "It's the other government's intent that we're all after, isn't it? Plans for a new gun, or a new aircraft, or even a new submarine are all well and good. But what is really important to us is the other fellow's intention. What is he going to do with those new toys? How soon is he going to use them on us? In how many days will his mechanized units be streaming across our borders? Has he the will of his people? Are they willing to fight?"

Chernov was a presence more than a simple flesh-and-blood man. Mahoney decided that he must have suffered before as well as during the war to have become such a cynical force so young. "How long?"

"I honestly don't know. And you can quote me on that to your

General Holister, but please wait until the conference is finished. Knowing will only muddy an already obscure issue."

"We're trying to feed people here."

"I know, Wallace, I know. And we are trying to survive."

"Then go home and attend to it."

"Hadn't you already guessed that the world has become too small for such a thing ever to be possible again? Didn't Pearl Harbor teach you anything?"

They stopped. "You were at Stalingrad during the siege, weren't you," Mahoney said, suddenly making the connection.

Chernov laid his hand on Mahoney's shoulder. The gesture almost fatherly. "I was born there, Wallace. Everyone and everything I love is buried in that city now. Burned to death, starved, shelled, machine-gunned, frozen."

"I understand hate . . ." Mahoney began.

"Oh, no, Wallace, you cannot possibly understand hate."

"The entire German population wasn't involved."

"Oh, but it was. And now you are friends with Rheinhard Gehlen, I think. You cannot possibly imagine what that means. And for that alone I could shoot you dead right now."

"You know, there is an old Russian proverb that says we are related: the same sun dries our rags," Chernov said. "But it has not been true between you and me since your Civil War."

They had found a small bierstube just off the Ku'Damm and had gone in out of the cold. Chernov had not had time for dinner, he said, so he ordered some fat sausages, sauerkraut, hard black bread, and a liter of beer. Mahoney had only a cognac. His stomach was unsettled this close to Chernov. He had toyed with the idea of pulling out his gun and bringing the man in. The Mercedes staff car waited outside, but by the time they realized something was going on, it could be over.

"Brother against brother, a nation divided," Chernov said. "They were terrible times for your people."

"It was a stupid war."

"All war is stupid, but your people understood suffering for a time, until the memories began to fade."

"The Russians didn't invent suffering."

"No, but we have become masters of the condition. Let the shortages be divided among the peasants. In Moscow they ring the bells often, but not for dinner. When you live close to the grave you cannot weep for everyone. We know the litany. Believe me when I tell you this. You do not know it, but we do."

"Perhaps it is time to forget."

They were seated in a back booth. The place was mostly filled with German workingmen. They were the only foreigners in the place, and already they had received a number of dirty looks. Chernov thumped his fist on the table, making the plates and glasses jump.

"We'll never forget!" he roared.

There was a momentary lull in the hum of conversation and laughter, and everyone in the place looked their way. But gradually the bierstube got back to normal. Chernov's face was red. It was the first time Mahoney had seen him lose control. He pushed his plate away.

"Why did you come here to Germany, Wallace?"

"To see if we could stop the blockade. It is a foolish, dangerous thing your government is doing."

"And when you saw me at the Rathaus, you thought here is a man with whom I can talk. We can cut through all of the bureaucratic red tape and get right to the heart of the matter, isn't it so?"

"I thought you would come out of curiosity, if nothing else," Mahoney said.

Chernov smiled and looked away momentarily. "It is *your* government who is playing the dangerous game, Wallace. You have no business being here in Germany."

"Mend our own fences at home, is that it? Fix our own system before it completely rots from within and tumbles down upon itself." It was Mahoney's turn to smile. "Is that about right?"

"Essentially."

"Well, save me the polemic, Yuri. You are a lieutenant colonel in the KI and that interests me. What are *you* doing here in Germany?"

"Making sure that our blockade continues, of course. I want nothing to go wrong."

"Innocent people are starving," Mahoney snapped.

They had been speaking in English. Chernov switched suddenly to German, his voice savage. "Let me tell you a little after-dinner story about the Nazis," he said, not bothering to lower his voice. Again all eyes turned their way. "I was on Gregori Zhukov's staff in November of '42 when we broke through the German flanks around Stalingrad. I wanted to get there personally to save all those people. It had been more than three months for them without food or any kind of medicine. But the stubborn Germans hung on, and we had to fight them street by street as winter came. It became their siege as well as the siege of my people. And now the Germans had no food, so they took what little my people had. When that, too, was gone, some of them resorted to cannibalism."

It was a story that Mahoney had not heard, though it didn't really surprise him. Those were desperate times. There was a dangerous silence in the bierstube.

"I was there, Wallace. I came into the city at last only to be told that my wife and little girl were dead and buried. But no one wanted to show me their graves. Everyone was afraid. But in the end I forced them to it, and I made the Germans dig up their bodies."

Chernov was looking at his hands that were folded in front of him on the table. He raised his head after a long moment and looked into Mahoney's eyes.

"There were only bones in that grave, Wallace. Some clothing, a few personal belongings, but no flesh. There were teeth marks on some of the bones. Human teeth marks. Do you know what that means? Do you know what that does to you?" He shook his massive head. "I personally murdered two dozen half-starved, defenseless German soldiers on that day. I made them beg for mercy and then I shot them. They were my prisoners. Young boys, many of them. Good German boys, from good German families. If they don't have sausage, let them eat Russian babies."

The proprietor behind the bar had picked up the telephone and was talking urgently to someone.

"I think they have called the police," Mahoney said in English. He thought about reaching in his coat for his gun. He could hold Chernov here until the police came. But to what end? Chernov had done nothing illegal. Nothing to be arrested for. He was a spy, so he would be sent home.

Chernov looked over at the barman, who stepped back a pace. "Then we should leave here now," he said. He got up, looked at his half-eaten meal, and shook his head. "I think I will not pay for this. They owe me a meal, I think."

Mahoney followed him outside. In the far distance he might have heard a siren, but then the sound was drowned out by a transport aircraft rumbling overhead in the dark sky.

Mahoney felt sad for Chernov, but he had seen Dachau and Auschwitz and some of the other death camps with his own eyes. It was time to forget the horrors now. "How long will you take out your revenge on Germany?"

The Mercedes staff car was parked across the narrow street. The three men inside were watching.

"More than twenty million of my countrymen were killed in the madness, Wallace. This is a number beyond comprehension. No family in the Soviet Union is untouched. Everyone suffers."

"Hungary wasn't involved. Neither was Poland nor Czechoslovakia. Why take it out on them?"

"They have become our buffer."

"Without choice."

"We weren't given a choice eight years ago!"

"The Germans have been defeated. The war is over."

Chernov looked sharply at him. "Do not be so sure, Wallace."

This time they both heard the sirens, much nearer now. Chernov stepped off the curb and started across the narrow street. The rear door of the Mercedes opened.

"It's time to forget," Mahoney called after him.

"Never."

"We'll stop you, then."

Chernov turned and looked back. "I think you will try. But I think you should always be looking over your shoulder. I will be there."

Chernov got in the car and closed the door. A moment later it pulled away from the curb and at the corner turned, disappearing into the night. Mahoney turned in the opposite direction and hurried away before the police arrived. Two blocks away he circled back toward the Tiergarten and the waiting Heiser, feeling very foolish and just a bit incompetent.

The train was slowing down. Mahoney looked outside as the lights of the Marienborn checkpoint into East Germany loomed up in the night. He had often thought about that strange night in Berlin with Chernov. Years later, during his first posting to Moscow, he had had a quiet trace put on Chernov's background, especially on his family history as far as it could be determined without kicking up too much dust. Chernov had been an only child, his father a simple house painter, his mother a piano teacher. He had never been married, nor had he ever fathered a child. The records were incomplete because of the destruction during the war, so the background was inconclusive, but Chernov had not been born in Stalingrad; he had been born in Moscow. Nor, as far as they could tell, had there been any incidents of cannibalism by German troops during the winter of 1942. Strange the lies we told in this business, he thought. Yet Chernov's had been the strangest of all because Mahoney had seen in his eyes that the man had honestly believed his own story, and would have been willing to fight every

German in the bierstube for it. By then of course he had come to understand the Russian penchant for making up histories to fit their current aims. They were experts at the game. It was why their fiction and their poetry and their music were so filled with beautifully involved tragedy. They could believe anything they wanted about themselves, and it was for them the absolute truth.

He got stiffly to his feet and left the train to line up in the customs hall next to the tracks. A short line for passengers getting off at East German points had formed behind one barrier, while a much longer line of passengers going on to West Berlin had formed behind another. Customs agents were going through the baggage while immigration officials were checking passports and issuing transit visas for one hundred marks. He did not try to spot Chernov in the crowd. It wouldn't have done either of them any good. In any event he was certain that the Russian would have no difficulty in returning. Nor did he believe Chernov would skip out, despite what had happened last night. He had his own particular truth of the moment to tell, and nothing was going to stop him.

"The purpose of your visit to West Berlin, Herr Oliver," the immigration officer asked pleasantly.

"Tourism," Mahoney said. He dug out a hundred West German marks and handed them over. The officer stamped his passport and handed it back.

Retrieving his overnight bag, he walked back out onto the platform where he hesitated just a moment before reboarding the train. Strong sodium vapor lights on tall aluminum stanchions illuminated the actual border, beyond which was absolute darkness. He had spent a lot of nights at border crossings like this one, his heart in his throat, not knowing if he would ever see Marge and the children again, wondering if he was going to spend the rest of his life in some East European jail. Had his life been correct, he wondered even now, or had it been an extraordinary waste of time? He was getting to the point where he honestly didn't know. Chernov had once spoken about a government's "intentions." It was the spy's primary ambition to find out what the other fellow was planning, and whether or not he had the willingness to carry out his plan. How often had he accomplished such a feat? How often had any of them accomplished the real task they had set out to do? In Berlin that year he had been sent by Dulles to find out how long the Russians planned on maintaining their blockade. He had returned with an answer that satisfied no one, and yet he had been as near the truth as anyone. "They have the resolve to keep it up for a very long time," he told Dulles. "Simply maintaining our airlift will not in itself cause the Russians to back down."

"What, then?" Dulles had asked.

"They want a show of force. They want to know that we are willing and able to defend Western Europe."

"We've certainly shown them the airpower these last few months. They can't deny that."

"If this North Atlantic defense alliance goes through, it will help," Mahoney said. (NATO was formed the following March, Mahoney recalled.) "But it will take something even more than that, I think, for the Russians to lift the blockade. Something internal to the Soviet Union."

"Somebody should assassinate Stalin. That would solve a lot of our problems."

Once again aboard the train moving through the night, Mahoney reflected on his past. In September 1949 the Soviet Union exploded its first atomic bomb, and within a few months the Berlin blockade was lifted, as Mahoney had said it would. But he did not feel any sense of vindication, then or now. The Russians had regained their pride, and they'd made their point. But they had the bomb. He had unofficially met with Chernov, so nothing ever found its way into his files, except for a quizzical note from Gehlen to Dulles concerning what became known as the "Ballhaus non-incident." *If you want to play cowboys and Indians, do it elsewhere, please,* Gehlen had written. "Someone I knew from the war," Mahoney explained. "I thought there was a possibility he could be turned. But nothing came of it. He never showed up."

"Soviet intelligence?" Dulles asked.

"During the war he was G-2 on General Zhukov's staff."

"We'll watch for him."

No encounter, no contact sheet. It was the same then as it is now. Mahoney thought about that first lie. All the good ones do it: it was Carlisle's favorite theme. Purely out of necessity though, sometimes. Or was that the excuse we simply told ourselves? Saving a little something for retirement. Or, rather, saving a little something so that you could live long enough to retire. A safety valve. A bargaining chip.

He looked at his own haggard reflection in the dark window. It had all been a terribly big mistake, the lies, that is—as well as that night in Berlin—that very nearly caught up with him a few years later. He had been doing time on the Soviet desk in Washington waiting for a new assignment. It was late summer, a month after the cease-fire had been signed in Korea. Sylvan Bindrich, who would later become Director of Central Intelligence, was working the night desk, which received reports from field stations around the world, analyzed them, and then made decisions based on their best guesses: can the material wait until morning, or do we call somebody?

On this late August evening all the bells were ringing when Mahoney showed up at his office. The Agency was housed in a series of buildings near the Lincoln Memorial, among them South Building, which housed communications and Bindrich's section, and temporary buildings, all interconnected, simply labeled with letter names, in which Mahoney's section was housed. The place looked like a three-ring circus on this late night. The director himself had come in for the confirmation and he had gone directly over to the White House to wake the president. The Soviet Union had exploded its first hydrogen bomb, and the Agency powers were suddenly smelling what they thought was a Soviet penetration agent. The Russians should not have been that far along with their technology. They had spied on America's atomic bomb project, but everyone had thought until now that the H-bomb was secure. A witch-hunt was about to begin and everyone was scrambling around to cover himself six ways to Sunday.

At three in the morning Bindrich broke from his desk and came down to see Mahoney who was up to his elbows in agent assessments, foreign embassy reports, and transcripts of Soviet radio broadcasts, telephone intercepts, and military communications traffic.

"Coffee?" Bindrich asked. He was a small, soft-spoken, dapper little man.

Mahoney looked up, annoyed that he was being interrupted. But there was something in Bindrich's eyes that was unsettling. Trouble, Mahoney remembered thinking, often came in small dapper packages at three o'clock in the bloody morning.

"How is everything up on the Hill?" Mahoney asked.

"Ominous. Can you tear yourself away, Wallace?"

"Is it important?"

"I think so," Bindrich said in his quiet voice.

The staff cafeteria was located in L building. Only a few of the tables were occupied. A lot of secretaries were coming in to fetch coffee for their bosses. Mahoney and Bindrich got their coffee and took a table alone in the corner. Even this far from the action they could feel that the place was on emergency footing. Everyone was moving fast, but no one seemed to be speaking above a whisper.

"Yuri Chernov," Bindrich said without preamble. "Does the name ring a bell?"

Mahoney felt as if he had been kicked in the stomach. "He's a Soviet intelligence officer. Or at least he was as of the late winter of '48. Lieutenant colonel, then. KI."

"That squares with what we have," Bindrich said. "Do you know him, then? Personally, I mean."

"I met him twice."

"Yes?"

"The first time was just before the end of the war. Vienna. He was a G-2 on General Zhukov's staff. Bill sent me over to check out the National Redoubt business for Eisenhower. I had to brief Zhukov's staff. Chernov was there. Didn't think much about my little project."

"I thought you worked with Zamyatin."

"I did," Mahoney said. Something at the back of his head was telling him to proceed with caution. This entire conversation was all wrong. Bindrich wasn't himself. There was a dangerous edge to his questions. "Chernov was his boss." Mahoney smiled. "He told me that if we got back in one piece, he'd buy me a drink."

Bindrich's eyebrows rose. "Did he?"

"Not then. When I got back to Vienna he was gone. We met again in Berlin after the war was over. During the Potsdam Conference. Us lesser types were comparing notes too."

"And?"

"He bought me that drink," Mahoney said. "What are you getting at, Sylvan? I don't know if I like the tone of this—"

"You met again, apparently," Bindrich interrupted. "During the airlift."

"It never came off."

"I've seen Gehlen's little memo."

"I don't give a shit what you've seen," Mahoney flared, hating the lie and being frightened because of it, and yet knowing that there was no way in hell for him to back out of it. Not now. It was too late for that.

"You apparently spotted him on the first day of the negotiations," Bindrich went on. "I've also seen Bryce's report."

"I spotted him, and I warned General Holister about him."

"That's when you went to see Gehlen's people?"

"That next morning. I wanted them to get a message to Chernov."

"What sort of a message?"

"I wanted to meet with him. In the western zone."

"Why?"

"Allen sent me over there to find out how long the Soviets intended on sticking to their blockade. We were getting nowhere with the negotiations—I saw that in the first five minutes—and I figured that if anyone would know, it would be Chernov."

"Why Chernov?" Bindrich asked. "I don't understand, Wallace. Talk to me."

"I had him spotted, we knew each other, so I figured he would come see me out of curiosity more than anything else. I figured he would try to work me."

"Just as you were apparently trying to work him."

"Yes. I thought he might let something slip."

"Did he?"

"We didn't meet," Mahoney said. "The BND's people got a message to him. We had it set up at a West Berlin nightclub. When I showed up, my waiter passed me a note, apparently from Chernov who said it wasn't safe to meet there. That I was to leave the club on foot."

"You told this to Heiser's people?" Bindrich asked.

Mahoney stared at him for a moment. Heiser's name hadn't been mentioned. Bindrich had done some homework. "Yes, I did. I was to lead Chernov, if he showed up, over to the Tiergarten where Heiser's people would be waiting."

"But Chernov never showed up."

"No," Mahoney said. "I explained it to the BND, and the next day returned to Washington."

"Have you seen Chernov since then, or had any contact with him?"

"No, I haven't, Sylvan," Mahoney said. "What the hell is this all about? It's your turn to talk to me."

Bindrich seemed to draw inward for a long second or two, as if he were listening to some internal debate in his own head. He pursed his lips. "They're running scared up on the Hill over this Soviet H-bomb thing. It seems your friend Yuri Chernov is now a lieutenant general. He's apparently carved himself an empire out of the shambles of Soviet military intelligence. It was probably he who engineered a technological hit squad for H-bomb information." Again Bindrich drew inward for a beat. "Everything I'm saying here this morning, Wallace, is strictly off the record. Between friends, nothing more. All of it is strictly top secret. We'll both have our asses in slings if it gets out I talked to you like this."

"It's a witch-hunt," Mahoney said.

"Full-scale, my friend. And anyone having any connections with Chernov is going to find himself on the hot seat. I just wanted to know where you stood. Just how far your involvement went. I think you're going to need friends in high places. It might get nasty."

"I'm not a Soviet spy, Sylvan."

"I know that, but I'm glad to hear you say it anyway," Bindrich said. He reached out and patted Mahoney's hand. "We'll come out of this all right, you and I, Wallace. Don't worry."

Of course he did worry about it, then and still to some extent these days. Perhaps, he told himself as the train approached Berlin, he had come here one last time to Chernov to expiate all of his sins, real or imagined. That is, if such a thing were possible so late.

Chernov was waiting in a light gray Ford Cortina on the Ku'Damm around the corner from the train station. It was nearly midnight and the main avenue was thick with traffic. For just a moment it was difficult for Mahoney to separate now from four decades ago. He could see Chernov at the bierstube talking about his nonexistent wife and daughter, and he could remember the witch-hunt that had very nearly destroyed the fledgling CIA, and he could remember all the years afterward. He knew now that he had been like a man wearing blinders when it concerned Chernov. Right up until 1961. Before that moment he had been operating in the dark. Only afterward had he made any progress.

He threw his bag in the back seat and got in the car. "Did you have any trouble crossing the border?"

"No," Chernov said. "You?"

"Not a bit."

They pulled away from the curb and merged with traffic. Mahoney hunched down in his seat. The day had been tiring. He felt as if he had wasted his time by coming here, and now he wanted to get on with it. Being this close to the one man who had caused him the most trouble in his life was upsetting, and confusing. He wanted to go home, to be surrounded with familiar things, to forget instead of remember.

"I think we have bought some time," Chernov said. He too sounded tired. They were getting old, Mahoney thought.

"For what? Let's get it over with."

"Very soon now, Wallace," Chernov said, glancing over at him.

"What are you waiting for? You called and I came, as you knew

144

I would. Now, what have you got to tell me? We're too old to be playing these games."

"It's no game, I can assure you."

"Pardon me, Yuri Yevgennevich, but your assurances fall on deaf ears. You are the great liar. You always were."

"Is that all you remember?"

"I remember the story about your wife and child in the siege of Stalingrad. Lies."

Chernov shrugged. "I came over that night with the idea that I could turn you. I was looking for your sympathy." Chernov had been remembering too. "I was paranoid about Germany in those days."

"Stalin was just as bad as Hitler."

"We survived."

They turned onto the broad Potsdamer Strasse, the Tiergarten behind them, and headed south toward the Grunewald and their hotel. It came to Mahoney that his life, for the most part, had been centered around three cities: Washington, Moscow, and Berlin. Three corners of a huge triangle with danger and sorrow at each corner. He was back on the circuit.

"It'll be just a little while now, Wallace," Chernov was saying from a distance. "Then you will understand what we must do, you and I."

Just a little while now, Mahoney thought. It's all the time they ever had. He'd squandered his, mostly. But the pattern was set. He could no more step out of it than he could step out of himself. Marge would have said that he was fighting himself. She had been a great believer in predetermined fate. She was a strong Catholic, but she had never despaired for his soul. "You are a good man," she told him. "Your life has made a difference, otherwise God would never have created you in the first place." But he wondered.

9

It was morning in the Federal Republic of Germany. The sun was peeking through a break in the low clouds. John Mahoney had managed a few hours of sleep on the flight over. He'd hitched a ride from the base into Kaiserslautern where he rented a small Fiat, and by nine he was on his way north to the ancient city of Bonn, gateway to the Rhine Valley, and hopefully to his father. He'd relived in his mind, over and over again, Kopinski's death. In his dreams he had vividly seen the old man falling back, felt the buck of the gun in his hand, and heard the speedboat exploding. Back in the field like this, however, he began to get the feeling he was streamlined. His past was being stripped away from him in huge layers. Nothing mattered now but the future. Renting the car, finding the right roads, minding the speed limit, negotiating the curves, slowing for the towns, making all the correct moves. Hayes had driven him out to Andrews Air Force Base by a roundabout way, taking a lot of care not to be followed. "We'll get you over there clean, but after that it's up to you," he'd said. "You know your father better than any of us."

But he didn't. He was operating just as much in the dark as any of them were. He just happened to have the same last name, which fit some perverse sense of orderliness that Carlisle so loved. Hayes or Cassidy would have been just as suitably qualified for this job. Perhaps even more qualified, because they didn't have the host of debilitating emotions to deal with that John had carried around since he was just a kid. He kept watching in his rearview mirror all the way up to Bad Kreuznach where he picked up the Cologne-Koblenz autobahn that followed the Rhine north. No one was behind him, and he sped up, merging with the morning work traffic. It had snowed here recently and there were patches of slick ice on the highway. The weather wasn't quite as cold as Minnesota, but Germany reminded him of the upper Midwest with its pine-covered rolling hills interspersed with farm fields and the hints of industry just over the next rise. Reaching Koblenz he took the bypass around the city, leaving the river for ten or twenty miles until the highway angled back toward Bonn. This was the Germany of his dreams, he thought. Here he would find his answers, perhaps even answers to questions he hadn't even asked himself yet. Everything pointed toward Berlin, but it was here that he would get his directions. Or, he thought, it would be here where he would fail before he even got started.

Finding Heiser was easier than he thought it would be. He parked his car in Münsterplatz near the cathedral basilica and walked across the market square to the ornate town hall on the Rathausgasse. Inside, a helpful clerk directed him downstairs to the offices of the city tax records. He was interested, he said, in purchasing a piece of property owned by a retired gentleman, Bernhard Heiser. It was a matter of a clear title, free of liens. No, he wasn't sure of the address because he was under the impression that Herr Heiser's holdings were extensive. The clerk, a young man with the pinched expression of the typical German bureaucrat, cross-referenced Heiser's name in his records and came back from the stacks lugging a large book, a smug, superior look on his face. "You are mistaken. There is only the one house," he said. "Perhaps you are seeking a different Heiser. Perhaps he lives in the Kreis but somewhere outside of the city." John assured the clerk that his Herr Heiser indeed resided within the city limits of Bonn, but perhaps he had been misled into believing that the man's holdings were larger than they were.

"*Nein, mein Herr.* He has only the single house very nearly in Bad Godesberg." John took out his notebook and pretended to read from it. "I have an address that I have no confidence in. Is it number Seventeen?"

The clerk smiled, closing the big records book. "No, evidently it is a mistake after all, mein Herr. The house is at Twenty-four Landstuhl Strasse. Not Seventeen, as you have been told."

"I was mistaken then," John admitted. "As I said, I was not certain of the address. But thank you for your help."

He crossed the square to the tourist bureau in the Bonn Center, where he picked up a city street map, then drove out toward the diplomatic suburb of Bad Godesberg, watching for the correct side street off Friesdorfer Strasse. Away from the city center there was much less traffic. The avenues were tree-lined and pleasant. In the summer this would be a beautiful, almost secluded area. Landstuhl Strasse turned out to be a short, cobblestoned lane barely a block long on which were situated well-kept three-story homes, mostly of red brick or brownstone. What few cars were parked in front at this hour were mostly Mercedeses and BMWs. The residents of this street were prosperous. He parked in front of number 24, shut off the car's engine, and sat for a moment or two watching the house, and watching in his rearview mirror. There was absolutely no traffic here at the moment. No one had followed him. Unlike Washington where he'd had the over-the-shoulder feeling from the moment he'd stepped off the plane, here he felt he was alone. Unwatched. At least for the moment.

He got out of the car, crossed the sidewalk, and climbed the three stairs onto the stoop. He rang the bell. An old woman in an apron opened the door. Her gray hair was pulled severely back into a bun, and she wore gold wire-rimmed glasses.

"Ja?" she said. "May I help you?"

"I have come to see Herr Heiser," John said. "It is a matter of some importance. Is he at home?"

"You are an American?" the woman asked, looking past him at his car.

"Yes. Tell him it concerns my father, Wallace Mahoney."

A very old man, small, slightly stooped, with jet-black hair slicked down and shining, appeared at the end of the corridor. "What's he done this time?" he croaked.

Any lingering doubts that John might have had that he'd found the right man were dispelled. But he got the feeling that Heiser wasn't going to be a very easy man to talk to.

The house was a museum of the man's career. Medals, letters of appreciation, certificates of achievement, and photographs, all of them framed nicely, lined the walls in the corridor, in the living room, and John presumed in every other room of the house. The smell of furniture polish and freshly baked bread mingled with the odors of age and decay, mothballs and disinfectant. Heiser had to be nearly as old as Kopinski had been, and he shuffled painfully rather than walked. John followed him into the rear parlor that overlooked what in the summer would be a wonderful flower garden. An antique reading table by the windows held a stack of magazines, mostly *Die Stern* going back to the fifties and sixties. Over the tile fireplace was a portrait of a young Heiser in the uniform of an Abwehr lieutenant. It looked very old. A pair of winged chairs flanked a small table on which a beautifully hand-carved wooden chess set was laid out halfway through a game. Across the room a mohair couch, matching chair, and spindly-looking antique coffee table faced the fire.

"Fetch us some coffee, Hilda," Heiser said without bothering to

148

look around. She left them. He opened a glass-fronted *Schrank*, took down a pair of snifters and a bottle of cognac, and poured two drinks.

"I think I should warn you, sir, that you may be in some danger by my being here," John said.

Heiser turned around. "At my age I'm in danger every time I take a breath. It's that Russian of his, I suppose." John was startled and it must have shown on his face. Heiser laughed, and handed him his drink. "If you're here about your father, you must have gotten my name from someone else. Who?"

"A friend of my father's. Stan Kopinski."

Heiser's eyes narrowed. "CIA? Archives?"

"Yes, sir," John said. "He said you knew my father from just after the war. In the early BND days."

"And Chernov, his test case."

"Sir?"

"Your father wanted to get to *know* the Russian. I told him he was a fool then, and I suspect he still is the fool." Heiser motioned John to the couch. "It was a dangerous game he was playing. Of course between rounds he could pack up his bags and go home for a rest. We couldn't do that here. I told him that once, but he wasn't impressed. He said he didn't pick the battlefields, they were just there. Is he missing?"

"Yes, he is," John said.

"Jolly. And you're looking for him. You are with the Agency? Like father, like son?"

John took a seat, cradling his drink in his hands. He could hear the woman, Hilda, rattling dishes in the kitchen. The odor of fresh coffee was strong. Heiser didn't like his father. It was very possible he would simply refuse to help.

"Yes, I am," he said. "I thought you might be able to help me."

Heiser swirled the cognac around in his glass, held it to his nose, breathed deeply, and then drank a little. He sighed and sat down across from John, crossing his spindly legs. His face was crisscrossed with blue veins, and his thin hands shook with a slight palsy. "I don't know if I can, Mr. Mahoney. I haven't had contact with your father for a good many years, nor do I have any friends in Pullach any longer."

"I don't need that," John said. "In any event we're trying to keep this quiet for the moment, as you might understand."

"What do you want?"

"Your memories."

Heiser smiled. "Your father's case files would be more helpful."

"There was nothing in them about Chernov."

Heiser's expression didn't change.

"They're meeting somewhere," John went on. "A few days ago a message from Chernov was relayed to Langley via our Moscow embassy. Chernov wanted to meet with my father. No time or place specified. When we asked my father about it, he denied knowing the Russian. Twenty-four hours later my father was gone. With several passports, some money, and presumably a gun."

"Perhaps he means to kill him," Heiser said.

"It's a very real possibility. But the Russians want them as badly as we do. One of their people was sent to my father's home in Minnesota, and another one murdered Stan Kopinski in Washington."

Heiser's eyebrows rose. "They're serious," he said.

"Yes, sir. At this moment the head of the KGB's Special Investigations branch is in East Berlin."

"Anyone I would know?"

John shrugged. "Major Trusov."

"It's not surprising," Heiser said. "Your people sent you and they sent her."

"What do you mean?"

"Didn't you know, Mr. Mahoney, that Tonia Trusov is Chernov's niece?"

"Christ," John said softly.

"A favored niece, from what I understand," Heiser continued.

"How do you know this?"

"Your father wasn't the only one to make a specialty out of Comrade Chernov. Only your father and I had different aims. Your father wanted to study the Russians. I wanted to kill them."

"I need to find them before the Russians do."

"I imagine you do," Heiser said. "But what brings you to Germany?"

"To see you."

"And?"

"I think they might be meeting here somewhere. Berlin, perhaps."

Heiser nodded. "Yes, I suspect it would be Berlin."

"Why do you think so?"

"Because Berlin is the ideological proving ground. The big

laboratory in which the grand experiment to prove who is right, us or them, has been going on since 1945."

"Where are they, then?"

"I don't know, Mr. Mahoney. What makes you think that I would?"

"Because this is your country, and according to Stan you knew my father and Chernov."

"Which is not to say that I know where they've gotten themselves off to. It was a favorite trick of your father's, hiding his intentions, didn't you know?"

"My father was a maverick."

Heiser smiled. "A successful maverick. But this time he may have gotten in over his head. Chernov was a very bad man, and I presume nothing has happened to change him. He is a liar and a murderer. A true Russian."

"He may have been responsible for my mother's death in the late seventies. Poison."

"Who told you that?" Heiser asked sharply.

"Someone who would know."

"Did you believe it?"

John looked away. "I'm beginning to. But if my father knows it, or even suspects, he will kill Chernov."

"Not until they've had a chance to talk. Your father will want to know what Chernov has been up to all these years. It's the curiosity that kills the cat—it very nearly ruined your father in the old days."

Hilda came with the coffee. She glared disapprovingly at the liquor bottle but said nothing. When she was gone Heiser chuckled. "She has been with me for a very long time," he said. "She feels that it is her duty to save my body as well as my soul for some perverse reason. Normally I humor her."

"Ruined my father how?"

"They thought he was a traitor, your people. Thought he'd turned his back and allowed Chernov to run the spy ring that stole your hydrogen bomb secrets." Heiser looked at his drink. "Of course we learned that long after the fact. They shared with us, but on a very limited basis. For a while I even thought it was possible myself."

"But it was not the case."

"No, he was proved innocent, but only because he lied to them. To us all. And *that* little bit I never shared."

"In what way did he lie?"

"There was a meeting between your father and Chernov in

151

Berlin in 1948. Very near Christmas, at the beginning of the Berlin airlift. I arranged it. Your father disappeared from the meeting place and when he showed up an hour later, he told us that Chernov had never made contact."

"Perhaps he didn't."

"But he did. I would be willing to bet anything on it. Your father gave up too easily, you see. After all the work of setting up the meeting, your father simply informed us that Chernov hadn't shown, and the next day he returned to Washington."

"Where was the meeting to have taken place?"

"A nightclub in the western sector. The Ballhaus Resi. Do you know this place?"

"No."

"They would not attempt to meet there again," Heiser said. "It is too public. They would be seen."

"My father met with Chernov sometime just after the war, in Berlin. Did you know anything about that?"

"During the Potsdam talks. There were many meetings going on between the Allies."

"Do you know of any of these places?"

Heiser shrugged. "Only from the history books, Mr. Mahoney. I was a prisoner of war at the time in Bavaria."

"Then you cannot be of any help to me?"

"Only in that I believe it is possible they are meeting somewhere in Berlin."

"East or West?"

"West, I should think. It would be easier for them both. There would be fewer questions."

John finished his drink and got to his feet. Heiser looked up at him but made no move to rise. "Why do you suppose Chernov wanted to meet with my father this time?"

"Not merely to discuss old times."

"They're enemies."

"Yes, but they have each other's respect. Chernov would be coming out, I suspect, with something that only your father would believe."

It was the same thing Kopinski had told him. Chernov had risked everything by coming out. The one man he chose to see was the one man in the West who presumably hated him the most, and would have the most to gain by killing him.

"And if that is the case, Mr. Mahoney, then the Russians indeed will be most anxious to find him. To find them both."

"You said that you yourself had made a study of Chernov."

Heiser nodded.

"What was his workname if he wanted to come to the West?"

"There were a lot of worknames. What good spy doesn't have his list?"

"In those days, though, what was his workname? You said that you arranged the meeting between him and my father. What was your contact procedure?"

"He came across as Carl Abbott Nostrand," Heiser said without hesitation. "It was some kind of a joke, I think. But I never found that out."

"Nostrand," John said. It was a start. He headed for the door.

"If anyone would know where they met during the Potsdam conferences, it would be the Russians," Heiser said. "Why don't you ask them?"

On the way out John could hear the old man laughing in the parlor and the old woman's soothing voice as she tried to calm him down.

Antonina Filipovna Trusov was tired and angry. There wasn't one man in the room who was her friend. Considering the fact that Chernov was her uncle, she wasn't surprised that they wanted to blame her for his defection. Not one of them could see through their blind prejudices or male superiority that there was more here than met the eye. His tradecraft had been too precise, his movements too studied, too well planned to be a simple spur of the moment defection. And there was his hurried trip to Finland last week—God in heaven, she thought, had it been that long already?—that had caught them all by surprise and by the time anyone had thought to react, he'd come back. An old fool on a shopping spree for liquor and cigarettes that he could just as easily have purchased at the government store. Why the trip? Had he met Mahoney there? Had he sent another message, made a telephone call? They might never know.

"By now they are long gone from Berlin," Feodor Drankov, deputy ambassador to the DDR, cautioned. "We have heard the Hannover report. They were spotted in the city less than twelve hours ago."

"And you lost them," Tonia snapped irritably. "Any amateur could have kept up with two old men."

"Two of the best, might I remind you," Nikolai Balachov, the KGB rezident said. "They are together in Hannover and we will find them. It is now only a matter of time."

"They have left the city," she said.

"I don't think so, Tonia. They went through too much trouble to get there. And if they did leave, as you suggest, it means they have abandoned their worknames."

"And are traveling under another set."

"Back to Berlin?" the deputy ambassador asked.

"Yes."

"Which would have necessitated them recrossing the DDR frontier. A dangerous maneuver for them both," Balachov said. He was a large, ponderous man, just the opposite of Drankov, the ambassador's puppy. Yet both of them thought alike. Both of them were frightened that somehow this business would reflect badly on them. Worse yet, the ambassador had insisted that no KGB operations be mounted in the western zone of Berlin or in the FRG, Hannover included. Of course her orders superseded the desires of a mere ambassador. Nonetheless he could make the operation even more difficult than it already was.

Perhaps it is time for you to think about leaving the service and finding a husband, Tonia, her uncle had told her less than a month ago. She should have recognized the signs. It happened to a lot of old men, the disaffection for the *rodina*, the motherland, for the lives they had lived. In the West among men it was called mid-life crises, and occurred when they were in their mid-forties. In the Soviet Union the crises often came when the man turned seventy. The philosophy began. Fear of death. Their lives had passed them by, and now they wanted to sample an alternative life, when it was too late.

Besides Balachov and Drankov, also present at this morning's meeting were Lieutenant Colonel Ivan Raina, who had come to her room last night with flowers and wine, and the GRU chief of station, Major Yuri Viktorov. Both of them seemed to be hiding something that she couldn't quite figure out. But she could see it in their eyes, the way they tried to avoid her gaze at the odd moment. Outside the embassy, traffic flowed along the Unter den Linden, but here in the *referentura* with its soundproofing and electronic antieavesdropping equipment they could have been in a space capsule three hundred miles above the earth. Isolated. Just like the old men in the Kremlin. Isolated, alone, and frightened.

"Why would they have returned, Major?" Balachov asked.

"To finish what they began," she said.

"Merely to talk?"

"Yes."

"About what? What is it your uncle wanted so desperately to tell Mahoney? And if they have left Hannover—I'll give you that

154

possibility only for the moment, Tonia—wouldn't it be more likely that they have gone on to Washington?"

"No, you fool," Tonia spat, sitting forward. "Because the CIA at this moment is just as desperately seeking Mahoney as we are my uncle!"

"It is a sham," Balachov said, unmoved by her outburst.

"Then why did they assassinate one of their own people?"

"You're speaking now of this Stanley Kopinski?" Balachov asked. He flipped through a file folder in front of him on the table. "We don't know that they were responsible. As you know, there is still no word from Sebryakov. Maybe it was an accident. Maybe it was a simple street crime."

"Perhaps they do not want Mahoney found," Viktorov, the GRU officer, suggested. "From what I understand, his son is in Germany at this moment. He was spotted at Ramstein, but then he dropped out of sight."

He was the one very large unknown factor in this entire business. Tonia had seen his file, of course, but there was no way of knowing how he would react, though she had warned them from the beginning that he would be sent out to look for his father. Who better to send? The logic was the same for him as it was for her. The blame equally his? She doubted it.

"All your hysteria aside, Comrade Viktorov, the Americans do not operate that way. They do not kill their own people merely to stage a disinformation plot. Whoever killed Kopinski did so to keep him from telling John Mahoney something. Something, I might add, that would help us in this search."

"When we see Sebryakov's report it may shed some light on Kopinski's elimination," Balachov said. "For the moment, however, we are simply in the dark."

"Either they killed him, Nikolai, in which case I want to know why. Or we killed him, in which case I also want to know why," Tonia said.

"Perhaps they were aiming for John Mahoney. Perhaps Sebryakov was a little overzealous and decided to stop their chief investigator in this matter," Balachov said. He spread his hands. "It would have been effective. They would have scrambled around, but we would have had the advantage."

"Except that Sebryakov is missing, and John Mahoney is very much alive and somewhere in West Germany. Meanwhile, you will continue to search Hannover long after the cows have left the barn by the back door."

"What do you suggest, Comrade Major?" Balachov asked, sitting back.

"Find John Mahoney."

"And then?"

"Bring him here."

"Yes? To East Berlin?" Drankov asked, his eyes wide. "Even if that were possible, what then?"

"I'll make a deal with him," Tonia said. She lit a cigarette and crossed her long, lovely legs. "He wants to find his father. I want to find my uncle. Between us we'll be able to find them."

The room was deathly still for a long time, until Balachov shook his head and laughed out loud. "You are mad, stark raving mad."

"I think she's right," Lieutenant Colonel Raina, the military attaché, said in his soft, almost hidden voice. He had been embarrassed last night, and had left Tonia's room like a young schoolboy who has been turned down by the first girl he'd ever asked for a date.

"The Americans would never cooperate," Balachov fumed.

"Not the Americans, Nikolai, just this one man," Raina insisted. "Tonia has got something here."

"How could you trust them?" Balachov asked. "Once they were found, who's to say that John Mahoney wouldn't call his people?"

"Because, Comrade Balachov, I will kill them all."

"Your uncle included?" Balachov asked.

"Yes," she said. "Or do you have another suggestion?"

No one said a word.

Tonia stubbed out her cigarette and got to her feet. At the door she looked back at them. Frightened little men, she thought. Bureaucrats with compartmentalized little minds who would believe what they were told if it were presented in just the right fashion. But there was more here at stake than any of them could possibly know. More even than Raina and his GRU lapdog thought they might know. "Find John Mahoney and bring him here, comrades. Alive and uninjured. And within twenty-four hours I will have my uncle and the elder Mahoney."

It was early afternoon by the time John arrived at West Berlin's Tegel Airport, and was picked up by Tom Bixby, the CIA's chief of station in West Berlin. He'd taken a Pan Am flight from Cologne where he had turned in his rental car. It seemed like years since he had slept last and he figured he looked it. Traffic was heavy and it had begun to snow again. Berlin looked dirty compared to Bonn.

"Where the hell have you been?" Bixby demanded. "Carlisle is having six kinds of kittens, and Hayes has called three times. You just disappeared from Ramstein. No word to anybody."

"They're here somewhere in West Berlin, Tom," John said. He was too tired to argue with Bixby. They knew each other from a few years earlier when John had spent a little time in Athens where Bixby had been COS. Bixby was a good man, but he was a stickler for detail, a nit-picker.

"How do you know that? Did you talk to somebody at Pullach?"

"Ex-BND," John said. "Knew my father and Chernov from the old days."

"Well, Carlisle wants to talk to you as soon as I bring you in."

"I'm not going back to the consulate with you, Tom. You can drop me off somewhere downtown. I'm going to get a hotel room and rent a car. In the meantime you can do something for me."

Bixby wanted to argue, John could see it on his face, but he held himself in check. Carlisle had said Berlin station would turn itself inside out for him if need be. And when Carlisle had a bone in his teeth, his station chiefs listened. "What do you need?"

"A list of every place where an American-Soviet meeting might have taken place here in Berlin just after the war. During the Potsdam conference."

"That's in the eastern zone, you know."

"Potsdam is, but there were meetings going on all over the city. I want a listing of the places in the western zone."

"You think they're here? Out in the open like that?" Bixby asked. "For old times' sake? C'mon, John."

"It's possible," John replied. "But I don't want you sending out your people. No legmen. Give me the list and I'll go looking."

"I'll do what I can," Bixby said glumly. "But keep in touch. Let us know what you're doing. This is my turf and I'm the one who's going to have to answer to Carlisle if something goes wrong."

The Bremen was a small, comfortable hotel just off the Ku'Damm. John checked in, had his bag sent up to his room, then took a cab over to the railroad station by the zoo, where he rented a Volkswagen sedan from the Hertz counter. He drove directly past the Bremen and found a parking ramp a block and a half away. He left the keys in the tailpipe and walked back to his hotel.

Both Kopinski and Heiser felt that his father and Chernov were meeting somewhere in Berlin. It had something to do, apparently, with a meeting between the two just after the war.

What the hell were they trying to prove? If his father had only said something to them, the meeting could have gone on as planned, but with fail-safes.

Both Kopinski and Heiser felt that Chernov would take the risk of coming out and meeting with his nemesis only for something very important. Something he was bringing out with him. Something he could only tell to the one man in the West whom he was absolutely certain would listen to him. What was it?

He had one name. Carl Abbott Nostrand. It was a start.

The telephone was ringing when he got up to his room. It was an anxious Alex Hayes calling from Washington. Bixby had wasted no time covering himself.

"They're here in Berlin," John said. "I'm certain of it now."

"Where did you go when you left Ramstein?"

"To Bonn to see an old friend of my father's."

"Did Stan give you his name?" Hayes asked sharply.

"Yes, he did, Alex."

"Why the hell didn't you tell us, John? You can't run off like that on your own. There's no way in hell we can protect you."

It was an open line and they were both aware of the possibilities. It's why they'd wanted John to come to the consulate where they could have spoken on an encrypted line.

"I may have something by this afternoon," John said guardedly.

"Tom told us about that. But listen, John, he doesn't know if such a list exists, and neither do I. But we're checking on it from here as well. Have you got anything else?"

"Something. But it's going to take a little time. Just get me that list if at all possible."

"What specifically, John?" Hayes insisted.

"Not on this line. Just get me that list."

The line was silent for a long moment.

"I need your help, goddamnit," John swore.

"I'll do what I can," Hayes said distantly. "But keep in touch. Don't go running off like that again."

"I don't want anyone on this hotel, Alex. No watchdogs." He was thinking about Washington.

"You have my word on it," Hayes said. "But as soon as you come up with anything, anything at all, don't try to be the lone ranger. Call me or call Tom, and we'll arrange a backup."

John ordered up a light lunch and a couple of bottles of beer. While he waited for room service he took a quick shower and changed his clothes. When his food arrived he sat down at the table by the window with the thick Berlin telephone directory and opened it to the listings for hotels and inns. There were dozens if not hundreds of them throughout the city proper as well as in the western zone villages of Reinickendorf, Wedding, Spandau, Charlottenburg, Neuköllon, Zehlendorf, and the others. Chernov and his father could be holed up at any one of them, or none of them. Perhaps they had arranged an apartment. Perhaps they were guests of another old friend. Perhaps they were at one of the many private unlisted establishments that catered to the well-heeled businessmen or the sort of person whose special needs did not bear up well to scrutiny. If he could have involved the West Berlin police, his job would be all but finished. But there could be no police. Not under any circumstances could there be police.

John telephoned the first name in the listing: the Aar Hotel u. Gasthaus in Wilmersdorf. "Good afternoon. I wish to speak with Herr Nostrand, *bitte*. Carl Nostrand."

"I am sorry, but we have no guest of that name here, mein Herr," a woman answered. "Perhaps you have the wrong number?"

"He is an older man. Tall. And he is with his friend, another older gentleman. White hair."

"Nein. Nichts hier," the woman said and hung up.

John took out his pen, made a tick in front of the Aar, and dialed the next number on the list, this one for the Aberg Hotel on Kant Strasse. They were only hunches he was going on, and half-guesses and weak possibilities. The imperfect memories of a couple of very old men, at least one of whom had his own ax to grind. And yet John felt there was a certain symmetry to the idea of a West Berlin meeting between his father and Chernov. Their long adversarial careers had had their beginnings here. During the war they'd been allies. It wasn't until afterward that they became true enemies. It had begun here, and here it would end. The notion, he decided, would fit the sensibilities of two old men. The name Carl Abbott Nostrand was another very long shot that nevertheless had its own symmetry. The first time Chernov had been called across the border for a meeting, he had come under the workname Nostrand. Might he not have chosen the same work-name for this final meet?

He finished his lunch and continued telephoning. He would be attracting some attention downstairs at the switchboard, but he was doing nothing illegal. Just another crazy American business-man trying to make a living here. A salesman no doubt.

The switchboard operator at the Bristol Hotel on the Ku'Damm apparently misunderstood the name. She connected him with one of the rooms. A man with a very gruff voice answered.

"Ja, wo ist?"

"Herr Nostrand?" John asked carefully.

"Nein. Ich heisse Nofsinger. Nofsinger. Nicht Nostrand."

"Entschuldigen, bitte," John started to apologize, but the connection was broken and he put down the telephone.

The clerk at one Charlottenburg hotel refused to speak with him, while the switchboard operator at another assured him that there were many Americans at the hotel. There were always Americans staying at her hotel, and if he would wish to make reservations, she would personally see that a room was made available to him. But no, she grudgingly admitted, no one named Nostrand—C. A. or otherwise—was currently a guest of the hotel.

A distant church bell was tolling the hour of three when someone knocked at his door. John put down the telephone. "Who is it?"

"It's the consulate, sir," a man speaking German called through the door. "Mr. Bixby."

It was the list, John thought, getting up. He had half expected that Bixby would make him drive over to the consulate to pick it up. In that way there would be no excuse for him not to speak with either Hayes or Carlisle on an encrypted line. He unlocked the door and started to open it when it suddenly dawned on him that a messenger from the consulate would not have spoken German. He would have been an American.

The door was suddenly shoved inward. Before John could react, a short, bulldog of a man had stepped lightly inside, a very large automatic in his right fist pointed directly at John's head. The muzzle looked enormous. A second man waited in the corridor.

"Shit," John said.

Under the overcast sky, snow falling quite heavily, streetlamps were on and traffic ran with its headlights. The Soviet embassy on the rebuilt broad Unter den Linden was a brooding, colossal structure that reminded John of the massive pyramids at Giza. He was wedged in the rear seat of a Mercedes sedan between the two men who had come for him. They'd had absolutely no trouble at the checkpoint. The American MPs and West German police hadn't even bothered to look inside the car as it passed, nor had they been stopped on the East Berlin side. The car's license plates were East Berlin diplomatic, and he would have been surprised had they been stopped. Their taciturn driver left them off at a side entrance, and John was hustled across the broad sidewalk and inside. Everything had been left back in his hotel room, including his gun which had been laying in plain sight on the bed. They had allowed him to put on his overcoat and hat, however, and then they had walked with him downstairs, across the lobby, and outside to the waiting car. He had not bothered talking to them because he knew that it would be useless. They obviously were operating under strict orders. He had probably been spotted at Tegel Airport when Bixby picked him up. Which meant they not only knew about the hotel, but in all probability they also knew about the car he had rented. He did not think they would have had time to put a tap on his telephone, however, though it was possible.

He knew what they were after, of course. The question was how they intended going about it.

Wordlessly they took him to the third floor on an elevator that opened onto a broad, busy corridor. Typewriters clattered, telephones rang, computer printers whined, and overall there was the hum of muted but urgent conversation. It could have been the corridor of any large country's embassy, or even the busy section of some large corporation. No one paid the slightest attention to them. At the end of the corridor one of his captors opened an unmarked door and stepped aside.

"In here," he said in English.

The office was small and very plain, with a single window that looked west over a tall brick wall toward the Brandenburg Gate. Tonia Trusov sat behind a small gray desk, her hands folded primly in front of her, and her KGB uniform crisp and correct. The door was closed behind him.

"You are an amazing man, Mr. Mahoney, did you know that?" she asked. "Very much like your father, from what I have read."

John looked past her toward the window. It wouldn't take Bixby very long to realize he was missing again. But they'd never dream he was here.

Tonia flipped open a file folder. "Your date of CIA enlistment is thirty-six years, almost to the day, after your father's," she said. "In five years flat you have managed to become one of the Agency's top operatives." She looked up. "It is said that you have a special insight. The same gift your father had, that of being able to see the abnormalities of a situation. You also have, from what

I have read here, an extraordinarily well developed instinct for survival. A very necessary ingredient, I think, for being a spy, wouldn't you agree?"

"What do you want with me?" John asked, moving away from the door.

"It is curious that you have come all the way from the United States on a moment's notice—through Ramstein Air Force Base, I might add—here to Berlin, the one Western city in the world that we have completely and utterly surrounded." Almost leisurely she opened a desk drawer and took out a nine-millimeter SigSauer automatic, which she pointed at him. "I think I would not like you to come any closer for the moment," she said. John stopped a few feet in front of the desk. "I think that your instinct for survival might be put to very good use over the next twenty-four hours or so."

"Cut the bullshit, Major."

"This is no bullshit, as you say, Mr. Mahoney," Tonia countered sternly. "You have taken some pains to mask your movements ever since you returned to Washington, and it was only by happenstance that we spotted you earlier this afternoon."

Tonia supported her gun hand against her left forearm on the desktop. John decided that the photographs Hayes had shown him, even the one of her on the beach, did her no justice. In person she was stunning in a non-Western, almost exotic way, that the severe cut of her uniform did nothing to hide.

"What interest do you have in me?" John asked. "You have gone through some trouble to get me here."

"Yes, I have."

"Within a very few hours my consulate will understand that I am missing. I'll ask you again, what do you want?"

"Your help," Tonia said.

"Help?"

"More than that, Mr. Mahoney. I am seeking your cooperation. You are a CIA intelligence officer, and I will not belabor that point, nor do I wish to suffer your denials. It is fact. It is also fact that I am a KGB intelligence officer of an unnumbered department that deals with what we call special investigations. I do not care what you think you know, or what you may have heard about me, but for the record I am not an assassin. I am a federal police officer whose chief concern is the investigation of suspected acts of treason or espionage, the penetration of my service by foreign intelligence officers, and the circumstances and damages caused by the defection of important Soviet citizens. Which is why I have come to Germany. We believe that a man you know as Yuri Yevgennevich Chernov may have defected to the West. He is a very important man to my government not so much because he is an active intelligence officer with up-to-date information, but more because he is a very old man and is looked upon as a national treasure. It would do neither our government nor yours any good to keep him. We would like him to come home. Nothing sinister in that."

"You forgot kidnapping in your job description, Major," John said. "That and stupidity."

Tonia's eyes narrowed. "If we find your father before you do, we will kill him."

"Thus disproving your self-analysis," John said. He didn't know why he was goading her. She was a dangerous woman by all accounts. If he hadn't already read her dossier, he would have seen it in her eyes now. Wherever she went she left behind a string of bodies. "Either shoot me or let me go, but don't tell me that you are the great humanitarian."

She smiled a little in frustration, shook her head, and laid the gun on the desk. "Yuri Yevgennevich is my uncle. He and your father got out of Berlin once, but they won't do it again. If need be, we would force their aircraft down in East German airspace and divert it to one of our fields before it ever reached the West." She sat back. "There would be a fuss, but we would apologize later. In the meanwhile your father and my uncle would be lost to us both."

John gauged the distance to the gun. "You say they have left Berlin?"

"They flew to Hannover where they booked rooms at the Inter-Continental Hotel under their worknames. Nostrand and Greenleaf. We lost them. They simply disappeared. I suspect they either drove or took the train back to Berlin. But they're here now. I'm sure of it."

Chernov's workname was the one Heiser had given him, but it was odd hearing Tonia Trusov mentioning it and his father's workname. She was watching him. He had the uncanny feeling that she knew what he was thinking.

"If you know all of that, then why bother with me?" he asked. "Send your people across and find them. Berlin is not that big a city. And, as you say, they are boxed in now."

"Berlin *is* that big a city. And your father and my uncle may be old fools, but their tradecraft is still very good. I imagine they are

163

armed, and the fact that they laid a track for us to Hannover proves that they know we are looking for them."

"And that they don't want to be found."

"That too."

"Then just leave them alone."

"We can't simply turn our backs on them and walk away any more than you can. I know my uncle, but I do not know your father as well as you do. Between us we have a chance of finding them before it is too late."

"Too late for what, Major?"

She got up and started to turn toward the window, but then thought better of it. She put the gun back in the drawer and locked it. She was tall. Perhaps five feet ten, John thought. But she didn't have the raw-boned look that so many tall women have, nor was she gaunt like a runway model.

"Yesterday evening you spoke with an old friend of your father's. A man named Stan Kopinski. In the middle of your conversation he was murdered, and you no doubt believe that it was done by a Soviet assassination team. I don't have the proof for you yet, Mr. Mahoney, but we did not kill him."

John was cold, as if they were standing outside. "Who, then?"

"The CIA."

"Why?"

"Obviously to silence him. Whoever it was doesn't want you to find your father."

"Then why not kill me?"

"I don't know," Tonia said heavily. "I haven't got that last part figured out yet, except that I suspect there may be two factions within the Agency who are at war with each other at the moment. Killing Kopinski they could get away with, but by assassinating you, the battle would be accelerated to unacceptable limits. I'm guessing—I don't know this for sure." She looked up. "I do know that your father and my uncle know something that when they put it together will be devastating."

"To whom?"

"To us, to you. My orders are to kill them both."

"And you will. You are a murderer."

"Not of old men! Not of my family!"

"You have already told me too much, Major."

"There are no recording devices in this room. Here for the moment it is just you and me. When we are finished I will have you driven back to the western zone."

"Why tell me all of this? Why did you bring me here?"

164

"For your help, as I told you. I want to save my uncle. Can't you understand this?"

"I can understand it," John said. "But I don't believe you."

"Then go!" Tonia snapped. "Get out of here now! I will have you driven back to your hotel." She came around the desk. "But next time I see you, Mahoney, I will kill you!"

It was snowing much more heavily now, and it had gotten dark. He could no longer see the Brandenburg Gate in the storm. There was much, he thought, that he was unable to see. Circles within circles. Plots within plots. Lies within lies. It had been a very long time since he had truly known what or whom to believe in. He wanted to save his father. It was the only constant now.

"My uncle hates your father," Tonia said softly. "Did you know that?"

"No."

"He told me once that your father represented everything that was wrong in the West. He said that your father had contempt for authority. It happens in unstructured societies, especially among men who believe they are better than the rest."

"Why should I believe you?"

"Because I am telling the truth. And because you love your father at least as much as I love my uncle."

"If there is someone within the CIA who does not want me to find my father, I will have nowhere safe to take him."

"That's your problem, Mr. Mahoney. I will have my own difficulties bringing my uncle back to the Soviet Union. All of which, of course, is a moot point unless we find them first."

"Who else is looking for them?"

"I brought a team with me. They have been supplemented by the rezident's staff, and even now half of them are in the western zone searching, watching, listening."

"And the others?"

"Still in Hannover following that dead lead, though they will soon tire of it and return here. As you can see we don't have much time."

"If someone followed me to my meeting with Kopinski and set up the kill, what would prevent him from doing the same thing here in Berlin?"

"You didn't know they were behind you in Washington, Mr. Mahoney. I trust now that you are armed with this information, you will take care of yourself."

But he had known in Washington, he thought. Or at the very least he had suspected. What was most extraordinary, however,

165

was the fact that he was here now, discussing with a KGB killer a search and rescue operation for two old men. It made no sense. And yet it did. There was an internal logic to such a joint venture. At least up to a point there was. He looked at her. She was an extraordinarily beautiful woman, he thought. But Carlisle had said she was called the Black Widow or the Scorpion. He could see the truth in that.

"They are meeting somewhere in West Berlin," he said, and a look of triumph crossed Tonia's features.

"Where? What have you found out?"

"Someone telephoned my father from Helsinki last week. They spoke for twenty-eight minutes. We have the telephone record, but there was no way of knowing for certain who he spoke with."

"It was my uncle. He went to Helsinki to buy a few things."

"A few days later he telephoned our embassy in Moscow with a message for my father. He wanted to set up a meeting."

"Where?"

"He didn't specify the time or the place. He just said he wanted to meet. But when we called my father he denied knowing your uncle. There was nothing in his files to indicate otherwise."

"But he disappeared."

"Yes," John said. "With several passports, money, and a gun." Tonia nodded. "My uncle is armed as well."

"Shortly after the war they met here somewhere. During the Potsdam conference."

"That's here," Tonia said, startled. "In the DDR."

"There were meetings, from what I understand, between Soviet and American officers all over the place. We have no listing, however."

"You think they have returned to the same place."

"If it still exists," John said, nodding. "Unless your uncle set something else up during his telephone call from Helsinki."

"It's the one thing I cannot understand," Tonia said. "If my uncle spoke with your father at such length, why did he expose himself by sending the message through your embassy?"

"Because my father probably told him no the first time. Your uncle forced his hand."

"Then why did your father come? Why didn't he tell his people, you, about the call?"

"I think my father finally decided to come to Germany because he wants to kill your uncle."

"Why?" Tonia asked sharply.

"An old grudge," John said evenly. His old grudge, too, he

thought. He would kill Chernov himself if his father hadn't already done it. "Why did your uncle set up the meeting? He knows that my father hates him, so he's not defecting."

"I don't know," Tonia said.

Oh yes you do, John thought. And whatever it is the old man brought out with him was scaring her silly.

"If such a list of postwar meeting locations exists, I will find it," she said.

"Divert your people. I don't want them stumbling all over the place."

"I'll do what I can. Who knows, the two old fools may have been spotted in Munich. I could very well be wrong about West Berlin. It will give them a certain pleasure to hear me admit it." She stuck out her hand. "We will be allies once again, just for this operation."

John ignored her outstretched hand. "If you cross me, Major, if you try anything, I will kill you."

She lowered her hand. "But you agree to work with me?"

"Yes."

"Then we will find them."

The same driver as before took John back across the border. This time they were stopped on the western side by American MPs who looked very closely at his identification before they let him go on. They didn't bother checking the driver's. Evidently they knew him. Ordinary people couldn't come and go across the border; only the people who had no business being on this side were allowed through with a wave. It didn't make sense, but then politics hardly ever made sense. Back at his hotel he checked with the desk to make sure he'd gotten no calls, then walked to where he'd parked his rental car and drove over to the American consulate on Clay-Allee in Dahlem.

He didn't believe for one minute that Tonia was telling him the truth, except that she was desperate to find her uncle. He just bet she was. Nor did he believe that she was calling off her people from the search in West Berlin.

He parked his car around the corner and walked back to the consulate where he waited in the foyer for Bixby to be called down.

Truth or not, he had given her more than she had given him. Yet he suspected that she would genuinely try to help him because at this point he had the best chance of finding them. It's what would come afterward that was most important. Someone in the CIA wanted to stop him badly enough to commit murder. Who was it, and why? What were they afraid of? What did they know?

Bixby, his jacket off, his tie loose, appeared at the head of the stairs and motioned for John to come up. At the top they went down the corridor and into a rear office that was so crammed with books, magazines, newspapers, and maps that it could have been the study of a college professor deep in some research project of vast importance.

"No such list exists," Bixby said. "At least not here. Hayes is trying to run it down in Washington, but he wasn't very encouraging."

"They may have left Berlin already."

"Are you sure?"

"No, I'm not sure, and neither was the hotel clerk or the ticket clerk at the airport. But two men who more or less fit their descriptions flew to Hannover yesterday."

"We'll start checking the hotels."

"That's all I want you to do. If they're there, I want your people to stay away from them. This is strictly hands off. Do you understand, Tom?"

Bixby's lips compressed, but he nodded. "You're calling the shots for the moment," he said. "Anything else?"

John sighed tiredly. "The Russian may be using Carl Nostrand as a workname. He's probably abandoned it by now, but it might provide a track."

Bixby was dying to ask how he knew these things, but he knew better. "Anything else?"

"Not for the moment. I'd like to talk to Hayes now on the secure line."

Bixby looked at his watch. "It's late over there."

"He'll be in his office," John said, slumping in a chair and lighting a cigarette. He was going to have to get some sleep soon, he decided. He could not keep on like this much longer. His judgment was going all to hell, and before long he was going to start making mistakes. This time, they could cost him his life. Be careful, he told himself. Careful.

When the call went through, Bixby left the office. Hayes's voice over the encrypted line was filled with little flats and hollows, as if he were speaking into a tin can during a windstorm.

"What have you got on Stan's killer?" John asked, sitting back and closing his eyes.

"Not much. We've pulled up what was left of the boat. It was a twenty-foot center console ski boat, reported stolen that night. Two bodies, burned beyond recognition. No identification."

"What kind of a weapon?"

"Haven't found one yet. But the bullets that were pulled out of Kopinski's body were .223 caliber, almost certainly fired from a semiautomatic rifle. I don't think there'll be much help there for us."

"Is Farley available?"

"He left a couple of hours ago with strict instructions not to be disturbed tonight. I think he's going around the bend."

"Oh?" John said. "How's that, Alex?"

"He's just different. Running around here like a crazy man one minute, and in the next disappearing or announcing that he will be incommunicado for the next hour or two. It's really weird."

"They may have left West Berlin. Tell him that as soon as he's communicado again, would you, Alex? They were seen in Hannover. Bixby is checking it out now."

"Seen by who?"

"An airline clerk. The descriptions match, more or less."

"Anything else I can do from this end?" Hayes asked.

"Have you come up with a list of meeting places?"

"Not yet, but under the circumstances it's no longer necessary, is it?"

"Keep digging anyway, would you, Alex? Who knows, maybe they didn't leave after all, or maybe they left something behind."

"I'll call you."

"Do that."

John scribbled a note to Bixby to call him at the hotel if anything came up in Hannover, then drove downtown to the big Ballhaus Resi nightclub on the corner of Gräfestrasse. It was early yet, and there were only a few people at the bar. John had a beer as he tried to imagine his father and Chernov here, with Heiser's people probably hanging from the rafters. Chernov would have been too sharp to fall for such a setup. He would have smelled a stakeout all the way across the border.

"I was supposed to meet two friends here this afternoon," John told the bartender.

"Yes? Maybe later this evening—we will have many guests then," the man said.

"They may have been here in the past day or so. Older gentlemen. One with white hair, the other much taller."

The bartender smiled and shrugged. "As I say, mein Herr, we

169

have many guests every day. Older gentlemen are not a rarity. Nor is white hair."

They wouldn't have come here, John thought. His father was too sharp for that. There were still people here who knew him, who might recognize him. And Chernov would know that the search would be on. They wouldn't be so open. In this he had to agree with Tonia Trusov. Their trip to Hannover was nothing more than a false track. They had returned to West Berlin, and they knew someone would be coming after them.

Back at his hotel he had a light early dinner and then up in his room began telephoning hotels again. For the moment it was the only lead he had. Sooner or later, he supposed, Tonia Trusov would be coming over. Heiser had joked that he should ask the Russians for the list of American-Soviet meeting places after the war. Well, he'd done just that. It was their only possibility now, unless his father and her uncle made a mistake, which wasn't likely considering who and what they were.

For more years then he cared to count, Bernhard Heiser had known that Yuri Chernov and Wallace Mahoney would meet again. It had been a hobby with him, following their careers, watching, waiting. More like an obsession, Hilda, his housekeeper and companion all these years, would say, and did often. "A fatal attraction," General Gehlen said at his retirement. "It is time to rest now, my old friend. It's a game for the younger men." Sitting in his study, watching the last of the gray light fade from his garden, watching the snow steadily come down, he sipped his second cognac of the day. In front of him on the library table at which he was seated was his journal that he had begun on the day Gehlen had rescued him from obscurity. In it was a distillation of everything he had seen and heard and learned over more than four decades of service to the BND. Disturbing things, all the more so in light of recent happenings.

"Big things are afoot, Hilda," he had told his housekeeper when the young Mahoney had left. "Now it's all coming together. At last."

"Hush, you old fool," she said gently to him. "No more of that nonsense now. It upsets you too much."

But it wasn't nonsense.

The doorbell rang, and he looked up. He could hear Hilda in the kitchen preparing their dinner. "*Ja,*" she called. The doorbell rang again. "*Gott in Himmel,*" she shouted. He heard her shuffling down the corridor and open the door.

He closed the journal. There was no telling who was coming to see him, and the journal was not something to be left out in the open.

"Oh," Hilda said softly. There was a popping sound, and then a second and the noise of a crash.

Heiser knew exactly what it was; he'd half been expecting something like this for a long time. He yanked open the drawer in the table and pulled out his old Luger. His fingers were arthritic and he had trouble pulling the ejector lever, stiff with age and disuse.

He turned and looked up as a large man appeared in the doorway. "You," he said, trying to bring the Luger around, but he was too slow and he knew it. As the first bullet entered his chest and he was driven backward, his last thought was that the bastards had finally won. And then he was dead.

10

Moscow was Mahoney's most fervent dream and his most haunting nightmare. To understand the Soviet mind it would take more than a look across the wall at one of them. Yet after Berlin he believed he knew them well enough to make use of his knowledge, and so did the Agency. But he was uneasy.

His posting came in the late summer of 1962, the year after the humiliating defeat at the Bay of Pigs when Agency moral was at its lowest ebb. The Russians weren't going to sit still for an abortive attack on Cuba. Big things were in the wind, and Mahoney was the very best man to be sent over for a close look. Besides, he figured that after Berlin Chernov would be back in Moscow, working out of the Lubyanka headquarters downtown while the KGB was building its new headquarters outside the city to match the CIA's newly opened building across the Potomac from Washington on what was officially Bureau of Public Roads property. He wanted to see him again. The Agency had survived the witch-hunt of '53 and '54, and they'd come out of the McCarthy era relatively unscathed, but this latest debacle was threatening to undo everything they had worked for since the late forties. A steady, knowledgeable hand was needed in Moscow. Not as chief of station, but as a special deputy assistant to the ambassador, responsible for looking at the Russians up close and analyzing their day-to-day posturing. By that time his spoken Russian was nearly fluent and he was considered an old hand on the Soviet desk. For the three months preceding his actual posting he was given his homework. The Soviet way of life, the peoples of the Soviet Union, histories of the Soviet Union, especially the period after the Revolution, Russian and Soviet literature, the lively arts, food and drink, customs, military strengths and aims, recent geopolitical goals and ambitions, Soviet presence in Third World countries, Soviet-Chinese relations (or lack of them), Eastern European satellite nations in relation to present-day Soviet politics, the history of the Presidium, the Politburo, the GRU, the

KGB, as well as literally hundreds of dossiers on the government's and military's top leadership.

The most difficult part was leaving the boys. John was seventeen and had just graduated from high school. He was planning on attending Stanford as a chemistry major. His plans were set, but Michael was only fourteen, just a baby with three more years of school before he would be safely off at college. He was very young for his age and couldn't understand why he was going to have to be left behind at a boarding school in Wisconsin.

"Moscow is no place for you, son," Mahoney told him.

"But I don't want you to leave me again," Michael cried miserably. "What will Mother do alone?"

The boys' school at Black River Falls in northern Wisconsin was run by a former OSS officer whom Mahoney had known from the war years. He promised to take good care of Michael. "I'll treat him like he was my own son, Wallace. But I won't coddle him. Not that."

He and Marge had stopped in Madison on the way back to see the ailing Norman Robie, his college professor, who was now living there in retirement. The reunion was sad. Robie was becoming senile, and when his mind would clear for a few minutes or so, he wanted to hear all about Mahoney's East Coast practice, for which Mahoney had to make up patient names and case histories.

"Not what I'd call my most favorite few days," Marge said on the plane to Washington.

He reached over and squeezed her hand. "He'll be better off in Black River Falls than with us in Moscow."

"I know that, Wallace, though a mother is allowed to worry," she said. "Actually, I was thinking about poor old Dr. Robie. Seeing him like that makes me think how old we're becoming."

Mahoney smiled. "Any regrets?"

Marge shook her head. "Not a one. You?"

"Not yet," he said.

She looked at him for a long time to see if he was kidding. Her lips were compressed. "Moscow is going to be dangerous for us, isn't it."

"Not terribly." He lied because he really didn't know. Chernov understood who he was. If the Russian wanted to make trouble, it would be very easy for him to arrange something. "But I don't think it'll be very pleasant. They do classify it as a hardship assignment."

"Can't be any worse than our first time in Berlin," she said,

173

smiling again, thinking back to the three years in the wretched railroad flat. She'd hated it, but she had never really complained.

"At least we'll be out of Washington," he said. She was going to miss Michael, and he knew it.

"At least that," she said wistfully. "But I'll have you. I don't expect you'll be gallivanting around the Soviet Union as much as you do Europe."

"No," Mahoney said. "Not that."

On the night before they left, Sylvan Bindrich called Mahoney into his office. They'd been in the new building at Langley for barely a year now and none of them were used to the newness. Bindrich poured him a drink, and they sat facing each other across his desk.

"You've done a good job for us these past few years, Wallace," Bindrich said. "Especially in Berlin and Madrid. The director sends his best wishes. Any last-minute jitters?"

Mahoney thought he was a bit pompous. "A few."

"This is the watershed for you, you know. We're all virgins until we've been to Moscow. And that goes doubly for you. No idealism. Over there it's the nitty-gritty."

"What are you trying to say to me, Sylvan?" Mahoney asked. He was thinking about Chernov.

"What I'm trying to say to you is watch your step."

"I will."

"They'll suspect that you're a spy. You'll be watched."

"I'll watch back."

"If they spot you they'll nail you to the cross."

"What *are* you trying to tell me?"

"You're the best we've got. We don't want to lose you. Take care of yourself, that's all."

"I will."

"And keep your eyes and ears open. We're not sending you over for a vacation."

"I expect not," Mahoney said, laughing.

Bindrich tossed his drink back, then got up and poured them another. Afterward they shook hands, and Bindrich wished him luck. "Do a good job for us," he said.

The next morning he and Marge flew to Orly in Paris, then on to Wiesbaden, Germany, where they spent a couple of days going over final briefings by the embassy staffing and housing officer, as well as a first secretary rotating back to the States. He had struck them as looking shell-shocked. He couldn't tell them much except that the ambassador was "good people," and that he was damn glad to be finally going home. At noon on their third day they flew to Stockholm and from there to Vnukovo Airport a few miles outside of Moscow. From the air the countryside had appeared vast and brooding, filled with dark shadows and mysterious roads that seemed to end in the middle of nowhere. But on the ground the sun was shining, the afternoon was warm, the customs and immigration officials courteous if a little slow with their diplomatic passports, and afterward they were driven into the city by an affable staffer from the consular section who kept up a running commentary on day-to-day life in the Soviet capital city. They spent the night at Spaso House, the ambassador's residence, though they didn't get to meet the ambassador himself. He was in Leningrad for the week, and the next day they moved into their own tiny but reasonably well maintained and furnished apartment on Arbat Street a half-dozen blocks from the embassy. They lived in a foreigners' building. Militia guards were posted outside the front door twenty-four hours a day. Mahoney had expected it, but he had worried about how Marge would react. He needn't have. Within a week she was bringing them coffee in the mornings, and tea and sometimes sweet rolls that she baked in the afternoon. They were her own personal doormen.

The embassy, even in those days, was old and ramshackle. Located on Tchaikovsky Street just a couple of blocks from the Moscow City Zoo, it was housed in a yellow brick apartment building with creaking wooden floors, rattletrap elevators, and hissing radiators that seemed to provide only two basic temperatures: blazing hot or arctic cold. Uniformed militia guards were stationed out front to check the identification of anyone trying to get into the embassy, and there were always a couple of plainclothes KGB officers parked in a car across the street. In the early days, as now, the embassy employed a few hundred Soviet nationals to do the mundane work such as cooking, housekeeping, some typing and translating, the maintenance, driving, and in some cases even baby-sitting and shopping. They were all KGB informers, of course, and fully one fourth of them were actual KGB officers. Among them were some very bright people and good-looking young women who always seemed to be hanging around at the odd hour down the odd corridor so that they would often end up alone with some hapless young staffer too long away from home and lonely. Another one of the ground rules was that except for a couple of electronically screened rooms on the third and fifth floors, as well as the cryptographic communications center where the KW-26 machines were housed in the basement, every square inch of the embassy was bugged. The KGB's Second Chief Directorate's First Department, which was charged with watching U.S. diplomats, was housed a few blocks away in a building called "the warehouse" from where they interviewed embassy employees on a daily basis, intercepted embassy telephone calls, sorted embassy mail that didn't come via the diplomatic pouches, and for a number of years actually scanned the embassy building with beams of microwaves, though to what end no one had ever been able to figure out. (They had also begun to dig a tunnel from the main sewer line in the street out front to the embassy's basement, but the project was discovered in due time.) Walter Frisque, a Donovan original whom Mahoney vaguely remembered meeting in London during the war, was chief of station. He was an exceedingly cynical old man who had always seemed to Mahoney to have been more suited for the Saturday evening critical columns of *The New York Times* than a foreign posting with the CIA. No one much cared for him, but he took Mahoney under his wing, and they soon became fast if not close friends.

"The problem, of course, is that they know what you're here for," Frisque said at lunch in the staff cafeteria. "What do you know about music and dancing?"

"I know what I like when I see it and hear it," Mahoney said.

"It'll do for now, I suppose. But you'd better take the short course on the subject, especially the Bolshoi, because you're going to become our resident expert."

"Why?"

Frisque grinned in his malevolent way that frightened so many of the junior staffers. "Everybody loves the ballet in this country. Department store clerks, taxi drivers, janitors. You know."

Mahoney did. "Colonels and generals and manufacturing plant directors, and Politburo delegates and staff."

"That's the ticket. Let them think what they want about you. By day you're going to be our analyst, and economic affairs officer, but by night you're going to become our little spy. Everyone's friend. You've just acquired culture."

Mahoney threw himself into his studies, learning as he did everything else, quickly and wholeheartedly. Marge helped him, though he hated lying to her like that. She knew that his motives were less than altruistic, but she never said anything. They learned about the Bolshoi company in Moscow as well as the world-famous Kirov in Leningrad. They learned about prima and prima assoluta ballerinas such as the Maya Plisetskayas and Maximovas. They learned about the virtuoso males such as Vasiliev and the much younger Baryshnikov; about the scores such as *Swan Lake*, *Romeo and Juliet*, and *Anna Karenina*; about the music of the Tchaikovskys and Prokofievs. And Mahoney began to develop an appreciation for a dancer's form and line. He read the books and the magazines and the special Russian newspapers devoted to the ballet. In his job as special assistant to the ambassador he was sent to numerous functions over the next few months with Stanley Jacobson, the chargé d'affaires, at which he spoke to Russians about the ballet, always with the same warm, gratified reaction that an American was actually interested in Russian art and not simply cold war diplomacy. He and Marge began to attend the ballet regularly, sometimes seeing the same program over and over again. Marge enjoyed the music, but she didn't care for the backstage meetings afterward, nor did she like the oftentimes late-night gatherings at the Arbat, the Metropole Bar, or the Minsk on Gorky, with the endless vodka toasts to the performers. Sometimes she would stay home, for which he was of two minds. On the one hand he missed being with her, and felt guilty that he was leaving her to go to bed alone in a very empty apartment in a strange country. On the other hand he felt even more guilty about involving her the way he had in his work. He was beginning to make friends among a certain set of the Moscow establishment. A dangerous game, Frisque cautioned him. "You can never tell when the bastards will suddenly turn on you. Watch your step." He was glad therefore when Marge began to drop out. She missed him, she missed the boys, and she missed home and familiar things, even Washington, yet she never complained. More than once he caught himself promising that he would make it up to her. Somehow, sometime. But he knew that he was kidding himself. Nothing could be done to make up for an absence. It was his job; it was part and parcel of what he did. Marge understood, and he loved her all the more for it.

In October Kennedy ordered the blockade of all Soviet ships heading for Cuban ports, and while the world held its breath wondering if it was finally on the verge of all-out nuclear war, Mahoney's Soviet friends and contacts dried up and he was left out in the cold.

The embassy drew back into itself. Almost every contact across the board was suddenly busy, missing, or knew nothing. The only intelligence to be gathered was from Soviet television, radio, newspapers, and other periodicals including a couple of *samizdat* newsletters published by Jewish dissident groups. It was meager pickings that were sent back to Langley, but it was the best that could be done under the circumstances.

While the blockade half a world away lasted, Mahoney pitched in with translation and analysis duties at the embassy. Quality, not quantity, had been their byword from the beginning. But that notion had been turned topsy-turvy, and it was only through the drudgery of quantity that they were making any headway at all, as meager as it was. The hours were long and tedious and sometimes riding home late at night in a staff car he would close his eyes and lay his head back on the seat and let his mind drift. If intent was what a secret service sought, we were failing miserably here, he thought. Just now especially so. No one, least of all Moscow station, knew what the Russians were going to do.

Two weeks later tensions began to noticeably ease, and in the next week he received an invitation to attend the opening of *Spartacus* at the Bolshoi. It was signed by Boris Shalayev, the director of the Ministry of Economic Achievement. Afterward there was to be a reception in honor of the ballet company.

"Peace overtures," Frisque said, looking up from the invitation. "You're going, of course, and you'd better take Marge."

"I'd rather leave her out of this."

Frisque nodded. "That's up to you, Wallace," he said. "Can't involve a man's wife in this business unless she feels comfortable with it. Not in my station, anyway." He glanced at the invitation again. "But she was invited. Says here, Mr. and Mrs. Wallace Mahoney."

It was a matter of cover, of course. And after the few weeks of enforced isolation Marge was glad for the chance to get out. The ballet was wonderful, and afterward at the reception they were introduced to Nikita Khrushchev and his roly-poly wife, Nina. There was no awkwardness, and in fact the Russians seemed particularly attentive and warm toward the several dozen Americans in attendance. The crisis had come, it had been dealt with, and it had passed. It was time now, the Russians were signaling them, for a normalization of relations between their two governments to begin.

The ballet season that winter was glittering. Mahoney had never before and never since been so busy. Practically every evening was devoted to the appreciation of the ballet and its habitués, which read like a who's who of Moscow. At performances, at backstage receptions, at the late-night parties, even at daytime luncheon meetings usually at the Metropole Hotel, Mahoney let the talk flow around him, adding his insights here and there when appropriate. "It is the Western view," he explained to Boris Shalayev, "that allows us to appreciate the grace and beauty of the performers onstage. But it is the Soviet soul in her music and dance which is solely responsible for the creation of such fine art." *Kulturny*, he'd learned his lesson well, was everything to the Russians. And they appreciated hearing an obviously erudite American say so. "The Soviet Union has given the world ballet," he said.

"What about your American Ballet Theatre or New York City Ballet companies?" Shalayev asked one evening at the Arbat.

"It's possible that in time we could challenge you," Mahoney said.

"Only a possibility?" Shalayev asked gracefully. "Surely you are being too hard on your own dancers. I was in New York not so very long ago and saw a wonderful *Swan Lake*."

Mahoney nodded his sage agreement and thanks for the compliment, and then he leaned forward so as to better make his point. The Russians were loving it. "Just what I have been trying to say all evening here, Boris Ivanovich. If we would stick with the classics, we would have a chance of matching you. But . . ." He shrugged. "But if we insist on experimental ballet, discordant music, questionable motivations—and it is motivation we are talking about here, after all, that and the moral issues you have been trying to reach for more than a century—if we allow our dancers to go off on such tangents, then we will never build a body of grace and expertise within our companies. Each year will be a season of new learning, not of development."

"You really do understand, Mr. Mahoney," Anna Chalkin, one of the younger dancers, said brightly. "It is fantastic to hear you say so."

On another evening he moderated a heated discussion about who was the very best prima ballerina, Galina Ulanova of forty years earlier, or Maya Plisetskaya, whose husband Rodion Shchedrin was currently writing great things for her.

"Plisetskaya, of course," Mahoney said with an assurance that stopped them all.

"Yes?" someone challenged.

"Just as twenty years from now a newcomer will be better. It is a matter of advancement. If Ulanova were dancing today, young and up on the stage, it would be a different matter altogether. It is unfair to her to make the comparison because she did not have the

179

benefit of an additional forty years of choreographic experience. She was the best of her day, as Plisetskaya is of hers."

Even as he was saying it he could see that he had won them over. Completely. It was the watershed that Bindrich had spoken of.

Only through culture could there be a meaningful understanding. Mahoney had ripened the garden and now it was time to reap the rewards. The next meeting came two weeks later in the form of a private weekend party at the Istra River dacha of Boris Shalayev. Besides ballet, their shared passion was furthering trade between the Soviet Union and the United States. For months Shalayev had been hinting at big possibilities in the field of electronics, which was a very touchy subject in Washington. Through intermediaries such as the Japanese and the West Germans, the Russians were attempting to purchase large mainframe IBM computing systems. Washington had denied the export permits and threatened to sanction even their normal trading partners because it was feared that the Russians would use the equipment for military purposes. Shalayev figured it was time to go directly to the source, starting with Mahoney.

Frisque knew exactly what the Russians were angling for with the weekend invitation, and so did Langley. It was a golden opportunity, they all thought, to gain some intelligence of real value. By playing along with them, at least initially, Washington would have a good chance of finding out exactly which equipment the Russians needed most. In that roundabout way it would be learned in which areas Soviet technology was most deficient. A back-door approach, but it was worth the shot.

"Marge is not included in this one," Mahoney adamantly insisted.

"I agree," Frisque said. "They might even be crude enough to try a honey trap on you."

Mahoney smiled. "It's the chance I'll have to take. What exactly do I give them?"

"Not that," Frisque said. "But anything else they want. Promise them the moon and the stars. But watch yourself, Wallace, they'll have all their big guns lined up out there. Anything can happen."

At home that evening he explained to Marge that he would have to go away for the weekend. To Leningrad, he lied to her. "Shalayev has arranged a series of meetings."

"Be careful, Wallace," she said at his side when they were in bed.

He wanted to turn on the lights and look into her eyes to see what she meant by that, how much she knew or guessed. But in the end he decided it was just his guilt again, and he was going to have to protect her at all costs. He couldn't imagine her involved in his business now, and he resolved then and there to keep her as insulated as humanly possible.

It was not a profession for a married man, he thought bitterly as he finally drifted off to sleep. Nor was it for the man with morals.

Shalayev was proud of the dacha, although it wasn't his. It belonged to a director at the Bolshoi who allowed his friends to use it on occasion. Mahoney figured it belonged to the KGB. Every room would be wired. Even outside he figured there would be microphones strung up in the trees. Shalayev went ahead in his Moskvich with a few friends, while Mahoney followed in an embassy Fiat with Shalayev's daughter, Natasha, in case they got separated. She was a young woman in her mid-twenties, good-looking in a Russian sort of way with tiny sloping shoulders and a square, pushed-in face, and very nervous being with an American. "It will be a very pleasant weekend," she kept saying. "There will be a lot of fun."

Snow had fallen most of the week, and the side road down to the river had not been plowed, making the driving difficult. The area reminded him of the Schultz Lake cabin, except the woods there were mostly pine; here they were mostly sad, narrow birch stripped of their leaves.

"It is very pretty," Mahoney said as they crossed a wooden bridge over the river. "Do you come here often?"

"Oh, no," she said. "Sometimes with friends, but not this year yet. Dominic has been very busy."

They turned down a very narrow lane, the tree branches brushing at times against the sides of the car, big lumps of snow falling on them. Around a tight corner the big house was situated on top of a hill overlooking the frozen river. Already there were several cars parked in the front yard, one of them a very large Zil limousine. Mahoney recognized several license plates as KGB, and the rest ordinary government official. His was the only foreign diplomatic plate. He pulled in behind Shalayev.

"Didn't I tell you this would be wonderful?" Shalayev said, beaming. The others went in.

Smoke came from three chimneys, and in the distance they could hear the faint tinkle of bells.

"Someone has taken the horse and sleigh down the river," Shalayev said. "You'll love it, Wallace. You'll see."

"My uncle used to have a place like this in northern Minnesota," Mahoney said, though it wasn't quite true. This place was huge, at least five bedrooms, he thought. No mere Bolshoi director owned it.

"Ah, then you know the value of a retreat such as this where a man can escape the pressures of his city life. Do you hunt, Wallace?"

"When I was a kid."

"Well, then, we'll try our hand this weekend," Shalayev said as they headed up to the house.

Natasha had gone ahead. She was talking to a young couple at a heavily laden buffet table. A big stone fireplace dominated the great room. Eight or ten men and a like number of younger women were talking and laughing and drinking. Music came from an expensive Danish stereo. Someone was smoking marijuana; Mahoney smelled it the moment he came in.

"Ah, the guest of honor," a tall, dark-haired portly man bellowed, breaking away from a young woman he'd been talking with and coming over. Mahoney recognized him from one of the recent post-ballet Metropole sessions. He was KGB. Second Chief Directorate.

"Nice to see you, General Aleksandrov," Mahoney said, shaking his hand.

"No last names or titles here, Wallace," the general said, wagging his finger. His face was greasy with sweat. He looked half drunk already. "Here is relaxation. No business."

"Perhaps only a little with Boris."

"Only a little, then, as you say. But come, meet the others and have something to eat and drink."

Shalayev hovered like an old woman who wanted everything to be just right. From time to time Mahoney caught his daughter looking at her father with an odd expression on her face. She wasn't very happy to be here, but it was only at those moments that it was plain. He felt sorry for her, but not for the other girls who were obviously professionals. KGB almost assuredly. Frisque had been correct in his warning. Several times that first evening he found himself sitting next to one of the girls, who had evidently been singled out for him. Her name, she said, was Lara, and she was a buyer for GUM, the big department store in Moscow, and her one desire was to someday travel to New York.

The music from the stereo was softer now, and the only light came from the fireplace. Some of the others had gone out for a midnight sleigh ride on the river. General Aleksandrov was dancing in the kitchen with Natasha. Shalayev had left an hour earlier.

"Is it true, what they say about New York?" she asked. She had been smoking marijuana and drinking wine most of the night. Her eyes were shining, and she kept flipping her long blond hair back off her face.

"It depends upon what you've heard," he said. "But most of it is probably true."

She laughed, her voice low and husky. "You have lived there, you know the city?"

"My wife and I had an apartment in Greenwich Village just after the war."

"Ah, the section of beatniks and poets and drunkards."

"There were some of them there too."

"Were you never afraid there at night?"

"Afraid?" Mahoney asked.

"For your life," she said. She had leaned very close to him, and he was very aware of her body, her clean feminine scent. She was dressed in blue jeans and a light sweater, her bare feet tucked up beneath her. She could almost have been Western with her makeup and long manicured nails. He figured she was in her late twenties, but she looked much younger.

"No more than I am right at this moment," he said.

It took a moment for the import of his words to sink in, and she reared back almost as if he had slapped her. "Oh, I'm sorry, Wallace."

Mahoney couldn't help but laugh a little. She was blushing. "No, it's all right, believe me. I was just feeling a little guilty."

"I didn't mean to offend you."

"You didn't, honestly. You're a pretty girl."

"Do you think I am pretty?"

"Yes."

"You can take me to bed if you like. I'd like it, very much. Here. Or we can go upstairs."

"I think not."

She glanced over toward the stairs. "It's all right," she said. She reached over and carefully set her wineglass down on the floor, and when she straightened up she pulled off her sweater. Her breasts were round and firm, the nipples already hard. "I think here by the fire would be nice," she said and she hunched back so that she could unbutton her jeans.

Mahoney reached out and stopped her. "It's not necessary, Lara," he said softly.

Oh, but it is, she almost said, but she stopped herself, a momentary look of fear crossing her face, to be replaced by a look halfway between disgust and cunning. "Are you a puffta, then?" she asked.

Again Mahoney had to laugh. "No," he said. "Just very married. And I came out this weekend to talk business with Boris Ivanovich, not to go to bed with a young woman, even one as pretty as you."

"Perhaps one of the other girls?" she suggested weakly.

"No," Mahoney said, getting up. "It's all right, honestly." He picked up her sweater and handed it to her. She was probably very innocent despite her brazenness, he decided.

"Where are you going?" she asked in alarm.

"Outside for some fresh air and a smoke. And then I am going to bed. Alone."

He left her sitting on the couch. In the front hall he pulled on his coat and stepped outside. The sky had cleared and the stars were brilliant. The temperature had plunged to well below zero. In the distance he could hear sleigh bells again and someone laughing. Sounds were magnified and crisp in the cold. The dacha had been very hot. It felt good to be outside for the moment. He unwrapped a cigar and lit it. Someone came from the house, and he turned around expecting it to be Lara, but it was one of the men.

"Hello, Wallace. I see you have a smoke too."

"It was a little warm in there for me," Mahoney said. "You're Ivan?"

"That's right," the Russian said, smiling nervously. "Ivan Sergeivich Lukashin. I am a lieutenant colonel in Line F of Department Viktor. Do you know this?"

It was the KGB's assassination and kidnapping squad. Mahoney involuntarily glanced up toward the eaves, looking for the hidden microphones.

"It is all right," Lukashin assured him. "The microphones just here are experiencing technical difficulties for the moment. But just for the moment. Do you understand?"

They spoke in English. Lukashin was agitated. They had tried with the girl, and now Mahoney had to wonder if they meant to kidnap him, or perhaps even kill him. They could claim it was an accident. Shalayev had mentioned hunting.

"What do you want with me?"

"We must talk, Mr. Mahoney. And very soon."

184

"About what?"

Lukashin glanced over his shoulder at the front door. "There isn't much time. I have information of very great importance to your government."

"I'm listening," Mahoney said noncommittally. If this was some kind of a trap, Lukashin was either a very good actor or a very frightened man.

"Not here, not now. We must meet somewhere in the city. But very soon. You can arrange the place, but it must be absolutely secure, and in this I must have your assurances."

"I don't know what you're talking about."

Again Lukashin glanced back at the door as if he suspected someone to be there. "Someone in America will be assassinated within the next ten months."

"Who?"

"I don't know yet. But I know some of the details. It will be someone important. Very important. It must be stopped."

"You're going to have to give me more than that before I can go to my government. How do I know this isn't some kind of a trick?"

"It is no trick," Lukashin whispered urgently. "It is called Operation CONUS. This is all I can tell you now. I must get back inside before I am missed."

"Who is in charge of the operation?"

"General Chernov himself," Lukashin said, and Mahoney was nearly staggered by the blow. "It is very big," the Russian said.

"It will take me a little time," Mahoney said, trying to regain his composure. Chernov here and now. If he was truly involved in some sort of assassination plot, it would indeed, as Lukashin said, be very big.

"There isn't much time," Lukashin insisted.

"How can I get a message to you?"

A look of relief crossed the Russian's features. "Come to the Bolshoi when you are ready. Leave your program in the men's room at the first intermission."

"It's going to take a little time."

"Not much time, Mr. Mahoney. I am already under suspicion."

"Operation CONUS, he called it," Mahoney told Frisque when he got back late Sunday evening. They met in the embassy's third-floor screened room. "He wants to set up a meeting place here in Moscow. Someplace secure."

"What about Shalayev? Did you get anything from him?"

"They need processing circuitry most of all, but this has nothing to do with computers. Lukashin was talking about assassination."

"It's one of the oldest tricks in the book, Wallace," Frisque said. "They get you accepting secret documents from a KGB officer, and then they'll arrest you."

"Not if they're working me for computer technology."

"Just another lever. If you balk, they'll threaten to use it against you. If you refuse and then run, then you weren't worth the effort and they'll have gotten rid of you. If you refuse but stay, they'll arrest you. They're masters of the game."

"I don't think so, Walter. He was actually frightened. I think he was sincere."

"You're saying that you want to go ahead with this?" Frisque asked.

Mahoney handed him a thin file folder. "I took the liberty of digging his file out of Archives. At least he's who he claims to be."

Frisque opened the file and quickly glanced through it. "I don't know," he said tiredly. He was a cynic and it was hard for him to rise above it. "Was he talking defection?"

"No."

Frisque said nothing. He rubbed his eyes.

"I think it's worth the effort."

"Do you realize the risk you'd be subjecting yourself to? You and your wife?"

"If I didn't want risk I would have become an accountant."

Frisque smiled. "The pay would have been a hell of a lot better." He glanced again at the open file. "I'll query Langley. If they give us a green light, we'll give it a shot."

"I'll get started on setting up a safe house."

"We'll need safeguards. Fallbacks. You're not going this alone. I'm going to insist on at least that much, and so will Langley."

"We can't drag our heels on this, Walter. If he was telling the truth, there's no telling how much time we've got. He said 'within' ten months. That could mean tomorrow."

"Right," Frisque said, getting to his feet. At the door he looked back. "Did he say who's running this operation?"

"No," Mahoney lied with a straight face, though he was suddenly sick with apprehension.

"Well, that doesn't matter for now. What does matter is keeping you out of Lubyanka and then finding out who the bastards have got targeted this time."

That night he lied again to Marge about the weekend, inventing dinners and endless toasts to economic cooperation between America and the Soviet Union, and endless tours of office buildings and factories. They made love and afterward, lying beside her in the dark, he wondered where it was all leading because he was still too young to wonder where it would end. For the next two days he worked out a meeting place with Frisque's fallbacks and safety valves while they waited for the green light from Langley. He considered sending Marge away with Frisque's wife, slipping Lukashin an American passport and bringing him past the militia guard to his apartment, but decided against it. Too much could go wrong. He considered arranging for a hotel room, but there were no guarantees the Russian wouldn't be seen and recognized. Besides, in the Soviet Union it was illegal to rent a hotel room in the same city in which you lived. He also considered a meeting on the run in one of the embassy's windowless vans. Again he rejected the idea. He didn't think the Russian would go for it, and in the event of a mechanical breakdown or an accident the entire operation could be jeopardized. In the end Housekeeping came up with a safe flat in a workers' district well past the Kazan Station. Barely a block from a metro station, with a back exit through a courtyard and a garage, the place would hold up for as long as they needed it, provided they took care with their tradecraft.

On Thursday he and Marge went to see a performance of *Sleeping Beauty* at the Bolshoi. During the first intermission he went to the men's room on the main floor where he left his program with the safe flat's address penciled in. He'd set the time of the meet for ten the next evening, then went back to his seat with the feeling that he had finally betrayed everyone: Marge, Frisque, the CIA, and even Lukashin. None of them knew about his connection with Chernov. It was a fatal attraction, but he couldn't help himself.

The apartment was on the second floor of a three-story building that once might have been used as a warehouse. It consisted of a small sitting room, and an even smaller bedroom. A chipped porcelain sink without plumbing and a small gas ring below two wooden shelves were closeted in a small niche just to the left of the door. The bathroom was in the corridor down two steps at the rear of the building. A single window looked down on the street. Frisque had been able to dig up only three people for the operation; Jim Reed stationed in the courtyard across from the back exit: Lyle Nelson parked in a canvas truck halfway down the block; and Howard Traub from the consular section waiting in an embassy van at the opposite end of the block. Mahoney was wired for sound with a voice-operated tape unit. If anything went bad he had only to turn off the apartment's single light and Nelson would come running. Once Traub in the van saw this he was to immediately circle around the block, picking them up on the run as he passed. "It's not airtight by a long shot, but it's the best we could come up with," Frisque said. Langley had been more indifferent than interested, and in the end had left the entire operation up to the discretion of the COS. "Which means it'll be their brilliance if something comes of it, but my ass if it falls apart."

Mahoney was in place by nine o'clock. He had brought a couple of bottles of vodka, a pack of cigarettes, and a bag containing a loaf of hard, crusty bread, some sliced cheese, and a big piece of sausage. He took off his coat, laid out the food, and turned up the heater. The tape machine was about the size of a large gun and was strapped to his side beneath his left armpit, the controls in his left pants pocket. One click turned it on, and one click turned it off. The tape would only last for an hour, so he had to remember to excuse himself and go to the bathroom at regular intervals so that he could change the reels. They all felt that Lukashin, if he knew he was being taped, might back out of the entire deal. If it was going to be impractical or even impossible for Mahoney to leave the room like that, he was to switch the recorder on only when Lukashin was about to say something important—though how anyone figured Mahoney was supposed to know that, no one said—and switch the recorder off during the intervals. It had been Mahoney's suggestion to do it this way, and no one had objected. "We need to know who they're planning on hitting, and when and where it's supposed to happen," Frisque said. "Beyond that, use your imagination. This guy could be a gold seam after all. Stranger things have happened."

Alone in the apartment Mahoney turned his thoughts to his nearly twenty-year relationship with Chernov. He was in too deeply now to back out. He had dug his own hole in '53 when he had denied having any personal contact with the man since the war. The results of the witch-hunt had been inconclusive. If there had been a mole within the Agency, someone working for Chernov, the investigation had driven him to ground. Mahoney had kept his ears open in the years since, but he had never gotten as much as a glimmer of such a person. If he existed, and was still in place, he was very good. Once again Chernov had surfaced like some ugly monster risen from the deep. This time Mahoney didn't know if he was going to be fortunate enough to escape notice as he had the last time. If he was guilty of treason, he thought, it was treason of omission. Yet he had gotten so much in an indirect way from the Russian. So many lessons had been learned. He'd gone to school on the Russian, but by God the tuition had been high, and he was still paying.

At ten precisely someone entered the building from the front door. Mahoney heard the door close, but then there was silence. Whoever had come in was standing down there in the semidarkness, waiting, listening. He reached into his jacket pocket and felt the pistol Frisque had made him carry. "I hate guns," he'd told the COS. "If your life depends on it, use it. Don't hesitate. We might not be able to get to you in time." Whoever had come in started up the stairs, his tread light, and slow. If it was Lukashin he was being exceedingly cautious: but, then, Mahoney thought, what man in his position wouldn't be? At the top of the stairs the person stopped again. Mahoney had left the door unlocked. He stepped back toward the bedroom door, and reached again into his jacket pocket, his fingers curling around the pistol grip.

Someone knocked at the door, softly, hesitantly.

"Da," Mahoney said.

The door opened and Lukashin, dressed in boots, an old dark gray overcoat and a leather cap, his face red from the cold, came in. "I spotted your people in front," he said, closing the door. "It is a good precaution."

Mahoney removed his hand from his pocket. "Are you certain you weren't followed?"

"Absolutely certain, Mr. Mahoney."

"What about the Bolshoi program?"

"It has been destroyed. No one suspects a thing."

"Last weekend you said you were under suspicion already."

Lukashin took off his hat and coat. "I was wrong. It was nothing more than a case of jumpy nerves." He spotted the food and liquor but made no move toward the table. "Is this apartment being monitored?"

"Would it matter if it was?"

"No," Lukashin said, sighing deeply. "Merely being here if I am caught is my death warrant. And yours, too, Mr. Mahoney. You cannot believe the secrecy on this operation."

Mahoney casually put his hand in his pocket and turned on the tape recorder. "We're together and it is safe, Ivan."

"No one is safe in Moscow."

"Would you like something to drink?"

"No," Lukashin said. "We cannot be too long together like this. It is too dangerous. I have come only to tell you that my department is planning on assassinating someone in America sometime this year."

"Who?"

"I don't know, Mr. Mahoney. I can only tell you that it will be someone important. Someone very important."

"A government official?"

"I don't know that either," Lukashin said. He stepped over to the window and carefully parted the edge of the curtain so that he could see down to the street. "It has to do with what has been happening in Cuba. Certain contacts were made in Mexico City with the Cuban consulate and one of our embassy officers."

"Why are you telling me this?"

Lukashin turned away from the window. There was a haunted, fearful look in his eyes. Mahoney didn't think he had been sleeping well. He could see it in the way the Russian held himself, as if he were afraid of collapsing.

"I love my country, Mr. Mahoney. I am what you would call a patriot. I want to survive."

"Adventurism," Mahoney said. Maintaining the status quo was everything to the Russian, that and saving face. One of the most heinous crimes for the high government official to be accused of was adventurism. Cowboy politics, they sometimes called it. Proposing or actually doing something that was outside the norm was forbidden; individual initiative that involved more than the individual in its effects was anathema.

"You know," Lukashin said.

Mahoney reached in his pocket and switched off the tape recorder. "It is Yuri Chernov who is planning this assassination?"

Lukashin nodded. "Yes," he said. "He is a madman."

"But a brilliant one."

They stood facing each other from across the room. "You know him?"

"I'll pass along a secret to you in return, Ivan. Yes, I know Chernov. In fact he is currently under investigation."

"For what?"

"We think he will become the director of the KGB one day."

Lukashin nodded. "Yes, this is possible. But it would be horrible. You cannot imagine how horrible. He has those old men in the Kremlin convinced that we could win a war. That we could survive an all-out nuclear exchange. We would use Europe as our battleground. We would not drop the bomb on your country and you would not drop it on ours. France and West Germany are your buffer zones, while Poland, Czechoslovakia, and Hungary are ours."

"I don't want his name mentioned again. Not to me, not to anyone else you might be asked to speak with."

Lukashin held up a hand as if to ward off a blow. "I will not speak to anyone else, Mr. Mahoney. Only you. And only this one time."

"It may be necessary—"

"No," Lukashin said, raising his voice.

"We'll see," Mahoney said sternly. "But I want your promise that Chernov's name will never be mentioned again."

"That doesn't matter. The time for stopping him is long past. He will survive no matter what. His kind always do. But this . . . this has to be stopped."

Mahoney switched on the tape recorder. "You mentioned certain contacts that were made with the Cubans and your own people in Mexico City. By whom, and what does this have to do with a supposed assassination?"

"Not supposed. Believe me, it will happen. It is only a matter of time. Unless you can stop it."

"Who contacted your people in Mexico City?"

"An American citizen."

"Who?"

"I don't know his real name, only his code name. He is known as A. J. Hidell. But he is married to a Soviet citizen. A girl from Minsk."

"Do you know her name?"

"Marina Nikolaevna Pruskova. She is very young. They were married two years ago."

"But you don't know his real name?"

"No, I haven't been able to see that file. Security is very rigid."

"He and his wife are in Mexico now?"

"I don't think so. By now they must be in the United States, getting ready . . ."

"Hidell is the assassin?"

"Yes."

"He has been trained? Here in Moscow?"

"No, no training, I think. I believe he was a U.S. Marine. But he is an amateur. If he is caught, there will be no real traces back to us."

"How about his wife? Is she a part of this? Is she KGB?"

"No. As far as I know, she is innocent. She is a very young girl. Perhaps twenty." Lukashin glanced at the window. It was clear that he was beginning to have second thoughts, and that he wanted to leave. "He is a crazy man, Mr. Mahoney. He wanted to become a Soviet citizen, but he was denied and was sent away."

"But it was he who contacted the Cuban consulate and one of your officers in Mexico City?"

"Yes."

"When was this, Ivan?"

"Just recently. Within the last month or so."

"Why did he contact the Cubans?"

"He wants help."

"It was his suggestion, this assassination?"

"I think so."

"And who exactly was it he spoke with?"

"The Cuban consul, Eusebio Azque, and with Valeriy Vladimirovich Kostikov, one of our consular staff."

"KGB?"

"Yes," Lukashin said, nodding.

"What did Hidell tell them? What exactly did he suggest?"

"He is very angry with your government, and with ours. He wants to return to the Soviet Union to live. He says he is a Marxist. But we will not allow him back."

"He first has to earn his way."

"Yes," Lukashin said.

"By assassinating someone."

"Someone very big."

"But he didn't say who."

"Yes, he did," Lukashin snapped. He was all strung out, and dangerous just now.

"But you don't know this name?"

"No."

Mahoney stared at the Russian for a few seconds, then turned and went to the table where he poured two vodkas. "Have a drink with me, Ivan."

"I must go now."

"Just one drink. I have only a few more questions."

"No more questions. It is too dangerous for me."

Mahoney turned around. "Then why the hell did you come here in the first place? You tell me this bullshit story and you expect me to believe it. You haven't given me one solid thing to go on. What am I supposed to tell my government? What do you want, Ivan? Do you want money? Do you want to go to the United States? It could be arranged."

"I don't want to go to the United States. I am not a traitor."

"Oh, but you are, Ivan. You yourself said that by coming here you have signed your own death warrant. Why?"

Lukashin stepped back a little as if by such a move he could somehow distance himself to what was happening. "I don't want another war. No one would win."

"A noble sentiment, Ivan. What makes you think a simple assassination would embroil us in a war? Assassinations occur all the time. Besides, you have told me that it can never be proved that the man you call Hidell could be connected to the KGB. And you told me that he was an amateur. A man like that couldn't possibly get close enough to assassinate anyone of such importance."

"In your country it could happen."

"You haven't been truthful with me, Ivan. There is something else that you are holding back."

"No, I swear . . ."

"Why, for instance, did you select me to approach?"

"You are a CIA officer and yet you seem to know something about us. I have watched you for months now. And you were available at the dacha."

Mahoney held up the drink. "Are you sure you don't want some?"

"No." Lukashin waved it off.

Mahoney set the glass back on the table. "Within ten months this assassination will take place."

"That is correct?"

"A very strange, very round number, Ivan. I would like to know how you came to such a figure."

Lukashin closed his eyes for a moment, and swayed on his feet. For a second Mahoney thought he was going to faint. But then he opened his eyes again and seemed to steady. "I have seen his termination order."

"Whose?"

"Hidell's."

"An order has been written out saying that Hidell is to be killed?"

Lukashin nodded.

"By whom? KGB?"

"Another American."

"And who is this other American?"

"I don't know the name. I only know the reason he will do it, which is also why I know that the first assassination must be stopped."

"Tell me," Mahoney said softly.

"Hidell's target is so important that his fellow American will kill him out of patriotic necessity."

Mahoney was totally perplexed. For the very first time in his career he simply did not know what to think. Either it was an incredibly involved story to somehow engineer his downfall, or the plot was incredibly sloppy. The KGB had made mistakes before, but this was bound to backfire. And if what Lukashin had told him were true, and if the plot indeed did backfire, there could very well be massive repercussions against the Russians. Not war as Lukashin feared, but disastrous for the KGB.

"I don't believe you," Mahoney said.

"You must," Lukashin said with much feeling.

"Nor will my government believe it. We will need more information. The actual name of the assassin, for instance, as well as his intended target."

"Impossible."

"Not only possible, Ivan, but necessary. You must understand my position."

"No," Lukashin said with finality. He grabbed his hat and coat. "Already I have told you far too much. It was a waste of time."

"Not if you will help us," Mahoney said.

The Russian went to the door.

"Come to the ballet when you have more. We'll arrange another meeting. But there must be more before we can do anything."

Lukashin hesitated a moment, then yanked open the door and left. Mahoney could hear him go down the stairs and out the front door. He shut off the tape recorder and at the window watched the Russian disappear up the street. He shivered. With Chernov, he thought, anything was possible. Anything at all.

It was after two in the morning. They'd listened to the tape recording all the way through four times, parts of it several times more. Jacobson, the chargé d'affaires, was with them in the screened room. "What do you make of it?" he asked.

Frisque looked up, and shook his head. "Beats me," he said. "Wallace?"

"We can't ignore it."

"No. But it's not a lot to go on."

"Will he come back with more?" Jacobson asked. He'd been included in the meeting at Frisque's suggestion because the ambassador would have to be told something. He was a brighter than average career diplomat. He and Frisque went way back together.

"I don't know," Mahoney said. "But if he's under any kind of suspicion, it would be dangerous to approach him."

Frisque sat forward suddenly. "Under no circumstances will you approach him! I want that clear."

"He might try me again."

"If it happens we'll just see, but until then you're going to keep a very low profile, except with Shalayev and his crowd. Langley is happy with the computer business. They want more."

"What about this business?" Mahoney asked, indicating the tape recorder.

"He's given us a couple of names, and the time line," Frisque said. "If this Hidell is scheduled for elimination in ten months, it means his little project won't happen until then. That puts it around November or December. If he actually succeeds in assassinating someone, they're not going to leave him running around loose for very long. I'll transmit everything to Langley and they can get the FBI in on it. If there's anything there, we just might get lucky."

"One thing puzzles me," Jacobson said. "You stopped the tape in the beginning of your conversation with Lukashin. Why, and what did we miss?"

"I had my hand in my pocket and hit the button by mistake," Mahoney lied, careful to keep his tone as light as possible. Once again he felt almost physically ill. "The only thing I missed was him telling me he didn't want to talk to anyone else. That it was too dangerous for him."

Jacobson seemed a little skeptical, but Frisque bought it.

"Go home and get some sleep, Wallace," the COS said. "In the morning you can write out your report for inclusion in the overnight bag. But you're going to have to go to the ballet as usual. It's going to be important for the next few weeks for you to maintain your normal routine."

"Sure," Mahoney said.

Sitting across the table from Chernov in the Grunewald Hotel bar, a great tiredness had come over Mahoney. The entire day had been a waste. He'd spent most of it alone with his own morose thoughts. At lunch and again at dinner Chernov had been uncommunicative. "A little more time," he'd said. "And then what I will tell you will make sense. Proof is what you always wanted—you were hardheaded about that from the very beginning—and proof is what I'm going to give you." It was late and he wanted to go back to Minnesota to his own bed, to rest, to tend to his wounds, and most of all to begin the long process of finally forgetting a lifetime of lies, of deceit and missed opportunities. The hate that had flared so brightly when Chernov had telephoned him from Helsinki and again when he had laid eyes on the Russian forty-eight hours ago had threatened to fade and dissipate. He hadn't been able to pull the trigger on the first night, and he was no closer now in his resolve, despite the painful memories that had tumbled one over the other out of the recesses of his mind. In a measure it was a sign of his aging, he thought. He had trouble remembering what the weather was like just last week, and yet he was able to remember in remarkable detail events that had happened to him four and five decades ago.

To what purpose, this summing up? he wondered. To what purpose his final meeting with the only man on this earth whom he had ever truly hated and feared?

Lukashin never made contact again. His name did come up a few months later during an end-of-season reception for the Bolshoi's last production of the year. "Poor Ivan Sergeivich," someone had said, and Mahoney's ears had perked up. He and Marge were seated next to Shalayev and his wife at the Arbat. It was very late and most of the Russians were drunk.

"Who's that?" Mahoney asked, leaning over toward Shalayev.

"Lukashin," the economic minister said. "You met him once at the dacha."

There was too much noise, so Marge had not caught the reference to the weekend. "The short one?" Mahoney asked, feigning ignorance.

"No, big and tall. Young. It is a shame."

"In what way?"

"Why, he's dead, hadn't you heard?" Shalayev said. "A heart attack. He just keeled over at his desk and there wasn't a thing they could do for him. Too bad, he left a wife and three children."

"Yes," Mahoney had mumbled. "Too bad."

The next morning when he had reported it to Frisque, the COS wasn't particularly impressed. "It happens all the time. He was under a lot of stress."

"It could be significant," Mahoney said.

"I don't think so. They'd simply have arrested him, and they most certainly would have come after you."

But Mahoney hadn't been convinced then, and he wasn't convinced now. But of course now he had the advantage of hindsight.

Moscow like any other big city had its season, and summer was definitely a time of slowdowns. In the fall he had picked up where he had left off with the ballet, making a few new contacts, and continuing to work Shalayev for computer information. By then they had been at their posting for a year, and Marge's initial restlessness had given way to a good-natured resignation. "As long as we're together, I don't really care where we are," she said. Though she would admit to being more fond of their posting in Vienna than here in Moscow, the city was interesting.

Mahoney remembered November 22 of that year. It was a Friday. He and Marge had decided to stay home for the evening. Around ten, just as the television news was beginning, he went into the kitchen to fix himself a drink.

"Oh, no!" Marge cried from the living room. "Oh, my God!"

With his heart in his throat Mahoney rushed into the living room. Her face was white, tears were streaming down her cheeks as she stared at the stern-faced news reader. It took several moments for Mahoney to realize what the man was saying, and he sat down, his legs suddenly too weak to support his body. President Kennedy had been assassinated in Dallas, Texas.

He remembered the telephone ringing. It was Frisque calling him to the embassy. "Better pack a bag, Wallace," the COS said, his voice choked with emotion. "Bring Marge along too. It might be better if you two stayed here at least for tonight."

Marge, numb with shock, let him pack for her and lead her downstairs where the embassy car had already shown up. "Why?" she kept asking. "Why would they do such a thing, Wallace?"

Ten months, Lukashin had told him. Somebody very important would be assassinated. He'd seen the FBI report of their investigation into Hidell, which was an alias for Oswald. They thought he might be a Russian spy, not an assassin.

The embassy was on emergency footing. The ambassador was on the secure line to Washington, and not one of their Russian contract personnel was being allowed through the front door. Everyone was in shock, he remembered. Though everyone was working at a frantic pace in an effort to figure out what this meant in terms of America's relationship with the Soviet Union, Mahoney also remembered that the next eighteen hours had seemed to pass as if in a dream.

"Another cognac?" Chernov asked, smiling.

Mahoney focused on him across the table. He nodded. Chernov had had the same grim smile twenty-five years ago. Mahoney had come out of the embassy at two in the afternoon to return home for a few things that Marge needed. Chernov was seated in a Zhiguli with KGB plates directly across from the embassy. Mahoney caught only a glimpse of his face in the back window as he passed. But the man had been smiling. He had won after all.

11

It was after ten when John woke up slumped in the chair next to the telephone. He had no recollection of falling asleep. He had been telephoning hotels without results and had simply drifted off. His back and neck were stiff and his mouth was foul from too many cigarettes. He got up and stretched. The city outside his window had come alive. Even from his room he could hear the noise of traffic along the busy Ku'Damm. Berlin like any large city never really slept, and like most large cities the evening activities seemed concentrated in one major area. In Tokyo it was the Ginza, in London it was Soho, and late at night in New York it was Times Square. Here in West Berlin it was the Kürfurstendamm, a broad boulevard of nightclubs, restaurants, sex shops, and private clubs. He stood at the window for a long time looking down at the street and the glow of the city. From here he could not see the wall, but like everyone else who came to Berlin, he was conscious of its presence out there in the darkness. Conscious of the vast differences in life on this side versus in the East. You couldn't come to Berlin without feeling it.

His father and Chernov were out there somewhere. He could feel their presence as well. Tonia Trusov was looking for them. And someone else was too. Who? Who had followed him around Washington? Who had killed poor Stan Kopinski? The Russians as he had believed, or some faction within the CIA as Tonia Trusov had suggested? In the bathroom he splashed some water on his face, straightened his tie, and looked at his haggard reflection in the mirror. He had come too many miles, he thought. More than any man should have to travel. His father had told him a few years ago that the very best men in this business burned out early, or simply quit before it was too late for them. "There comes a point at which we are ruined for anything else, though," he'd said. "This business is de-civilizing. And when that is stripped away from us, what do we have left? Perhaps only a primal instinct for

199

survival in which we lash out at anything in our path—friend or foe." Had he come that far already? He supposed he had.

Before he left his room he checked his gun, cycling a live round into the firing chamber and making sure the safety catch was in the on position before he holstered it at the small of his back. He pulled on his coat and took the elevator downstairs.

To trust or not to trust. It had been his problem from the time of his earliest memories when his father was disappearing sometimes for months on end. From an age when he began to question those disappearances, and the little things his father was saying—or not saying—to his family by way of explanation. The late-night telephone calls and messages, the strange people just at the fringes of their lives. And finally the murders of his wife and children. How much could a man possibly endure before he lashed out blindly, as he had been doing for the past five years? How long before he completely fell apart?

He headed up to the Ku'Damm past the Schiller Theater. Whatever had been playing was just letting out, the street choked with traffic for the moment. He stopped to look in the window of a bookstore, the crowd surging past on the wide sidewalk, so that anyone following would not lose him. The afternoon's snowstorm had not abated, and by now many of the side streets had become nearly impassable, funneling most of the traffic along the main arteries. The Ku'Damm was filled with people in a gay, holiday mood. He walked to the end of the block, then crossed with the light to the other side past the Kömodie Theater ablaze with lights, but not yet let out from its evening show. Reaching yet another corner, he crossed again to the other side where a long line had formed at the door of a nightclub. No one seemed to mind the wait in the cold and snow. There was a lot of good-natured joking back and forth. In the middle of the next block he suddenly stepped out into the street and looked back the way he had come, scanning the faces and the cars, obviously looking for someone or something. A taxi came up the street and he motioned for it, telling the driver the Ballhaus Resi when he climbed in the back seat. It was impossible to isolate a face or a car on a single sweep, but in these matters he had patience. Someone was behind him, he knew it, just as he had known it in Washington. Only this time he was prepared to do something. At the nightclub he hesitated outside for a couple of minutes as if he were deciding whether or not he should go inside. The traffic here was much lighter than on the Ku'Damm, but still sufficiently thick to conceal a good legman. He didn't notice anyone from before and he finally went inside

200

where he paid his cover charge and was shown to a small table well back to the left of the stage. The club was mostly filled, a dense pall of smoke hanging from the high ceilings. A band was onstage playing American and British rock tunes. The dance floor was packed.

"Is the manager here this evening?" John asked the waiter.

"Yes, of course," the waiter said.

"Could you tell me his name, and how I might reach him?" John asked, laying down a hundred-mark bill.

"He is Herr Allmann," the waiter said, scooping up the money. "If you have a special request of him, merely pick up your telephone and dial 'one.' "

On the dance floor a couple fell down and the other dancers laughed and helped them to their feet. They were quite drunk. John picked up his telephone and dialed. A woman with a soft, sensuous voice answered. "Good evening, may we be of service?"

"I would like to speak with Herr Allmann if that is possible," John said.

"May I inquire as to the nature of your request?" the woman asked.

"It is something very personal for which I would be willing to pay well."

"Of course, mein Herr. A young woman will come to your table in a few moments. Just go with her."

Wilhelm Allmann's office suite was on the second floor at the rear of the club. In the anteroom John was expertly searched by two young men who relieved him of his gun. "It will be returned to you, mein Herr, the moment you leave the establishment," one of them said politely. Allmann turned out to be a youngish-looking man with thick horn-rimmed glasses and a precisely tailored three-piece dark business suit. Except for his shirt and tie, which were obviously silk, he could have been an accountant. His office was small and unpretentious, though expensively furnished.

"How may I be of service?" he asked, motioning John to a chair across from his desk.

"I was hoping you would be much older," John said.

Allmann's left eyebrow rose slightly. "I am sorry to disappoint."

"I am looking for two men who met here just after the war, and who may again be in the city."

"Are you a policeman?"

"No."

201

"But you are trying to find these two gentlemen who met in this club some forty years ago?" He smiled.

"Perhaps it is a wild-goose chase."

"It is important, your finding these two gentlemen?"

"Of extreme importance. I would pay well for any help you may be able to provide me."

"Yes," Allmann said. "But why have you come to me? Why haven't you simply gone to the police with your request? They are very efficient and Berlin is not such a big city."

"The matter is delicate. The police would not understand," John said.

Allmann sat back in his leather-upholstered chair and looked at John through tented fingers. "But you wished that I was older. Much older so that I would personally remember these gentlemen from the past. Their meeting then was of some significance. Is either of them a former German military officer? Perhaps wanted for some crimes real or imagined?"

"No," John said. "In fact one of them is an American."

"And the other?"

"I must ask first if you are in a position to help me."

"I cannot say that, mein Herr, but I can give you my assurances that our conversation will remain confidential no matter the outcome."

"Fair enough," John said. "The second man is a Russian. A former officer of the KGB."

If Allmann was impressed he didn't show it. "You believe it is possible that they will come back here, for old times' sake, shall we say?"

"It's possible."

"Do you have photographs of these gentlemen?"

"Unfortunately not. But I can pass on to you the names under which they are traveling, and of course their descriptions. But I must stress your discretion, Herr Allmann."

"Of course," Allmann said thoughtfully. He was an accountant, after all. He was weighing the costs and the profit potential of such an operation. John could see it in his eyes.

"They may not come here, however. In fact they may be anywhere in the city at this moment, though it is likely they will not remain for long. Perhaps a day or two at the most."

"I see," Allmann said. He glanced toward the door. "You came here armed. Are these two gentlemen dangerous?"

"They are very old."

Allmann waited patiently.

"But, yes, they must be considered dangerous. Your job would be simply to locate them, if at all possible without their knowledge. Certainly under no circumstances would I want them to be approached, or in any way interfered with should they be on the move."

"Where could you be reached should we meet with success?"

"I would keep in contact on a regular basis."

"Not here at the club. In truth it would be for the best if you were never to return here." Allmann smiled. "That is, of course, if we agree to work together."

John nodded.

"I would provide you with a telephone number."

"I understand," John said. "There is another aspect of this business that your associates would have to understand. At present these two men are being sought by the American authorities as well as by the Soviets."

"But not by the West Berlin police or the BND?"

"No," John said. "The search is very intense, but very quiet."

"Have there been any, shall we say, injuries to date?"

"Not in West Berlin," John said.

"But elsewhere?"

"In the United States."

"I see," Allmann said.

"Speed and stealth are important at this point," John said. "Not muscle."

"May I be permitted to ask your interest in finding these two gentlemen?"

"You may not," John said.

"Or your employer?"

"No."

Allmann nodded sagely. "But you are permitted to pay well, and in a timely fashion?"

"Well, but within reason."

"One hundred thousand marks," Allmann said. It was around fifty thousand dollars. "In advance."

"Fifty thousand marks in advance," John said. "The remainder to be paid providing certain conditions were met."

"And what would these conditions be?"

"First, of course, that you locate them. Let's say within thirty-six hours."

"If we didn't?"

"You would keep the initial payment for work already com-

203

pleted. Any continuation of our contract would have to be renegotiated."

"Agreed," Allmann said. "And?"

"That neither of them be harmed in any way. And most importantly that your efforts are conducted in complete secrecy. From the German authorities, naturally, but from American and Soviet intelligence officers now searching."

Allmann thought about that for several seconds. "This last condition would be the most difficult to meet without your help. Are you in a position to supply us with information on exactly what the . . . shall we call them the opposition . . . is doing?"

"Yes."

Again Allmann considered the proposition.

Finally he nodded. "I will give you an account number with a certain bank in Bern, to which funds can be telexed twenty-four hours a day. As soon as I receive confirmation of deposit, we will begin."

"Begin immediately. I will personally guarantee that the funds will be deposited within a few hours."

"You will guarantee this with what?"

"With my life," John said.

Allmann smiled and permitted himself a chuckle. "Your life is worth nothing to me, if you will pardon me saying so. But I will begin and continue for three hours at which time we will switch the object of our search to you."

"All right."

"Now, I will need some details."

It was the same hour in East Berlin. Tonia Trusov, bundled up in a fashionable silver fox coat and matching hat, sat behind the wheel of a light gray Ford Cortina one hundred yards from Checkpoint Charlie. The automobile's headlights were out, but the car's engine was ticking over slowly, the heater keeping the inside reasonably warm. The car had West Berlin plates, and in her purse she carried the identification of Marlene Hoffburg, a dietitian from Munich. She had watched the steadily diminishing traffic crossing the border into West Berlin for the last half hour. No one had come East in that time. Soon, she thought. She felt no fear, of course, only anticipation for the hunt.

Ivan Raina, the foolish military attaché, had come to her room again earlier in the evening with a list of postwar meeting places she had requested he dig up for her. "There were several dozen in what is now the western zone," he said. "I've narrowed the list down to twenty-three places where your uncle might have met with Mahoney. Of course there can be no guarantees that my list is complete, or that some of these places even exist today."

"I understand," Tonia had said, taking the file folder from him. She had changed from her uniform into an obviously expensive Western European skirt and blouse and patterned black nylons. She'd done up her hair in the back exposing her ears and long, delicately formed neck. She had turned away from the door expecting him to leave, but he grabbed her from behind and drew her close.

For an instant she resisted, but then she forced her body to relax, and she turned to him with a smile.

"They want to stop you, Balachov and that old woman Drankov," Raina whispered huskily. "They know that you are going over to the West tonight after John Mahoney. I can cover for you."

"I appreciate your concern, Ivan, believe me," she said. "But it is not necessary. I am a big girl. I can take care of myself."

"You don't know them as I do," Raina said. "They are jealous of you."

She reached down with her right hand and brushed his penis through the material of his trousers. He reared back, startled for just a moment, but then a big smile spread over his face.

"Tonia," he said.

She grabbed his testicles and squeezed. He rose up on his tiptoes, his face flushing, a thin squeal coming from his throat.

"If you ever lay your hands on me again, Comrade Colonel, I will kill you."

Raina's eyes were wide. He was trying to pull her hand away, but she was too strong. She squeezed harder.

"Do you understand?"

"Da! Da!" Raina squeaked.

"For your sake I hope so," she said, releasing him and stepping back. She kept a long, thin-bladed knife strapped to her chest beneath her breasts. If need be, she thought, she would kill him here and now. There would be a fuss, of course, but the old men in the Kremlin were more interested in her search for her uncle than they were in some lieutenant colonel military attaché. In any event she would be justified.

"I only wanted to be your friend," Raina said, looking at her as if she were some wild animal.

"I have no friends," she said. "Remember that—it may save your life."

There was no time for friends in this business, she thought, watching how the falling snow formed halos around the lights atop the Brandenburg Gate. "Something is missing from you, Tonia," her uncle Yuri told her once. "For your sake I hope you find it someday before it is too late." Curious, she thought, for such a man to say something like that. But by then he was old and somewhat maudlin. In her own way she had loved him, she supposed. But she loved the other thing more, she thought, her grip tightening on the steering wheel. There was no room in her heart for friends, or loves. Not now, perhaps never.

A Mercedes sedan with West Berlin diplomatic plates came down the Friedrichstrasse and stopped at the checkpoint. Two border guards came out to meet it. Tonia flipped on her headlights, pulled out from the shadows onto the broad boulevard, and approached the gate, stopping just behind the Mercedes. She cranked down her window and got her passport and East Berlin entry permit that showed she had come through a few minutes before noon that morning.

One of the guards came back. He was very young. His uniform made him seem like a toy soldier, but the AK-47 strapped to his shoulder was real enough. She handed him her papers.

"*Guten Abend*," she said, smiling sweetly. She had let the bottom of her coat fall open. Her skirt had hiked up a little, and the young guard was ogling her legs.

"The purpose of your visit to the DDR?" the young soldier asked.

"I had business at the Palast Hotel," she said. She'd thought it better that she maintain the fiction on this side of the border as well as on the other, in case they were watching closely from the western zone. She spread her legs a little, giving him a better view. "I am a dietitian."

"Ah, yes, Fräulein, I understand," the boy said, handing back her papers. The Mercedes had gone ahead and was on the other side.

"*Danke*," Tonia said, laying her papers on the seat beside her. She followed the Mercedes through the barrier into the western zone. A young American MP checked her papers, his eyes on her legs too. She smiled. They were all the same, East or West. Young or old. They thought through their balls. She held up her left hand on which she wore a plain gold wedding band. The MP smiled. "Too bad," he said good-naturedly. He handed back her papers, stepped away from the car, and waved her on. Driving away she looked up into her rearview mirror. The young MP was staring after her.

She turned left into Potsdamer Platz and joined the thick traffic past the Philharmonic Hall and National Gallery to the Tiergarten where she found a parking spot and doused her lights. Of the places on Raina's list, most had been hotels or inns in the days during and immediately after the war. A few had been private residences. There were no guarantees, as he had said, that his list was complete, or that some of those places even existed any longer. There had been a lot of tearing down and rebuilding in the intervening forty years. But John Mahoney had thought it was a very real possibility that the two old fools had come back to Berlin to wherever it was they had met just after the war. For old times' sake. Something old men were likely to do.

Making certain that no one was watching her, and that there were no police cruising by, she bent down and reached up under the dashboard. She had taped her gun to one of the heater ducts. Pulling the tape loose she yanked it out, cycled a round into the chamber, and then pocketed the gun. It was a German-made 9mm SigSauer. It was large, but she liked the automatic because it was reliable and it held fifteen rounds. An advantage at times.

She pulled out into traffic again, circling the park on Budapest Strasse and then turning down the Ku'Damm, traffic even more dense here. Three blocks later she turned down Bleibtreustrasse and slowly drove past the Bremen Hotel. A snowplow had just passed and the street was clear but slippery. John Mahoney was still the major unknown in the equation. He had been sent here to search for his father, just as she had been sent to search for her uncle. But her orders had been specific. If they had already met and talked, they both were to be killed. It was a testament to her abilities and to her loyalties to the state that they had sent her on such a mission with such orders. They knew that she would do exactly as she was told. With flair and dispatch. "It is a very bad thing, Tonia, to send you after your uncle like this," Kryuchkov, the director of the KGB, had told her personally. Unlike Andropov, he was a young man who knew and understood the realities of the Western world. "But what he is doing to us is even worse. My heart grieves for him, as well as for you."

"I understand," Tonia had told him at their secret meeting before she left Moscow.

He touched her cheek and shook his leonine head sadly. "If there were any other way, anyone else to send, it would be so. Believe me."

"He is a traitor."

"Yes."

"Then I will kill him. It must be so, as you have said. But it will make me sad."

"I hope so, Tonia. I truly hope so."

What were John Mahoney's orders? Killing an uncle was something completely different from killing one's own father. She suspected he had come looking for them so he could take them back to the States. But she didn't know, yet.

A block and a half beyond the Bremen she found the parking garage where John Mahoney had kept the Volkswagen sedan he had rented. She had expected it would be gone, but she found it on the third level, and parked three cars away from it.

Slinging her overnight bag over her shoulder, she walked back to John's car and looked inside. There was nothing in the passenger compartment. At the trunk, she took a thin, case-hardened steel needle from her purse and in a few seconds had picked the lock and opened the trunk lid. But he had left nothing there either. He was a careful man. An enigma she was going to have to figure out if she was going to be successful in her search. Relocking the trunk she turned and made her way back down to the street, and then to the Bremen where she booked a room for two nights on the same floor as John's.

The hunt, she thought, was about to begin.

There were two of them. John had picked up the tail when he left the Ballhaus Resi and started on foot back toward the Ku'Damm. One of them wore a green felt hat and an old military parka, and the other one wore a fur cap and a sheepskin leather coat. They were good. He only spotted them from time to time across the street, sometimes one of them ahead of him and one of them behind. But always they were there. If he could not see them at every moment, he could feel their presence.

He stepped into a telephone booth near the Tourist Information Bureau on Kant Strasse and dialed the consulate. Bixby was in a meeting and it took a full three minutes for him to come to the telephone. Sheepskin Coat was across the street in the doorway of a boutique. Military Parka was nowhere to be seen, but he was nearby, John was certain of it.

"Anything from Hannover yet?" John asked when Bixby was finally on.

"They are checked into the Inter-Continental Hotel," the chief of station said excitedly. "Their passports are still at the desk."

"Are they in their rooms?"

"We don't think so. I called Farley, and he told me to wait for you."

"I may be a while," John said, looking across the busy street at the boutique. He couldn't see Sheepskin Coat, but he supposed the man was still there in the shadows. "Keep a watch on the hotel, but under no circumstances approach them when they show up."

"They might have skipped out," Bixby said. "It could have been a false track."

"We won't know that unless your people keep a sharp lookout there. In the meantime something else has come up. I'm going to need some money, a lot of it within the next couple of hours. You're going to need authorization. Get it from Farley or from Alex, but get it."

"How much?" Bixby asked guardedly.

"Fifty thousand West German marks."

Bixby whistled.

"It is to be wire-transferred to an account at the Crédit Suisse bank in Bern." John gave him the account number. "I'll telephone you in a couple of hours for the confirmation."

"Who is the money for?"

"I can't tell you on an open line, Tom. Just make sure it gets there within the next couple of hours. I don't want any screw-ups."

"Farley is going to have to have more than that before he'll authorize—"

"Just do it!" John snapped. "He'll okay it."

"What the hell are you up to?" Bixby demanded.

"Tell him that I've hired some help."

"Here? In Berlin?"

"That's right."

"Jesus," Bixby said. "You're out of your goddamned mind."

"Just do it," John said. He caught a slight movement from the boutique's doorway. Sheepskin Coat was getting impatient. "Have you got anything else for me? Did Alex call yet with the list?"

"Does the name Bernhard Heiser mean anything to you?"

John's heart skipped a beat. "Yes?" he said cautiously.

"I thought so," Bixby said. "He and his housekeeper were found shot to death. It's on the FRG wire, and Interpol will have it within the hour. They've got a description of a man who was there at the house. Your description."

"Head them off, Tom. I was here in Berlin, you know that."

John's mind was racing ahead to a dozen possibilities, foremost among them that someone had followed him from Washington. Evidently, someone had known he had gone through Ramstein and had followed him to Heiser's home in Bonn. The connection, or at least one connection, led back to Washington. For the first time since he had taken this assignment he was truly frightened. He had no idea where it was leading. Or what he could do to prevent the entire operation from falling to pieces.

"I'll do what I can, but you'd damn well better keep a low profile."

"Have they got my name?"

"No. Is that a possibility?"

"If they saw my car, they might get it from the rental agency where I turned it in, in Cologne."

"Did you fly out of there?"

"Yes. When were they killed?"

"Just a few hours ago. A friend discovered their bodies."

"Then my alibi is my flight out of Cologne. But I don't want some cop gunning for me. You're going to have to take care of it."

"I'll do my best."

"See that you do," John said, and he hung up. He waited for a moment, his eyes on the boutique doorway, then dialed the number that Allmann had given him. It was answered on the first ring by a man.

"*Ja.*"

"Do you know who this is?" John asked.

"Yes."

"A man named Bernhard Heiser was shot to death in Bonn a few hours ago. The police may think I was involved, but I was not. However, he did supply me with information pointing me here to Berlin. Whoever killed him will probably be coming here as well. Tell your people to be careful."

"I understand. Is there anything else?"

"I'm being followed at the moment. But I will take care of it."

"Who is following you?"

"I don't know yet. I'll keep you informed. As to your money, it will be telexed in the time specified."

"Anything else?"

"Not for now."

"We have something for you. The gentlemen you seek were spotted leaving Berlin by air yesterday."

"I know this. They are back here in Berlin."

"Hannover is a false lead?"

"Yes, it is. Tell your people to concentrate their efforts here. I may have more information for you later this evening."

"Very good," the man said and broke the connection.

John hung up the telephone, and turning sideways so that his movements were shielded from Sheepskin Coat across the street, he took out his Beretta and transferred it to his coat pocket. He stepped out of the telephone booth, hesitated for just a second or two, and then headed past the post office up toward the Tiergarten a dozen blocks away. It was time now to find out just who the hell was following him, and put a stop to it.

Farley Carlisle left his table at the fashionable Rive Gauche restaurant on M Street in Georgetown to make a telephone call from the pay phone near the men's room. It was six-thirty and he had been drinking steadily since just after five. He was going to have to slow down, he thought. He was going to need his wits about him. Everything they had worked for, for so long, was now threatening to blow up in their faces. The fallout, if it actually happened, would be devastating.

"He's asked for fifty thousand marks to be deposited in a blind Swiss account."

"How did you find this out?" Carlisle asked sharply.

"The usual sources. Our Bern people are checking on it now. We should have the account holder's name or names within the hour."

"I'll have to authorize it, of course."

"Under the circumstances there's nothing else you can do."

"If this falls apart, it will be the end for us. You know that," Carlisle said.

"For all of us, yes. I understood that from day one. You're going to have to hold yourself together. It shouldn't be long now."

"I hope not. I hope to God you're right." Carlisle glanced over his shoulder toward the dining room where his wife was waiting for him at their table. "What about Heiser? Christ, if that gets out . . ."

"I feel just as badly about it as you do. It was a mistake, plain and simple. An error in judgment."

"But we have the journal?"

"Yes, and it's as bad as we suspected."

Carlisle did not think it had been an error in judgment. He suspected that the operative had been working under very specific orders. He didn't know which frightened him more: Heiser's murder, the old man's journal, or John Mahoney.

211

"Have we identified the two men in the boat?"

"Contract assassins. Cubans."

"Working for the opposition?"

"Just as we suspected."

"Where will it end?" Carlisle sighed.

"When we have the proof we need, and not before. It won't be long now."

The perimeter of the Tiergarten glowed with lights, but within the park the night was dark and secretive in the heavily falling snow. Sheepskin Coat had followed John from the boutique all the way to the park, but the man in the military parka had either given up or he was so good that John never spotted him. To the east the park was cut by the busy Potsdamer Strasse just beyond which was the brightly lit wall. Paths led in all directions through the trees. In the summer this place would be alive with people strolling, with lovers hand in hand. Now it was deserted. A distant, dangerous world.

Why had Heiser been killed? The timing made no sense to him. If someone had wanted to prevent the meeting, if someone was worried that the old man would have some information for him, then why hadn't he been killed beforehand? Unless Heiser had had more information. Something written down, perhaps. Something he had not told John. It would have had to have been very important for it to have cost him his life.

He waited in the trees across from the English Garden after he had circled back from Holfläger Strasse. Sheepskin Coat would have to cross the open space to come after him. A car horn tooted on the busy street off to the east, and in the distance he could hear an ambulance siren. Something moved at the far side of the garden.

John pulled out his gun and eased a little farther into the shadows off the path. Sheepskin Coat appeared at the head of the path across the way. He hesitated for several seconds, obviously searching the dark woods in which John was hidden. He would be weighing his decisions now. If he remained where he was or circled around the open space of the garden, it would be likely he'd lose his quarry. But if he crossed the garden he would be exposed the entire way.

Sheepskin Coat stepped out of the woods and hurried across the garden. John flipped the Beretta's safety off. It bothered him that he had not spotted the other one. Between the two of them, if they were as good as he thought they were, they could have effectively boxed him in here. Careful to make absolutely no noise he looked over his shoulder, but there was nothing to be seen in the dark, snow-shrouded woods. Sheepskin Coat reached the near edge of the garden and stopped again. John could suddenly smell his cologne. He was a large man, his form made even bulkier by the heavy coat. If he was armed he wasn't carrying his gun in his hand. Apparently he didn't believe he was in any real danger. He was being circumspect only to avoid detection.

The man stepped onto the path, and as he drew past, John stepped out from behind the tree and raised his gun.

"That's far enough," John said softly.

The man spun around, nearly losing his balance on the slippery path. He opened his mouth to say something, but then shook his head.

"Who are you?" John asked, stepping out of the woods and onto the path, but keeping a respectful distance.

Sheepskin Coat said nothing. He just watched John.

"Wer sind Sie?" John demanded, switching to German. "Why are you following me?"

"Pardon me, sir, but I am merely out for a walk," the man said. His German was terrible. It was not his native language.

"You're an American," John said. "Let's see your identification."

"I will call the police," Sheepskin Coat said in German.

"Then I will shoot you!" John snapped in English, raising the Beretta a little higher. "Your identification! Now!"

Sheepskin Coat stepped back a pace, and an instant later someone fired a shot from farther up the path, the bullet ricocheting off a stone fountain in the English Garden. John spun left, back into the protection of the trees, as Sheepskin Coat started to sprint away.

"Stop!" John shouted.

A second shot was fired from somewhere down the path as John rolled over on his stomach and snapped off a single shot toward the retreating figure. Sheepskin Coat stumbled and fell forward on his face. His body twitched once and then was still.

John scrambled farther into the woods, and then keeping low made his way back, parallel to the path, where he figured the shots had been fired. But there was no one.

The shots would have been muffled by the woods and by the falling snow. Unless someone else had been in the park, he didn't think anyone would have heard them.

He waited in the woods for a full ten minutes, moving from spot

213

to spot all the way back to Holfläger Strasse, without spotting anyone. It had been the one in the army parka, of course. But he had run off rather than continue the confrontation. They had wanted only to follow him, not interfere with him.

Hurrying back along the path to the man he had shot, he was conscious of the danger of being caught here like this. If the shots had been heard, and if the West Berlin police arrested him, the entire operation would fall apart. He did not suspect he would survive his custody. They would have him killed; he was convinced of it.

Pocketing his gun, he pulled the body off the path and, twenty yards into the woods, turned it over. His single shot had caught the man in the back of the neck, blowing away most of the front of his throat. John opened his jacket, pulled out his wallet, and opened it. "Christ," he muttered. His name was Stewart Turner. His home address was somewhere in Alexandria, Virginia. He was, or had been, CIA.

"Christ," John said again, rising. He pocketed Turner's wallet. What the hell was the Agency doing following him around? More importantly, why had the other one taken a shot at him? What the hell was Farley trying to prove? If, that is, they were here at Farley's orders. It made him think about Bernhard Heiser.

12

The Grunewald Hotel was like an ancient sentry in the German woods: it seemed to be timeless. It had always been and it would always be, despite the men who came here for a while and then left as all men do. More lights were showing in the upstairs rooms now. Several more guests had shown up this afternoon and evening, among them a jolly couple from Schwäbisch Hall, who called to each other in the corridor in the German equivalent of baby talk, and a taciturn old man who nevertheless told them that he had served as a drummer boy in the first war and a top sergeant in the second. The snow, which had fallen all day, hung in great lumps on the tree branches. Standing outside, Mahoney could hear when the slight wind would rustle a branch, sending a heavy clod falling to the ground with a dull plop. The distant city glow was lost to the storm. He felt as if he were in a cocoon, warm and safe, almost as if he had finally gotten back to the womb. You're getting maudlin, old man, Marge would say. And it was finally true. In the going back over old wounds, he had become sentimental, though not in the positive sense of the word.

He looked at the glowing end of his cigar, hunched up his coat collar against the cold, and at that moment, acutely aware of just how tragic a figure he cut, he trudged through the snow toward the lake.

If Moscow was Mahoney's most fervent dream, Berlin was his most difficult reality. It had been in Germany where his career had had its real beginnings. It had been in Berlin where he had first met Chernov, and it had been in Berlin where he had finally come to understand the Russians. It also had been in Berlin where he had his very last chance in which to win his struggle with Chernov. The year was 1971; Moscow was like a distant bad dream left far behind him. They'd returned to Austria, had spent eighteen fretful months in Santiago, Chile, a year in Mexico City, two in Athens, and the past year back in Washington, so they were

215

ready for a change, and they weren't too upset about being sent back to Berlin. The wall was a ten-year-old established fact of life. Vietnam was grinding to its unsatisfactory conclusion, and the U.S. was in turmoil with demonstrations, one after the other. Stop the war. Ban the bomb. Close even the nuclear electrical generating plants. Berlin was different. Life there seemed somehow more important, less idealistic. "The exigencies of the situation." It was the favorite bon mot that season to explain America's continued presence as a force not only in West Berlin but in the entire FRG and in fact all of Western Europe. Sylvan Bindrich as DDO had explained himself: "The minute we pull out, you know and I know—and so does the average German know—that Soviet tanks will be rolling across the border. It's a simple fact of life."

World War III, if and when it came, would begin there.

"The German military is tops, absolutely first class. But it would be like sending a gnat armed with a machine gun up against an elephant brigade. It might cause a momentary irritation, but not much more."

The Mahoneys were going over as deputy undersecretary of state and his wife. They were to work liaison between the British and French consulates in Berlin, to keep the Germans in Bonn happy, and the Russians in the eastern sector at bay. His real job, this time, was to establish and operate an agent network in the eastern zone. Washington had gotten word that the DDR was installing Soviet medium-range nuclear missiles all along the East-West border, in what from air reconnaissance would look like nothing more than ordinary barns.

"It's a goddamned mess over there," Avery Woodman, his briefing officer, told him. "Currently we're running—amend that—currently we're trying to keep intact six separate networks, only two of which—PLUTUS and COSMO—are worth a tinker's damn. And even they are on shaky ground."

"Pull them all out and start over again," Mahoney suggested.

"Good God, man, have you any idea, have you the slightest notion what you're saying? Some of those poor bastards have never seen the light of day. Lord, they have families going back six dozen generations whom they are supporting through our largess. Do you know what I'm saying here?"

"I think so," Mahoney said.

"Pull them out and we wouldn't have a chance in East Germany until the next millennium. Talk about the Thousand-Year Reich . . ."

"How about an end run? Leave them in place, in fact work them, but at the same time establish a new network."

"Elitism," Woodman said. He was gaunt almost to the point of looking cadaverous. But his voice was deep and mellifluous. "The word is, we work with what we already have in place until the networks are stabilized before we branch out. Pull them together. Give them the old Knute Rockne speech."

"A dangerous game," Mahoney said. He had already heard that Chernov was in East Berlin. Trying to make some semblance of order out of what apparently were a half-dozen networks that were in shambles would be made doubly dangerous because of him. Once again he was caught with his back against the wall because of his mistake of omission in 1953.

"It's the only game in town," Woodman said. He sat back in his chair. "You've been there before."

"Yes. Just after the war, of course, during the airlift, and again in the sixties."

"How's your German?"

"Passable."

"Have any friends left over there?"

"A few here and there."

"Any contacts with Gehlen's people?"

"I knew the general himself," Mahoney said. "His memoirs are coming out this year."

"So I understand," Woodman said. "Anything we should know about before we send you over? Any loose ends from your last visit? Just anything at all?"

There it was again, Mahoney thought. The oblique fishing expedition. Every agent worth his salt submitted to it. Every now and then the tree would be given a good shake to see what would fall out of the branches. If nothing fell, it didn't mean there was nothing up there, necessarily, just that the fruit wasn't ripe yet. But he was getting used to it by now. He was no longer the new kid on the block. He'd been around. A lot of the section chiefs were beginning to look young to him. That, along with the fact that in the last couple of years his hair had turned absolutely white, were sure signs of his aging. "It makes you look distinguished," Michael said, referring to his hair. "Bullshit, it makes me look old," he'd replied. "It happens to us all," Sylvan said. "Don't fight it."

"I won't be picking up from where I left off, if that's what you mean, Avery. Most of the old crowd is gone by now, I suspect. But I'll manage."

"Oh, I suspect you will," Woodman said strangely.

It was summer. Before they shipped out, Mahoney and Marge drove out to see Michael at the University of Wisconsin where he was studying forestry. It had been a little strange coming back to their old alma mater and not seeing anyone they knew from the forties. Dr. Robie had died nearly ten years earlier, and no one was left from the old days. Michael had spent the last two summers working on a research project in Montana, and he was on his way back for a third summer. After their visit in Madison they drove with him, spending a few days in Missoula, which they found to be a lovely town. Michael was already well known and liked there, and it was likely that when he got his doctorate he would join the staff of the U.S. Forestry Research Station.

Later they drove to Los Angeles to see John and his wife, Elizabeth Mary, and their son, Carl, who had just turned two. Marge doted on their grandson, spoiling him rotten in the ten days they were there, shedding a few tears when it was finally time to leave. For the first time in their marriage she was outwardly unhappy about heading to an overseas posting. "We'll be so far away from our grandson," she said. "I'll miss him growing up."

"We'll visit," Mahoney had promised her. "And they can come to Europe to visit us. Elizabeth has never been. Think of the fun of showing them around."

"I won't create a fuss, old man," she said.

"You'd better not, or I'll trade you in on a new model." It was their standing joke.

Berlin in those days, as now, was technically neither a part of the Federal Republic of Germany nor the German Democratic Republic. There were no embassies in West Berlin, only consulates, though the United States/Great Britain did maintain small embassies in East Berlin. It was a confusing situation, made all the more so because of the unemployment created by the wall. West Berliners who until 1961 had held jobs in the eastern sector were barred from crossing the border on a daily basis now. Many of them had moved away, but the welfare rolls in West Berlin were large. It had become a sad city. Without massive infusions of money from the FRG and from the U.S., West Berlin simply would not have survived. Young people were leaving Berlin in droves. As soon as they graduated from high school they took off, leaving behind a big gap in the service industries that came to be filled mostly by Turks who were willing to work at those kinds of menial jobs for one tenth the pay of the average German. Berlin, in a way, had become a lopsided city. The one constant was the wall. Always, wherever you were in West Berlin, day or night, you were conscious of the barrier; you could either see it with your own eyes, or you knew that just around the next corner, down the next street, beyond the next park, your progress would be blocked by it. West Berliners had taken to writing slogans on the wall: *Lebe einzeln und frei, wie ein bayer üm Baum, aber Brüderlich wie ein Wald* ("Live alone and free, like a tree, but in the brotherhood of the forest"). Tensions had eased slightly that year when the so-called "Quadripartie Agreement" was signed in which East Germany guaranteed West Germans free and relatively easy access to West Berlin across DDR territory. East Germany also agreed to allow West Berliners thirty days each year in which to visit with friends and relatives in the East. In return the U.S. agreed to recognize the East German state, and two years later East and West Germany were finally allowed to join the United Nations. Curiously the Wall had become the stabilizing factor in East-West relations. Without it the DDR would have lost its brightest and ablest workers and would probably have done something even more drastic than the wall purely out of self-defense.

He and Marge found a nice house in Zehlendorf, a suburb in the American sector well to the southwest of Tempelhof Airport. They had a German cook and a young French girl to help keep house and serve at the parties an undersecretary of state was expected to host. For the first few months their lives settled into a reasonably agreeable routine that in many ways reminded them of their first posting to Vienna. Their quarters were nice, and they worked an interesting cross section of people from the British and French consulates, as well as their own, to establish their bona fides. Background noise, it was called.

"You're going over as a deputy undersecretary of state, so you damn well better make the proper noises so that every time one of them glances your way all he'll see is a glad-hand diplomat with a good wine cellar," Woodman had preached.

During the day at his office in the U.S. consulate on Clay-Allee, he set out to learn all there was to know about the networks he had inherited, going back in the histories to their creation. He studied their operations, the product they developed as a result, and even the personalities of the individuals. The average-sized network in those days was six or seven people. Ideally they would all be involved in the same general endeavor. PLUTUS network, for example, included two customs officers, a gate guard, and three administrators at East Berlin's Schönefeld Airport. They did not know each other, though they understood that they were not alone. They had been providing lists of important arrivals and departures. Usually within twenty-four hours. Their contact routine was a series of letter drops in the huge Alexanderplatz in downtown East Berlin. Over the past ten or eleven months, however, the frequency of their drops had fallen off sharply. Their previous agent runner, Brian McCann, had dropped dead of a cerebral hemorrhage at his desk two months earlier, his own records a complete mess. Some of the other networks, such as HAMMERSTRIKE, which consisted of four enlisted men and one low-ranking officer in the East Germany Army; TONTON, which involved hotel workers at the Palast and the Stadt Berlin where high-ranking Soviet officers visiting East Berlin often stayed; and ALLEGRO, which consisted of five prostitutes who were often called to the KGB's headquarters in the Horst Wessel Barracks, had all but shut down operations. Nothing of any real value had come across in months. In some cases it wasn't even known for sure if the networks hadn't been compromised, the agents arrested.

Three or four evenings a week they either hosted dinner parties at their Zehlendorf home or were guests at someone else's party. Often they would begin with cocktails at the British consul's residence, go on to a show at the Philharmonic, and end up at the Mahoneys' for nightcaps. The French were usually distant, the British reserved, and the Americans oftentimes too boisterous. Over all, however, there was a spirit of bonhomie among them. They were all here in West Berlin trying to maintain the status quo. Not one of them for a single instant thought that what they were doing would have any effect whatsoever toward tearing down the wall. They wanted only to keep the boat as steady as possible in a very rocky stream.

Among them, of course, were Mahoney's opposite numbers: Wynn-Harris from the SIS, and Henri Bachautte, the chief of station for the French secret intelligence service, *Service de Documentation Extérieure et de Contre-Espionage*, commonly referred to as the SDECE. Sharing of product at anything below the European Operations level with its headquarters in Paris was strictly forbidden. Station chiefs did not have friendly chats to compare notes. Nor did agent runners. But from the beginning Bachautte had set his sights on Mahoney.

The Frenchman was tall, well built, and exceedingly handsome in a Gallic sort of way, and he was a charmer. He never failed to bring flowers for Marge, or a good box of Cuban cigars once he found out they were all that Mahoney smoked. He was also free with his little bits of "gossip," as he called his tips. A certain Soviet Air Force colonel, for instance, who was having a problem with alcohol, and would probably be sent back to Moscow very soon for disciplinary action. Or the wife of a certain West German politician who was having an affair with an East German officer who was almost certainly reporting everything he heard to the KGB. Or a series of intriguing coded messages that were discovered in the nightly news broadcast by a certain East Berlin radio station. No one had made sense of the messages yet, but they were worth looking into.

"Perhaps this will be of some use to you, Wallace," Bachautte said with a little laugh.

"I'll pass it along," Mahoney said each time. "Somebody will make use of it, I'm sure."

"*Certainement.*"

"*Je vous en remercie,*" Thank you for it, Mahoney had replied in his limited French.

"*De rien,*" the Frenchman said. But it was more than just nothing. Bachautte was working him, and he didn't know whether to feel flattered or resentful. He had been given some useful if not terribly important information, and the French expected that he would not only reciprocate, but that he was in a position to do them some good.

The tips, of course, were included in his daily summaries, but he did not report his source at first. He wanted to see just how far the Frenchman would go before he began demanding something in return. It was a moderately dangerous game he was playing, but by then he had become quite adept at it.

He had been in Berlin nearly five months when Bachautte, who was a bachelor, invited him to his apartment in Reinickendorf, up in the French sector, for some poker. The French military attaché and a couple of others from the French consulate played with them. The game broke up around midnight, and Bachautte asked Mahoney to stay for a few minutes.

"I'm certain by now, Wallace, that you know who and what I am," the Frenchman said. He had poured them both a good cognac.

"I have an idea," Mahoney admitted.

"Then you must also know what I am after, *mon ami.*"

Mahoney smiled and put down his glass. "Pardon me, Henri, but you should also know that it is impossible for you and I to liaise."

"*Merde*, it is a stupid rule imposed by your service. It does none of us good, this bureaucracy."

"Maybe you are a Russian spy."

Bachautte laughed. "Perhaps I am. But I have given you good information to date, *n'est-ce pas*?"

"What do you want?"

"Some assistance. Not much."

"With what, specifically?"

Bachautte sat forward. "You have a network that you call COSMO."

Mahoney hid his surprise. COSMO was the only decent network remaining of the original six. It consisted of five people in the Soviet's East Berlin embassy, one of them a young stenographer who held a top-secret clearance and worked regularly in the *referentura* section where sensitive KGB conferences were held.

"You have access to the Soviet embassy," Bachautte was saying. "We do not."

"What are you getting at?" Mahoney asked, a hard edge to his voice.

"There is a girl working in their embassy. Her name is Marie Fournier. She is a French Communist. Three years ago she defected. It is time for her to come back out, but we cannot get a message to her. We do not even know if she is still alive. We have heard nothing in the last six months."

"What is this girl to you?" Mahoney asked.

Bachautte looked miserable. "She is my fiancée."

"It was your idea that she go across?"

Bachautte nodded. "So you can see why this is so important to me, *mon ami*. And why I cannot go through the proper channels. I am asking you, man-to-man, to help me."

"I can't guarantee a thing, Henri," Mahoney had said. "But I'll see what I can do."

"You'll get a message to COSMO?"

"You know I don't know what you're talking about, but I'll try to find out what I can."

"Of course," Bachautte said. "I understand completely."

The next morning Mahoney typed up a highly amended report of his conversation with Bachautte, leaving out the months he had been worked by the Frenchman and omitting Bachautte's reference to their COSMO network. The chief of Berlin station was Allen G. Bennington, a Harvard graduate from old family money who had known the Roosevelts as a young man. He was a xeno-

222

phobe who absolutely despised the Russians and didn't think much better of any European, certainly not the French. Mahoney laid his report on Bennington's desk, and then went back to work. The explosion came at two in the afternoon.

"What kind of a goddamned game are you playing behind my back?" Bennington bellowed.

"What are you talking about, Allen?" Mahoney asked calmly, closing the office door.

"This," Bennington said, tapping a blunt finger on Mahoney's report on the desk in front of him. "I'll have your ass as well as his for this."

Bennington was on his last posting before retirement. A retirement, Mahoney had come to learn, that was long overdue. "Fine," Mahoney said. "You'll have my resignation on your desk within the hour."

"What are you talking about?" Bennington practically screamed.

"Bachautte approached me, not the other way around. He simply asked for some help."

"And you agreed?"

"Only to look into it."

"Thus blowing your cover."

"He knew who and what I am. So does Wynn-Harris, I suspect. I neither denied nor confirmed his suspicions."

Bennington was frustrated. He was less angry with the content of the report than he was with the fact that Mahoney had actually written it, thus making it official, thus putting him in the position of having to act on it.

"In any event, Allen, if I have lost your confidence, send me home."

"I didn't say that," Bennington backpedaled. "I didn't say that at all." He swiveled his chair around so that he could look out the window. "I want to keep this away from Bonn, and especially Paris," he said. "At least for the time being."

"Wouldn't do his career any good."

"What do you think of him?"

"I don't know yet. I thought I'd make a few quiet inquiries into his background."

"And then?"

"COSMO needs a test run."

Bennington swiveled back. "What?"

"We don't know whether COSMO has been blown, or has simply petered out for lack of direction. I've been trying to come up with something for them to do that if they are blown wouldn't tip our hand."

"You want to use an inquiry about this Frenchy as your test case?"

Mahoney nodded.

Bennington grinned. "You are a cold bastard, aren't you," he said. If the network were blown, so would Marie Fournier the moment he mentioned her name to them. But Bachautte said they'd heard nothing from her for months. The chances were that she was presently sitting it out in some jail awaiting trial.

"We'll know one way or the other," Mahoney said.

"Go ahead," Bennington agreed, shoving the report back across his desk to Mahoney. "I never saw this, and I never want to see it. The Frenchy is nothing more than a test case. No need to go any further."

In three days Mahoney was ready. He had checked into Bachautte's background as far as it was possible without causing a fuss, and everything had come back clean. He'd been born and raised in Nice on the Riviera and had attended the Sorbonne in Paris studying art for two years before switching to a military academy in Lyon. He had been attached to military intelligence with the French Army in Algeria. After his service he had been recruited by the SDECE. Berlin was his fourth posting, coming directly after Mexico City. Marie Fournier, on the other hand, was for all intents and purposes a raging Communist. Her father, Gisgarde Fournier, was secretary of the Paris district of the French Communist party. Her mother worked in the office as a writer, and her sisters were both graphic designers and sometimes political fund-raisers for the party. There had been some trouble in Algiers a few years back, but the report Mahoney saw was confusing and not very complete. It was there, however, that Bachautte met and presumably fell in love with her. Though in that Mahoney was only guessing. But it was the only period in which they had been at the same place at the same time. Marie Fournier had publicly defected to the East three years ago, though the right-wing and moderate press didn't give her departure much attention.

It proved in Mahoney's mind at last that Bachautte had been telling the truth. If indeed he had been engaged to Marie Fournier when she defected, his career as a French secret service officer would have been over. The fact that it was not, however, made it more likely that Marie Fournier was in actuality working for the SDECE. But the thought had also occurred to Mahoney that the

224

direct opposite could be true as well: that Marie Fournier and Bachautte were both double agents working for the Russians while pretending to be French loyalists.

As part of the original four-power agreement between the Soviet Union, France, Great Britain, and the U.S., diplomats were allowed free access to all sections of Berlin, East and West. The American embassy in the eastern zone was on Kirschstrasse in the section called Neustadtische. On a daily basis a courier made a run from the U.S. consulate in West Berlin to the embassy in the eastern zone with the diplomatic pouch. It was not uncommon for a consular section officer such as Mahoney to make the run.

"I'll be taking the bag over for the rest of the week," Mahoney told Bennington. "It's time I made contact with COSMO."

"Has Bachautte approached you again?" Bennington asked. They were having coffee in the officers' dining room. They kept their voices low.

"Not since last week. He seems to check out all right. It's likely that his girl friend is a penetration agent working for the SDECE."

"With her fiancé as her runner," Bennington added smugly. "Nice people, those French."

"I don't know if COSMO will pick up on it. We haven't heard anything from them in months."

"What are you going to tell them?"

"Not much at first. I'm just asking for a meeting."

"Where?"

"Leninplatz. Right out in the open."

"If they're blown, you could be walking into a trap."

"If they're blown, no one will show up," Mahoney said. "At any rate we can't just leave them hanging out there. One way or another it was going to have to come to this. Bachautte's request will be nothing more than our test case. If it works out, we can try to activate them."

"When is it going to air?" Bennington asked.

"It went out last night, and again this morning." Their contact procedure with the network was in the form of a message on a West Berlin radio station that played mostly American and British rock music. Once in the evening and again in the morning a half-hour talk show was aired. During a portion of the show, birth and anniversary messages were sent. "Marie and André are celebrating their second anniversary today," was the message for Raya Astayef, the stenographer from COSMO, to meet with her runner at two in the afternoon in Leninplatz. Other messages would indicate different places or different agents for the initial meet. They would recognize their man by a tear in the left pocket of the jacket he would be wearing. The secondary identification signal was the blue, red, and black club tie he would be wearing. He, on the other hand, had dossiers complete with photographs of his agents. He was expected to recognize them on sight.

"Then we'll know one way or the other shortly," Bennington said ponderously. "Whatever happens, Marie Fournier was your invention. Let's keep it that way."

"Of course," Mahoney said.

At eleven Mahoney left Clay-Allee in the consulate's well-used Mercedes 190 sedan, actually crossing into the eastern zone a few minutes before noon and arriving at the embassy at around twelve-thirty. It was a quiet afternoon; most of the staff had gone off to lunch. The consular clerk signed a receipt for the bag.

"Anything to go back?" Mahoney asked.

"You're a little early. If you want to wait for a while . . ."

"Not unless it's important," Mahoney said. He didn't want to be burdened by the returning bag.

"Whatever we've got will keep 'til tomorrow. If anything does come up we'll ring."

"Right," Mahoney said, and he turned to leave.

"Sir," the clerk called after him. Mahoney turned back.

"Yes?"

"Your jacket," the clerk said. "It's torn."

"I know. I caught it on the doorhandle. I'll have my wife fix it tonight."

"Don't want the East Germans to think we're poor cousins."

"No," Mahoney said with a laugh as he walked out the door.

Traffic was fairly heavy downtown. It was a weekday and all the shops and department stores were open for business, and many of the office workers were out for their lunch break. The day was pleasantly warm for the season, and the sky was cloudless. A few restaurants had put their tables back out on the broad sidewalks. Mahoney parked the car just off the square and walked up to a small bierstube where he was given a table outside. He ordered a beer and settled back to wait. He was an hour early. If COSMO had been compromised, and the KGB was watching for this meeting, the signs of their presence would soon become obvious.

He was keeping his exposure to a minimum. He carried the proper diplomatic identification, he was carrying no diplomatic pouch, nor was he carrying so much as a scrap of paper that would in any conceivable way incriminate him. He was simply an American on lawful business in East Berlin who had stopped for a glass or two of beer before returning to his consulate in the West. Though why he had stopped here was anyone's guess; East German beer wasn't very good.

Mahoney unbuttoned his jacket so that his tie would be clearly visible, and sat so that his torn pocket could be seen by the passersby. They never tell you to figure that perhaps your agent forgot his glasses and couldn't see very well. He'd had meets fail for more prosaic reasons than that.

By two o'clock much of the pedestrian traffic had thinned out. He had not spotted any obvious signs that the KGB had staked out the square or its approaches, although the *Bereitschaftspolizei*, which were East Berlin's civil police, were in constant view.

Leninplatz, unlike Alexanderplatz a few blocks away, was ringed mostly with new apartment complexes, shops, and bierstubes on the ground floors. There was no way, of course, for him to know if the KGB had set up a surveillance team in one of the apartment buildings. If they wanted him badly enough, they'd take him no matter what precautions he took. The risk was a part of the business.

It was five minutes after the hour when a short, swarthy man got off a bus at the corner, hunched up his coat collar, and headed toward where Mahoney was seated. He was Grigori Pashchenko, a relatively low-level clerk in the Soviet embassy's consular section. He was also the senior member of COSMO. He was married to an East German girl and had been stationed here for the past five years. The Russians, at times, were compassionate in their assignments. As he walked he scanned the people just ahead of him. Even from where he sat, Mahoney could see that Pashchenko was nervous. He walked, like most Russians, flat-footed, but the way he carried himself made it seem as if he were getting set to take off running at the slightest hint of trouble.

Approaching the bierstube he glanced idly at Mahoney, then down at the torn pocket, and back up to the club tie, and the relief was almost comically visible on his face.

He passed the bierstube and then apparently thinking of something, he turned back and entered the restaurant. Mahoney remained seated where he was. A few moments later Pashchenko came back out and sat down at the table next to Mahoney's. He ordered a beer, some bread, and a plate of sausage.

When the waiter was gone, Mahoney turned his head so that he was looking across the street. He could just see the back of Pashchenko's head.

"I'm glad you could come, Grigori," Mahoney said.

"Where have you people been?" the Russian said under his breath. "There has been no word from you for months. Where is David?" It was McCann's code name.

"He's gone. I'm his replacement. Is everything well with you?"

"As well as can be expected."

"We must meet somewhere."

"It may be impossible."

"I was surprised to see you here this afternoon," Mahoney said. As senior member of the team, Pashchenko was the fallback for everyone else.

"Raya is under suspicion. She has been temporarily suspended from her office. She is working with me now."

"Is it about us?"

"I don't think so. But I'm not sure. There is a rumor that someone is stealing supplies from the embassy and selling them on the black market. They may think it's her."

"We must meet, Grigori. But first there is something I would like you to do for me."

"I think it is too dangerous now."

"This is simple. I want you to find out about a young woman. Her name is Marie Fournier. She is a French Communist who defected about three years ago. She works in the embassy."

"It is a big place."

"Have you heard of her?"

"I think so," Pashchenko said. "What do you want to know?"

"I want to know if I can get a message to her," Mahoney said.

Pashchenko almost turned around. "Is she working for you as well? I know nothing about this. Nothing at all."

"No, she is not working for me. Under no circumstances do I want you to approach her. Just find out if she is still working at the embassy. I will return here tomorrow."

The waiter came with Pashchenko's food and beer. It was obvious he didn't like Russians. His attitude was surly. When he was gone, Pashchenko started on his meal.

"Tomorrow at two," Mahoney said. He finished his beer and laid down a West German ten-mark bill.

"No, it is too difficult for me to get away. I will meet you at the Palast Hotel. In the men's room at the main bar at eight o'clock sharp."

"If something goes wrong, leave a message at the bar for Rudi."

"Is that your name?"

"I am Horace Greenleaf."

"Well, Horace Greenleaf, if something goes wrong, there will be no messages, there will be no me."

"Are you under suspicion as well?" Mahoney asked, getting up.

Pashchenko looked up at him. "All of us are under suspicion all of the time, didn't you know?" He turned back to his meal and Mahoney walked off.

"Is there a message for Rudi?" Mahoney asked the bartender at the Palast Hotel. "A friend was to meet me here."

"No, there have been no messages for you, Herr Rudi."

The bar, as was the hotel, was filled with a convention of East German and Soviet automobile factory engineers. A new plant was being constructed for the manufacture of East German Wartburg automobiles. A small band was playing in the lobby, the music barely drifting into the bar over the noise of talk and laughter. It was a few minutes before eight.

"No funny stuff," Bennington had told him yesterday. "If it looks like it's going wrong, get the hell out of there. At this point I'd rather sacrifice the entire network than you." He'd been disturbed by the fact that Pashchenko and not the girl had shown up. "God only knows what will happen over there."

"I'll take care of myself," Mahoney assured him.

"You'll take your real diplomatic passport with you."

"I told him my workname."

"It's not likely he'll be asking to see your identification," Bennington had insisted. "And you will not be armed. That, mister, is an order."

"I'm going in alone."

"I agree. But once you've met and he passes whatever it is he's got for you, I want you to get the hell out of there. Hightail it back here, and call me. No matter what time it is."

"Will do," Mahoney said.

A dozen Russians sat at a large table in the corner. They were already drunk. Someone across the room was singing. Some girls had come in earlier and were hanging around the East Germans. Mahoney thought he might have recognized one of them from the ALLEGRO files, but he wasn't sure. The engineers had apparently been working together for a week or ten days and this was their last night before the Russians returned to Moscow. It was a going-away party. It was likely, Mahoney thought from listening to bits of conversation, that the East Germans and the Russians were happy for opposite reasons tonight. He thought about all the other networks he had been involved with over the past twenty years or so. They were like people: each had distinct personalities, with specific strengths and weaknesses. And they were like fickle lovers, hesitant at first to give of themselves until at some point the dam burst and they couldn't do enough to please. But like love, there was a season for a network, and when it was over it could never be recaptured. He thought now that it was likely COSMO and the other networks were on the long downhill slide into oblivion. Chasing after them, as he was now, was like chasing after a former love who is beginning to find the character traits in you that she once so admired to be nothing more than irritating little habits. Hell hath no fury like a woman scorned, it seemed applied equally to networks. Woe betide the agent runner who tried to hang on too long; like as not he would get shot for his foolishness.

Mahoney finished his drink and left a small tip for the bartender. Everything was normal, everything was as it should have been, and yet he was beginning to get the feeling that he was being set up. It had come over him on the way across the border, and the feeling was much stronger now. At the doorway to the lobby he hesitated a moment, wondering if he should turn right, go outside, retrieve his car, and drive back to the consulate. "Sorry, Allen, but Pashchenko never showed, so I got the hell out of there." "Sorry, Henri, I could find out nothing." He turned left, following the broad corridor that ran back to the men's and women's rest rooms. "Abandon the networks now," he would suggest. "Pull out anyone who wants to defect, and write the others off. Start fresh. In a year, maybe less, we'd be back in business better than before." He could do it. He'd done it before, and he would do it again.

The music from the lobby was much clearer now. A Strauss waltz, he thought, which was oddly in contrast to what was going on in the bar. But music was one of the opiates of the masses, wasn't it?

The men's room was filled. Mahoney had to wait for a minute or two before he could get to a urinal. Pashchenko hadn't arrived yet. When he was finished he went to one of the sinks and began washing his hands. There was trouble. He could feel it thick in the atmosphere. It was time to bail out.

If something does go wrong, there will be no messages, there will be no me, Pashchenko had said. He had known something would go wrong. He had tried to say so, but his words had fallen on deaf ears.

Mahoney looked up into Yuri Chernov's smiling face in the mirror, and his heart skipped a beat.

"Hello, Wallace," he said. "Or should I address you as Horace Greenleaf?"

Mahoney straightened up and turned around. No one was paying them the slightest attention.

"You and I are long overdue for a little chat, I think," Chernov said reasonably. "I have my car just outside. Did you bring anyone over with you, or did you have the good sense to come alone? I don't want to cause a scene for either of us, you know. I just want to talk."

Shivering in the woods, looking back toward the Grunewald Hotel, Mahoney remembered exactly what had run through his mind at that moment in the Palast Hotel. He felt that he had been betrayed, and that he himself had also betrayed. For years he had kept Chernov as his own secret, and for years, he realized at that exact moment, Chernov had known it, and had used that knowledge to his best advantage. Years of lies, of deceit, especially to Marge, had just caught up with him. He felt old and defeated. As if every other thing he had done in his career, all the good things, the successes, the rescues, had been for nought, suddenly wiped out by the smiling face of this one Russian. Christ but it had hurt. He especially remembered the pain that threatened to completely swamp him. He had been outclassed and outmaneuvered for his entire career. Here it was happening to him again, and he knew no way out of it. Perhaps, he thought morosely, he'd never had a choice.

Mahoney dried his hands on a paper towel and went with Chernov across the lobby. Outside, a Mercedes sedan pulled up, and they climbed in the back seat. Chernov sat back and the car moved out into the street and sped southeast toward Treptow along the Spree River. Sometimes they drove fast, at other times they slowed down, turning down side streets, and twice they doubled back the way they had come. They were shaking any tail that might be trying to follow them, and Mahoney understood that their driver was very good. Nothing short of a well-planned, long-term team effort could have kept up. But he had been telling the truth: he had come across alone. "We can't afford to be careless," Chernov said at one point. "It wouldn't do either of our careers much good to be seen together like this." Curious, Mahoney thought, but he had used almost the same words about Henri Bachautte's career. Passing down a long, well-lit avenue, Mahoney studied Chernov's face. The Russian had definitely aged. His face was lined and weathered as if he had spent a great deal of time out of doors. If anything he had gained a little weight, especially in the chest and shoulders. His hair was still thick and dark, and although the years had somewhat softened his features, his eyes and mouth were still set in the same posture of a smug, superior knowledge. He understood things that no one else understood. He brooked no argument.

"Are you kidnapping me?" Mahoney asked.

"Heavens, no," Chernov laughed. "You're far too valuable for me to do something as stupid as that. No, my old friend, you are perfectly safe. I wish only to talk for an hour or two and then you will be returned to your automobile."

"We have nothing to talk about," Mahoney snapped.

"Oh, but we do. Unless you want me to take you in. We could be in Moscow by morning. You would have a very good reception there. Believe me."

"What are you doing here?"

"Working out of my embassy, just like in the old days. And you are trying to put together your networks, which is, if you don't mind me saying so, a futile effort. I think you would be much further ahead writing them off and starting from scratch. We're all vulnerable, all of us, you know."

"I don't know what you're talking about."

Chernov laughed again. "I could have allowed Pashchenko to meet with you this evening. He could have told you that Marie Fournier is alive and doing well. You would have gone back feeling very good about yourself, and your great abilities. Bachautte would have felt well, too, though I think the both of you would have wondered just a little bit that it had been too easy. Am I right?"

He knew about COSMO, but that didn't necessarily mean he knew about the others, though Mahoney thought it was likely. Chernov was simply too good to miss them.

"Better yet," Chernov continued, "I could have sent Raya to meet you at Leninplatz. Marie and André, who are perpetually celebrating their anniversary, is her message, I believe. But she is not doing too well these days."

"I see," Mahoney said. "Is Marie Fournier working for you?"

"Yes, now she is, though at first her thinking was confused. When she came over she still had stars in her eyes for poor Henri Bachautte."

"Why are you telling me this?"

"Because I need your help."

It was Mahoney's turn to laugh. "You must be joking."

"No, I am not," Chernov said. "Call it a trade if you will. Go back and close down COSMO, PLUTUS, ALLEGRO, and the others. They are doing you absolutely no good. McCann wasn't a very capable administrator. In fact he knew nothing about the business. He was an amateur, not like you. Then when you have cleared the decks, you can begin again, this time doing it right. You will be a hero."

"What happens to Raya and Grigori and the others?" Mahoney asked.

"How do you mean?"

"If they want to come across, will they be allowed to defect?"

"No, I'm afraid that would be impossible, for a lot of obvious reasons."

"Perhaps we could get them out."

"It's already too late. But if you persist, perhaps I will arrest you tonight."

"On what charge?"

"You're a spy, Wallace. That's the charge."

"Prove it."

Chernov smiled wanly. "I think you have said enough tonight for me to make a case."

They had passed the Pioneer Palace in Treptow and now they were out in the countryside, the weather clear, the sky lit up behind them with city lights. It brought him back to 1953 and the hunt for the penetration agent within the CIA. No such person had been found. He thought now that it was possible Chernov had managed to plant someone within the Company after all. But it was too late now for him to go back to try to fix it. Far too late. All that was left would be for him to salvage something here and now. Somehow turn this meeting to his advantage.

"We can both benefit from this situation, Wallace," Chernov said as if he had read Mahoney's thoughts. "I'm not asking you to spy for me. Nothing so melodramatic as that. I am asking only for a simple trade that will not hurt your government."

"I'm listening," Mahoney said.

"I'm giving you all six of your East Berlin networks on a silver platter. They are blown, every one of them. You understand what

I am giving you? We could simply have managed the intelligence they pass to you. Disinformation. It would have set you back by months, possibly even by years. You understand this?"

"I'm still listening," Mahoney said. They crossed the Spree River towards Köpenick, the Grosser Müggelsee to the north through the woods.

"In trade I am asking only one thing. That you pass a simple message back to Bachautte that Marie Fournier is doing well. That she was in the hospital for an appendectomy, and that she is well and will soon be back to work."

"Thus compromising the SDECE," Mahoney said.

"Not for the first time, nor for the last, as I believe you know. She is a very pretty girl with a very large ego. She was actually quite easy to turn. Wallace, she practically jumped into our laps. She is very close friends now with a lieutenant colonel on my staff. They have already been to Odessa on vacation."

"Perhaps I'll just return tonight and write up a complete report on this meeting. Tell everything, share it with the French. Our networks are gone in any event, as you say. Perhaps we will be able to salvage something out of this. Your effectiveness here would be at an end."

"I don't think you will do that," Chernov said. "No, I don't think so. For the same reason you told no one about me in the forties when we met in West Berlin. Do you remember that meeting? The BND certainly had their doubts about you there for a while."

"I would include that in my report," Mahoney said. It was a weak lie and he was sure that Chernov saw through it.

"Thus ruining your own effectiveness as well as mine. A trading of queens on the chessboard works only for one of the players. The one who either had the most strength or the best position. You have neither. At least not at this moment."

That part was true. The entire Berlin operation was in more of a shambles than even Woodman could possibly understand. And what would happen if he did blow the whistle? Jail possibly. At the very least some very hard questions for which he would have no realistic answers. Defeat. Humiliation certainly for him as well as for Marge. What does a fifty-two-year-old spy who had fallen from grace with his service do for a living? Become an expatriate writing his memoirs on some Greek isle? Watching over his shoulder every day for the rest of his life in fear that someone would be there to put a bullet into his brain? Or could he go along with Chernov? Lose this one time so that he could continue another day? He had been effective. He had been a good spy. He had even saved lives. His was an honorable profession, after all. But he didn't feel honorable.

"I would like to go back now," he said. "Unless of course you were lying and you do mean to arrest me."

Chernov smiled a little sadly, and patted Mahoney on the knee. "No, you have my promise." He leaned forward. "We'll return to the Palast now," he told his driver.

"What will become of Marie Fournier?"

"That depends entirely upon you, my friend."

Mahoney looked at him. "I am not your friend, understand at least that."

"I do," Chernov said solemnly.

"And also understand that I will do everything within my power to bring you down."

Chernov smiled again. "This too I understand. We are at war, you and I. We always have been. In war some battles are won, others are lost. It is up to us to continue, leaving the final analysis of who was right or wrong to the historians long after we are dead and buried."

The season belonged to Mahoney as no other season had before or since. It was also one of his darkest eras. "The man is working himself half to death," Bennington explained to anyone who would listen. "Of course he's tired—send his replacement at once." But Langley was hearing none of that. They kept urging their brightest star to newer and greater heights. Only Marge, dear sweet Marge, understood that all said not well with her husband. But in her typical fashion she said nothing to him about his sudden mood swings, his snappish temper, and his sleepless nights. Instead she was simply there for him with her love and companionship. Unquestioning loyalty. Stoic strength. Without her, he would never have made it through that period.

He had waited at the hotel bar for more than an hour, he explained to Bennington that same evening. "When he hadn't shown up by nine, I decided to get the hell out of there." Hating the lie of omission, he wrote in his report that Pashchenko was waiting outside the hotel. They had only a couple of minutes to talk. The Russian was extremely agitated, and kept saying that he was being followed, but that he had managed to shake his pursuers for the moment.

Everything is blown, Mahoney reported. All their networks. Pashchenko mentioned each of them by name. No one is safe now.

Everyone is compromised. How Pashchenko could know this was never made clear, but the man had sounded convincing.

Mahoney had suggested running a few test balloons across, just in case Pashchenko was lying or mistaken, and was subsequently given authorization to do so. No one showed up at any of the rendezvous. All information from East Berlin had suddenly ceased. Pashchenko's information was apparently valid.

"If no contact is possible," Mahoney wrote, "the feasibility of trying to get our agents out of the eastern zone is doubtful."

Regrettable but true, Langley concurred. Cut our losses and run. Number one priority would be the establishment of the new networks, a task at which Mahoney worked steadily and with much success over the next twenty-four months of his posting.

As to the business of Marie Fournier, Bennington thought it would be best all around if Mahoney's report to Langley included a highly amended version of the actual story. Pashchenko knew of Marie Fournier and thought that she was a loyal Communist. But he had heard certain unspecified rumors about her. Considering the fact that Pashchenko and COSMO were blown, his information about the French girl would have to be looked upon with suspicion at the very least.

"If," Mahoney wrote, "she is or has been in contact with Henri Bachautte, then we should regard the entire SDECE operation in West Berlin as equally suspect."

Langley looked upon this as another regrettable piece of news. But the French had not been terribly cooperative in recent years, so there wasn't much of a relationship to damage. Mahoney was instructed to keep one eye cocked for Bachautte, but to leave it at that. Thus isolating the Frenchman from doing them any harm through Chernov's machinations, Mahoney told Bachautte that as far as he knew Marie Fournier was still a loyal Frenchwoman, and that she had stopped communicating for a time simply because of her ill health.

"Did you get to see her, Wallace?" a highly excited Bachautte asked.

"No, I only heard of her," Mahoney said. "And you must understand now that this can go no further between us. I cannot give you any more help."

"I understand, *mon vieux*. Thank you for what you have done."

Mahoney's very last chance for redemption came in the spring of the following year. The West German Police had arrested a Soviet diplomat outside Bachautte's apartment building. The captain of detectives had called the American consulate because he was a personal friend of Bennington, and because the Russian had been carrying a large sum of American money. More than ten thousand dollars. The Germans didn't know what to do with the Russian, who was claiming diplomatic immunity and who gave no reasonable explanation as to why he was hanging around the apartment building of a French diplomat, or why he was carrying so much money. "If he was dealing with the French, I would have assumed he'd be carrying French francs," the detective explained. "Is he one of yours? Should we send him back, or what?"

Mahoney had gone with Bennington for a quick look. The diplomat turned out to be Yuri Chernov, who sat in the interrogation room calmly smoking a cigarette. They could see him through the one-way glass, but he could not see out.

"Look familiar?" the detective asked.

"Not to me," Bennington said. "Do you know him, Wallace?"

Mahoney remembered staring through the one-way glass at Chernov, wondering what the hell he had been trying to prove this time. Perhaps he had come over in an attempt to use Marie Fournier to turn Bachautte. But why the money, and in American currency? "I don't think so," Mahoney said. "What's his name?"

"Vasily Zhigulenkov," the police captain said. "We've absolutely nothing on him in our records."

"I've never heard the name," Bennington said.

"Neither have I," Mahoney said. That, at least, he mused, was the truth.

"If he's done nothing wrong, I suppose you'll have to send him back," Bennington said.

"What about the money?"

"No crime in being rich. Not even for a Russian. At least not on this side of the wall." Bennington stepped a little nearer to the one-way glass. "Intriguing," he mumbled. He turned back. "I wonder what the bastard is up to," he said.

"I was thinking the same thing," Mahoney said. "But you're right—we can't hold him if he's done nothing wrong." He turned to the detective. "He hasn't asked for political asylum, has he?"

"First thing we asked him."

"And?"

"He laughed. He just laughed at me, the *Schweinhund*."

"Then let him go," Bennington said.

The final footnote came six weeks later when Henri Bachautte's maid found him slumped over his desk in his apartment, his service revolver in his right hand, his brains splattered all over the wall. He had left no note, but Bennington figured he knew why the "Frenchy" had done it. "Thank God you saved us from that mess," he told Mahoney. "He was working for the Russians all along. Him and his girl friend, Marie Fournier."

13

Standing across the street from the Bremen Hotel, John Mahoney wondered who was there now waiting for him. Once you cross the frontier you can never return. How often had he heard that? Until this moment he had never felt quite so detached, quite so disassociated from something that had been a part of his entire life. The ID could be fake, of course. But somehow he thought that Sheepskin Coat—Stewart Turner—had been legitimate. Who had sent them and why? It was this last question that was so disturbing. "Leave yourself a back door, an alternative," his father had told him. "But remember that the other fellow is doing exactly the same thing." There was more than one path to an objective. When you were someone's possible object, however, the flavor of the game was changed.

The doorman was talking with a cabdriver who had pulled up beneath the canopy out of the snow. Traffic had begun to slow down, at least here it had. The night had taken on an ethereal quality for him, in part because of his lack of sleep, but in part because of the darkness and the snow and the fact that for most Berliners at this moment, life was occurring at a normal pace, while for him it had become frantic and dangerous. He had stopped at the parking garage to check his rental car. As far as he had been able to determine, no one had been there, nor had he seen anyone posted to watch for him. He had taken great pains to get here, turning down back alleys, doubling back, suddenly turning in his tracks to hail a cab to the opposite side of the city, and then wandering, apparently aimlessly, on foot until he had finally convinced himself that he was clean. For the moment. But Bixby knew this hotel. His first instinct told him that it was time to move on. Time to burrow deeply. Yet another more studied part of him resisted the notion. You shall be forever marked by how and when you finally run. Time now to run? For the first time in his life he didn't know.

He crossed the street. The doorman looked up, recognized him, and hurried to open the door. Inside, John went to the desk. "Any messages?" he asked the clerk. "Mahoney, Four-oh-five."

"Yes, sir," the clerk said, plucking a pink slip from a pigeonhole. "Herr Bixby has called for you several times in the past hour."

"Thanks," John said. Crossing the lobby he pocketed the message and unbuttoned his overcoat. He used one of the telephones across from the elevators to call the consulate. Bixby himself answered on the first ring.

"Where the hell have you been?" Bixby demanded. If the agent in the parka who had taken a shot at him had reported back, Bixby gave no sign of it.

"Out. What have you got for me?"

"Plenty. Farley okayed the wire transfer. Your funds are in place. But he made a lot of noise. He wants to know what the hell is going on."

"Does he want to talk to me? Should I come in?"

"No. He said that you knew what you were doing, though I'm not so sure. The West German police have your name from the Hertz people in Cologne."

"You'll have to quiet them down."

"I have, for the moment, though they're not particularly happy about it. We had to promise that you would come in for questioning on your own."

"When?"

"I've got you until tomorrow afternoon. Here in Berlin. Are you calling from a reasonably secure telephone?"

"Reasonably," John said, glancing across the lobby at the desk clerk who wasn't paying him any attention. He could see the doorman through the glass doors talking with the cabby. A plant? It was possible.

"Our friends in Pullach have perked up their ears. Heiser was one of theirs. They want to know if we're running anything that they should know about."

"What did you tell them?"

"I stonewalled it. Referred them to Farley, who of course will be out of his office until morning. But they're going to get insistent real soon."

"Anything on the list from Alex?"

"Not a thing."

Time to run now? Time to get out? He had thought about it for several years. His father had built an entire career on knowing how to sidestep the most pressing issues, how to turn an apparent disaster into an advantage. But that took intelligence and a certain almost fatalistic feeling: if you believe that what you are doing is morally correct, you push your luck to the limit. It was a question for which he didn't have the answers right now. He could feel the weight of his gun in one pocket, and the dead CIA agent's wallet in his other.

"Have you put a team on me, Tom?" he asked, making his decision. He heard the wind go out of Bixby.

"What's happened?"

"Am I being tailed?"

"Not by this station. Has something happened, damnit?"

John looked again toward the front doors. The doorman was still there talking with the cabby. "Someone took a shot at me tonight."

"When? Where?"

"In the Tiergarten an hour or so ago."

"Did you get close enough to ID them?"

John's grip tightened on the telephone. Bixby said "them." Did he know? Most surveillance was done in teams. Pairs, not single watchers. Had Bixby made a simple assumption?

"I got the hell out of there."

"Christ. The Russians are here in West Berlin, you do know that."

"I figured as much."

"We think Major Trusov herself came over earlier this evening, although we're not certain. A woman answering her description, but with West German identification, came through Checkpoint Charlie."

John had figured she would be coming over sooner or later. "Check the airports," he said. "She's probably on her way down to Hannover."

"That's a dead end."

"They might not know that. There's no reason anyone should think they're here in West Berlin. At least nothing official. Hannover will be their only real lead."

"They've probably got you spotted nevertheless."

"I agree," John said. "I'm switching hotels tonight. I'll call you as soon as I'm settled."

"Maybe you should come here. It makes a lot of sense."

"No," John said. "But I want you to call Farley and ask if he's put a team on me."

"We're not tailing you—" Bixby started to say, but then he

realized exactly what it was John had been telling him. "You know them? You saw them after all?"

"Talk to Farley. I'll call you later this morning."

"Wait—" Bixby shouted, but John hung up. He waited a moment, then dialed the number Allmann had given him. It was answered immediately by the same voice as before.

"Your money is in place," John said.

"Yes, we appreciate the timeliness. Have you something further for us?"

"Two complications. I'm being followed. There was a shooting." He explained what had happened in the Tiergarten, including the fact that Sheepskin Coat had been carrying a CIA identification.

"Is it possible his identity card was fake?"

"Very possible."

"In that case who might these men be?"

Turner had been an American, not German or Russian. He had heard it in the man's accent. "I don't know."

"There may be a third party interested?"

"It is possible."

"I see. You mentioned two complications."

"The KGB has placed agents here in West Berlin. They will be searching as well. Under no circumstances are they to be interfered with."

"Yes, we understand."

"Have you anything for me?"

"You were correct that your gentlemen have returned. They were spotted last night arriving by train. However, since we were not at that point involved, no thought was given to having them followed."

"Were they together?"

"On the same train, yes. After that we do not know."

"Very well," John said. "I will caution you again not to approach either of them, under any circumstances, should you discover their location."

"We understand this."

"I'll call again soon."

With the same abruptness as before, the connection was broken, and John hung up. He stood by the telephone for a minute longer. Chernov and his father had laid their track out of Berlin, and then had immediately snuck back to Berlin on the train, apparently leaving their workname passports at the hotel in Hannover. Were they now traveling under new names? If that was the case, his search for Greenleaf and Nostrand was useless. They could be posing as anyone. The possibilities were nearly endless.

He glanced at the elevators. Tonia Trusov had come across. Sooner or later she would be making contact with him here. He was going to have to wait for her. He had no other option at the moment.

The instant he opened the door to his room he knew that she had already arrived: he could smell perfume. For an unknowably short split second of time he was transported to another age in which he was married, to a homecoming in which he smelled perfume, and the pain was so overwhelmingly sharp that he was nearly blinded. He stumbled backward, groping for the gun in his pocket. He wanted to lash out, to fight back, as he had been doing since the cabin had gone up in flames with his wife and children inside. Little sparks were going off inside his head; he could feel the heat of the flames against his face, hear the explosion, smell the smoke. Sometimes at night, alone in his bed, he thought he could hear screams coming from the cabin. But that was only his overworked imagination fed by his grief. They had never screamed, not once. He couldn't accept that.

Tonia Trusov sat propped up in his bed, her shoulders bare. She held the sheet demurely over her breasts with her left hand. In her right she held a large automatic.

"Come in and close the door," she said, lowering the weapon.

"What the hell are you doing here like this?" John asked, coming back into focus. He shut and locked the door, then snapped on the lights.

Tonia laid the gun on the nightstand. She moved languidly, allowing the sheet to fall away from her body, exposing breasts that were beautifully formed, high and firm, the nipples slightly erect. She sat back again, one knee cocked, her stomach flat, a slight duskiness to her flawless skin. She smiled.

"You were spotted coming across the border tonight," John said, concentrating on her eyes and not her nakedness. She was an exotic woman, made all the more so by the extreme danger she presented.

"No one has followed me here," she said softly.

"If they have, I'll arrest you."

"You might try," she said. "But I didn't come here to fight with you. I came because we have work to do."

"Nor did I agree to work with you so that I could fuck you." Her face darkened. "What are you then, a queer?"

"Just someone who prefers to keep his balls intact," he said evenly. "I've killed once tonight. Don't tempt me into making it twice."

Her nostrils flared slightly. "Who was it? One of my people?"

John took Turner's wallet out of his pocket and tossed it over to her. While she was looking at the ID he took off his coat and laid it over the chair. She looked up.

"He's not one of my people," she said. "What happened?"

He told her what had happened, leaving out his telephone call to Bixby, and of course his calls to Allmann's people.

"Somebody in the Company doesn't trust you, I think," she said. "They fired first?"

"Yes."

"To warn you, or to hit you?"

"If it was simply a warning, it was damn close," John said. "Get dressed."

"Yes," she said absently. She pushed the sheet back and got up. Her legs were long and graceful, with a hint of muscles like a dancer's. Her jet-black pubic hair had been removed to a narrow swatch. She had been in the sun a lot. Her tan line was very narrowly defined. Being naked in front of a stranger didn't seem to bother her in the least. She talked as she got dressed. "Does your station chief, Tom Bixby, know that you're here at this hotel?"

"Yes, but he'll expect me to move around."

"Good," she said. "Then we'll use my room. It is just down the hall. In that way we'll be able to watch who shows up."

"Did you come up with anything from your end?" he asked.

"A list of twenty-three places here in the western zone where they might have held their meeting after the war." She took out a document from her purse and brought it over to him. This close, still only partially dressed, he could feel her warmth as if she were an open-hearth furnace. He concentrated on the list, which had been stamped CONFIDENTIAL top and bottom, with the GRU chief of East Berlin Rezidency's signature over a file number and date that went back to September 1945.

"Who knows that you have come across to work with me?" John asked, scanning the names and addresses. Many of the places were hotels. He recognized some of them as ones he had already called. Others appeared to be Third Reich office buildings that most likely were no longer in existence, while others were private residences, those, too, most likely gone, or almost certainly under completely different ownership.

"No one of importance."

John looked up. "You brought a team with you. Where are they?"

"Two of them are running down the Hannover lead. The rest of them are here in the western zone watching both airports, all four train stations, and the four highway exit points."

"They're bottled up here, then."

"They're here in Berlin? You know this for a fact?"

"They came in by train yesterday."

"Hannover was a false lead?"

"It would appear so. It might mean that they're no longer traveling under their original worknames. We're going to have to go down the list one at a time in the hope they're at one of these places."

"Meanwhile keeping out of everyone's way," Tonia said distantly. "Somebody is trying to stop you for some reason and my own people are not too happy that I made contact with you. They think I have gone too far this time."

"Perhaps you have," John said. It was going to be a pity to kill her, he thought. But he knew that he wouldn't have much of a choice in the matter. Her orders, he was certain, were very specific: kill his father, her uncle, and him.

"How do you know they are back in the city?"

"They were seen coming in."

"By whom? Had Berlin station staked out the stations?"

"No, this was after-the-fact information. Someone recognized their descriptions, that's all."

"Then you can't be absolutely certain they are here."

"I am," John said, getting up.

She looked at him and nodded. "So am I."

While she finished dressing, John stuffed a couple of pillows beneath the blankets. For a moment or two in the darkness the ruse might fool someone. It wouldn't last, of course. But all they would need was a little warning. Nothing more. He packed most of his things in his bag, leaving a shirt and a few toiletry items laying out. Again the fiction wouldn't hold for long, but he hoped it would be just long enough. Before they left the room he hung the Do Not Disturb sign on the doorknob, then switched off the lights. Once again he had the uneasy feeling that he had absolutely no idea how this was all going to turn out, except that it wouldn't end neatly, or to anyone's satisfaction. So easy just to turn and run, he thought. But the time for running had passed. He was

245

caught in the downward spiral now, with no way in which to extricate himself.

It was the same moment in Moscow two time zones to the east. The military hotel on Gor'Kogo Street, a block and a half from the Moscow City Soviet, was housed in a dumpy red stone building with no sign out front. The weather was extremely cold, and the GRU Chief of Staff, Captain-General Leonid Seregin, briefcase in hand, did not linger in the tiny unheated lobby. His aide, Major Vladimir Filatov, had gone ahead and was waiting on the ground floor with the elevator. No one else was around. The hotel could have been deserted, and except for the maintenance staff and a few unobtrusive guards, it was. Seregin was a large man by Russian standards, with thick, ponderous features that were almost Siberian, much more Asian than Slavic.

"Has Zadvinsky arrived?" he asked his aide as they started up.

"A few minutes ago, sir," Filatov answered.

Colonel Vasili Zadvinsky was the liaison officer between Moscow GRU Operations and the KGB. Technically he was on the KGB's payroll. But Seregin had secretly used his patronage over the past eight years to ensure the younger man's rapid rise within the intelligence community. Zadvinsky owed his loyalty to Seregin. Since his posting as liaison officer between the GRU and KGB—which were often embroiled in bitter rivalries—a new age of harmony had come to the relationship between the services.

"Everything is in readiness at the airport?"

"There is a MiG-31UTI trainer standing by on transfer orders to Schönefeld. It can be in East Berlin in under an hour and a half."

"Anything further from Colonel Raina?"

"She has definitely gone across."

"Bitch," Seregin swore. "She is a crazy woman. She could ruin everything."

"It is the bloodlust, sir," Filatov said. "It runs in the family."

"Yes," the general said. "Well, we have our own bloodhound."

Zadvinsky was waiting for them in one of the top-floor apartments that was reserved for the exclusive use of the GRU. It was one of the few safe flats the military intelligence service maintained in the city that were perfectly safe: there were no bugs.

"Comrade General," Zadvinsky said. He had poured himself a vodka. His hand shook slightly when he raised his glass in a toast.

"I called you here tonight because I want a witness," Seregin said without preamble, and he was satisfied to see that Zadvinsky's complexion paled. It meant he understood the significance of what was happening.

"There will be questions."

"Most assuredly there will be a full-scale investigation. After the fact."

"She's gone over?"

"Yes. But we will stop her before it's too late."

"How?" Zadvinsky asked. "We don't even know where that old fool Chernov has gotten himself to."

Filatov had poured a glass of tea to which he added lemon. He brought it to the general.

"We now have a very good idea where he and Wallace Mahoney are meeting. It is in West Berlin as we suspected. Raina came up with the list."

"Which he handed over to the Black Widow."

"A stupid name," Seregin snapped.

"Her orders were to find them and kill them."

"She might kill her uncle, though I wonder," Seregin said. "But in making contact with John Mahoney, she has gone too far. We have all heard the tape of her interview of him. Much too far. She can no longer be trusted."

"I agree," Zadvinsky said. "I can arrange to have her recalled."

"No."

"What, then, Comrade General?" Zadvinsky asked in a small voice.

Seregin glanced at his watch. It was three in the morning. He had a meeting in the Kremlin within an hour. He was playing a very dangerous game here. They all were. But the prize they had worked for since after the Second World War was finally within their grasp, if only they could plug the leaks. Such a short time. Only days now. He looked at Filatov and nodded. "Bring him in."

"Yes, sir," Filatov said and left.

Seregin extracted four file folders from his briefcase and slapped them down on a low table in the living room. Zadvinsky stood to one side, his gaze alternating from the door through which Filatov had gone, to the file folders. Seregin opened them one at a time. Each contained a personal dossier and photographs. In the first, Tonia Trusov stared up at them from a glossy eight-by-ten photograph. In the other files were photographs of John Mahoney, Yuri Chernov, and Wallace Mahoney.

"What do you mean to do, Comrade General?" Zadvinsky asked.

Seregin looked up. "Why, have them all killed. What other choice is there?"

The door opened. Filatov came in followed by a good-looking man who might have been in his late twenties or early thirties. He was dressed in a smartly cut business suit, his sand-colored hair trimmed neatly, his face closely shaved. He could have come from anywhere: Helsinki, Munich, Vancouver, Los Angeles. He was athletically built but not overly musclebound. When he smiled, one was drawn to his warmth. Here is a friend, a man to be trusted. Gentle. Kind. In fact the man was a sociopath. He had absolutely no conscience. Killing for him was as routine an act as scratching one's own nose. And he was very good at it.

"Captain Serafim Timoteevich Kochetkov," Filatov said, closing the door.

"Good evening, Comrade General," Kochetkov said pleasantly. "Colonel," he said, inclining his head toward Zadvinsky.

"You will be leaving within the hour," Seregin said.

"Yes, sir."

"The files on your targets are there on the table. Study them on the way, but leave the files in East Berlin. Are you clear on that?"

"Perfectly," Kochetkov said, moving gracefully toward the table.

Zadvinsky moved aside as if the younger man were the carrier of some deadly disease. His name was less well known than Tonia Trusov's and completely unknown outside of the Soviet Union. He was every bit as good as she was. An added advantage, Seregin thought as he watched Kochetkov study the dossiers, was that he now knew Tonia's face, while she did not know his.

Kochetkov looked up. Zadvinsky shuddered.

"Are you clear on your instructions?" Seregin asked.

"Yes, sir."

"You are to kill all four of them at the very first possible moment, and nothing, absolutely nothing will stand in your way."

"Yes, sir," the assassin said. When he was five he had killed his baby sister by holding her head in the toilet until she drowned. No one could believe that such a sweet-looking little boy could do such a thing deliberately, so the death had been ruled accidental. Three years later his mother fell down the stairs of their apartment building, breaking her neck, killing her instantly. Two years after that, Kochetkov slit his father's throat with a straight razor, and he was put in a mental institution. The doctors could find nothing wrong with him. Instinctively he knew which were the "correct" answers on the mental inventory tests. He was transferred to a military school where he was educated, finally coming to the attention of Seregin five years ago when he killed a roommate who had been guilty of nothing more than humming off-key during study period. He had been tried by a military tribunal and sentenced to death. Seregin had been there for the last days, directing that food be withheld from the condemned man, and that he not be allowed to sleep during the last seventy-two hours before his scheduled execution. At the appointed hour, Kochetkov had been manacled and led out to the execution yard where he had been stood against the wall. The execution squad had been marched out, they had cocked their weapons and had aimed them at the young man's breast. Seregin had stopped the execution. "Do you wish to live or die?" he asked Kochetkov. "Live, of course," the young man croaked. He could barely stand. "Then you shall live, Serafim, but only for me." "Yes, sir," Kochetkov said, understanding perfectly then as he did now.

"I asked Colonel Zadvinsky here as a witness. There almost certainly will be repercussions from this act."

"Yes, sir," Kochetkov said unconcernedly. He looked at Zadvinsky, obviously memorizing his face. "Yes, sir," he said again.

"Good hunting, Serafim," Seregin said softly.

Kochetkov's face lit up. "Yes, sir," he said.

It was still snowing. The hotel was very quiet. Outside a snowplow rumbled by on the street. Tonia Trusov had switched the television to an all-night news channel, but she had turned the sound almost completely off. She sat on the bed, her shoes off, her feet curled up beneath her. John sat in the chair by the writing table. They had decided to remain here until morning when they would attract much less attention moving around the city. They were wasting valuable time, but neither of them could afford to attract any attention to themselves. Tonia had agreed at first, but over the past hour she had become increasingly nervous. Something was wrong. She was waiting for something. He could see it in the way she held herself, in the way her eyes darted toward him whenever they heard a noise from outside. "What's wrong?" he had asked. "Nothing," she'd said, but she had been lying. He could tell.

He needed sleep, but he could not turn off his mind. Twice he had gone to the window and carefully looked down at the street. Nothing moved below. Up on the Ku'Damm there were still a few private clubs open, but for the most part the city had shut down with the late hour and because of the heavy snowfall. He could barely hear the television news reader's voice as a distant mumble, and he found himself straining to listen. He got up to turn it off.

"No, don't," Tonia said.

"What are you waiting for?" he asked her sharply. "What are you expecting?"

"Nothing."

"You're lying."

She smiled faintly. "Yes, I am," she said. "What spy doesn't?"

"Assassin," John hissed. It had been insanity to work with her. He wanted to take his gun and shoot her now. But she had brought out the list. Without it, he didn't know how far he would have been able to carry the search on his own, even with Allmann's help.

"Your hands are not so free of blood," she said.

"I'm going to attempt to take them back and you're going to try to kill them," he said. "It will be interesting to see which one of us succeeds."

She sat forward suddenly, snatching the SigSauer from beside her, levering a round into the firing chamber, clicking the safety off, and pointing it at him. He stared at her for a long hard moment, then shrugged and turned his back to her. A weather chart was showing on the television screen. He shut it off. He could see her image in the blank television screen. She lowered the gun, and laid it down.

"I'm not going to kill them," she said. "I don't care what you think."

"You are a killer, just like your uncle. You weren't sent here to hold my father's hand."

"They are a couple of old fools," she said tiredly. "Neither of them have been active in years."

"But your uncle knows something that he came out to tell my father." John turned around to face her. "At very great risk to his personal safety."

"We're all at risk," she said, missing the hint.

"Being with my father, for him, is the ultimate risk."

"I don't know what you're getting at. Your father was an analyst, not a triggerman."

"But he'll kill your uncle."

"Why?"

"Because of what your uncle has done."

"It was his job," Tonia said. "He didn't create the war we are

250

in. You know this." She looked away and sighed, the gesture almost theatrical.

"He murdered innocent people."

"There are no innocents," she flared.

He'd heard that line before, and it was no less a horrible lie now than it had been that other time. "My mother was an innocent," he heard himself saying, although he had not wanted to bring it up.

"What are you talking about?"

"He poisoned her. When they were in Moscow last. A carcinogen. It was a program that was designed to demoralize our people."

"You have proof of this?"

"Proof doesn't matter if my father believes it."

"Does he?" she asked quietly.

John thought about it for several seconds. At last he nodded. "I think it's the only reason he agreed to meet with your uncle. They have been enemies for a long time."

"Then perhaps it is already too late," she said. "Perhaps it no longer matters."

"What did he bring out with him?" John asked. "Why was it so important for him to take the risk? Why were you sent after him? And why did you come to me?"

"I don't know. I don't make policy. I was ordered to find them, that's all."

"And kill them."

"That's right."

"But you're a humanitarian."

She said nothing.

The only light came from outside and from the glowing tip of the cigarette John was smoking. He thought Tonia had fallen asleep, but she got up and went into the bathroom. He could hear the water running, and then silence.

He went to her gun on the bed, removed the clip, ejected the live round out of the firing chamber, and replaced the clip. Pocketing the bullet he sat down. She came out of the bathroom a moment later, the light on.

"I'm going to take a bath. You should get some sleep, I think. We have a long day ahead of us."

"Your concern is touching, Major."

"I didn't kill your mother. Or your brother, or your wife and children."

It took everything within John's power not to kill her then and there. He could see that she knew it.

"Have you anything for me?" John asked softly into the telephone.

"The airports and train stations are being watched. If your gentlemen decide to leave they will be stopped."

"It is the Russians. They are watching the highway exit points as well."

"That is good to know. We have begun at the various hotels and private clubs within the city, but there may be delays because of the weather. We would wish to talk about an extension."

"When the time is up we will discuss extensions," John said. "In the meantime I have a list of twenty-three locations where they might be staying or meeting. Have you the capability of recording?"

"Yes. Proceed."

John quickly read the names and addresses from Tonia's list, translating from the Russian directly into German, including the explanation that the information was more than forty years old. "There will be many changes. You will have to use your ingenuity and imagination."

"Does the opposition have this information?"

"I don't know," John said after a hesitation. "But it certainly is a real possibility. One which your people should consider carefully."

"We will."

The connection was broken. John hung up and looked at his watch. It was after five already. Nearly time to go. Sleep would have to wait.

When Tonia came out of the bathroom she wore a robe, her hair wrapped in a towel. Without makeup she seemed even more exotic than before. She had relaxed; there was no tension in her eyes now. She could have been on vacation. No troubles. No worries.

"You are rather well known in Moscow," she said, sitting on the edge of the bed. The bottom of her robe parted. She pulled it together.

"I was given your file before I left," John said.

"I don't want to fight you over this business. Our battles will come in time, if we survive. For now let's cooperate. The sooner we find them, the sooner we will be able to go home."

"What do you know about my wife and children?"

"They died in a fire at your father's dacha in Minnesota. But it was not KGB who did it. Your father knows that. He must have told you."

He had. John remembered their conversation in great detail. He had replayed it in his head often, looking for the flaws, looking for the errors of perception, because Farley Carlisle had told him a completely different story, and he'd had the facts to back it up. It had come down to a choice of whom to trust (his father, of course) versus who seemed to have the most reliable information (in this case, Carlisle). He had never told Carlisle what his father had said about it, nor had he told his father what Carlisle had told him. By then he had made his own decisions, his hate solidified into a very hard core at the center of his soul.

"And my brother?" he asked, knowing what she would say.

"An accident, as I'm sure you know. Your father, at that same time, had arranged for the kidnapping of three Soviet children. Let me tell you, their family still worries about them."

"It's a cruel world," John said, and Tonia searched his face for his exact meaning. Finding nothing she could understand, she got up and began taking clothes out of her suitcase.

"It will be dawn soon," she said. "We'll begin at the top of the list."

"Yes," John said, and he got up. As he went into the bathroom he heard the television set coming on. She was waiting for something. What?

At that hour it was still the previous day in Washington, D.C., just a few minutes before midnight, and Farley Carlisle wondered how long the situation could last. Driving up the parkway, Fort Marcy off to his right, he kept watching in his rearview mirror expecting someone to be back there. The Soviet embassy had been ominously quiet all evening, only the most routine calls going in or out of the place, not a single one of them from overseas. Even their satellite links had been silent for the most part, except for a single burst transmission, duration 150 milliseconds, that had occurred around nine. So far they'd made no real noises about their missing agent who'd been sent to Minnesota, though that would come, he was sure. "The trouble with maverick operations," his instructor had told him years ago, "is that as many as succeed spectacularly also fail with a very big splash." And when they fail everyone suffers. To every season comes such an operation, he'd been taught. No service is without them. Not theirs, not ours.

He and Gina had gotten home early from dinner, and he had laid off the booze, though the thought of drinking himself into oblivion just this once had its appeal. He'd felt out of touch, certain that he wouldn't be able to stand an entire evening listening to his wife's inane prattling about their friends, so that when Alex's call came he'd been almost glad of it.

"You'd better get over here on the double."

"What's going on?"

"Not what you think," Hayes had said cryptically. "Just get here."

"On my way," Carlisle had said, the sudden sharp fear that he hadn't felt since Vietnam gnawing at his gut.

The night was clear and reasonably warm for the time of year. Traffic was light, so he made good time, pulling through the CIA headquarters' gates just twenty minutes after Hayes's call. He got his ID badge from the door guard and took the elevator to his office. Operations was busy, but no more so than usual. He took off his coat and hung it up as Hayes, carrying a thick stack of files, hurried across the hall, an intensely worried look on his face.

"Donald's here. He wants you upstairs on the double."

Carlisle closed the door. His heart was thumping. "Is it Mahoney?" he asked, lowering his voice.

"It's the goddamned Russians. They're up to something." He handed Carlisle the files. "I pulled the Soviet Operations summaries for you. But we didn't have so much as a hint."

"What the hell is happening?"

"I'll explain on the way up," Hayes said, starting for the door. Carlisle stopped him.

"No, for God's sake. First of all, what is happening with John? Have you talked to him tonight? Or with Bixby?"

Hayes looked at him oddly. "The money you authorized has been transferred to the Swiss account, but no, I haven't talked to John all evening. Bixby called a few hours ago asking if we had put a tail on John. I assured him that we hadn't. That John was there clean. It seems the Russians are getting itchy. Someone apparently took a potshot at him."

"God in heaven."

"We've got other problems, Farley . . ."

"Did he get a look at them? Was he certain they were Russian?"

"He didn't say. But it's likely. Tonia Trusov is in West Berlin. I think we should put some more people on it. John is out there essentially all alone."

"No, not yet," Carlisle said, distracted. When Chernov had

254

called and Mahoney had gone walkabout, it had seemed like the perfect opportunity. Now he wasn't so sure. He was afraid now. Truly afraid.

Again Hayes was looking at him oddly. "Are you all right, Farley?"

Carlisle looked up. He nodded. "You said Donald is here. What does he want this time?" Donald McClean, unlike many of his predecessors, kept a firm hand on day-to-day operations.

"The Soviet Third and Fifth Air Forces have gone to Amber."

"We know that. It's on the schedule."

"The Chinese are starting to raise hell. They're trying to tell us that it's not just another exercise."

"What else is new?"

"They claim to have intelligence indicating that the Soviet Missile Defense Service has been moving some heavy hardware up to the border over the past thirty days."

"We have that too."

"There has been a general buildup of Soviet submarine activity in the South China Sea, the Yellow Sea, and the Sea of Japan."

"We're also aware of that, Alex. You're telling me nothing new so far."

"The Chinese, like I said, are getting very worried. Tonight the Chinese premier called the president."

"What in God's name do they think is going on? Are they afraid the Russians are about to start World War Three?"

"Something like that."

"Donald can't have swallowed it. Is he going to send us on another wild-goose chase?"

"This time they might have a legitimate gripe. The president thinks so too."

What Hayes was saying, and just how he was saying it, finally began to penetrate Carlisle's anxiety. "Just what is it you haven't told me, Alex? What have you left out? We didn't have so much as a hint about what?"

"The Chinese ambassador saw the president this evening. He brought along a batch of photographs from the Chinese intelligence agency's Mourning Dove–One." It was a spy satellite in geosynchronous orbit over the Chinese-Soviet border.

"Which showed?"

"Some unusual activity in a remote area south of Semipalatinsk. Our KH-11 satellite was rerouted before nightfall, and the photographs just came up from analysis about an hour ago."

"Don't spin it out, Alex."

"The Chinese suspect, and our own photo analysis seems to confirm, that the Soviets are getting set up for an above-ground test of a nuclear weapon. And a large one, from the looks of it."

"Oh, Jesus Christ," Carlisle groaned.

The dawn was gray. Spits of snow melted on the windshield of Tonia Trusov's Ford Cortina, turning almost immediately to ice that the wipers and defroster were having a hard time with. She drove. They had left the hotel through a back door and had made their way separately to the parking garage. No one had come to the hotel in the night. No one had been waiting outside, and no one had been watching the garage. For safety's sake they had decided to use Tonia's car, at least for this morning. Whoever had taken a shot at John last night possibly knew his. It was only a thin margin, but it was something.

Only the main thoroughfares had been properly cleared. Some side streets were still blocked with snowdrifts and were impassable. Others were difficult at best. The city had taken on a holiday mood. Music played from speakers. Traffic was at a minimum, but a lot of people were out and about. School had been canceled, and many of the shops and offices downtown would be closed at least until noon according to the radio news broadcasts Tonia insisted on listening to. She was waiting for something, and it was important. He had decided not to press her. If it was a message she was waiting for, something in code, he would know it by her reaction.

Children were skiing in Charlottenburg Park as they came up from Otto-Suhr-Allee. Mothers and fathers and old grandmothers had come up with them. Everyone was happy and excited, which served only to deepen John's mood. His anger had grown with the night, and now in the morning, tired, hungry, and just a little confused, he was barely able to maintain control. He wanted to lash out at something, anything, just as he had five years ago. He knew that somehow he was going to have to hold on for a little while longer. Either Allmann's people would find Chernov and his father, or he and Tonia would stumble across them. In the meantime the two old men were effectively bottled up inside West Berlin. The wall had become not only a barrier between their two separate philosophies, but their cage as well.

He was angry with his father for not sharing what Tonia had called his "obsession" with her uncle. It had been going on for a lot of years. But only once had his father ever mentioned Chernov's name, and then only in passing.

"It was a two-way street, believe me," Tonia had told him. "Your father was held up to me as some idea of perfection. My uncle didn't think much of the CIA in terms of its effectiveness, except that it always had a lot of money that could buy technology. But he thought your father was very good. The very best. Except, of course, for his one flaw."

"Your uncle," John said.

"Yes, but my uncle had the same obsession. I've looked through his case files and only once or twice was your father's name ever mentioned in them. And yet my uncle devoted his life to him," Tonia admitted. "So many times it would have been possible for my uncle to stop him. But he always held back. He wanted to understand your father. He felt that if he could fathom what made this one individual tick, he could understand the rest of you. He had a fatal attraction for the West that oddly enough actually enhanced his career. He knew, given any particular situation, what the CIA would do. How you would react. And it was an obsession that in the end he tried to foist off on me."

"You've followed in his footsteps," John said. "You are a killer."

"Yes, I have killed," she said. "Like a soldier kills."

"Christ," John said, looking at her. "Save the apologies, Major. They call you the Black Widow."

"If you know that much, then you know who I have killed and why," she flared. "Spies. Some of them assassins themselves. Traitors. Scum. In America you root for the underdog. In the Soviet Union we root for our government. We are not so kind to our turncoats. When we discover a cancer we eliminate it."

"Up the party. Lenin lives."

"Yes, he does."

"You're proud of what you do."

"Yes," she said. "Aren't you?"

No, John thought as they came around the corner onto Schiller Strasse and stopped. He had not been proud from the moment he had been recruited. He tried to remember if he had ever been proud of his father, but his thoughts and memories were too confused, too wrapped up with emotion for him to make any clear sense of them. A modern six-story office building rose from the end of the street. A record shop, a bookstore, and a restaurant, all closed now, occupied the ground floor.

Tonia was studying the list she'd brought out with her against two street maps of Berlin, one from 1944 and the other current. "Not the same building, of course," she said, looking up. "But during the war this was the Reich's research department. The *Forschungsamt*. They tapped telephones, intercepted radio broadcasts, and came up with codes. The OSS took over the place. There were apparently many meetings held here between our military intelligence groups."

"Nothing is left of the original building," John said, gazing at it through the blowing snow. None of the windows were lit.

"It doesn't look like it. I don't think they'd be here."

"Neither do I," John said. "But I'll just have a quick look."

"I'll go with you—" Tonia started to say.

"Swing around the block and see if there's a back way out. I'll meet you at the corner."

Tonia studied him for a moment, trying to come to a decision. She finally nodded. "If my uncle spots you he'll kill you."

"I suppose he'll try," John said, getting out of the car. He closed the door, waited for a taxi to pass, then crossed the street and hurried up the block. As he reached the lobby entrance, Tonia passed him in the car, turned the corner, and disappeared.

He glanced over his shoulder one last time. No one was there. No one had followed them. So far. Inside, a directory was posted in an aluminum frame next to the elevator. A dozen attorneys, one diamond importer, and an insurance and title company occupied the upper floors. They would be closed now because of the weather. Any one of them could have been a front. Something Chernov could have arranged, even at arm's length from Moscow. But he doubted it. This wasn't the place. If they had come to Berlin to get together at the same place they'd met just after the war, it wouldn't be in a new building. It would have to be someplace old. Something they would both know and recognize without having to compare maps from then and now. Someplace that would instantly bring back memories of the other time when they technically were still allies. A common ground. Not here.

Back outside he walked to the corner and crossed the street as Tonia came around the block from Hardenberg. She pulled up and he got in. "Nothing," he said.

"There was a service entrance in the back for the shops, but I didn't think they would have come here," Tonia said, again studying his face.

"What's next?" he asked.

"Still downtown, there's the Abwehr's Ausland Division," she said, reading from the list. "But we'll probably run into the same thing. Most of the inner city was in shambles at the end of the war.

258

And a Nazi secret service office building is not the kind of a place that would have been saved."

"We'll try it," John growled.

"As you say," she replied, putting the car in gear and pulling away. "What was back there anyway?"

"A few attorneys, a diamond merchant, and an insurance company. Your uncle could have set up something ahead of time. But I don't think they would be sleeping there."

"Neither do I. They are at a hotel or an inn somewhere," she said.

"Probably," he said, thinking about Allmann's people and wondering how far they had gotten.

The *Auslandsorganization* headquarters building no longer existed. Even the street it had been on along the southern edge of the Tiergarten had been rerouted, so they could only approximate from the old map where it had been located. Back in Charlottenburg the Nazi party's Foreign Intelligence Headquarters—RSHA/VI—was gone, replaced by drab apartment blocks, as were the RSHA/VI's F7 Radio Intercept Unit and F6 Technical Group buildings. American-Soviet meetings had taken place during the summer and winter of 1945 throughout Berlin. Going back and trying to locate the old places was like walking through an ancient graveyard.

Tonia was leaning against the car and smoking a cigarette as she watched the children playing in Charlottenburg Park when John came on foot up from the broad Mier Strasse after checking the apartment block that had once housed the RSHA's Technical Group. He was behind her, and about twenty yards away. She was not aware of his presence. He stopped, his heart hammering in his chest. Eliminate the variables whenever, wherever possible. The simple instruction had been hammered into his head by his instructors at the Farm outside Williamsburg. He didn't need her. She'd brought the list out, and she'd given him not only the insight he needed to understand her uncle, but she'd also inadvertently led him to understand that there was more here than a simple meeting between two old men. Something was about to happen. Something so important that she would agree to cooperate with him like this. Something that she would know had happened by listening to news broadcasts. It would be so easy now, he thought, to kill her. He'd probably get a medal when it was all over.

He needed rest. He needed time to think. By this afternoon, when he didn't report to the West German police for questioning into Heiser's death, they would come looking for him. And there were others out there too, looking for him. The man in the parka from last night would know that his partner was dead. He would be searching the city. Under whose orders? And why? The BND was becoming anxious; according to Bixby they would be entering the fray before long, as would the KGB who had to be nervous by now knowing that Tonia was here.

Something was missing, though. He had felt it from the beginning at his father's cabin when Carlisle and the others had shown up. There had been something in Carlisle's eyes, in his attitude that had been only slightly bothersome then, but now it had grown into different proportions. Look for the anomalies, his father had taught. The bits and pieces that don't seem to fit anywhere.

Tonia straightened up suddenly and turned around. She spotted John standing there, and for just a moment they stared at each other through the snow that had begun to fall again, until finally she flipped away her cigarette and climbed back into the car.

John hurried up the street and climbed in beside her. "Nothing. Just like the others," he said.

She was staring at him. "How long were you there?"

"A half a minute."

"And what did you see?"

"The chief of Department 8," he said. "A good and loyal Communist."

"I was watching the children," she said after a beat.

He turned away. "Don't talk to me about children."

"You're tired. When have you slept last?"

"It doesn't matter. We have work to do. People will be looking for me."

"And me too," Tonia said. She glanced down at the list beside her on the seat. "The Europäischer Hof is a hotel on Messedamm. We'll check there. If it's clean, we'll stop for lunch."

"And then what?"

"Then we continue. They are here in the city. We will find them."

A lot more traffic was moving now through the city, even though it had begun to snow again. Most of the streets downtown were open for the moment. The day had turned dark. At noon streetlights had come on, and traffic ran with headlights. The Europäischer Hof turned out to be a large hotel with a roof garden café-restaurant. No one named Nostrand or Greenleaf had been guests of the hotel during the past four days, nor were there any guests currently in residence who matched their description, according to the bell captain who pocketed John's hundred-mark bill with an insolent sneer.

"A regular run on those two," he said.

Tonia was across the lobby checking at the desk.

"Someone else has been here this morning looking for them?" John asked.

"You a cop?" the bellman wanted to know.

"No. Would it make any difference?"

"About what they said. Mafia if you ask me. What do you want them for?"

"They're Russian spies and I'm going to kill them."

The bellman's face lit up in a big grin. "Well, they're not here. Too bad for us all."

John met Tonia at the elevators. "Nothing?" he asked.

"No. You?"

"They're not here," John said. He glanced up at the elevator indicator. The car was on the sixth floor and on its way down. "We'll have something to eat and then continue. With any luck we'll find them this afternoon."

Tonia looked at her watch. "I hope so," she said.

He looked across the lobby toward the front doors. A young man with sand-colored hair, dressed in a three-piece business suit, a light gray overcoat over his arm, had just come in. Something about him didn't seem quite right to John. The way he held himself, the way he moved. John couldn't put his finger on it, but alarm bells began jangling along his nerves. The young man looked their way, then headed toward the front desk.

"Me too," John said vaguely. Something he should know. Something he should be aware of.

The young man said something to the desk clerk, and a moment later turned and started their way. He was smiling.

There was something about his coat, the way he held it draped over his right arm. Covering his right hand.

"Move!" John said urgently, suddenly putting it together.

"What?" Tonia asked, looking up.

"Now!" John snapped, grabbing her arm and pulling her away from the elevators. Before they'd gone two steps a woman behind them suddenly shrieked and fell backward, a big red stain spreading across the front of her dress just below her neck.

The young man stood smiling as if he were in a daze, the overcoat pulled slightly away from his hand to reveal the silencer of a big automatic.

261

Tonia, suddenly realizing what was happening, broke away from John and rolled left as she yanked her gun out of her purse. John already had his gun out and snapped off a shot that went wide as he swiveled on his left heel, and then started in the opposite direction.

The young man fired again, the shot plucking at John's sleeve, and then stepped gracefully behind three men and a woman who were too confused to realize that they were in mortal danger, and were just standing there.

A large man in a security officer's uniform, a pistol in his hand, came racing across the lobby from behind the desk. The young man turned and calmly fired two shots, the first hitting the big man in the chest, the second taking off half his face.

Tonia had already reached the safety of the corridor that ran toward the rear of the hotel. She raised her SigSauer and pulled the trigger, but nothing happened.

John got to her a second later as another shot ricocheted off the wall just above his head, and then they were running together down the long hallway, the sounds of shouting and screaming behind them.

14

Berlin was a triumph. In eighteen months Mahoney had managed to place three highly successful networks that continued to produce a viable product for many years after his departure. Langley was offering him the sun and the moon, but he wanted none of it. He was a simple fieldman. He'd always been at the front lines, and it was there he wanted to stay. Humility became a virtue, but in part his decision to forgo promotion to the hallowed halls of the third or even the seventh floor at Langley was due to a certain guilt. His unfinished business. Chernov was the devil incarnate who had to be fought in the field, not from some safe office. When his notice of pending reassignment came up, he wasn't terribly upset to be leaving. All the old crew had gone or was leaving, and he'd heard that Chernov had left thirty days earlier.

When Allen Bennington left he'd warmly pumped Mahoney's hand. "It has been a rare pleasure working with you, Wallace," he said. "I'll put in a good word for you at Langley, but I don't think you need it. In fact if I weren't going back for retirement, I'd be begging for a few of your crumbs."

"None of it would have been possible without your direction, Allen," Mahoney said gracefully.

The farewell party at the consulate had been a noisy affair. Bennington stepped a little closer and lowered his voice conspiratorially. He was half drunk. "Don't fret about Weddel. You'll be out of here yourself in a couple of months."

Walter Weddel was the new chief of station fresh out of Washington, but with back-to-back tours in Poland and Hungary under his belt he was considered the resident East Europe expert. He was a relatively young man, only in his early forties, and he had his own very definite ideas how things should go, which did not include letting his people run, as he put it, "like wild Indians chasing after buffalo."

"You've done a creditable job here, Mahoney," Weddel said in his second week. He'd instituted 7:00 A.M. daily staff briefings that a grumbling Bennington was obliged to attend during the four-week transition period while the incoming COS was getting his feet wet.

"He's done more than that, I'd say," Bennington interjected.

"I'm not denigrating Mr. Mahoney's accomplishments, Allen. I'm merely trying to tie up the loose ends before all the old hands run off on me."

Something was up. Mahoney had seen it in Weddel's eyes. He'd dismissed the others so that it was only the three of them meeting in the basement safe room.

"There are ongoing projects," Mahoney said. "You're up to date."

"The networks are fine," Weddel said. "I have no problem with the networks. You have done yourself proud, though looking back at the record I don't know if I would have allowed you to handle the various situations the way you did. Not exactly." Bennington started to protest, but Weddel held up a hand to silence him. "I'm not here to start a fight, or to tell anyone that he's done questionable work. Langley is pleased. Very pleased with your accomplishments to date. Nothing will change that."

"What loose ends did you have in mind?" Mahoney asked.

Weddel glanced down at a file in front of him. "Does the name Marie Fournier ring a bell with you?"

Mahoney stopped himself from looking over at Bennington, though he knew the man's blood pressure had probably gone through the roof. No one had ever looked too closely at that operation, nor, presumably, had Bachautte said anything to the SDECE about his query to Mahoney concerning her. Whatever Weddel had come up with, Mahoney hoped it was nothing more than the man's concern about the discrepancies in the files.

"She's a French Communist who defected to the East a number of years ago," Mahoney said, keeping his voice even. "Her fiancé at the time worked here with the SDECE."

"Yes," Weddel said, looking up. "He killed himself."

"An unfortunate incident," Bennington said, his voice a little shaky.

"The West German police have her in custody," Weddel said.

Mahoney's heart skipped a beat.

"Or I should say they *had* her in custody. The girl hanged herself this morning in her cell."

"Good Lord," Bennington said.

"What was she doing back here?" Mahoney asked.

"Apparently trying to re-defect."

"Have the French been notified?"

"Not yet," Weddel said. "They're not to be trusted, as you well know."

"Why wasn't I notified?" Bennington blustered. "I am still chief of station here."

"Of course," Weddel said smoothly. "I only happened to stop by the police this morning on my way in. Something I've taken to doing. It makes good sense. They asked me about her and the name struck a chord. I came back here, looked up the record, and began to wonder."

"About what?" Mahoney asked.

"She admitted that she worked for the Soviet government. And she mentioned a name that I've seen in your case files, Mr. Mahoney. From a long time ago."

"Yes?"

"Yuri Yevgennevich Chernov. Apparently he was her case officer. Had you known that?"

"No," Mahoney said. "In fact the name is only vaguely familiar. Refresh my memory."

Weddel stared at him for a long moment. "We don't have much on him. He's only surfaced off and on over the past twenty years or so. You had set up some sort of a meeting with him some years ago here in Berlin. There was a BND cross-reference."

Mahoney pretended to think. Chernov wouldn't have been so foolish as to mention his name to the girl. At best he would have viewed her as only a temporary resource. She'd been too unstable. "During the Berlin airlift," he said suddenly. "The end of 1948. I tried to set up a meeting, but it never came off. He didn't show up. That's been a few years ago."

"Why did you want the meeting?"

"He and I had worked together, briefly, just after the war. I was OSS. He was GRU. I thought I might be able to get something out of him."

"Concerning the Soviet blockade?"

"Yes."

Weddel sat back. "You are a maverick, Mr. Mahoney. I don't mind telling you that. Nor do I mind telling you that I will be pleased to see you leave my station."

"I'll leave right now if you wish," Mahoney said.

"Oh, no, at the moment you're the fair-haired boy. I'm not

going to have it on my record that you and I couldn't get along. Famously."

Bennington got up angrily. "It will be on your record once I report this conversation."

"No," Mahoney said. "Mr. Weddel is simply doing his job, Allen."

"He's the new breed," Bennington said at the going-away party. "A piss-ant. Glad I'm getting out. The service has changed. Everything has changed, goddamnit."

Mahoney had been glad too when he followed a couple of months later. Weddel had not liked or trusted him. And for good cause, he reflected. For very good cause.

"We're not going to keep you very long here in Washington," Sylvan Bindrich, who was by then deputy director of Operations, said. "I'd just as soon send you back to Moscow, but I think it's too soon."

"What have you got in mind, Sylvan?" Mahoney asked. Marge had gone out to California to be with John and Elizabeth, who was pregnant again and had asked for help. But if he was to be off again, he would be burning the midnight oil studying for his new assignment, so there wouldn't be much time to miss her.

"This time Hungary or Greece," Bindrich said. They sat together on the leather couch in his office, drinking coffee and brandy. "Though I'd prefer you take Hungary, I think maybe you and Marge might be needing a little time in the sun."

"I appreciate the thought, Sylvan. I'll talk it over with Marge. But in the meantime, what's happening in Hungary?"

"It's the Russians again. This time they're pumping a lot of money into the AVB"—the Allami Vedelmi Batosag, the Hungarian secret intelligence service—"and they've managed to double their staff in the last nine months. Quite simply, we'd like to know what the hell they're up to."

Mahoney was the logical choice for the assignment, fresh from his successes in Berlin. His most effective network had been HOMESPUN, which had penetrated the East German secret service. They were hoping for a follow-up.

He mentioned it that afternoon to his old friend, Stan Kopinski who was chief of Archives. Just any help I could get would be worthwhile, Mahoney told him. They agreed to meet for dinner that evening at an out-of-the-way Italian restaurant in Georgetown. They had worked together for enough years so that they understood each other perfectly. Kopinski especially understood personal loyalty. His induction into the OSS and subsequent naturalization as a U.S. citizen had been partially Mahoney's doing. And he had no great love for bureaucracy. Any bureaucracy.

"So, the conquering hero returns home and already they want to send him off again," Kopinski said after they'd ordered a drink.

"A lot of things have changed in Germany since the war," Mahoney said. "You should see it."

Kopinski shuddered. "No, thanks. Was it awful?"

"Actually it was interesting, Stan. And busy."

Kopinski looked at him for a few seconds. "It would be just as interesting for you in Budapest, I think," he said carefully.

"Oh?"

Kopinski nodded. "I've heard a rumor that Yuri Chernov might be running the show over there."

"Where did you hear something like that?"

"Military communications intercept. Routine transfer orders. His name was buried."

"Hasn't created much of a stir, then?"

"Hardly a ripple."

"Not a promotion, I suspect."

"Hardly, after your success in Berlin. He has to be smarting from that blow. They thought they were home free with our old networks. But you showed them otherwise, didn't you?"

Mahoney smiled. "It's a dangerous world we live in, Stan."

"Yes it is. But be careful in Budapest, Wallace. It's a lovely old city, but don't let it fool you. There are a lot of grudges there."

Hungary would suit him just fine, he told Bindrich. But never having been there before he would need some time to do his homework. To that end his assignments officer would be detached from his normal duties as assistant to the DDI for however long it would take, though he'd heard the figure of thirty days bandied about. He telephoned Marge in California and told her that they were off again, this time to Budapest, and although he heard the disappointment in her voice, she only asked if he wanted her in Washington immediately. "Stay with Elizabeth for now," he told her. "I'm going to be at least a month with my homework." He spoke with John who was disappointed that Mahoney wouldn't be out there for the birth of his second child, but he said that he understood. Michael was off in the mountains and could not be directly reached, but Mahoney left a message for him to call as soon as he got back.

Hungary was a land of mirages, according to his briefing officer, Farley Carlisle, who had spent two tours of duty in Budapest since 1963. He was a man who'd always been filled with an overinflated sense of self-importance, Mahoney thought, remembering their first meeting. But Carlisle knew his stuff, even if he sometimes got some of the motivations wrong.

"We'll send you over as a deputy undersecretary of state again," Carlisle said. "Worked in Berlin, no reason for it not to work in Budapest. Hungarians more than any other people in the world are impressed by titles. And they love to talk."

"Who is the COS over there?"

"You, if you want the job."

"I don't think so, Farley. I'm going to have my hands full as it is without trying to administer other operations as well."

"I tend to agree with you," Carlisle said. "In that case, you'll be working for Herbert Tilley. A good man. Absolute tops. He's a Hungarian speaker, and this is his fourth tour there. We'll talk him into staying another six months until we can find his replacement."

"I'll want some autonomy this time," Mahoney said carefully.

Carlisle took a moment or two to answer him. "Allen Bennington had some high praise for you, but Weddel hasn't said much. Did you two have some trouble?"

"Let's say our methods were different."

"We have a very busy station in Budapest. More so these days because of the increased Soviet interest in the AVB. Loads of in-place operations and established networks of resources that have stood us in good stead."

"I'd prefer to develop my own resources."

"Within limits I agree with you," Carlisle said. "I'll be working the Eastern European desk, so I'll have to know what you're up to."

"I hadn't planned on hiding anything from Tilley. But I'll want to call my own shots this time."

Carlisle managed a weak smile. "From what I've seen of your service record, you've always called your own shots. We didn't expect anything different this time."

"Then I'll have your cooperation?"

Carlisle sat forward. "Herb Tilley is a damn good man. He'll have something to say about what you want to do. For now let's just say that we'll leave that relationship for the two of you to work out."

Mahoney had to laugh. "In other words, take it or leave it."

"Either that or take over the entire station," Carlisle said. "It's yours for the asking."

"We'll work it out," Mahoney said.

"The Mahoneys will have to be validated," Bindrich told Carlisle. "I want them expected."

Mahoney was shipped off to the State Department where he wandered around for two days speaking with the so-called Hungarian experts, not one of whom could speak the language. They had the geography down pat, though: "It's a terribly flat country, nothing between the Danube and the Soviet Carpathian foothills except wheat fields. Just like Kansas."

"I've heard the people are friendly," Mahoney said with feigned enthusiasm.

One evening he and Marge had dinner with the assistant secretary for European Affairs, and the director for Czechoslovakia, Hungary, and Poland and their wives. They seemed to know even less about Hungary than their staff. "You'll be doing some good work for us out there," he was told.

"I'm anxious to get started," Mahoney said. "Anything in particular I should know?"

"Oh, I think the best way to get to know Hungary is simply by going there. Get your feet wet, so to speak."

The Hungarian legation to the United States in those days was up on 15th Street, just across from Meridian Hill Park. He and Marge were paraded up there four days before they were scheduled to leave.

"How I envy you your first sight of Budapest," the wife of the Hungarian legate, Nicholas Hogyesz, told them. Her English was quite good. "It is actually two cities, you know."

"Yes," Mahoney said. "Divided by the Danube. We're looking forward to serving there."

"My brother, Jan, is the director of the Erkel Theater. You will simply have to stop by and say hello for me." She had taken Mahoney's arm and had guided him toward the buffet. "Unfortunately he is not too happy where he is. He has the idea he would like to come to New York. Talk to him."

"I'd be happy to, madam," Mahoney had said, not at all certain exactly what she'd meant. Did she want someone to talk her brother out of his notion, or help him realize it? He avoided the issue for the rest of the evening.

"No one seems to know much about the place," Marge said on

the way home that evening. "Can't be any worse than Berlin or Moscow."

"We'll soon see," Mahoney had said, suddenly feeling very guilty about having turned down the Athens assignment, and yet looking forward to Budapest.

"Herb Tilley has been killed in an automobile accident," Bindrich said on the eve of their departure. "Will you take over as COS?"

Mahoney could hardly believe his ears, yet he knew that it had not been an accident. It stank of Chernov. "Only as long as it takes for you to come up with a replacement, Sylvan."

"Six months. You have my word on it."

"I'm going to hold you to it."

The Hungarian operation was much like Berlin when Mahoney finally arrived; it was in shambles. With Tilley's death—he was actually run over by a trolley, his body horribly mutilated—the in-place networks seemed to melt into the vaporous night. Letter drops dried up, contact routines were ignored, and in one instance a young army cipher clerk turned around in mid-sentence at a meet and walked off. Within twenty-four hours he had been transferred to Debrecen on the Rumanian border.

"We don't know what the hell's happening, Mr. Mahoney," Sid Kline, the assistant COS, told him. They met in the screened room on the second floor of the embassy on Szabadság Tér, just south of the Hungarian parliament building and a couple of blocks up from the river.

"There were no warnings?" Mahoney asked. "He was taking no precautions?"

"Not here," Kline responded. "Budapest is a safe city. I'd let my wife walk alone at night down a back alley."

"Until now."

Kline nodded. "This came out of the clear blue, I'm telling you."

But it hadn't, Mahoney thought. Tilley's death was Chernov's signal that Budapest wasn't going to turn out to be another Berlin.

"What do we do now?" Kline asked. "Write them all off?"

"We start over again, Sid, picking up whatever pieces we can, developing new networks where possible, but most of all keeping our ears to the ground and becoming a hell of a lot more careful than ever before."

The Mahoneys were settled in immediately. Their grand apartment was in the inner city district known as Belváros, across from

Margaret Island. It was an area of outdoor terraces and lovely cafés. In the summer they could hear the operas and ballets staged in the open air on the island. And all the while, Mahoney expected to see Chernov, but the man had become a phantom.

Budapest was a lovely old city, not flat as he'd been told at the State Department, and actually composed of two cities as the Hungarian legate's wife had told him. The city of Buda on the west side of the Danube was dominated by rounded hills and bluffs rising directly up from the broad river. Pest, on the east side of the river, was mostly flat and commercial, most of the city rebuilt since the war. They hired a housekeeper and cook who stayed with Marge during the day while Mahoney was at the embassy. Their routine was similar to the schedule they had maintained in Berlin, in that at least three evenings a week they attended functions at the various other embassies—including the Soviet embassy—at which they were introduced to Hungarian society, among them quite a number of deputies in the National Assembly. He also met Jan Gönc, whose sister was the wife of the Hungarian legate in Washington.

"My sister said that she had met you," he said. He was a man easily in his fifties, but with boyish features and very thick black hair.

"Yes, she told me to say hello," Mahoney said, shaking his hand. They were at cocktails at the British embassy on Harmincad Utca.

"Have you been to the theater?"

"Not yet," Mahoney said.

"Ah, but then we are closed for the summer and you have never been here before. How do you like our city?"

"It's lovely."

"Not very much like New York."

"No," Mahoney said noncommittally.

"But then I will have to go someday," Gönc said. "We must do lunch soon."

"Let's do," Mahoney said, and the man drifted off. Moments later the British chargé d'affaires came over, drink in hand.

"Wallace Mahoney, isn't it?" he asked. "Deputy undersecretary of state for something or other?"

"That's right," Mahoney said, shaking his hand.

"Have you known that one for very long?" the chargé asked.

"Not really. I met his sister in Washington."

"I see," the chargé said, glancing over his shoulder toward the bar. "Just a word of advice, old man. I'd watch out for him if I were you."

"Oh? Why?"

The chargé smiled faintly. "Word is that he is a major in the AVB, and a man of voracious appetites, if you catch my drift."

"No," Mahoney said. "Not quite."

"He has a penchant for good food, good wine, and young girls. *Very* young girls."

Mahoney smiled. "And unwary Western diplomats."

"Something like that," the chargé said. "Just be careful."

"Thanks," Mahoney said.

"It's nothing, old top."

Back at their apartment that evening Marge was strangely silent, but it took Mahoney a while before he noticed her mood because he was wrapped up in his own thoughts. "I don't like this place, Wallace," she told him. It was the very first time she had ever lodged a direct complaint against one of their assignments. "Everybody says one thing while they mean another," she explained. "And everyone is frightened."

He held her in his arms. "You too?" he asked.

"Yes, but I don't know why. I just feel it."

In the morning back in his office, Mahoney went back through Tilley's files and especially his contact sheets, coming up with Jan Gönc's name twice: once three months ago when they'd been introduced at the Soviet embassy during a reception for the newly elected mayor of Budapest; and the second time barely ten days before Tilley's death when they had lunch at the Duna Inter-Continental Hotel. The first meeting had merely been noted on Tilley's encounter sheet, along with the names of a dozen other Hungarians and a like number of Soviet diplomats. After the second meeting, however, Tilley had noted in his log that he suspected Gönc had possible AVB affiliations. "Check it out with K. A possible for us?"

"I don't know a thing about it, Mr. Mahoney," Sid Kline said when Mahoney showed him the entries.

"The K. would be you?"

"Yes, sir, but he never mentioned it to me."

"Dig up what we have on Gönc. We're going hunting."

Kline looked up from the encounter file. "Do you think Herb was murdered?"

"I think it's a very real possibility. The question is we don't know why, or even how he was pegged as chief of station, although I have a fairly good idea on that score."

At three that afternoon Mahoney telephoned Langley on the KO-6 encrypted line, and spoke with Carlisle. It was just nine in the morning in Washington. "I've had an approach made to me by an AVB captain. I need some quick information, Farley."

"You'd have more on that score over there," Carlisle said, his voice oddly distorted by the encryption. "Who is he?"

"Name is Jan Gönc. He's the director of the Erkel Theater. But I'm not calling about him. I need to know when Herb Tilley was last in Washington."

"That's easy. It was about three months ago, maybe four. I can dig up the exact date for you if need be. He was recalled for a conference about the time we realized the Russians were becoming generous with their largess. What are you on to?"

"Do you happen to know if Herb stopped by the Hungarian legation when he was in Washington?"

"Yes, he did. A cocktail party."

"On whose suggestion?"

"What are you getting at?"

"Who sent him, Farley?"

"I don't know," Carlisle said after a hesitation. "I suspect State got the invitation, and Tilley was keyed in. What exactly are you getting at?"

"You'd better talk to Sylvan on this one, but I suspect that the wife of the Hungarian legate is an AVB spotter. She claimed that Jan Gönc is her brother, and asked me to look him up when I got here."

"Good Lord," Carlisle said. "Which means you've been blown as well."

"It's likely," Mahoney said. Marge would be glad, he thought. It meant they would probably be going home soon. "I'm going to get in a couple of licks myself."

"I don't know if that's such a good idea. I think maybe we're going to pull you out of there."

"Give me a couple of days, Farley. If Gönc set Tilley up for assassination, or actually had a hand in it, I want to know."

"No heroics out there," Carlisle said. "I absolutely forbid any unilateral action on your part."

"Sure," Mahoney said.

There was almost nothing in the files on Jan Gönc, except that he was the director of the Erkel Theater, and indeed was the brother-in-law of the current legate to Washington.

"We're going to run a little operation, Sid," Mahoney told Kline. "And when we're finished, the little bastard Gönc will probably spend the rest of his life in a Hungarian jail—that is if they don't shoot him."

A big grin crossed Kline's face. "What can I do?"

"For starters we need a nice hotel that's a little bit off the beaten track. Somewhere we can have some privacy."

"How about a safe house?"

"You'd bet your life that the AVB doesn't know about it?"

"I don't know if I'd go that far, but close."

"All right. Secondly, I need some Dom Perignon champagne. Say, a case of it. A couple of pounds of Beluga caviar. Half a dozen Maine lobsters—live. Truffles. Pâté de fois gras. Whatever else you can think of along that line."

Kline whistled softly. "It'll put a hell of a dent in our budget."

"If need be we'll take up a collection."

"You got it," Kline said, grinning.

"We'll need a cameraman standing by, along with a sound technician and equipment."

"That's easier than the lobsters."

"How's your conscience, Sid?" Mahoney asked.

Kline's eyes narrowed. "Sir?"

"If Gönc actually had a hand in Tilley's death, what would you be willing to do about it?"

"Just about anything, sir," Kline said grimly.

"Then I want you to find me a prostitute, and set her up in the safe flat."

"We're going to burn the bastard . . ."

"A young one, Sid."

"How young?" Kline asked warily.

"Very young."

"Fifteen, sixteen?"

"More like ten or eleven," Mahoney said. "Or at least one who looks it."

Kline sighed deeply. "He's a perverted bastard, then?"

"That's what I've heard."

Kline turned away for a moment. He was married and had two children. One of them was a nine-year-old girl. "How soon?"

"Yesterday."

"Right. I'll get on it."

Hungary. Whenever Mahoney thought about his truncated assignment to Budapest station a sharp pain of realization would come to him what a terrible fool he'd been. Chernov was there, of course, but he never once showed himself. There was no need for

274

it. Had Mahoney been thinking straight he would have realized that Chernov had given him far too much in Berlin, and sooner or later he was going to take some back.

The safe house was nothing short of picturesque, on the Buda side of the river in an ancient section of the city near the Gellért Hill that was topped by a stone fort and a memorial to the Soviet liberation of the city in 1945. Ostensibly it was let on a long-term lease to a Canadian businessman who came and went at irregular intervals and had been doing so for nearly a year. When he was in residence he often had frequent callers, both foreign and Hungarian. The house was perfect, with a small garage and narrow courtyard in the rear through which Kline's people spirited their equipment, the food, and in the end the girl out of sight of the neighbors. The entire apartment was wired for sound, the equipment in the basement. From an attic crawl space each room of the apartment was clearly visible through the ceiling light fixtures. An added bonus to the setup, as Kline explained, was that none of the equipment installations was of a permanent nature. "Within fifteen minutes flat—less, actually, if we were pressed—we could have the place stripped clean. There might be a lot of questions about holes in the ceilings and walls, but nothing would point our way. Absolutely nothing."

It took Kline forty-eight hours to make his arrangements. In the meantime Mahoney stopped by the Erkel Theater to see Gönc in person, taking him out for a drink at a nearby café.

"I'm hosting a party at my apartment tomorrow evening," Mahoney said.

"Yes, and why not at your embassy? Isn't this unusual?"

Mahoney forced a smile. "It's not that kind of a party, Jan. Shall we say, wives are not invited?"

For a moment Gönc seemed startled, but then he broke out in a huge grin. "Ah, yes, I see," he said.

"Just a very few friends. Gentlemen. I've managed to come up with some lobsters from my state of Maine, and a few other interesting things."

"I would be honored, Wallace."

"Let's say around ten o'clock?"

They were keeping the operational personnel to a bare minimum. Kline would be stationed down the street, listening to what was going on in the apartment on a short-range radio. The cameraman was in the attic above the bedroom, and the sound technician was in the basement, both with instructions to get out as soon as they had what they needed. After tonight the safe house would be blown, of course, so most of the equipment had already been removed, and what remained would go that night.

The girl's pimp had been paid enough so that no matter what happened up there, she wouldn't say a thing. Kline had a lot of trouble dealing with that aspect of the assignment, as Mahoney suspected he would. But there was no help for it. If they meant to burn Gönc, it was the only way. Or at least it was the most effective short-term method. The girl had been kept completely insulated. She had been hired and installed in the bedroom by one of the station's personnel who had been scheduled for rotation back to the States. She was in place by eight-thirty, and the man was on the Malev Hungarian Airlines flight to Paris by nine forty-five, his part in the operation completed. The young girl's instructions were simple. She was to remain unclothed in the bedroom and under no circumstances whatsoever was she to come out, or try to see what was going on elsewhere in the apartment. Whoever came through the bedroom door, however, would be coming to see her, in which case she knew what to do.

"Makes me sick to my stomach," Kline said.

Mahoney entered the apartment just past nine-thirty. The food had been laid out, the champagne was cooling in a tub of ice, and the live lobsters were writhing in the bathtub. The lights were low, and music was playing on the tape deck. He took off his coat, laid it on the couch, and then unholstered his station-issue Beretta 9mm automatic, checking to make sure a live round was in the firing chamber and that the safety was on. He stuffed it in his belt at the small of his back, so that it would be easier for him to reach if he needed it, and then settled back to wait.

Several times he caught himself looking toward the bedroom door and wondering about the girl. He agreed completely with Kline: the whole thing was sickening. So was murder, he thought in justification. So was the entire business. He was in a glum mood. If Chernov was involved, and Mahoney expected he was, there would be more than one surprise before the night was over. Thinking back on it, he was amazed that he hadn't made the connection, that he hadn't instinctively known what would happen. As it was, he thought later, he'd been blinded once again by ambition, and by his own unfortunate ego.

The cameraman tapped the ceiling rafters twice, softly. Gönc had arrived. Mahoney got up from where he had been seated, opened the champagne, and poured two glasses. A couple of minutes later Gönc knocked on the door and Mahoney let him in.

"You're a little early, Jan, but that's all right," Mahoney said, filled with good cheer. "You didn't notice if you were followed here by any chance?"

"Followed?" Gönc flinched. "Why would someone be following me?"

Mahoney grinned lasciviously. "Guys get together like this, and you can't be too careful. A lot of them out there wouldn't understand, you know?"

Gönc wasn't following him at all, but he took a glass of champagne and eyed the banquet laid out. There was enough food for a dozen people. "I don't understand, Wallace. What wouldn't they out there understand?"

"You know." Mahoney winked. "Your sister asked me to take care of you, so what the hell. You know." Mahoney lowered his voice. "The others won't be along for a while yet. No reason you have to wait." He nodded toward the bedroom door.

"What is there?"

"Why don't you have a look? You're among friends now, Jan. People who understand."

Gönc went hesitantly to the bedroom door, opened it, and looked inside. He sucked in his breath.

"Hello," the young girl said. Mahoney could just hear her tiny voice. He moved farther back into the shadows.

For a long time Gönc just stood there. What if she was wrong? Mahoney thought. Too young or, heaven help us, too old for the bastard? What if the British chargé had been wrong? Something like that could only be known as a rumor. Gönc glanced over his shoulder, an unreadable expression on his face. Mahoney nodded for him to go ahead. He turned, hesitated a moment longer, then went into the bedroom closing the door behind him.

Mahoney went to the window and opened the curtain, allowing a little light to spill outside—once, then twice. The bait has been taken. The signal was a fallback in case something was wrong with Kline's radio.

He checked his gun again, then dumped out his champagne and poured himself a stiff measure of bourbon, drinking it neat in one swallow. Still he couldn't get the very bad taste from his mouth. He didn't want to know what was going on inside the bedroom, and yet he couldn't help but imagine. He was just glad that Kline wasn't running the camera upstairs. Pouring himself another drink he went out into the corridor and listened at the stairs. There was no one else in the building at this hour. On the ground floor was a small leather goods shop closed at six every evening. The owner lived with his wife's mother, renting out this apartment for some extra money.

Something dropped with a heavy thud up in the attic. Mahoney spun around. "Christ," the cameraman swore. "Oh, Christ!"

Something had gone drastically wrong. With a sense that everything they had done, everything they would do this night was nothing but a wasted effort and terribly futile, Mahoney was across the living room in three bounds, the pistol in his hand, the safety off and the hammer cocked. Chernov! It was all Chernov's doing! He could suddenly see it all. The legate's wife. Tilley's death. And now his own downfall. With every ounce of his strength he smashed open the door and stumbled into the bedroom. Gönc, his clothes off, sat straddling the young, thin girl, his hands still around her neck, her eyes open and bulging, blood filling her mouth where she had evidently bit through her tongue. He had murdered her. He was Chernov's handmaiden. He was a madman. All of it came to Mahoney as a whole.

"Why?" Mahoney hissed, raising the gun with shaking hands.

Someone was racing up the stairs, not bothering to keep down the noise.

"It was him!" Gönc cried. "It was—"

Mahoney fired, the bullet catching Gönc in the middle of the face, driving his head backward, blood and bone and white matter spraying the wall and the white curtains, as he fell and kept falling, it seemed, forever into a great bottomless pit that was so close it threatened to swallow Mahoney as well.

15

John waited in the recess of a doorway across the alley from the rear loading platform of the hotel. Tonia was positioned about twenty yards to his left. His heart was pounding. The one in the three-piece suit was no CIA fieldman. He'd bet almost anything on it. The Agency, for all its mistakes and blunders, simply did not open fire in crowded hotel lobbies. The Tiergarten at night was one thing; this was something entirely different.

Look for the anomalies, his father had told him. The concept had been drilled into his head for years. Look for the odd bits that seem to be out of focus, or out of sequence. Look for the inexplicable. Nothing happens without a pattern. A fact or a sequence of events that seems outside your immediate ken are merely telling you that there is another pattern. Search for it!

Snow was still falling steadily, muffling sounds. In the distance, however, he could already hear the first of the sirens converging on the hotel. They were running out of time. Soon the alley would be blocked both ways. The door at his back was locked. He'd already checked it, so there would be no escape that way. If they waited too long they would have to take their chances back in the hotel.

The assassin had only three choices that John could see. He could have turned and left the hotel by the front door. No one would have tried to stop him, not after what had happened. If they did he would simply kill them. Once outside he would have a car waiting and would be able to disappear in the confusion. Or he could have gone to another part of the hotel, perhaps to a room, perhaps even to the basement where there could be an exit to one of the neighboring buildings. Or he could have come after them, in which case he should already have appeared at the back doorway unless he had run into trouble, or unless he was being overly cautious. The kitchen staff had been startled when he and Tonia had raced through, but no one had tried to stop them, nor had there been anyone to impede their progress through the supply area and out onto the loading dock.

Where the hell was he? More importantly, who was he? John had seen the look on his face. He was a professional, but beyond that he had seemed to actually enjoy the killing. He had been smiling.

The sirens were getting closer. A blue windowless delivery van turned the corner and came down the alley. John hunched farther back into the doorway. The driver swung the van around and backed it up to the loading platform.

If the assassin had come after them he would have been here already. Aware that he was exposing himself to anyone watching from the hotel windows, John stepped out of the doorway, and holding his gun out of sight at his side, he quickly crossed the alley.

The van's driver was a young man dressed in white coveralls. Leaving the engine running he got out of the van and started around to the back. He looked around as John approached him, his eyes suddenly growing wide as he saw the pistol.

"I mean you no harm if you do exactly as I tell you," John told him in German, pointing the gun at him.

The driver stepped back, raising his hands above his head. He looked past John and flinched as Tonia hurried up the alley.

"Put your hands down!" John ordered, and the driver complied. He was very frightened.

The sirens were much closer now. There were a lot of them.

"Get in on the other side," John told Tonia. She went immediately to the passenger side and got in. "I'll be in the back," he told the driver. "You're going to drive away from here. No funny stuff or we will kill you instantly. Do you understand?"

"Jawohl, mein Herr," the frightened driver stammered.

"All right, get in. I'll be in the back."

The driver got in behind the wheel. John hurried to the back of the van, yanked open the doors, and climbed inside over a stack of plastic crates that contained new linen napkins, the hotel's monogram in the corner. When he had the door closed he worked his way forward so that he was right behind the driver.

"Let's go, nice and easy now."

The driver pulled away, turning left the way he had come. At the end of the alley he stopped. Three police cars had pulled up in front of the hotel; a fourth and fifth were just coming around the far corner. "Turn right," John ordered.

The driver complied and they headed the two blocks up to the

Kaiserdamm. The traffic light was red. Other police cars were converging on the hotel from all over the city. One ran the red light, passing them, and then the light turned green and John directed the driver to turn right again, taking them back toward the center of the city.

Tonia held her silence. She looked back at John. It was clear she wanted to say something, and it was just as clear that she was mad that her weapon had misfired. She was professional enough to realize what had happened and why. But she was also professional enough to realize that now wasn't the time to talk about it. The less information the driver had to give to the police when they released him, the easier it would be for them to remain at large a little longer. And only that. John had no illusions that they would escape West Berlin. Everything was against them. Their only strengths now were their own tradecraft as well as the list Tonia had brought out with her. As long as no one else had it, they would have at least the chance to find Chernov and his father. But only just a chance.

They entered the Ernst Reuter Platz and John ordered the driver to turn right again down to the Ku'Damm. Traffic was piling up downtown. Some shops and offices had opened, but still the holiday mood pervaded the city. There was a lot of pedestrian traffic.

John leaned forward. "We're going to get off here," he said. "Once we're out I want you to drive back to the hotel and make your delivery as if nothing happened. Do you understand?"

"Yes, sir," the driver said.

"Pull over here."

They stopped in front of the Europa Center with its shops and department stores.

"Do not talk to the police," John said. "If you do, we will know about it, and I can guarantee that we will come looking for you. Do you understand that as well?"

"Yes, sir," the driver whispered.

John scrambled back over the boxes, pocketed his gun, then opened the back door and jumped out. Tonia had already gotten out. The moment John slammed the back door, the van took off.

"He'll stop the first policeman he sees," Tonia said.

"No doubt," John replied. They waited until the van was out of sight, then turned and headed directly over to the parking garage where John's rental car was still parked on Bleibtreustrasse, losing themselves in the crowd. Sometimes John lagged behind watching both sides of the streets, until Tonia would suddenly stop to admire some bit of merchandise in a shop window, giving him a chance to pass and allowing her a moment to see if anyone was coming up from behind them. In a small measure it felt good to be out in the field like this, especially with someone who knew what she was doing. But always riding on his shoulder like a terrible weight was the knowledge that everything was coming to an end for him. There no longer was any doubt of it in his mind. The pattern was clear, or at least some aspects of it were. Someone wanted him stopped before he reached his father and Chernov. And he was finally beginning to understand the why, if not the who.

The Grunewald Hotel was snowed in. From the second-floor window of his room, Wallace Mahoney could see the drift-covered road that led back up to the Zehlendorf Highway and hear the high-pitched whine of the approaching snowmobile. "One man," he said.

"Official?" Chernov asked behind him. They had been talking most of the morning, though Chernov had risen late, complaining of chest pains. It was his heart, Mahoney suspected, though the Russian wouldn't admit it.

"Doesn't look like it," Mahoney said. "Just the one machine."

"We'd better check it out. Do you want to take the front or the back?"

Mahoney turned away from the window. "He could be out for a joyride."

"There's been enough time for them to catch up with us if they're sharp," Chernov said.

"Let's call it quits. Go home. I'll do the same," Mahoney said. If he had learned one thing by delving back into his memories, it was that the past can never be altered: triumphs and defeats, accomplishments and failures, were all of the same thing; they were nothing more or less than the simple fabric of our past. Untouchable no matter how urgent the reasons.

"Not yet, Wallace," Chernov said. "But very soon, I promise you."

"What are you waiting for?"

"The truth."

"From you?" Mahoney asked disdainfully.

"Even from me, and then you will see what must be done, and why you and I are the only ones for it."

Mahoney glanced again out the window. The snowmobile had stopped at the edge of the trees where the road swept up from the lake to the front entrance of the hotel. The driver had dismounted and was studying the hotel through binoculars. "I'll take the lobby," he said, turning back again. "If need be I'll lead him out the back door and up the path toward the hill."

"He may be here only to check at the registration desk with orders not to make contact."

"If that's the case, I think I can manage to convince him to take a little walk with me."

"I suspect you can," Chernov said with a faint smile.

When he was gone, Mahoney pulled on his overcoat and hat. He checked to make certain that the silencer cylinder was screwed firmly to the barrel of his .38 police special. Leaving his gloves behind, he stuffed the gun in his pocket and went downstairs to the lobby. Schemmerhorn, the young clerk, was behind the desk.

"Oh, Herr Greenleaf, you're going out, I see. Unfortunately there is no transportation into the city at the moment. But we have been told that the plows will come sometime this afternoon or early evening. I hope this is no inconvenience?"

"None whatsoever," Mahoney said, smiling pleasantly. "I thought I would take a walk."

"Yes, please be careful, sir. The snow can be treacherous."

"Thank you, I will."

The snowmobile came up the driveway and stopped outside. Mahoney stepped a few paces away from the desk and at one of the tables picked up a magazine. The driver, dressed in a black snowmobile suit, came in and stomped the snow from his boots in the vestibule. As he crossed the lobby he pulled off his helmet, glancing only briefly toward Mahoney.

"Good afternoon," Schemmerhorn said.

"I have a message to deliver," the driver said. "For Herr Greenleaf, or Herr Nostrand."

Before Schemmerhorn could react, Mahoney put down the magazine and stepped up behind the man. "Then you are in luck. I am Herr Greenleaf."

The driver spun around. Mahoney put his hand in his coat pocket, his fingers curling around the grip of the pistol. The driver, realizing the mistake he had made, started to step away, but Mahoney took his arm with his free hand and smiled.

"I think you can give me your message in person," he said. "In private. If you will just come this way."

The driver stiffened for a moment, but then let Mahoney lead him across the lobby, past the dining room, and out the back door.

283

"I have a gun in my pocket and I will not hesitate to use it if you do not cooperate with me," Mahoney said once they were outside.

"I mean you no harm, Herr Greenleaf."

"Nor I you," Mahoney said. "In this you must believe me." They headed away from the hotel up a gently sloping path into the woods.

"Where are we going?"

"To meet Herr Nostrand, and to find out about this message of yours."

The driver held back. "I will talk to you, not him."

They were just at the edge of the woods. In the falling snow they could barely see the hotel behind them. "Very well. Tell me the message."

"There is none. I was merely sent to find out if you were registered here at this hotel under those names."

"Who sent you?"

"I'm not at liberty to say, sir."

Mahoney took the gun out of his pocket, careful not to catch the barrel of the silencer on the material, and pointed it at the driver. "I suspect you know that I must insist."

"I wish no trouble with you, Herr Greenleaf, nor do I wish to deal with the Russian."

"Then I will ask you again, who sent you?"

"Wilhelm Allmann."

"The name is not familiar to me."

"He is the owner of the Ballhaus Resi."

"Why does he wish to find me?" Mahoney asked. He couldn't imagine the connection, unless the BND had somehow become involved. It was possible that Carlisle had asked for their help.

"It is a contract of a private nature, sir. I swear that is all I know."

"Why did you come to this hotel?"

"There is a list, from what I understand, of locations where you and the Russian may have met once before. Just after the war."

"What was the source of this list?" Mahoney asked.

"I do not know."

"Are there others searching for us?"

The driver was clearly nervous. He kept glancing up the path toward the woods. "The CIA and KGB are both said to be searching West Berlin. They consider your disappearance a matter of some importance, especially after the killings."

"What killings?" Mahoney asked sharply.

"A man in Washington and another in Bonn. I do not know the

284

American, but the police are looking for the murderer of the German citizen."

"Who was?"

"A gentleman named Bernhard Heiser."

Mahoney realized he had been holding his breath. He let it out with a sigh. So many memories. So many past mistakes for which truly he could never atone. Only someone who could have known about the incident here in Berlin in 1948 could have also known about Heiser. The connection led back to the CIA. Specifically one name.

Chernov stepped out from behind a tree barely ten yards up the hill and came down to them. He had his gun drawn. The driver backed up and appeared ready to bolt and run.

"I am an excellent shot," Chernov said. "I suggest that you consider very carefully the alternatives."

It was over finally, Mahoney thought, almost gratefully. They had run out of time. They would have to leave as soon as possible.

"I wish neither of you gentlemen any harm," the snowmobile driver said. He was obviously deeply frightened of Chernov.

"You are nothing more than a nuisance to us," Chernov said. "And because of it you are going to be very uncomfortable for the next few hours." He stepped aside and motioned up the path toward the hill. "We're going to walk you over the top of the hill, beyond which is a forest. The highway is about seven or eight kilometers almost straight west. By the time you reach it, hail a ride, and then get to a telephone, we will be long gone."

"Yes, sir," the driver said, relieved.

"We do not like being spied upon," Chernov said harshly. "It would be most unfortunate for you should we see you again."

"Yes, sir, I understand perfectly," the driver said. But Mahoney did not. According to the desk clerk the hotel road to the highway would not be open to normal traffic until later this afternoon or possibly not until this evening. It would be hours before they could leave.

Chernov motioned again up the path and the driver started up it, Chernov right behind him. They got barely twenty yards, just within the protection of the woods where there was no chance of being observed from the hotel, when without warning Chernov raised his automatic and fired a single shot at point-blank range into the back of the driver's head.

"No!" Mahoney shouted.

The driver pitched forward onto his face, his helmet rolling a few feet away, his right leg twitching for a moment, and then he was still.

Mahoney had rushed up the path. He raised his pistol and pointed it directly at Chernov's head. He cocked the hammer, the noise loud.

Chernov looked up. "Just a few more hours and then you will understand everything."

There was no use asking why Chernov had killed the man. There was no possible way they could have let him leave here. But the cold-bloodedness of the murder was impossible for him to accept. Oh, he had made mistakes, all right, but he had never been what Chernov was. Never. Still it would be good to pull the trigger now.

"I know what you're thinking, Wallace, and I know why. But you must wait."

What hold did Chernov have on him? Mahoney wondered. For more than forty years it had not changed one iota. He lowered his pistol. "What about his machine?"

"We'll hide his body, and then I'll don his dark suit and helmet, walk around to the front, and drive the machine into the woods somewhere."

"What about your heart?"

"You're slipping, Wallace. Concern about my health while wishing to shoot me dead would seem to me to be mutually exclusive concepts." He laughed, and Mahoney suspected that the man was probably quite mad, and all this could have been for nothing.

It was a few minutes before seven in the morning. Carlisle felt like hell. He hadn't had a chance for as much as a cup of coffee all night. Since midnight, their operations and desk officers had come filtering in one by one. The Agency was now on full emergency footing. The DCI had gone over to brief the president at six. The Russians were definitely up to something in the region of Semipalatinsk, as well as along the Soviet-Chinese border. It was going to be up to the president and his advisers whether or not U.S. military forces would be elevated in readiness to a DEFCON THREE or even a TWO, which could do nothing but increase the tension in an already nearly explosive situation. The problem was, according to McLean, that no one at State or in the Pentagon had the slightest idea what the Russians were up to this time. It was scaring the hell out of everyone. In the meantime he hadn't heard a thing about Mahoney in the past seven hours.

Stepping off the elevator on the seventh floor, he walked past the DCI's office and entered the anteroom of the deputy director. His secretary was at her desk. She looked up. "Oh, Mr. Carlisle, go right in. He's expecting you, sir."

"Thanks," Carlisle mumbled.

Sylvan Bindrich was on the telephone when Carlisle walked in. "I'll call you back in a few minutes," he said and hung up.

Carlisle closed the door and crossed the big room.

"We've finally traced that Bern account," Bindrich said.

Carlisle involuntarily glanced over his shoulder.

"We're secure here, Farley. The recorders are off, for the moment." Bindrich's face had visibly aged over the past few days. His jowls sagged, his complexion was pale, and there were dark circles beneath his red-rimmed eyes. "We had to twist a few arms to get a follow-up. The account was hidden through a blind corporation in Italy. Belongs to a Wilhelm Allmann. Owns the Ballhaus Resi nightclub in West Berlin."

"With underworld connections," Carlisle said, seeing it all.

"Apparently John has hired himself a personal army," Bindrich said.

"Then he must know something we don't."

"It gets worse than that, Farley. Much worse," Bindrich said heavily. "I want you to get on the phone to this Allmann and buy whatever John gave him, and then buy him off."

"What about the budget line? How much can we hide?"

"I don't care. The sky's the limit. John has gone completely crazy. He shot and killed Turner in the Tiergarten, and at this moment he's apparently joined forces with Tonia Trusov."

The enormity of what Bindrich was telling him was staggering. They were on the right track after all. Everything they had done, the laws they had broken, the lies, the skulking around dark corridors, the phone calls in the middle of the night, all of it could be forgiven now because they were right. "Then it proves—" he began, but Bindrich cut him off crossly.

"It doesn't prove a goddamned thing, Farley. You haven't been in this business long enough to know what constitutes a proof."

The remark stung, all the more for the fact that he *had* been in this business for a long time. Too long a time, he was thinking right now. "What else do you want, Mr. Deputy Director?" he asked coldly.

Bindrich looked at him intently. Then he shook his head. "It's the job, it's finally gotten to me," he said. "Sorry."

"We're all under a lot of tension, Sylvan. I'll call Allmann and see what I can come up with. In the meantime where's Byrd?"

"At the Bristol waiting for instructions. He's mad as hell. He wants revenge."

"What exactly did happen?" Carlisle asked. They might cover the major portion of the operation satisfactorily but how would they explain a dead agent killed in the middle of an illegal operation? Congress would have a field day with it, so would *The New York Times* or *The Washington Post* if they got hold of it.

"I don't know, I haven't got the entire story, but evidently Turner got careless and John was suddenly there behind him in the park."

"He shot Turner in cold blood?" Carlisle asked. "What more do you want?"

"Byrd fired the first shot. Thought he could scare him off. Turner evidently tried to run and John shot him."

"Good Lord almighty. Have the West Berlin police got it yet?"

"As a John Doe. His ID was missing."

"Did John take it?"

"Evidently," Bindrich said. His telephone rang. He picked it up. "Hold my calls for another minute or two, Sally," he said.

"He asked Bixby if we had someone on him. He probably knew or suspected from the beginning. Let's pull him in, Sylvan. Now. Before this goes farther astray."

"It won't be that easy."

"If we put enough people on it . . ."

"You're forgetting about Wallace and Chernov," Bindrich said. "The Russians are after them in a very big way. Their people are all over West Berlin, and Hannover. They've already had at least one run-in with the BND—who by the way are screaming bloody murder."

"You said it was all in Heiser's journal."

"Not that, Farley," Bindrich said, leaning forward. "Chernov came out now not simply for a chat about old times. He came out bringing something with him."

"What are you getting at?"

"Just this: The timing is damn curious to my way of thinking, considering what's happening along the Chinese border right now."

Carlisle suddenly did understand what Bindrich was getting at. "Do you think they're actually going to start something, and Chernov wants to warn us?"

"Who else would listen to him other than Mahoney?"

"The goddamned old fool," Carlisle said. "This time he really doesn't know what he's gotten himself in for."

"No," Bindrich said softly. "In some ways I hope to God we're wrong."

"But we're not."

"No, I don't suspect we are."

"What do you want me to do, Sylvan? Tell me. Whatever it is I'll do it."

"Find out what Allmann knows, and then pass it on to Jack Byrd. If need be we'll get Bixby and the entire Berlin station on it. Number one priority is to find Mahoney and Chernov. Find out what Chernov brought out with him."

"And?" Carlisle asked. There always seemed to be *ands* in this business.

"Transmit the file on John and on Tonia Trusov over to Pullach. We'll get the BND and the West Berlin police in on it as well."

"On what charge?"

"The murders of Bernhard Heiser and his housekeeper. What else?" Bindrich asked.

Now that Mahoney had come this far, he felt an urgent need to continue, to see this one last terrible thing to its end. Chernov wanted him to hold on for a few more hours, so hold on he would. Once again he stood by the window in his room looking up the snow-clogged road, seeing the tracks, already beginning to fill in with drifting snow, of the snowmobile coming in and going out. The hotel was deathly still. The messenger's arrival had barely been noted, and his departure had caused even less of a stir. There would be others, though. They were gathering out there. Time was ebbing, as it had in another time and another place. Moscow. Around every corner, down every dark alley he had expected to see Chernov waiting for him. After the Hungarian debacle he'd expected the man would at least show himself long enough to gloat. But he hadn't, though Mahoney suspected he was in Moscow again. The president was due for a state visit, and KGB headquarters in Dzerzhinsky Square suddenly seemed to be on emergency footing. A lot of people were getting nervous in Moscow. Find out what the bastards are up to, Wallace. This can't be coincidental, Wallace. Shall we advise the president to cancel his visit, Wallace? What should we do? Where should we turn? You're the bloody expert. Where should we turn? To another Yuri, this one Zamyatin, a colonel in the KGB's Political Services Division with a wild story about a kidnapped Soviet scientist and a state-of-the-art laser device small enough to be portable yet powerful enough to be used as a weapon of assassination? "An assassination?" Mahoney asked the Russian on a deserted Moscow street corner one night. They had worked with each other during the war. Zamyatin had been on Chernov's staff.

"Yes, my friend. There may be an attempted assassination. But not of Brezhnev. Of your own president. Here in Moscow on Soviet soil as he steps off Air Force One."

Mahoney had pulled a gun on him.

"One of two things is happening," Zamyatin said. "First, the kidnapping was arranged by a Soviet group to assassinate your president. But that would be insane."

"We're not talking about sanity," Mahoney said.

"The other possibility—the one more likely—is that this operation is being carried out by your own people."

"We would not kill our own president."

"What about Kennedy?" Zamyatin had said. "If it is a Soviet group, I will find them and stop them. But if it is an American operation, *you* must stop it."

But it had been nothing more than a fishing expedition, a carefully orchestrated operation designed to test the capabilities of the Agency's Moscow operation. Engineered by Chernov, no doubt, and conducted by him from behind the scenes. A second retribution for Berlin. Hungary hadn't been enough. He'd wanted even more. In the end Zamyatin had been shot dead, and Mahoney's son Michael had been kidnapped from his laboratory in Missoula and driven on a mad ride through the Montana countryside which ended in an automobile accident. Sorry, Mr. Mahoney, but your son is dead. Sorry, dear sweet Margery, but our son is no longer with us and I am to blame. Not Chernov, though his hand is in it, but me for a single mistake that has compounded itself all out of proportion with any known reality.

16

John saw Tonia at the end of the block hesitate for just a moment and then enter the parking garage. She looked very capable and sure of herself. Just another Berliner coming for her car. The thought briefly crossed his mind that he could be walking into a trap. She could have been sent out to stop him. The one in the three-piece suit who had shot at them was a Russian, he had decided. Other than Allmann's people, the Russians were the only others who could possibly have the list of meeting places. If he was one of Tonia's people, they could both be waiting upstairs in the garage.

A police car cruised past, its rear wheels spinning in the deep snow. John turned away to study something in a shop window until it disappeared around the corner, and then he hurried the rest of the way down the block to a side entrance into the garage. The attendant in a glass booth looked up as John came up the ramp. He pushed open the window. "This is for exit only," he said in broken German. He was a Turk. "For cars, not for walking."

John held up his ticket. "I'm just going up for my car."

"Take the elevator, or walk the stairs. This is for exit only."

"Where?" John asked, pretending not to understand.

A car came from an upper level, and John stepped aside as the driver stopped at the window and handed up his ticket and money. While the attendant was distracted, John hurried the rest of the way inside and started up around the first switchback where he stopped in the gloom and listened. His car was parked on the third level halfway between the up and down ramps, and directly across from the stairwell that Tonia had used. "If someone is up there waiting, we'll have them between us," John had told her.

"Why take the risk?" she'd asked. "I don't understand. We don't need your car. We can get another."

"I want to know if someone is there."

She had looked at him closely. "A dangerous little diversion.

Your last with my gun nearly cost us our lives." She'd been annoyed, but she'd held her anger in check.

"It wasn't coincidence that he was at the Europäischer Hof. Your people are the only ones who have the list. But my people are the only ones who know about my car."

"And the hotel," she snapped. "We could have been followed. If he was Russian I'd know him."

"He's not CIA," John said. "I'd know him. Besides, the Agency doesn't open fire in crowded hotel lobbies."

She'd laughed disdainfully. "Then we shall go to the parking garage and see what we shall see," she said. "What about afterward?"

"We're not going to stop until we find them."

"I agree," she said.

Somewhere above a car door slammed and a moment later an engine roared to life. He listened as the car was backed out of its stall, its tires squealing lightly on the cement and then it started down. Stepping between two cars, he reached in his pocket for his gun but didn't pull it out. A few seconds later the car appeared at the head of the ramp, drove slowly past, turned on the switchback, and was gone. An elderly couple had been in the front, a young girl in the back seat. The garage was quiet again, and he continued up the ramp to the next level, pausing at the switchback to watch and listen from the shadows, but nothing moved. At the third level he stopped again behind a thick concrete support pillar. He pulled out his gun and switched off the safety. From where he stood he could see the rear bumper of his Volkswagen parked between a Fiat and a much larger dark red Mercedes. On the opposite side of the ramp a red *Ausgang* sign illuminated the stairwell door which was partially ajar. She was already in place.

"Tonia?" he called out just loudly enough for her to hear him, his voice echoing off the low ceilings.

"Here," she said from the stairwell.

John stepped around the pillar, and keeping low, he raced to the nearest car, expecting a gunshot at any moment. But the garage remained deathly still. Getting down on his hands and knees he looked beneath the car. As far as he could see up the line of parked cars on this side of the ramp, no one was in hiding unless his feet and legs were blocked by a tire, or unless someone was inside one of the dozen or so parked vehicles.

He moved around to the front of the car and worked his way between its front bumper and the cement wall to the next car in line.

The stairwell door began to open just as John heard a car coming from below on the up ramp on the far side of the garage. "Wait," he called softly, and the door closed. He eased down a little lower, still just able to see the end of the ramp.

A blue and white police cruiser came around the corner and slowly moved down the row of cars. What the hell were they doing here now? John ducked lower so that he was completely out of sight. He heard the patrol car stop and a moment later both doors opened. He could hear the blare of the police radio. Looking beneath the car he was hiding behind he could see the legs of the two police officers. They were at his Volkswagen, and it came to him all at once that Bixby had not been able to fix his alibi with the West Berlin police. They knew his name, and they were looking for him now in connection with the murders of Heiser and the housekeeper. They'd probably checked all the car rental agencies in town and had been searching for the Volkswagen.

One of the cops went to the door on the driver's side. John started to straighten up, when a tremendous explosion shattered the stillness, the flash filling the entire ramp with a blinding light, the concussion sending metal, flaming fabric and oil, and huge chunks of concrete flying everywhere. He was shoved up against the wall, his ears ringing, his entire body battered. Blood streamed from his nose. For several long seconds he sat where he was trying to make his brain work. They'd planted a bomb in his car against the possibility that he would be coming after it. It had been a simple contact fuse that went off the moment anyone so much as touched the car. They hadn't given a damn that an innocent person would get hurt.

Slowly he crawled over a pile of rubble, realizing with a sick feeling just how close they had come to being killed.

"Tonia?" he called, getting shakily to his feet.

The explosion had completely destroyed his car, the cars on either side of it, the police car, and had blown a huge hole in the wall and the ceiling. Two other cars were burning furiously. It would only be a matter of seconds before their fuel tanks exploded. There was absolutely no trace of the cops.

"Tonia?" he called again, stumbling forward. Through the dust and smoke he could just make out the wall where the stairwell exit had been. The door was gone and an engine block lay smoldering in the opening just where she had been standing. Christ, he thought. He looked over his shoulder. Someone would be coming very soon. And the moment the burning cars began exploding, this place would become an inferno. Leave her, he told himself.

Turn around and get the hell out. She'd brought over the list, and he'd seen it and memorized it. He didn't need her any longer. If she were already dead, so much the better; it would save him the trouble. If they found her body, they might suspect that he'd been blown to bits, and the search for him would ease up. It was hard to make his brain work. It was hard to decide.

Holding his arm up to protect his face, he ran forward around the burning remains of the police cruiser, stepping in something wet and red, the heat singeing his coat and his hair. He had to jump over the engine block to get into the stairwell. The heavy metal door was wedged between the twisted metal railing and the wall on the first landing down. Tonia was nowhere in sight. She could have run, he realized. Her gun was lying on one of the treads. He picked it up and pocketed it, the motion causing a wave of dizziness to wash over him.

"Tonia?" he called again, starting down the stairs.

She moaned, the sound coming from beneath the door. He had to scramble up over the rail in order to get over it. She had been shoved up against the corner, the edge of the door just inches from her head. She appeared dazed, but there was no blood anywhere, and she didn't seem to be seriously injured.

"Can you move?" he asked her.

She looked up, blinking. "The car?" she mumbled. "Was it your car?"

"Yes," he said, helping her out from beneath the door. "We've got to get the hell out of here now."

"What about the police?" she asked. She was still dazed, but she was coming around fast. She still had her shoulder bag.

"They're dead. Can you walk?"

"I think so," she said. They started down the stairs, John helping her. Halfway down to the second level she suddenly stopped. "My gun . . ."

"I've got it."

They could hear the first of the sirens in the distance. Someone was shouting below on the stairs. On the second-floor landing John hauled open the door and dragged Tonia out onto the ramp. No one had come this way yet, but it would be only a matter of seconds before someone would be showing up.

He started toward the down ramp.

"Wait," Tonia said, holding back. "We won't get out of here on foot."

"How—" John started to ask, but she broke away and hurried off to a Mercedes parked just across from them. John followed after her. She took something from her purse, bent over the door lock, did something with it, and then pulled open the door.

"Get in," she said. Her speech was still slightly slurred, but she was beginning to move fast. She flipped open the passenger door lock, and then began working on the ignition lock with her steel pick. It took her precious seconds before she finally had it, and the engine roared to life just as another explosion boomed above them on the third level.

"What was that?" she shouted.

"A gas tank."

They could hear someone screaming in the stairwell. The burning fuel must have spewed through the opening on the third-floor landing.

Tonia slammed the car in gear, backed out of the stall, and careened down the ramp toward the exit. A police car had already shown up and had pulled over on the street. Tonia lowered her window.

"There was an explosion!" she shouted hysterically. "A fire! There are people trapped up there! My God, someone help them!"

The parking ramp attendant was running toward them, shouting for them to stop, but the cop from the police cruiser was waving them on. "Get out of here! Get away!" he shouted.

A sizable crowd had already gathered. As they shot away from the ramp up Bleibtreustrasse toward the Ku'Damm, John was sure he had spotted the assassin from the Europäischer Hof in the crowd, but then they were past and racing away.

"It was him," John said, looking out the rear window.

"Who?" Tonia demanded.

"The one from the hotel."

"Did he see us?"

"I think so," John said. "Christ, I think so."

Even now, so many years after she was gone, a day never passed in which Mahoney didn't think about Marge. Dear sweet Marge who had been the mainstay of his life through the wars, through the operations good as well as bad, through his assignments—Washington, Berlin, Moscow, Budapest, and the others—through their troubles. The lowest point in their lives had come when they'd learned of Michael's death. He was so young, he had hardly begun to live. From that time on she had been a changed woman. And it wasn't long afterward that she got sick and died. He was sincerely glad that she'd not been alive to bear the pain of the deaths of their daughter-in-law and the grandchildren. Not a day went by, either, in which he didn't feel an overwhelming sense of guilt for what he had put her through.

His guilt and his longing for his wife, of course, had finally crystallized into an abiding hate for the man who had put him through it all. At times he thought that his hate was the only thing that kept him going, the only thing that allowed him to face each day: There will come the day, he used to tell himself, in which I will once again come face to face with Chernov, and I will not hesitate to kill him. In the early days after Marge's death he dreamed about his revenge. But with time the dreams faded, leaving in their aftermath a bitter realization that it was too late. He had grown old and so had Chernov. His friends and contacts in the business had retired or died, or had simply drifted off.

Chernov's color was a pasty white. He'd managed somehow to find a portable black-and-white television set and he sat watching one of the West Berlin stations. Mahoney had seen him trudging up the road, how he had stopped every few yards to catch his breath, and how once he had stumbled and nearly fallen. In the lobby Mahoney had met him and helped him upstairs to his room.

"The machine is hidden," he wheezed. "About a kilometer up the road. Not well, but the snow will soon cover it."

"Do you need a doctor?" Mahoney had asked dispassionately.

Chernov looked up, shook his head. "No doctors."

"Someone else will be coming, you know. It won't be long now."

"No, it won't be long now," Chernov had said, and he turned on the television and sat down in front of it.

Mahoney stood by the door. He had transferred his gun to his jacket pocket. The bulge was obvious, but he didn't really care. "And then what?" he said.

"Then I'll talk and you'll listen."

"Yes?"

Chernov turned around. "And then you'll run back to Washington and tell your people what has happened here. You will give them the proof and something will be done about the . . . madness."

"There will be some out there who would want to stop me."

"No doubt," Chernov said with a harsh laugh. "Nor do I have any doubt that you will somehow manage. You always did."

The news came on and Chernov turned back to the television, but it was only a weather bulletin. The stern-faced news reader explained on a weather map of Europe how the front was intensifying, and how the snow would not only continue, but would increase over the next twenty-four hours. Mahoney turned inward once again to his own thoughts, every now and then reaching in his pocket to touch the pistol. Soon, he thought. Very soon now.

Farley Carlisle felt that he was finally going to be vindicated, because no matter what Sylvan Bindrich said to the contrary, he was, and had been for some time now, convinced that John Mahoney was a traitor. A spy. A penetration agent in the employ of the Soviet Union. On the surface, of course, the notion had been ridiculous. A man who had lost his mother and brother to the Russians, and a man who had watched his wife and babies burn up in a fire caused, he was led to believe, by the Russians, could hardly be considered a likely employee of the same bastards. But we lived in a strange world in which a man's motivations could only be truly known by himself. It was like throwing a football down from a great height onto the pavement: you knew that it was going to bounce, but there was no way in heaven or on earth to know which way it would go.

The difficulty had come because there had never been a single all-damning bit of evidence. John had been guilty of no one act that could be construed as an act of a traitor. He had simply known too much. He had been in the right places at *too* right a time. He had, of course, inherited some of his father's old contacts, but they were not gods. They didn't know everything. And there had been too many operations that should have worked but that had gone sour for inexplicable reasons . . . reasons that were inexplicable unless a penetration agent had been active within the Agency.

"Like father, like son," he mumbled to himself alone in his office waiting for his call to go through to the Bristol Hotel in West Berlin. He'd seen Bindrich's files from the fifties during the big witch-hunt. Wallace Mahoney had been a prime suspect. He, like his son, simply knew more than was humanly possible for one man to know. The investigation had been dropped for lack of evidence, but in some of the oblique references Bindrich had made in the past, Carlisle knew that the elder Mahoney was still suspect. Who knows? he thought. Maybe they had worked together all these years with Chernov as their control officer. At this moment John was running around West Berlin with the KGB's top assassin. What more proof was needed?

Wilhelm Allmann had been very cooperative once he understood that Carlisle not only knew his Bern account number, but had in fact been the banker. For two hundred thousand marks he had been effusive in his desire to "be of some assistance," as he put it.

"There has been some trouble already," Allmann had said delicately.

"Of what nature is this trouble?" Carlisle had asked.

"There was shooting just a few hours ago at one of our better hotels. Witnesses apparently saw a man and a woman escaping." Allmann gave their descriptions. "Would this be them?"

"Yes," Carlisle had said. "Who did they shoot?"

"We are not quite clear on this as yet, but reports seem to indicate that a third person, a young, handsome, well-dressed man, may have opened fire first. A woman was killed, as was the hotel's security guard. The West Berlin police at this moment are looking for a man named John Mahoney."

"For these shootings?"

"No," Allmann had said. "In connection with the murders of an old man and his housekeeper."

"In Bonn," Carlisle said.

"Yes, that is correct."

"You are no longer in his employ, Herr Allmann."

"Of course. I understand perfectly. However, should the promised funds not appear in my account, shall we say within the next three hours, I will be forced to report our conversation to Mr. Mahoney. You understand this?"

Carlisle held his anger in check. He hated Germans and anything German. Always had. "You'll get your money."

"Then I will withdraw my people from the field, leaving it all to you."

"First I want you to find Greenleaf and Nostrand."

"Yes? And report this to whom?"

"A man will be contacting you very soon. You will know him when he tells you that F. C. sends his regards."

"A bit melodramatic, if you do not mind me saying so, but effective. We will await his call."

But who the hell was the young good-looking man who had opened fire in the hotel? The description did not even remotely fit Byrd, nor could it apply to anyone on Bixby's staff. A Russian, Carlisle thought. It was the only other possibility. But why would they want to kill one of their own people . . . hell, two of their own people. It didn't make sense.

His call finally went through to the Bristol, and seconds later he had Jack Byrd on the line. "You're back in business, Jack," he said without preamble.

"What the hell is going on? When can we bring Stewart's body home?" Byrd said. He sounded nearly hysterical to Carlisle.

"Very soon, Jack. But in the meantime I have the proof for you, and I've gotten you some help."

Byrd was silent for a long moment. "It's true? He is a traitor?"

"He's with a Soviet KGB major at this very moment. But I can't say anything else on an open line like this. Get yourself over to the consulate and call me back on a secure line. I'll clear it with Bixby."

"The bastard," Byrd said. "The fucking bastard! I would never have believed it."

As soon as Carlisle hung up, Alex Hayes knocked once and came in, carefully closing the door behind him. He looked very tired and just a little bit puzzled.

"Would you mind telling me just what the hell is going on around here, Farley?" he demanded.

"What are you talking about?" Carlisle asked, looking up.

"Since when do we send dossiers complete with photographs of our agents to the BND? Not only that, but in the same transmission with the dossier of a Soviet assassin?"

"Have a seat, Alex," Carlisle said smiling. "I've got something to tell you that you're going to find a little hard to believe."

17

The Askanischer Hof was a cheap hotel on the Ku'Damm that didn't bother with passports for the right price, especially when the guests were a good-looking couple obviously worried about being discovered in a love tryst, and presenting themselves without bags. Upstairs after the bellman had shown them to their room and was paid well for his services, John and Tonia split up, checking out the stairwells at either end of the long narrow corridor. One led directly down a hall to the lobby; the other led to the rear of the hotel and the storeroom area. Satisfied that they had two ways out other than the elevator, they met back at the room.

"Whoever the hell he is, he wants us both dead," John said.

"It could be anyone," Tonia said distantly. She stood at the window looking down on busy Ku'Damm. They'd insisted on a front room so they would at least have a chance to see when the police showed up.

"Not the Agency or the BND—they simply don't operate that way," John insisted. "First the lobby of the Europäischer Hof, and then my car. The Agency wouldn't have done that."

"No," she said. She turned back. "Neither would my people, John. In this you must believe me. Our methods may be extreme at times, but we don't kill innocent people. Only enemies of the state."

John thought about his brother, and his mother and his wife and his children, hate welling up in his chest. "Then who the hell is it?" he snapped. "And why the hell is he after us?"

They'd come to the hotel to clean up and to catch their breath. The police would be after them now with a vengeance for the deaths of the two officers in the parking ramp. They needed time to think, to plan their next moves. They'd left the Mercedes across town and had taken cabs separately to the Europa Center and had met in front of this hotel. They had not been spotted, nor had they been followed.

"He knew about your car," she was saying.

"And he probably has the list," John said. "The Europäischer Hof was no coincidence."

"I agree. Which means he's probably one of ours. Not KGB though, I don't think."

John started to object, but she held him off.

"No, not KGB. But it could be GRU, all things considered." She was thinking as she spoke. Trying to remember something. Trying to dredge something up from her past. Something she might have heard.

"Why military intelligence? What the hell have they got to do with this? Was your uncle bringing out military secrets? Was he privy to your general staff?"

Tonia looked up out of her thoughts. "My uncle was privy to everything. And I mean everything."

"But he was retired, you said."

"From active duty. But he knows everyone. He still works liaison between the KGB and the Politburo."

"You said GRU, all things considered. Why?"

"I can't tell you that."

She'd also insisted on a television set when they checked in. It was on now. The American show *M*A*S*H*, dubbed in German, was playing. "What are you waiting for?"

"If you knew, I would have to kill you for it," she said evenly.

"I could force you."

"You could try, John. We've already covered that. And in the end one of us would be dead, but you wouldn't know any more than you already do."

"Then why the hell did you come over?"

"To find my uncle and your father and get them the hell out of here before it's too late for them. For all of us."

"But it has to do with the military. Is your government planning on some action. In Afghanistan? Cuba? Is that what you're waiting for?"

"Don't," she warned.

"But it would have to be big, very big for your uncle to risk meeting with my father. Big enough for the GRU to send an assassin out to shoot up hotel lobbies and blow up cars. The repercussions, once it gets out that a Soviet military intelligence officer has been shooting up West Berlin, killing innocent people, killing policemen, would be massive. Yet they're willing to risk it. Why? For what? Something very big. What?"

"In the meantime we have to find my uncle and your father," Tonia said, ignoring the direct question.

John looked at her for a long time. It would be so easy to pull out his gun and shoot her dead then and there. "We're going to have to stay alive while we're doing it," he said.

Tonia went to her purse on the bed and took out the list of meeting places. At the desk she checked off the places they'd already investigated. John joined her.

"We've already been to eight of the places," she said.

John took out his pen and quickly scratched out a half-dozen other spots, all of them hotels. She looked up at him questioningly.

"I started calling hotels before you came over. I got about a third of the way through the phone book."

"Which still leaves us a dozen places," she said, studying the list.

John looked at the remaining entries, a few of which were hotels and others private residences. Most were in West Berlin proper, but at least three were outside the city: two in Grunewald and the other in Wilmersdorf. Allmann's people would have checked the spots in town first, he reasoned. Especially in this weather. He went to the window and carefully looked down at the street. It was going to be very dangerous for them to be out on the streets during the daytime. By now, undoubtedly, his description and probably hers had been circulated to the police. They had eyewitnesses from the Europäischer Hof, as well as the garage attendant and the staff at the Bremen, if they'd gotten that far. In addition there was the GRU assassin.

He turned back. Tonia was watching him.

"We'll check the two places in Grunewald," he said.

"What about the places here in the city? Several of them are within walking distance."

"Someone else is checking them."

"What are you saying to me?" she asked evenly.

"I hired the local mafia to check it out for me."

"You gave them the list?"

John nodded. "And enough money to ensure their loyalty with instructions not to interfere, only search."

"What have they found?" she asked, her voice still reasonable.

He had expected an explosion. "I'll call them now."

She thought about it for a moment, then shook her head. "I don't think I want you using the telephone."

"Then you'll have to stop me," John said. He went to the

telephone and picked it up. When he had the hotel operator he asked for Allmann's number. While the call was going through he turned around. Tonia was right behind him, the barrel of her gun inches from his head. She was shaking with barely suppressed rage.

"Put it down," she said softly.

He didn't move. The connection was made and the number began ringing. Once. Twice.

"Put down the telephone," Tonia said, moving a little closer so that the gun was pointed directly at his left temple. If she fired, it would take the entire side of his head off.

The telephone rang a third and fourth time, but still there was no answer. It wasn't right. Something definitely was wrong.

"There is no answer," he said, holding the telephone out for her to hear.

She cocked her head slightly. At that moment John let the telephone fall out of his hand. She jerked involuntarily and in the next instant he batted the gun aside with his left hand and clipped her lightly on the jaw with his right fist.

Her head snapped back and she went down, momentarily dazed but not unconscious. He grabbed the gun away from her and hurriedly stepped away. She started to jump up, but then slumped back realizing she didn't have a chance.

John picked up the telephone. The number was still ringing. He got the hotel operator back and had her try it again with the same result. After five rings he hung up. Allmann had quit. The only possibility was that Carlisle or Hayes had managed to trace the Bern bank account back to Allmann and had bought him off. The implications were staggering.

"We're going to have to get out of here now," he said.

"Who has the list?" she asked from the floor. A small trickle of blood ran down from her mouth.

"Most likely the Agency," he said. He uncocked the hammer, switched the safety on, and tossed the gun on the bed. Then he helped her to her feet. She looked at him warily as he took out his handkerchief and wiped the blood from her lip. "I don't like having guns pointed at me," he said.

She appraised him for another long moment. "The next time I point it at you I won't hesitate to pull the trigger."

"Somebody in the Agency thinks I'm a Soviet agent," he said, ignoring her threat.

Her left eyebrow rose. "All that from one unanswered telephone call?"

"And everything else that has happened," he said. "Langley paid through an account in Bern. They must have found out it belonged to Allmann and bought him off. It's the only reason he'd back away."

"Allmann?" she asked.

"I'll tell you on the way. In the meantime we're going to have to move fast."

"Where do you want to start?" Tonia asked, glancing over at her gun on the bed.

"Grunewald."

"How?"

"You'll steal us another car," John said. "How else?"

Chernov was dozing in his chair in front of the television like an old man in a nursing home. His hair was askew, his breathing shallow, and his color pale. He was an old and battered war-horse who had overextended himself physically by driving the snow-mobile up the road, hiding it in the woods, and then walking back through the deep snow.

Mahoney watched him with mixed emotions. His call had come like a prayer answered. After all these long years revenge could be mine. If only I had the courage to pull out my gun, put it to his head, and pull the trigger. So easy to do then, and even more easy to do now.

He reached in his pocket and felt his gun, the metal warm from being so close to his body.

It is hard to imagine the end of a career that spanned forty-odd years, and even harder for a man to contemplate his own death and then resurrection. Even with the benefit of hindsight Mahoney wasn't so sure what had happened or why. Chernov's hand was in it. He hadn't been so certain at the time, but now he was. His retirement was in full swing. Marge was dead and he was just beginning to deal with her absence, if such a thing can ever be fully dealt with after so many years of togetherness, when the Israelis came for him in the person of Sonja Margraff with the story about a penetration agent in high places within the Mossad. . . .

Go or stay. He remembered clearly his indecision at the time. There would be a blind drop at the Athens airport with instructions to meet his briefing officer, Ezra Wasserman, the head of the Mossad. An extraordinary man, extraordinary circumstances, and an extraordinary request. His fame had preceded him. They'd asked for him specifically because he was retired, he was very good, and he was apparently above bribery. Diogenes with his light looked for an honest man; Mahoney's forte was looking for the dishonest man, the traitor, the mole: the nigger in the woodpile, as Carlisle had once so indelicately put the entire problem of penetration agents.

"We need your help," Sonja had said.

"Who sent you?"

"Ezra Wasserman," she'd said. "No one else knows except for Prime Minister Begin and General David Ben Abel who is chief of Aman, our military intelligence service. Will you help us?"

A couple of days later in Athens, Mahoney made his way to the meeting with Wasserman at Papaspirou, a sidewalk café on Syntagma Square across from the American Express office. The night had been brilliant but Wasserman was deeply troubled. Sonja Margraff was his niece, yet she was one of his prime suspects.

"I've known her since she was born," Wasserman said in anguish. "I changed her diapers, wiped her snotty nose, bought her a toy when she had the measles."

"And grieved for her."

"That too. But it was she who suggested your name," Wasserman said. "No one else knows. You'd be coming to Tel Aviv primarily as a tourist as cover for an arms deal you're trying to negotiate."

"None of that is really necessary," Mahoney had said. "Your mole knows I am coming, and exactly why I am coming."

The Russians had a hand in it. A lot of Israeli intelligence data was showing up in the wrong places, and only the KGB could have been that organized. What they were looking for was the conduit so that they could stop not only the in-place penetration agent, but permanently plug the gap so that others wouldn't pop up just as fast as they were uncovered.

Wasserman was a short man, his face round, his nose large, and his eyes small, dark, and very intense. He looked nothing like a man you would expect to head one of the world's most effective secret services. His name along with the actual location of Mossad headquarters was a closely guarded national secret. "We need your help. We simply cannot do it without you. If Ben Abel had his way he'd shake up the entire structure—top to bottom—to see what fell out. It would ruin us."

Everything pointed to Sonja Margraff, at least it had in the beginning.

Tel Aviv welcomed Mahoney a few days later as it would any other tourist—with indifference. And during the long cab ride into the city from Lod Airport he had to ask himself what the hell he was doing here. He had no business messing in the affairs of a foreign country. He was retired. And yet he was like a general going into battle against an unknown enemy. But in this war his only allies were the prime minister of the country, an aging general, the head of the secret service, and Sonja Margraff, all of whom were suspect.

He could not quit in his quest for Chernov. Everywhere he turned he saw the man's influence if not his actual presence. It had become like a sickness with Mahoney that had finally grown into a full-blown hypochondria at the end of his life. He wanted to lay the blame for all of his ills, real or imagined, at Chernov's doorstep.

Israel that year was in a tough spot. The Syrians were threatening them from the north, the Jordanians from the east, the Egyptians from the south, and the traitor from within. Not too many years later it would be discovered that the Israelis had actually been spying on the United States, but at that moment America was her only real ally. Calling Mahoney out of retirement, had it been discovered, would have had repercussions all the way back to Washington. So when Mahoney finally did arrive, Begin wanted to call off his investigation before he'd even begun. But by then he'd had the bone in his teeth and wasn't about to give it up. Wasserman, as a result, had been in a very difficult spot. Mahoney was his salvation. He wasn't about to give it up. Mahoney had been set up in a safe house in downtown Tel Aviv on Kfar Saba Street about three blocks south of the thirty-five-story Shalom Mier Tower, the tallest building in the Middle East and the new center of Tel Aviv's business district, where he set about his work to catch the spy, starting with dossiers on every conceivable possibility for the mole.

"I've already worked up a suspect list," Wasserman had said.

"You can redline the suspects for me, but I want a list of the *possibles*. That means anyone and everyone who knew what al Qaryūt really was, or who might even have guessed."

Israel had put up a secret spy satellite. Al Qaryūt was its receiving station out on the desert. It had been a closely guarded secret. Before it had become fully operational, however, the Jordanians had staged a raid, completely destroying the installation. They had been betrayed at the highest levels. There was no other way around it.

"No," Wasserman said firmly. "The list would be too large to be of any use. Many of the people on it are my closest friends. I don't want you prying into their lives and affairs needlessly."

"One of those people is a traitor."

"I have a list of suspects—" Wasserman started, but Mahoney didn't let him finish.

"Then let me go home! You don't need my services!"

Wasserman had been momentarily stunned by the savagery of Mahoney's tone.

"Put a watch on your list of suspects. Sooner or later the traitor will make a mistake and you'll have him. If he or she is on the list."

"We can't do that and you know it."

"Then cooperate with me, for Christ's sake. You want help, then get the hell out of the way and let me help."

Wasserman sighed. "It will take time."

"Give me the dossiers as you get them, but don't stop until you've covered the entire list."

"All right," Wasserman said. "What's your first move going to be?"

Mahoney got up, went to the window and looked down at the traffic on the street. There was no one lounging there. No one out of place. No suspicious cars parked along the curb. "Hares and hounds," he said half to himself.

"What?" Wasserman asked. "I didn't quite catch that."

Mahoney turned away from the window. "My methods may be a little unorthodox, but no matter what happens over the next few days or so, I want you to give me plenty of elbow room. I don't want the cavalry called out."

Wasserman nodded uncertainly.

"You've heard of the old gumshoe game, hares and hounds?"

Wasserman nodded again. "Send a top-notch legman out on the streets and have your trainee try to stick with him."

"Exactly," Mahoney said. "It's usually a one-on-one exercise. I'm going to develop it into a team sport."

A few days later he was introduced to Israel's greatest modern-day friend and patriot, Chaim Malecki, who had been educated in the U.S. and in England as a Rhodes Scholar, and now raised money for his adopted nation. He was an ex-officio member of Wasserman's staff and nobody's suspect except Mahoney's.

* * *

Had he had the gift of foresight, would he have continued? How many times in the past had Mahoney asked himself that question? The answer, of course, had always been the same; it was as difficult an answer as it had been simple. The fact of the matter was that he did not have foresight. Oh, he had plenty of educated guesses and the vision that only intelligence and experience can bring to an operation, but no foresight, so he'd always plunged on.

"Is his name on your list of possibilities?" Mahoney had asked Wasserman.

"No," Wasserman snapped. "I trust him more than I trust you."

"Then he did not know about Al Qaryūt? The truth about it?" Mahoney asked. The secret was a big one. Even the CIA knew nothing about it. If they had, he reflected, they would not have allowed the technology into the region, friend or not. The obvious advantage would have to be too destabilizing to an already explosive situation between the Jews and the Arabs.

"No," Wasserman said, but this time his voice was weak.

"No possibility? Not even the faintest possibility? He had no glimmers?"

There was a silence on the telephone line.

"The truth," Mahoney said.

"It's possible," Wasserman finally replied.

"I want his dossier and I want it fast."

"He's a friend of Begin and Moshe Dayan. Hell, they have dinner together at least once a month."

"I don't care whose friend he is," Mahoney said, and he didn't. If Malecki knew what the station at Al Qaryūt had really been, he was a suspect. But he was smooth, urbane, and all of Israel was at his feet. He was not an easy man to catch because he didn't work for the Russians—not directly—although he was the spy, and ultimately his architect was Yuri Chernov though nobody knew it at the time.

One does not set out to catch a panther with a mousetrap, Mahoney had told Wasserman, and to that end he created a monstrous fiction: Operation Wrath, it was called, something so enticing, the spy would be forced into stealing it.

It began with three assessment documents contained in thick file folders marked with triple red stripes denoting critical matters, all marked For Your Eyes Only and S-1 distribution, and all heavily marked with authorization stamps as well as TOP SECRET in red, top and bottom, in support of two critical files.

The first was a brief letter from Menachem Begin to General Ben Abel, with a numbered copy to Wasserman, asking for recommendations to a number of sweeping defense and political posture questions. From a superficial standpoint the Begin letter would have been suspect as a phony. Such questions were not usually asked of intelligence units that often tended to be self-serving. That is unless the head of state had a specific objective already in mind and was looking for the kinds of answers he already expected. On second reading, then, the deeper significance of the letter became apparent, raising the likelihood that it was genuine.

The second critical file, which was actually in two parts, consisted of a recommended line of action and a specific implementation timetable. That second critical file was a summary, in part, of the bulkier assessment units, and was backed in full detail by budget lines, personnel allocations, field effect reports, and by hardware data.

Finally, as a sort of pin-the-tail-on-the-donkey file—something that Mahoney strongly suspected Ben Abel might have initiated—was a request for a Mossad political repercussions analysis.

The prime question posed by the documents was, What shall we do? Ben Abel's answer had been clear, concise, and to the point. His counter question was, If we do it, what can we expect in the way of retaliation?

The documents and supporting data were nothing more than an outline of a plan of action strongly recommended by Ben Abel and supported by Wasserman. The general had recommended that Israel make preemptive nuclear strikes on the capital cities of Syria, Iran, Iraq, and Jordan.

"Israel must not only be guaranteed her borders," Ben Abel had presumably written, "but she must also have control over much of the Middle Eastern oil fields if she is to gain a permanent place of world prominence, and therefore safety."

"If this does get out, it will be suicide," Wasserman breathed. He was deeply frightened.

Within the week it was over. Wasserman had his mole—who turned out to be Sonja Margraff, the hardest blow of all for him—and Mahoney had his answers, which were even harder for him to accept. Chernov's hand had been nowhere visible and yet everywhere evident. Chaim Malecki had taken the documents and had flown them out to Brussels, where he turned them over to a NATO intelligence officer, who in turn passed them over to a former British SIS officer who was an adviser to 10 Downing

Street. His name was McNiel Henrys, and like Wasserman, he desperately needed Mahoney's help.

"We're out to stop World War Three," Henrys had told him when they finally met face-to-face.

"By assassination?" Mahoney had asked. Ben Abel had been shot to death.

"By any means at our disposal," Henrys had said.

"The Israeli nuclear strike documents are fakes," Mahoney said.

"We know," Henrys said. "We suspected the bundle as soon as we had confirmed that you had followed Malecki to Brussels."

"We?"

Henrys smiled. "There's so terribly much to tell you and so little time in which to make our position clear. The fact of the matter is, we need your help."

"With what?"

"To clear up the mess you've created for us with your meddling in Tel Aviv."

"If I refuse?"

"You won't," Henrys said confidently. "Not after I've told you what I brought you here to tell you."

It was an old boy network, according to Henrys, that had had its beginnings during the war when the U.S. was in the midst of developing the atomic bomb. Nuclear secrets were being shared with the British aboveboard, and with the Russians under the table. Balance of power, Henrys said, in order to assure that there would never again be a world war. Skirmishes, yes, but never an all-out fight in which nuclear weapons would be used. "We can't afford that luxury any longer," Henrys said. Malecki was the contact within the Mossad, Sonja Margraff, who was in love with him, his unwitting assistant. There were others in the network—the SIS, the KGB, NATO intelligence—and within the CIA it was Robert McBundy who had gone all the way back to the OSS days. His was a respected name in the business.

"If the war is to come," Henrys said, "it will come because of a country like Israel actually making a nuclear strike in the Middle East. The Arabs would have to retaliate with Soviet-supplied weapons and soon we would all be pulled into it. Or perhaps some madman will sell nuclear weapons to an Idi Amin or an Ayatollah Khomeini or a Muammar Qaddafi. Or perhaps the next time the Soviets will be successful in their placement of offensive nukes in Cuba, or your own government in its placement of nukes in Turkey."

Henrys stood up, went across to the sideboard, and brought back the brandy bottle. He poured some more in Mahoney's glass and then his own.

"We've been more or less successful in our efforts these past years, Mahoney. We've managed to weather some serious storms, managed to avert some devastating moves by politicians, yet you're the first to really hurt us. Unless you help us now, everything we have worked for will come tumbling down around our ears. Sooner or later this could all go public."

"Maybe that wouldn't be such a bad thing," Mahoney said.

"It would be ruinous," Henrys disagreed. "The first effect would be that the general public the world over, who have little if any respect or trust for their own intelligence services or their leaders, would revolt. And the second obvious effect is that we would be at war, Mahoney."

The network had begun with the atomic bomb. It was a by-product as insidious and deadly as radiation. Mahoney felt like a caveman: having discovered fire, he was burning his fingers in the flames, so that it was very difficult for him to see the benefit of the heat.

Looking at the television and watching Chernov, Mahoney was suspended in time. The El Al jetliner was lifting off the main north-south runway at Tel Aviv's Lod Airport, accelerating up into a perfectly clear blue sky, the Mediterranean in the distance dotted with boats, and the city spread along the coast like a sugar and cream fairy tale. Touching the pistol in his pocket he was reminded of the violence that had been so much a part of his life, from the afternoon at the lake cabin when he saw his uncle Fred's lifeless body, to the war, and all the assignments that seemed to stretch backward and forward in an incredibly complex pattern that even hindsight could not satisfactorily unravel.

Chaim Malecki and Sonja Margraff were both dead. The Mossad was clean for the moment, and if Wasserman was not happy he was at least satisfied, though he was giving it up: he was retiring to his kibbutz at Gan Haifiz. He had gone too far, had seen too much, and like Mahoney had lost nearly everything that was dear to him. In a way Mahoney had felt sorry that he had not gotten to know them better. He had had the grandiose notion that somehow he might have redeemed them. They had struck him as being empty, lost souls, ripe for salvation. And yet in his heart of hearts he'd known it could never have happened that way. Marge

311

would have laughed and called him a romantic old fool. Sonja had killed Malecki and then officially had turned the gun on herself. Unofficially her death had been an accident. She had struggled with Mahoney and her gun had gone off. He would never forget her.

McNiel Henrys, on the other hand, had struck Mahoney as a man of such huge arrogance that he felt it was his duty to operate the world according to his own twisted philosophy for his own strange pleasure. For the moment Henrys was out of reach, insulated by his network. But only for the moment.

They were already high over the Mediterranean, and there was nothing to see out the window except blue sky and the deeper blue water far below. He ordered a drink from the steward and sat back in his seat. McBundy would have to be neutralized first. His was the one name that didn't seem to fit the pattern. He had been a friend at times, a confidant, a mentor in some respects. And among all the other bitter pills Mahoney had to swallow in this mess, McBundy's apparent complicity—if Henrys was to be believed—was possibly the worst.

The steward came back and set Mahoney's drink on the pull-down tray. Mahoney opened the little bottle, poured the whiskey in his glass, and then sat back again as he sipped the drink. He wished now that he were going home, not just to Washington, and that Marge would be there waiting for him. It would have been so much better if he could have explained everything to Wasserman; because of what the man had suffered, he deserved to know the entire story. He was sipping at his drink when the first pain, sharp and very hot, stitched across his chest making him gasp. It passed, and for a few moments he was confused about what had happened. Perhaps it had been a gas bubble, he thought, but then the second pain, massive and exceedingly sharp, caused his vision to dim and he realized only vaguely that he had either spilled his drink on his lap or he had wet himself. He started to reach, trying to catch his breath so that he could call for help, when a third pain wracked his body with unbelievable strength, and before his vision went totally dark, he was looking into the face of his steward. The man was smiling.

Hours, days, weeks later, he had no recollection of the passage of time, only of the intense pain and the last fleeting glimpse of the steward and the realization that he had been poisoned and was dying; he opened his eyes onto a bleary world of a farmhouse in Greenwich, Connecticut, and the face of an obviously relieved

Agency doctor. "Welcome back to the land of the living, Mr. Mahoney," he said.

"An epinephrine compound called Sus-Phrine," McBundy told him. "We arranged it to get you out clean. It was in your drink. An overdose, which is what you were given, produces all the symptoms of a heart attack. You were in a deep coma within seconds after you took the first sip. Dead, for all intents and purposes; your heart slowed to almost nothing. Once we had you back here you were given some Inderal to stabilize your heart and Valium to keep you under. At this point, Wallace, as far as the rest of the world is concerned, you are a nonperson. You are dead."

The final madness had begun then, and looking across the table at McBundy and the others on the team, he truly didn't know if he would be able to handle it. McBundy was the network's penetration agent in the CIA according to Henrys. Yet McBundy had gone through a great deal of trouble and risk to pull Mahoney out so that he could uncover the entire network and smash it. Who to believe? It was a question, he reflected now, to which there never was a completely satisfactory answer. Yet he had gone looking at McBundy's bidding; it was his life.

The morning sun was streaming through the third-floor windows of Farley Carlisle's office. He had just gotten off the secure telephone for the second time with Jack Byrd at the consulate in West Berlin. He felt a sense of triumph: he had been vindicated. No matter what Hayes thought to the contrary, John Mahoney was definitely the traitor in the Agency that they'd been looking for all these years. And now with the list Allmann had supplied Byrd he would have him.

"You're crazy," Hayes had said earlier.

"Your loyalty is as touching as it is misplaced, Alex," Carlisle had said. "We have the proof—"

"You have nothing, goddamnit!" Hayes shouted, his face red. "He's out there doing his job, finding his father just like you ordered him to do."

"With a Soviet killer."

"You don't know that for sure," Hayes said. "And besides, if it is true, he's working her. Using her because she knows something he doesn't know."

"Indeed. It was probably she who came over with the list of places where Mahoney and Chernov met after the war, and where they are probably meeting at this moment."

"So he'll find them and bring them in."

"He's been working with the Russians all along," Carlisle said. He was beginning to lose his patience. He didn't have time to explain his every move. Especially now with everything else that was going on. The Russians were definitely up to something along the Chinese border. Everybody in Washington was scared silly.

"I've seen the reports from your ongoing investigation," Hayes was saying. "We had the problem of failed operations all the way back to the fifties. If you recall, John Mahoney only came on five years ago. You were his recruiting officer, for Christ's sake."

"Before that, it was his father!" Carlisle blurted, not really wanting to bring that up at this moment. He'd never liked Mahoney, who in his estimation had always been a sanctimonious son of a bitch. They'd worked together in Moscow, and those days still rankled.

Hayes sat back, an incredulous smile on his face. "I see," he said. "Probably the greatest agent we've ever had, who lost his wife, a son, and his grandchildren, is now revealed as a Russian spy." He shook his head. "Christ, Farley, what the hell have you been smoking?"

Carlisle felt his face coloring. He got to his feet. "You are either one of us, or one of them," he said dramatically, a petulant edge to his voice that even he didn't like. But he couldn't help himself. He had waited for this time for a long while.

"Bullshit," Hayes said, getting up. "You're way off base, and you're going to turn out the asshole when it's over."

"One more word, mister, and I'll relieve you of duty," Carlisle snapped, livid.

"You haven't that authority," Hayes said contemptuously. "And if you push me I'll take it to the director himself and let him decide." He went to the door. "Recall him, Farley. Once he's back here we'll go over his background with a fine-tooth comb. I'll personally lead the interrogation team. But if something happens to him over there, and I find out that you were responsible, I swear to God I'll have your ass."

Carlisle said nothing. He was seething.

"I'll be watching you," Hayes said. "I'll be watching every move. We're going by the book on this one. In this country we're still innocent until we're proven guilty."

As soon as Hayes left, Carlisle bundled up his notes, left his office, and took the elevator up to the seventh floor. He had to wait in Bindrich's anteroom for a couple of minutes before he was allowed in.

"We've got him," Carlisle said, closing the door and approaching the desk.

Bindrich looked all in. He glanced up, his eyes bloodshot. "What's happening, Farley?"

Carlisle spread the list out in front of Bindrich. "John gave this list to Allmann. These are the places where Mahoney and Chernov may have met just after the war. They're probably at one of these places now."

Bindrich glanced at the notes.

"Allmann's people have checked out all but one of the places. All that's left is a hotel out in the Grunewald section of West Berlin. Their man who was supposed to check it out is long overdue. They suspect that something happened to him."

Bindrich looked a little closer at Farley's notes, circling the Grunewald Hotel listing. "What about John and Major Trusov?"

"They're presumably going down the list themselves. There was a shooting in the Europäischer Hof Hotel. It's one of the places on the list."

"You're saying that we can get out to this hotel in Grunewald before John and Major Trusov?"

"Jack Byrd is on his way right now."

Bindrich sighed in relief. "Good, Farley, very good."

Carlisle hesitated a moment. "But something else has come up. Something that may cause us a little trouble, especially if the business with Heiser gets out."

Bindrich waited for him to continue.

"It's Alex Hayes. He knows about our investigation, or at least a part of it."

"Does he know about this?" Bindrich asked, tapping a blunt finger on the list.

"Yes," Carlisle said. "He wants John recalled and interrogated here. He doesn't believe he's our penetration agent."

"I see," Bindrich said thoughtfully. "Just keep up with what you're doing. I'll take care of Hayes from this end."

"Yes, sir," Carlisle said, pride welling up in his chest. After all these years his career was about to take a quantum leap, all the way up here to the seventh floor. He could feel it in his bones.

The afternoon light from the dull overcast sky made the city of Berlin appear flat, two-dimensional, unreal, as if it were a scene from a woodcarving in an old history book. The storm over central Europe had intensified, bringing with it more snow. Most of the offices and shops that had opened around noon had closed, but the

Ku'Damm if anything was even more clogged with traffic—both vehicular and pedestrian—than before, and everybody seemed to be in a cheerful, holiday mood.

Captain Serafim Kochetkov stopped and looked in the window of a closed travel agency. A poster showing swimmers on a sun-drenched beach on the Spanish Costa del Sol beckoned, but he wasn't seeing the bikini-clad girls. Instead he watched the reflections in the window glass as a West Berlin police car cruised past. He had changed out of his business suit, and was now dressed in snow boots, heavy trousers, and an expensive down-filled nylon jacket, a fur cap on his head. He was not particularly worried that anyone would have been able to provide an accurate description of him from the Europäischer Hof Hotel, but he was a man, despite his madness, who was very bright and knew enough to eliminate as many variables as possible. Blend into your environment, wasn't that what they had taught him at School One outside of Moscow? Wasn't that what Zaytsev had drummed into his head in Krasnoyarsk? Make yourself into a sheep and you'll meet a wolf nearby.

He was frustrated, however. Major Trusov and the American CIA agent should not have escaped from the parking ramp. He had watched from outside as they had approached from different directions, knowing that he could take either one of them out with ease, but not both of them now that they were alerted. The bomb wired to the car, he figured, would do it. He had also watched as the police car entered the ramp a couple of minutes later. When the explosion came he had resisted the urge to leave. Make certain they are dead, Serafim, he'd been told. He'd been dismayed but not surprised when he saw them emerge from the ramp in the Mercedes.

Now they were gone. They had simply vanished.

He turned around and looked down the broad expanse of the Ku'Damm. They were here somewhere. He could feel their presence. But West Berlin was a very large, open city. Even if all exits had been sealed to them, the city was still far too large.

Directly across the street was the Askanischer Hof Hotel. It wasn't on the list he'd been supplied with, but he felt something. Instincts are fine, provided they do not rule your life and your actions. He'd been told that, too. How to separate fact from feeling.

He turned and walked down the street, stepping into a Gasthof bar and restaurant. He ordered a beer at the bar, paid for it, and then walked back to the corridor to the men's room where a public telephone hung on the wall. He dialed a West Berlin number that was connected through a secret relay directly into the *referentura* of the Soviet embassy in East Berlin. It was answered on the first ring.

"It is me," he said. The bar was noisy and he had to strain to hear.

"One moment," a voice said.

Kochetkov looked over his shoulder as a man came down the corridor from the bar. He stiffened. But the man just glanced idly at him and went into the men's room, totally unaware of just how close he had come to death had he paid even the slightest attention to the man on the telephone. A moment later Lieutenant Colonel Raina was on the line.

"I am glad you called."

"They have disappeared," Kochetkov said.

"I have new information for you," Raina said.

"From where?"

"Washington."

"Yes?" Kochetkov said. He was a cautious man. General Seregin had taught him that most difficult of all lessons to learn. The future is his who knows how to wait, the general said. You are a valuable resource of the state; we do not want to waste your special talent.

"They are at the Grunewald Hotel," Raina said. "Ignore the other addresses on your list."

"You are certain of this?"

"It comes from the highest source. Abel and Baker will be on their way out there sooner or later." They were the code names for John and Tonia. "You can wait for them there after you take care of your secondary targets."

"Yes, I understand."

"But there is a complication," Raina said.

"Tell me."

"Someone else is on the way out there. He has a head start."

"The Agency?"

"Yes."

"Only one?"

"Yes. You will recognize him by the olive green army parka he is wearing. His name is Jack Byrd."

"Is he good?"

"Competent."

"I will deal with him," Kochetkov said. "Is there anything else?"

317

"No," Raina said. "Good hunting."

Kochetkov hung up, walked past the bar, and stepped out into the street to hail a taxi. One came down the street and pulled across two lanes of traffic to get to him. He glanced again at the Askanischer Hof Hotel down the block. Still he had the feeling. It was very strong.

"Tempelhof Airport," he told the cabby.

"The airport is closed now," the driver said.

"That's okay, I'll take my chances," Kochetkov said, smiling. "I'm meeting a stew out there."

"Ah, I see," the cabby said with a leer. "Good weather for it, I'd say. You can give her a lay for her layover."

18

John stared at the television in stunned disbelief. He was seeing his and Tonia's photographs. Not composite drawings such as those made by police artists from eyewitness descriptions, but actual photos. His he recognized at once from his Agency dossier.

Tonia came out of the bathroom, her coat and purse on the bed. They'd been about to leave. She saw the pictures as John glanced over at her.

He turned up the sound. The announcer was speaking: ". . . be considered armed and extremely dangerous. Under no circumstances should they be approached. If seen, report immediately to West Berlin police."

"How?" Tonia whispered.

"The Agency," John snapped. He went for his coat. "We're getting out of here now."

"But why? What the hell are they trying to do?" She was staring at him. "Who are you? What have you done?"

"I'm going with or without you, Major," John said. "Somebody in my Agency is a Soviet penetration agent and they want me stopped. They don't want me to get to your uncle and my father for the same reason you won't tell me what you've been waiting for. Whatever your uncle brought out with him is so important someone wants us to fail. We must fail."

It came to her in a rush: John could see the sudden change in her expression. "They think I'm working with you," she said, aghast. "They think . . . I've told you . . ."

She bolted for her purse on the bed, but John had anticipated her move, and he was quicker. He dropped his coat, shoved her roughly aside, and scooped up her purse, tossing it away. Regaining her balance she reached down the front of her blouse, came out with a seven-inch-long stiletto, and charged him.

John sidestepped her attack, the blade just missing his face. She swiveled on her heel and was at him again, her reflexes lightning fast. This time she nicked the back of his hand and drew blood before he managed to grab her wrist, and they fell back against the nightstand, knocking the lamp to the floor with a crash. Tonia slammed her knee expertly up into John's crotch with all her strength, driving the air out of his lungs. But he held tightly onto her knife hand and rolled left, his superior body weight pulling her down onto the floor.

"No!" Tonia screamed, battering him with her free hand and trying to bring her knee up again so that she could kick him. "My wrist!"

"Drop it or I'll break your arm," John grunted. The pain had exploded all the way up into his chest. He was having a hard time catching his breath. He bent her wrist back a little farther, increasing the pressure. At any moment he was sure he would hear the sharp snap as the bones broke.

"You bastard!" she screamed wildly, but then she slumped back, the knife dropping from her hand.

For a few seconds, John did not release his grip. He reached over with his free hand, picked up the knife, then released her arm and rolled away from her. She was lying half propped up against the wall beside the bed, and he sat a couple of feet away from her, their eyes locked. Her chest was heaving. She cradled her bruised wrist in her other hand, and rubbed it to get the circulation back. Deliberately he reached beneath his coat and pulled out his Beretta, slipping the safety catch off, but he didn't point it at her. Not yet.

"Now, Major, you are going to tell me what's going on," he said. "Otherwise you won't leave this room alive."

Tonia looked wildly around for something, anything with which to fight back. But there was nothing. Her purse with her gun was on the other side of the room, and the shards of the broken lamp were just out of reach.

"We don't have much time," he said. "The desk clerk downstairs will be calling the police soon, if he hasn't already. He must have recognized us from the television."

"I can't!" she cried. "They'll kill me!"

"They're already trying to kill you. Kill both of us. It was probably the GRU who took a shot at us in the Europäischer and again tried to kill us in the garage. And now my people have sent the West Berlin police and probably the BND after us. As I said, we don't have much time."

"If I tell you, I can't allow you to live."

"Then one of us will not be leaving here alive," John said. He raised his gun, pointing it now directly at her chest. "And I think you will agree that I have the advantage at the moment." It was hard to talk; the pain in his gut was deep and sharp. He cocked the hammer.

"My uncle knows everything," she said miserably.

"Knows what?"

"He was against it. Not at first, but later he turned. Tried to talk them out of it."

"Out of what? The clock is running."

Again she looked for a way out of her dilemma. John raised the pistol a little higher.

"It's the bomb!" she blurted. "The hydrogen bomb!"

"What bomb, where . . . ?" John started to say, when they both heard the sirens pull up outside.

He scrambled painfully to his feet and went to the window, Tonia right behind him. Three police cars had pulled up outside. A fourth was just coming down the street along with two civilian cars. "You won't get out of here alone," he said, turning on Tonia. "Are you with me, or do we stay here until they take us? Quickly!"

"I'm with you," she said. "For now."

John handed her the knife, brushed past her, grabbed his coat, and raced across the room. He eased the door open and looked out into the deserted corridor. At the end of the hall the elevator indicator showed that a car was on its way up.

Tonia had resheathed her knife and had pulled on her coat. She joined him in the corridor, her gun in hand, and they raced down to the stairwell door. The elevator doors were just opening as John yanked open the door and started through.

"Halt! Polizei!" someone shouted from the elevator.

Tonia turned and fired three shots in rapid succession, the first driving a West Berlin policeman back into the elevator into the arms of two other officers, and the second and third shots hitting at least one of the others.

Now they were guilty of murder, John thought as he started down the stairs. But there was no time to make amends. Their room was on the third floor. They reached the second-floor landing as the door on the ground floor slammed open with a loud bang and someone started up. It sounded to John like several people, obviously in a very big hurry. He shoved open the door onto the second-floor corridor and stepped through. He didn't want another shoot-out with the West German authorities, but he wasn't going to be cornered like this. Not yet. What in God's name had she meant by the hydrogen bomb? What were the

321

Russians up to? What had Chernov been against? What had he brought out with him? And who was trying to stop him?

He and Tonia waited just within the corridor as four West Berlin policemen raced past on the stairs, and then John pulled open the door and started down, careful to make as little noise as possible. At the bottom he hesitated for just a moment. They could hear the sounds of commotion above. It would be only a matter of seconds before it was discovered that they had gone.

"Put your gun away," John said, pocketing his own. He pulled open the door that opened onto the broad service corridor that ran from the lobby past the hotel's office back to the kitchen area, and stepped directly into the arms of a tall man dressed in civilian clothes.

"*Scheisse,*" the civilian swore, stepping back and reaching inside his coat for his gun.

John shoved him into two uniformed police officers to his left, knocking them all off-balance, and he turned right, Tonia still with him.

The commotion in the lobby grew as John ran toward the back of the hotel. A woman in the office was screaming into a telephone. She looked up as he passed. A waiter was just coming out of the kitchen. John grabbed the man by the lapels, spun him around, and shoved him past Tonia back down the corridor in the direction of the lobby. A shot was fired that went wide, and he and Tonia were in the large kitchen, racing past the startled cooks to the rear doors.

They passed through a narrow service corridor and then through a broad steel door and they were suddenly outside, a concrete staircase leading down to the snow-clogged alley. Twenty yards away the alley opened into the side street which was blocked by a single blue and white police cruiser. A lone cop had been leaning against the side of the car, and he straightened up as he spotted them.

"Put your hands up," John hissed, stepping around her so that her movements were blocked from the policeman.

For a moment she hesitated, trying to read the expression in his eyes, but then she did as he'd told her, and slowly raised her hands.

John shoved her roughly down the stairs. He pulled out his wallet, opened it, and held it above his head with his left hand, and yanked out his gun with his right.

"Move, you pig," he shouted in German just loud enough for the cop to hear him.

Tonia slipped and nearly fell. John pushed her with his foot. "BND," he shouted to the cop. "Come and help me with this bitch."

The cop, whose hand had gone to the holstered gun at his side, hurried toward them. If he was alone they had a chance, John thought.

"BND," John shouted again, waving his wallet. The cop's eyes were distracted, and John suddenly stepped away from Tonia, diverting his aim from her to the cop, who stopped short and clawed for his pistol.

"The moment your gun leaves its holster you are a dead man," John spat.

The cop's eyes went wide. He backed up a pace, his hands moving carefully away from his sides.

"Who else is out there with you on the street?"

"There are six others," the cop said, the slightest of hesitations in his voice.

John cocked his gun. "The truth!"

Tonia had gone to the end of the alley.

"No one else here yet," the cop said.

Tonia waved them on.

"You're going to do exactly as I say," John said. At any moment someone would be coming behind them through the steel door. "We're going to get in your car, you're going to put on your siren, and you're going to drive away. You're not going to touch your radio or your gun. When we're far enough away, we'll let you go. If you cooperate. Do you understand?"

"*Jawohl*," the cop stammered, raising his hands.

"Put your hands down and let's go. Now!" John ordered.

The cop turned and walked back down the alley toward his cruiser. Tonia was waiting just within the protection of the building. She was watching the steel door they'd come through, her hand in her pocket where she had stuffed her gun.

At the corner the cop went first to his side of the car. Tonia stepped out of the alley and got in the back seat. As the cop was getting in behind the wheel, John pocketed his wallet, and holding his gun out of sight at his side, he stepped out onto the street. A fair-sized crowd had gathered at the front of the hotel, but no one was paying them any attention. John slipped in beside the cop.

"Make a U-turn and get out of here," he said. "But skip the siren unless we run into traffic."

The cop did as he was told, and seconds later they were headed

323

down the broad Joach Strasse past the busy Europa Center, where some of the shops and restaurants were still open.

Tonia was watching out the rear window.

"Anyone coming?" John asked.

"Not yet," she said softly.

The communications radio had been blaring with traffic all along. More units were being ordered from all over the city to the Askanischer Hof Hotel, where the shooting was already being reported. The cop kept looking at Tonia in the rearview mirror and at John seated beside him.

They passed a cab rank where two taxis were waiting on Bundes Allee Strasse. "Turn right at the next corner," John told the cop. "We're getting off here."

"Yes, sir," the cop said.

John reached over, unbuttoned the cop's holster flap, and removed his gun. He pocketed it.

They turned the corner and the cop pulled over to the curb.

"If we see you again we will kill you, do you understand?" John said.

"I will have to report this sooner or later—you must understand this. There is no way you can escape the city. Why don't you give yourselves up?"

John yanked the radio's handset off its hook and ripped the wires out of the connector. "You'll have to do it in person now," he said. "Remember, just keep going. If we see you again we'll kill you."

He got out of the car, let Tonia out, and the cop sped away even before the door was closed. The moment he was out of sight, John and Tonia pocketed their weapons, hurried back around the corner, and took the first cab parked at the stand.

"Can you get us out to Grunewald?" John asked.

"I doubt it," the cabby said good-naturedly. "The roads are *Scheisse* with all this snow. But I can give it a try. What the hell, yes?"

"Is this what you have been waiting for?" Mahoney asked, more shaken now than he wanted to admit, even to himself.

"No," Chernov said, staring at the television set. "It's your son, of course. But do you know the woman?"

Mahoney studied the television screen, but he had never seen her before. His heart was hammering. He should have known that Carlisle would send John here. But what was happening? What had happened? His son was now a hunted man.

324

"She is Tonia Trusov. Major Trusov. KGB. Department 8," Chernov was saying. "My niece."

Mahoney's eyes left the television set. "What is she doing here with my son?"

"I have no idea other than that they are looking for us."

"She's an assassin."

"Yes," Chernov said sadly. "Sent here to kill me." He looked up. "And you. Clever of them to have come so far. But then they're both very bright. They must make a hell of a team."

The announcer had reported that they were wanted for the murders of Bernhard Heiser and his housekeeper in Bonn as well as two policemen in West Berlin. How had they come to Heiser? The snowmobile rider from Allmann had told him that Heiser was dead. He'd also said that a man in Washington had been killed. The only possibility, Mahoney decided with a sick feeling, was Stan Kopinski. He might have talked to John, told him about the past, probably told him about Chernov. But he would never have talked to the KGB in the person of Tonia Trusov. There was more, though. John would not have killed Kopinski, or Heiser and his housekeeper, nor would he murder innocent policemen even if his own life had been threatened. He would have run or he would have allowed himself to be taken. Something else was happening. Something dark and ominous.

Chernov had been watching him. "It is essential that we not be taken. Not yet."

Mahoney heard the words but they didn't immediately penetrate. He was thinking about his son who was now presumably running for his life. How had they come this far in such a short time? How much had Heiser told them, if indeed they had gone to see him? And what was the list that the snowmobile driver had talked about?

"Could your niece know about this place?" he asked.

Chernov thought about it for a moment. He shrugged. "It's possible, Wallace. Anything is possible, of course. There are old records. Perhaps—"

"What old records?"

"Each meeting we had with you or the British or the French was recorded in somebody's daybook. It's possible they thought you and I might have chosen a place such as this to meet now. They were here in West Berlin. What did Heiser know?"

"He set up the meeting between us during the airlift. God only knows what he knew or guessed."

Chernov looked back at the television. "It will not be long now. I promise you."

"The snowmobile driver didn't check here by chance," Mahoney said. "He told me that he had a list of our meeting places. Your niece must have given it to him."

The color left Chernov's face. "Why didn't you tell me this?" he demanded.

"For the same reason you have not been truthful with me."

Chernov was thinking furiously; it was obvious from the expression on his face. "It doesn't change anything. He came here and checked the hotel, and he hasn't reported in yet."

"They'll have West Berlin sealed. They'll be watching all the exits."

"Yes," Chernov said. "Getting away will be difficult at best. But we will manage, you and I, because we must."

In the meantime, Mahoney thought, his son was in mortal danger. He had no doubt that if John was with Tonia Trusov, and they were cornered, she would not hesitate to open fire. Where were they at this moment? What were they doing? How were they managing? And why wasn't Carlisle, the Agency, helping him . . . ? That thought stuck, and Mahoney turned it over and looked at it from another angle. Why *hadn't* the Agency done something? John had presumably been assigned to find his father. There should have been some backup. Someone here from Berlin station should have been on it. Even if John had murdered someone, the BND would have cooperated once they were made to understand what was at stake. No, something was definitely wrong. And now John had joined forces with a KGB assassin. It didn't make sense, and yet he had a terrible feeling of foreboding that he knew what it was, that he had known all along. What had stopped him? His guilt? All these years, had it been his pride and then his guilt that had blinded him?

Mahoney turned his back on Chernov and walked quickly to the door. He opened it and looked out into the deserted corridor. The hotel was quiet. Too quiet? he wondered.

"What is it?" Chernov asked sharply.

"We're going to have to leave immediately."

"Not yet."

"Yes, as soon as possible," Mahoney said, looking back at Chernov. "Get your things together. I'll check with the desk to see how soon the roads will be open. Short of that, we'll use the snowmobile."

Chernov struggled to his feet. "Not yet," he croaked. "We've come too far to give it up now. I won't allow it."

"You're right, Yuri. We have come too far," Mahoney said. He slipped out into the corridor and hurried toward the stairs, not seeing that Chernov had been desperately fumbling for his gun.

Downstairs the lobby was also deserted, although a fire burned cheerily in the big hearth. At the registration desk he stopped a moment to listen. The wind had risen a little, he could hear it in the flue, but there were no other sounds. It was as if the hotel had been evacuated. He and Chernov were the only ones left. He was getting spooked.

Schemmerhorn suddenly appeared in the doorway from the office, smiling when he saw Mahoney. "Ah, Herr Greenleaf, will you and Herr Nostrand be having dinner this evening? We missed you at lunch."

"Where is everybody? This place is like a morgue."

"Gone, mostly. Last night and early this morning before the road became impassable. Of course the Shumanns are still in residence." He smiled again. "Is there anything we can do for you?"

"Yes," Mahoney said. "Please be so kind as to prepare our bills. Herr Nostrand and I will be leaving this afternoon."

"I'm afraid that is impossible, mein Herr. At least for the moment the road out remains impassable because of the storm."

"No one can get out?"

"No, sir, nor in. But rest assured we are well supplied. By tomorrow the storm will have stopped and the plows will be able to get through. Out here in the countryside we are always the last to be rescued."

"I see," Mahoney said. He started to turn away, but then changed his mind. "Are the telephones working?"

"For the moment," Schemmerhorn said. He glanced toward the front windows. "But if that keeps up, one can never tell. Do you wish to place a call?"

Mahoney had considered it. "No," he said. "Perhaps later this afternoon."

"Very good. Will you be having dinner with us?"

"I don't know yet. I'll have a word with Mr. Nostrand."

"Yes, sir."

Back upstairs Mahoney hesitated a moment at Chernov's room and put his ear to the door. He could hear the television playing softly, but nothing else. Allmann's man had come by snowmobile. The storm wouldn't stop someone determined. But unless Chernov had done something to the machine, rendering it inoperative, they had a chance of getting away from here. Just a chance in this weather. John would have to be drawn out of the chase. At this point there was only one way Mahoney could think to do it. His son had come looking for him; it was time now to make certain that he was successful.

He went to his room to get his overcoat, hat, and gloves. It was going to be a very long, cold ride out to the highway. Beyond that it was difficult to plan. But he knew what he would have to do. God help him, he hoped that he would have the strength for it, and for what would almost certainly happen in the coming days and weeks.

At the window he looked out at the deepening gloom of the late afternoon and thought about his son. Finally he would extricate his son from the Agency. Finally he was going to be able to give his son's life back to him. It was the only gift Mahoney had left to give after an entire lifetime.

How the madness had seemed to encompass Mahoney's world when he'd faced Robert McBundy in that Connecticut safe house. He'd felt like no Lazarus being raised from the dead; instead a sense of doom had come over him when he was made to understand that there was a network mole within the CIA, and that it was McBundy who wanted him unmasked. McBundy his friend, his savior in a measure, his Jesus Christ raising him from the dead, his chief suspect until this point was now his king sending him off to do battle. Against whom? Against what? Against a world gone insane? Against a group of men who wanted to control the world according to their own bible?

They were odd, terrible times, the months that followed. Before he'd left Israel for the last time he'd written everything down that Henrys had told him and had mailed the entire package to John. He'd named McBundy as the likely penetration agent, and he'd named Darrel Switt, another friend from the Moscow days, as someone to trust.

But Switt was gone. He had left Washington without a trace after Mahoney's sham funeral.

"And my son?" Mahoney asked.

"He thinks you're dead," McBundy said. "He saw your body in the coffin. There was no other way."

"Where did he go?"

"Your cabin," McBundy had said.

"Switt is the network man," Mahoney said. "My God, now that he thinks I'm dead, he'll go after John."

He remembered with a terrible clarity standing at the end of the driveway that led back to his cabin, staring at the burned-out remains of his home. How to endure that? How to live beyond that? Elizabeth and the babies had been inside when it had exploded and burned. Their bodies had been positively identified. But John was missing. John had run. God in heaven, he had left his wife and children, and he had fled. *Tell Switt to be careful with this information,* Mahoney had written to his son. But it should not have turned out this way. He had never envisioned this. There should have been no danger for John. Switt was one man to be trusted. John had turned over the notes to Switt just after the funeral and had come back here. To close down the cabin. To remember his father. To remember the better times.

Tell Switt that this information is very dangerous. Several people have already died because of it. Now John was on the run. Frightened. Alone. There was no telling what he'd do, or where he'd go in his present state of mind. The notes had gone from Mahoney to John. From John to Switt. And then presumably to Henrys who had given the order: Kill him. The madness was just beginning.

Even now Mahoney found it difficult to put those times into any sort of real perspective. John had read the notes, he knew about the network, he knew about Henrys, and he knew that McBundy was suspect. He'd also known the names of the others in the network—in the German BND, the Italian SISM, the French SDECE—so he had gone to Europe gunning for them. Against all odds John had succeeded. He had the natural instinct. The ability, like his father, to see beyond the obvious, to search for and understand the anomalies.

Across Europe he had fled, leaving in his wake a trail of death and destruction. Vengeance will be mine, the Lord said. But no one had counted on John's strength of will. And in the end with McBundy revealed as the traitor after all, dying on a Geneva street corner, Henrys dead, the network smashed, Mahoney had wondered why. But he'd never got a satisfactory answer until now. Chernov. It had been Chernov all along. From the very beginning he had been the mastermind. But then, as all along, he had been out of reach. Always just beyond the horizon. Behind the scenes, hidden yet apparent by the stamp of his hand.

* * *

The rebuilt Minnesota cabin had become Mahoney's elephant graveyard where he was surrounded with the bones of death and destruction. He went back to spend his final days. A failure, then, in the end. The one thing he'd so wanted to accomplish in his life, the downfall of Yuri Chernov, was finally denied him. The only people he'd held dear to him were dead . . . all except for his son, his only surviving genetic link with any kind of a future. It was especially difficult now to think of those most recent times. To think how his days had begun to have a numbing sameness to them. In the summer he was able to fish on the lake, but even that activity gave him no real pleasure because he was constantly reminded of Uncle Fred, and the summers they'd had together. The evenings, with the television and his bourbon and his hand-rolled Cuban cigars a friend from State supplied him, were even worse. Marge's ghost sat next to him in her chair, knitting him another sweater. From time to time he would cock an ear because he thought she'd said something to him. But she never repeated herself, so he had to be content with merely the possibility that he'd heard something. In the night when the cold winter winds howled around the eaves, he'd wanted to reach out for her comforting warmth, but she wasn't there, even in his imagination unless on some rare night when he had been sleeping particularly soundly something would wake him up. For just a disorienting moment or two it was years earlier, and she *was* there beside him, lending him not only her warmth, but her strength which had always been her inner peace, for Marge had been a woman supremely calm. John had visited the rebuilt cabin only once and had left after a couple of hours, terribly upset. It had been a mistake, his coming, Mahoney realized, and a few months later he had gone out to California to visit. They'd taken a couple of days drive out to Missoula to visit the graves, and then had parted. John disappeared after that. For a couple of months there had been no answer at his Los Angeles home, and his supervisor at Monsanto Chemical had said he'd taken an indefinite leave of absence. To forget, or perhaps to find himself. Mahoney had waited patiently for his son's return because he knew that both quests were impossible and that sooner or later John would realize it and get on with his life.

The call came at four-thirty in the morning from Sylvan Bindrich, who at that time was acting director of Central Intelligence. The former DCI had been killed in a plane crash and Bindrich had been given the top spot until the president could appoint a new man.

"Something has come up, Wallace. Something I'm going to need your help with."

Something had always come up. "Leave me alone, Mr. Director. I don't want to hear whatever little dirty problems you have on your hands this time."

But of course in the end he had packed a bag and taken the morning flight to Washington. Somebody had tampered with the records in Archives concerning the last assignment Mahoney had worked on. The entire agency was in an uproar. McBundy and Switt were both dead. What else was happening? They wanted Mahoney's memory, which he was happy to give. There had been a funeral for the DCI and afterward Mahoney had had lunch with Stan Kopinski. "Bindrich needs me to hold his hand," Mahoney had said.

"Can't say as I blame him," Kopinski had said. He had aged badly over the past couple of years. He looked wan and tired. He had lost a lot of weight and the skin hung slack on his thin neck and birdlike face. "How about your son?" he'd asked offhandedly. "I hear he's doing well these days."

"What?" Mahoney asked, his heart skipping a beat.

"John," Kopinski said. "He's finished with his training. Eric was telling me about it. Doing well from what I heard. Didn't you know?"

John had been out of touch for a couple of months. It was about the length of the Agency's primary training course. Hand-to-hand combat, psychological stress management, equipment, weapons, techniques. A potpourri of tradecraft. The school served to pump the proper esprit de corps into the new recruits. Sometimes the spirit actually lasted a month or so, but it always faded in the end. Reading foreign newspapers and making friends with foreign government officials and their families was generally not the work the new people had envisioned. But now and then something would come up, something dangerous. Most of the new ones had no idea what was happening to them; the Farm hadn't really prepared them. If they were lucky they survived. After a few field assignments, if their luck held, they became pros. Most did not make it that far. It was not the life Mahoney wanted for his son. Not after all they had lost.

"Fire him," Mahoney had said, storming into Bindrich's office.

"It's not that easy," Bindrich said.

"Then I'll do it for you."

Bindrich said nothing. He was looking out the windows. There was something about the set of his shoulders just then, one lower than the other, that was bothersome.

"You've already sent him off," Mahoney said. "He's out there already, isn't he. You've got him listed as an expendable."

Bindrich sighed deeply. "We couldn't keep him. I don't know all the details, Wallace. I swear to you. But your son wants this more than anything else. He says it. His profiles say it. His physical testing is all positive. He's at the top of the scale in almost every category. The psychologists say he has one of the strongest instincts for survival that they've ever seen."

Just the smallest bit of pride crept into Mahoney's breast, and it frightened him. "No!" he said, more as a cry of anguish than a command, more a sense of self-denial than the rejection of the idea.

It was Brussels that final season. British General Sir Robert Isley Marshall, chairman of NATO's Nuclear Defense Affairs Committee, had apparently gone walkabout with a briefcase filled with top secrets. NATO's new contingency war plan, should Soviet tanks roll across the East-West border, was to turn both Germanys into a nuclear wasteland, containing the Soviet's forces far to the east. Had the British general been snatched, or had he defected? The secret services from every NATO nation had sent agents to Brussels to find him and the explosive documents. Bindrich had sent John, and Mahoney had followed after his son.

"You're out, John," he told him. "You'll return to Washington in the morning. Talk to Bindrich. This is all his doing. But I'm taking over the assignment."

"And if I don't go?"

"I'll have you declared persona non grata in Belgium. And believe me, son, I can have it done."

John hadn't quit the field, of course. He had simply sidestepped for a moment, allowing his father to hunt alone. And what a hunt it was. Sir Robert had, from his earliest school days, been a lover of Germany and things German. He'd studied in Germany, had played in Munich, and before the war had even known Hitler. He had been a man obsessed with the notion that the divided Germany would have to be put back together if there was ever to be any stability in Europe. He was a revanchist in the simplest of terms, and NATO's contingency plans for the two Germanys in case a war developed had finally unhinged him.

All roads led to East Germany that year. Had Mahoney been thinking straight he would have realized that Chernov was involved somehow. But he wasn't thinking straight. He was on his own final quest. A diversion toward the end of his life. A simple, clean assignment in which the choices were clear, in which his conscience would be clean no matter the outcome. Bonn was the capital of the new West Germany, and Mahoney reasoned correctly that Karl-Marx-Stadt would be his mecca in the East. Bonn, the city created by the Allies to be the capital of a democratic Germany, was the counterpoint to Karl-Marx-Stadt, no less a creation of the Soviets as the capital of the worker.

It was a discovery of intuition. Sir Robert had gone to the East to speak with East German leaders and businessmen, and Mahoney had simply outthought the man in a flash of characteristic brilliance. It was his stock in trade. He crossed the border in Berlin and drove directly down to Karl-Marx-Stadt where he was captured by Sir Robert's people. He would never have gotten out alive except for John who had followed him across the border and shot Sir Robert to death. Together they had run back to the border, expecting at any moment to be stopped, but it never happened. At the frontier crossing itself they were allowed to cross. The Soviets had been no more interested in a unified Germany than NATO had. Sir Robert had been stopped and NATO's strike plans had been secured, though in time they would be rendered obsolete, and much of what had happened had actually been for nothing. But all through that final assignment Mahoney had had the feeling that he was being manipulated. Which of course he had. He'd been nothing more than Chernov's tool. The Russians wanted Sir Robert's dangerous plan stopped. Chernov was the man for the job. He had the contacts. He had the knowledge.

And someone had been working for him in the Agency. Had been all along. It was this final thought that Mahoney turned over in his mind now, as he readied to leave the hotel. It explained everything. All these years the simple fact had been staring him in the face, but he had not been able to see it for his own guilt. He had been used, but not in the sense he had been led to believe. One name kept popping up all through the last four decades. The madness, he decided, was finally coming to an end.

A door slammed somewhere. Mahoney looked up, listening for footsteps in the corridor. A moment later someone was pounding at his door. It was Chernov.

"It's happened!" Chernov was shouting.

Mahoney opened the door. Chernov stood there out of breath, his face flushed.

"It's finally happened," Chernov repeated. "Come and see, Wallace. It's on the television. Now you will have to believe me."

At eleven in the morning the CIA was on full emergency footing, but Carlisle waded through his work as if he didn't have a care in the world. Vindication was almost his. John Mahoney would not be able to stay at large for very long now, and when he was captured with his Russian girl friend it would come out that he had been a spy from the beginning. Like father, like son, he thought. It was even possible—Christ, likely—that Chernov had been their control officer. There wasn't a hope in hell they would escape to the East. All exits out of West Berlin had been sealed tighter than a gnat's ass, as he had told Hayes barely an hour ago.

Hayes had actually threatened him. His career was as good as finished. He was good, but no one was indispensable. Not in this business, not in any business.

Chernov's message to Wallace Mahoney and the old fool's subsequent disappearance were dead giveaways. All of it was some elaborate plot on their part to get away scot-free. Somehow they must have known or suspected that the game was over. That someone was on to them, so their control officer had simply pulled the plug on them.

Well, Carlisle thought smugly, their little plan had backfired on them. Now they were all stuck in West Berlin. There would be no escape for them this time. No escape.

The phone rang. He picked up the receiver. "Yes?"

"It's Sam Duff, Mr. Carlisle," his secretary said. "He would like a word with you. He says it's urgent." Her voice sounded odd. Strained.

"Send him in," Carlisle said.

"Yes, sir."

Duff was chief of the civilian security force that guarded the CIA's headquarters building and grounds. He was a big, gruff man who had previously been number two man on the presidential security staff. He filled the doorway, a very stern expression on his face, his eyes hooded.

"What's up, Sam?" Carlisle asked. "Have we got a problem?"

"Yes, sir," Duff said. "We certainly do. I think you'd better come have a looksee."

Carlisle got to his feet, suddenly noticing that Duff had pushed the left side of his suit jacket back and hooked it behind his holster. He came around the desk. "What is it?"

"Better if you see for yourself, sir," Duff said.

Carlisle followed him through the outer office and into the third-floor corridor. Just down the hall several people had gathered in front of the men's room. Two of Duff's men were keeping them back.

"What the hell is going on here?" Carlisle asked, raising his voice. "Get back to your desks," he ordered.

Everyone seemed shook up. They moved aside as Carlisle went into the rest room just behind the big security chief. Duff stepped aside, and Carlisle stopped dead in his tracks.

Another of Duff's security people stood at one of the toilet stalls. He was holding open the door. Alex Hayes, his trousers down around his ankles, was slumped over to his left, his body wedged between the toilet and the metal partition. He had been shot in the forehead just above the bridge of his nose, apparently while he was sitting on the toilet. His eyes were open but filled with blood, and his mouth was open as if he had cried out, or had tried to say something. Carlisle's stomach was heaving.

"This happened less than an hour ago, sir," Duff was saying. "His body is still warm. I'd say his killer used a silenced pistol. Probably a large-caliber revolver. We haven't found a discarded shell casing."

Carlisle was trying to make his brain work. Trying to think what was happening here. What it meant. Christ, he had just talked to Hayes an hour ago. Probably minutes before he came in here and was murdered.

"Seal off the building," he said.

"It's already been done, sir," Duff said.

Carlisle looked up. "I don't want anybody in or out of here until we get the Technical Services people out."

"Yes, sir."

"I'm going up to see Mr. Bindrich."

"We tried to call him, sir," Duff said. "His secretary said he stepped out."

Carlisle focused on him. "Stepped out? Out of the building?"

"No, sir, he hasn't left the grounds. Just out of his office. It's why I came to you."

"Right," Carlisle said absently. "Find him, and let me know as soon as you do." He looked again at Hayes's body. Christ, barely one hour ago he had been alive. And now. . . .

The big sign on the hangar read Messerschmit-Bölkow-Blohm, GmbH. The Soviet GRU assassin, Serafim Kochetkov, hesitated at the service door for a moment and looked up into the sky. The ceiling was very low, probably under one hundred meters. But it wouldn't matter; he had no need of height, only speed and the ability to go where a car could not in this snowstorm. He'd rented a car from the Hertz counter and had driven across to the private aviation sector of the big airport. The pilots' lounge was just inside. He glanced over toward the control tower, barely visible in the blowing snow. All flights had been canceled. A fuss would be made, but no one would be coming after them. Not immediately. And by the time someone did get around to taking action, his job would be finished and he would be gone.

He pulled open the door and stepped inside the big hangar. Two Augusta-Bell 206A helicopters were parked beside each other across the hangar, their rotors drooping. Closing the door behind him, he stopped to listen. From somewhere in the back he could just make out the sound of music. Probably a radio, he thought, starting across.

In a small measure he felt bad about this assignment. Not because he was going to have to kill—that was all he lived for—but because he had failed so miserably so far. Without the information Colonel Raina had supplied him, he would have failed completely. Major Trusov and the American had simply disappeared after the explosion in the parking ramp. In this weather they could have been anywhere. It would have taken an army to find them. Now, however, he wouldn't fail. He couldn't fail.

At the door to the pilots' lounge at the rear of the big hangar he stopped again to listen. From within he could hear the sounds of music, but nothing else. No movement, no conversation. It was possible that no one was here. He looked back at the helicopters. If the hangar had been deserted, he reasoned, it would have been locked. Someone was here.

He put his hand in his coat pocket and opened the door, a big smile on his face. Two men were seated at a small table in the middle of the room. They were drinking coffee. One of them was reading a magazine, while the other played solitaire. They looked up when Kochetkov came in.

"You guys the pilots?" he asked.

"How the hell did you get in here?" the one with the magazine asked.

"I was told I could find a pilot for one of the 206s out there," Kochetkov said apologetically.

"We're both pilots," the man with the cards said. "Who sent you over here? Nothing is flying in this weather."

Kochetkov took out his gun. It was an Austrian-made 9mm Glock-17 automatic with a state-of-the-art Kevlar silencer. He fired two shots, both of them catching the card-playing pilot in the chest, blowing out half his spine and shoving him violently backward away from the table. He switched his aim to the other man, who barely had time to react. His mouth was open, spittle drooling down his chin.

"You will fly me to Grunewald," Kochetkov said calmly. "Now, without hesitation, and I promise that you will come to no harm."

The pilot was stammering, barely able to control himself. He got up slowly and lurched drunkenly to the left, almost tripping over his own feet.

"Control yourself, man!" Kochetkov said sharply. He hated weakness of any kind.

"We can't fly in this weather . . ."

"Then you will die here like your companion," Kochetkov snarled. The pilot nearly jumped out of his skin.

"Yes, sir," he stammered.

Kochetkov grabbed a flight jacket from the coat tree and tossed it to the pilot. "We'll go now," he said.

They walked out into the hangar to the nearest helicopter. The pilot opened the door, and Kochetkov pushed him aside. He looked at the control panel, and finding the communications radio, ripped the microphone and headset from its jack and tossed it away.

"How do you open the hangar doors?" he asked.

"A button on the left side of the—"

"Start the machine. I'll get the doors," Kochetkov ordered, and he stalked off across the hangar confident that the pilot would do exactly as he was told. He had seen it in the man's eyes. He would offer no resistance. His will had been completely broken.

As the hangar doors began to rumble open, the helicopter engines began to whine to life. By the time Kochetkov got back to the machine and climbed in on the passenger side, the rotors were already coming up into the green.

The pilot had taken out a chart of the area of West Berlin. Kochetkov took it from him, studied the chart for a moment or two, then pointed to the Grunewald Hotel.

"There," he shouted over the noise of the engines. "In the back somewhere, or down by the lake, I don't care. As long as you get me within a kilometer of the main building."

The pilot was nodding.

"Do you know the area?"

"Yes, sir," the pilot said. "Yes, sir."

"Then take me there—now!" Kochetkov shouted, securing his seatbelt.

The pilot hesitated for a moment. The wind wasn't blowing too strongly, but the apron directly in front of the hangar was choked with snow. "I'll have to lift off in here," he shouted to Kochetkov. "Otherwise we'll get stuck."

"Do it. I am tired of waiting," Kochetkov said, pointing his gun at the man.

The helicopter lifted shakily off the hangar floor, drifted a few feet to the right, and then steadied. The pilot took a deep breath, let it out slowly, and then they were heading toward the open doors. The instant they cleared the doorway the machine slewed violently to the right, the tail just missing the building before the pilot regained control and then they were climbing up over the apron, someone running from the main office building fifty meters away.

"Keep low," Kochetkov said.

"I don't have any other choice," the pilot mumbled, and they peeled off toward the west, the airport lost behind them in the snow within ninety seconds.

19

An American soap opera dubbed in German was playing on the television in Chernov's room. Mahoney, his overcoat on, stood with his back to the door watching. It came to him that he had done this sort of thing often in his career: waiting, watching for something to happen. Some signal to arms, some message or significant bit that would suddenly put everything into perspective. He'd also stood like this a thousand years ago in a hospital room in Duluth. It was winter then, too, and he was waiting for Marge to die. It was inevitable. He'd had no control over it and he felt the same sort of helplessness then as he did now, though the comparison, even as he made it in his own mind, was not a good one. With Marge he had lost the only person who ever meant anything to him in his life. With Chernov he would be losing a hated enemy. One was painful, this would be sweet, though not as sweet as he'd always imagined.

Chernov angrily switched channels, this one showing an opera that Mahoney didn't immediately recognize. He was searching for something, and he was impatient.

"The fools," Chernov snapped.

"It's time we left," Mahoney said. "Get your coat."

Chernov switched channels again, this one showing another soap opera. Germans loved American television, the more melodramatic the better.

"Now," Mahoney said. "Before it is too late for us."

Chernov pulled a pistol out of his pocket and turned on Mahoney. "Not yet!" he cried. "I didn't come all this way for nothing! They'll broadcast it again. The fools. They must!"

"What is it?" Mahoney asked.

Chernov was waving the gun around like a madman. He was finally losing control. But Mahoney could also see that the man was frightened. It was unsettling now after everything that had happened to them.

"Just wait!" Chernov shouted. "You'll see!"

The television beeped five times, and the soap opera was replaced by a grim-faced news reader seated at a desk, a map of the Soviet Union behind him.

"At approximately one-fifteen, Central European Standard Time, an aboveground nuclear explosion estimated to be as large as one million kilotons of TNT occurred in a remote region of the Soviet Union south of the city of Semipalatinsk in the Republic of Kazakh."

Mahoney's breath caught in his throat. What in God's name were they trying to do? It was insanity. No one had tested nuclear explosives aboveground for years. This was sure to provoke a harsh reaction not only from the United States but from the Chinese as well.

The television camera had focused on the map where a large X marked the site of the explosion, on which was overlaid a series of weather map symbols. The news reader was continuing: "Strong northwesterly winds are expected to carry a large amount of fallout over the People's Republic of China within the next twenty-four to thirty-six hours. Meanwhile, reaction from Washington and Beijing was swift and strong."

"This is it," Chernov said, lowering his pistol. "And now you must believe me. You have no other choice." He sank down in his chair, his eyes glued to the television screen. "The fools," he murmured. "The utter fools."

Mahoney came the rest of the way into the room and stood between Chernov and the television set. "Is this what you came out to tell me?"

Chernov looked up tiredly. "They've been watching the weather patterns over the past year, waiting for just the right moment. A storm. Strong northwest winds so that the fallout would be blown down over Tibet and Mongolia. The jet stream will carry it even farther. And it was a dirty bomb. A low-level firing so that it would pick up a lot of debris."

"Why? What does your government hope to accomplish?"

"A response from the Chinese," Chernov said. "What else, Wallace? There will be a series of border incidents over the next couple of days that will escalate into a full-fledged war. But contained to the region. No missiles will fly to the West. Europe is safe. The United States is safe. It's not their fight." Chernov seemed to sink lower in the chair. "Our problem has always been the great yellow horde. Now the solution is at hand."

"This could touch off an all-out nuclear war . . ."

"Carl Sagan was wrong, you know," Chernov interrupted.

340

"Our scientists are convinced that the notion of a nuclear winter is myth. Even in an all-out exchange of nuclear weapons, the worst that would happen is a couple of years of nuclear autumn. Survivable, even if the United States should decide to involve itself, which no one believes will happen. But the worst-case scenario is survivable, Wallace. Do you know what this means?"

It was the ultimate madness. Mahoney was at a loss for words. There was nothing to be said.

"You would never have believed me. You had to see this first," Chernov said.

Mahoney looked at him. "This is what you came out to tell me?"

"Yes."

"What if I don't believe you? What if my government won't accept it? You have been a master of the game, Yuri."

"I have brought you something else as well, Wallace. Something almost as important. Especially to you, and to the Agency. Something you have been waiting to know for a very long time. A very long time indeed."

"You?" Mahoney asked, a bright fire suddenly burning in his gut. "Are you defecting? Is that it? Are you coming back with me?"

"No," Chernov said, smiling. "Not that. Something even more important."

"You can't return to Moscow. Not now. Not after this."

Chernov shrugged. The gun was on his lap; he looked down at it. "No, I don't expect to be going home." He looked up. "They know why I came out. They know what I am telling you. You'll have to get this information back to Washington immediately. Before they stop you. Before my . . . Tonia arrives here. You can take the snowmobile."

"They'll never believe me without you."

"Yes, they will, when you tell them what else I brought out with me."

"What?"

An infinite sadness seemed to come over Chernov, and his size diminished as his shoulders sagged. "I didn't kill your wife, Wallace. She died a natural death."

Mahoney's gut tightened. "It's a little late to lie."

"No, it is no lie. But the clues were put there for you to believe I had killed her."

"By whom? Why?"

341

"To break your will, and eventually to be used as a control on your son. And it worked."

"By whom?" Mahoney asked, barely at the edge of his control. He wanted desperately to lash out at someone, at something.

Chernov looked away. "For a long time you were suspected of being a traitor. Did you know that? My agent."

"It was Bob McBundy."

"He was one of them. But not the best. Certainly not the best. Neither him nor Darrel Switt."

"There were others?"

"Just one. The best. My triumph."

"Who—" Mahoney started to say, when he thought he heard the sounds of a helicopter outside. He turned and went to the window. The storm had intensified, snow falling much more heavily now, and the wind had risen. Again he thought he heard the chop of a helicopter's rotors, but he could see nothing and the sounds were gone as quickly as they had come.

"Who?" he asked again, turning back to Chernov.

"First I want your word that you will help stop this insanity, Wallace."

"You have it," Mahoney said, feeling that once again he had been drawn into Chernov's web.

They'd seen a few lights on in the hotel as they'd flown past, but now there was nothing but blowing snow and the vague outlines of the forest above them on the hill. They were fifty meters from the edge of the lake and less than a hundred meters from the access road.

"Shut it down," Kochetkov ordered.

The pilot was shaking so badly now that they were down, he could barely make his hands work as he began flipping switches. The engines died and the rotors began to slow immediately. The pilot had been good, but the flight had been terrible in this weather. Twice they had nearly crashed into trees, and west of Schöneberg they'd missed power lines by inches.

"Am I to wait, sir?" the pilot asked, his voice cracking.

"No," Kochetkov said, smiling. He nodded toward the road. "Go ahead and get out of here. You should be able to catch a ride up on the highway."

The pilot undid his seat belt, popped the door open, the wind and snow filling the interior of the helicopter, and scrambled out.

"Oh, pilot?" Kochetkov said.

The pilot turned back.

"You did a good job."

"Ah, yes, sir, thank you—" the pilot started to say, when Kochetkov fired once, the shot catching the man high in the chest, just above his sternum, shoving him back into a snowdrift.

Kochetkov took his time unbuckling his belt and climbing out into the wind. He glanced up toward the hotel, then walked around to the other side of the helicopter. The pilot was still alive, thrashing in the snow. He was bleeding heavily. He looked up, his eyes wide, and he began to babble incoherently.

"A very good job," Kochetkov said. "Thanks." He raised his pistol and fired one shot, taking the side of the pilot's head off. The thrashing stopped.

It was unwise in this business to take unnecessary chances, Kochetkov thought, pocketing his gun and turning back to the helicopter. He climbed up on the side, lifting himself up by the open door until he could reach the engine cowling and the big air intake scoop. He studied it for a moment, then climbed down and went to the pilot's body. He stripped off the dead man's flight jacket, and once again climbing up on the side of machine, stuffed the jacket into the air intake scoop. Climbing down he stepped back and studied the machine. The obstruction was nearly invisible from the ground.

He started up the hill wondering if anyone from the hotel had heard the helicopter. It wouldn't matter if they did, he thought. Not a bit. At the edge of the road he stopped long enough to remove the clip from his automatic and reload the four bullets he had already used. The Glock-17 held eighteen rounds. But you could never be too careful in this business, he thought again, smiling to himself.

The helicopter was just visible behind him as he hurried across the drift-covered road and worked his way through the woods toward the rear of the hotel. The snow at times was nearly waist deep and it took him nearly twenty minutes to make the quarter mile to where the trees gave way to a broad clearing slightly below his position. He waited for a full minute. Nothing moved below except for the wind-driven snow. A couple of cars parked in the front were half buried. They'd been there at least twenty-four hours, he figured. No one had come or gone today, which meant he'd made it in time. He had certainly beat Major Trusov and the American, and unless the CIA agent Jack Byrd had come on foot from the highway, he'd beat him as well.

Gun in hand, and moving fast, Kochetkov emerged from the woods and raced down into the clearing. When he reached the rear entrance to the hotel he stopped for a moment. Nothing moved yet. No alarms had been raised. They would be expecting him, Chernov and Mahoney, or someone like him. And they were very good, the general had told him. "Watch out for those two. Treat them with respect or you'll get a bullet in your brain for your carelessness."

He opened the door cautiously and looked inside. Straight ahead a broad, carpeted corridor opened into the lobby. He could see the fireplace, and suddenly smell the woodsmoke. Directly to his right was the dining room down two steps. No one was there.

Inside, he closed the door softly and moving silently on the balls of his feet made his way down the corridor to the edge of the broad staircase. He peered up into the gloom. Nothing moved in the corridor above. Keeping the gun out of sight at his side, he smiled broadly and stepped out into the lobby, his eyes sweeping automatically from left to right. A buxom young woman, her complexion flushed, stood in the doorway of what appeared to be the hotel's bar. No one was in the vestibule, nor was anyone seated around the fireplace. A large man dressed in a green parka stood at the registration desk speaking with a young man who evidently was the clerk.

"Oh," the buxom woman cried, spotting Kochetkov.

She was no immediate threat, so he ignored her for the moment. The man in the green parka was turning around, reaching inside his coat as Kochetkov moved swiftly to the left, raising his gun as he did, and firing three shots in rapid succession. The first caught Jack Byrd high in the right shoulder, shoving him up against the registration desk. The second went high and wide, hitting Schemmerhorn in the neck, completely destroying his throat. The third hit Byrd in the left thigh and he went down hard.

Kochetkov spun on his heel and shot the bartender in the forehead, taking off the back of her skull and driving her into the bar.

He turned back as Byrd was raising his gun in his left hand, and he fired again, the silencer reducing the noise to a dull slap, the bullet hitting the CIA agent in the chest, destroying his heart. He was flung backward by the force of the impact, his head slamming against the registration counter.

Steam rose from the wounds in the pilot's body. John bent over him to check his pulse, knowing even before he did that it was no use. The man was obviously dead. But where the hell was his

344

jacket? Tonia had gone to the helicopter and she was studying the control panel.

"He's dead," John said, straightening up.

Tonia glanced up toward the hotel. They both saw the footprints in the snow at the same time. The tracks were fresh. The wind hadn't had a chance to fill them in.

"It's the one from the Europäischer Hof and the parking ramp," John said, yanking out his gun and starting up the hill in a dead run, slipping and nearly falling.

They'd walked nearly three miles from the highway where the cabby, unable to go any farther, had dropped them off. The lack of rest was telling on John. At the top of the hill he had to stop to catch his breath. His legs felt like rubber. Tonia wasn't in much better condition.

The tracks in the snow led across the road and through the woods.

"That's the long way around," Tonia said. "He probably approached the hotel from the rear."

"Then we'll go straight in," John said, pushing through the snow onto the road itself, and starting directly toward the hotel. "We still might have a chance. He doesn't have that much of a head start."

"We should have heard the helicopter," Tonia said, catching up.

"Not in this weather," John said. "He probably came down from Tempelhof. The wind was blowing away from us."

"That means they heard it in the hotel."

John had figured the same thing. His father and Chernov would not be taken so easily. But they were old men, and the GRU assassin, from what he had seen so far, was very good. The question was how he had decided to come here. Someone had to be feeding him information. With a sick feeling John knew who it was, and why. None of this was going to work out. Yet he was driven to continue as he had been driving these past five years. Again he could hear the explosion in his mind, he could feel the pressure wave shoving him off the dock, and he could see the flames and sparks rising into the night sky. "*Elizabeth!*" he screamed. But he was too late. The cabin had collapsed inward on itself, trapping his wife and children, with no way for him to get to them. They were dead. Gone from him, and he had run with a vengeance. As he had been running ever since.

A line of trees angled down the hill where the road curved away from the lake and opened up into a clearing in which the hotel stood. John and Tonia stopped just at the curve. Smoke came from one of the chimneys, but only a few lights shone from the windows. Two cars, partially covered by drifts, were parked in front. From here nothing seemed out of the ordinary. The only sound was the wind sighing in the trees above them. They could have been somewhere in a deep wilderness a thousand miles from civilization, and not just a few miles from the center of West Berlin.

"He could be waiting for us," Tonia said.

"Probably," John replied, not taking his eyes off the hotel. "We'll split up. You take the back, I'll go in the front way."

"What's going to happen if they're still alive?"

John turned to her. "You take your uncle and I'll take my father."

She studied his face for a few seconds. It was clear that she wanted to say something to him, but she held off. She nodded. "I'll take the helicopter out. We can be across the border in a couple of minutes."

"And after that?"

She shrugged. "We'll both have problems, you and I. Nothing new."

He looked again at the hotel, then nodded. "Let's do it, then."

They sprinted away from the trees, expecting at any moment for shots to be fired from the hotel. But nothing happened. As soon as they reached the parked cars, Tonia cut right and raced around to the rear of the hotel. John waited until she was out of sight, then hurried up under the front entrance overhang and mounted the two stairs, flattening himself against the wall beside the main door. He flicked the Beretta's safety off, took a deep breath, then yanked open the door and leaped inside, rolling immediately left as soon as he had cleared the vestibule.

Someone fired from above on the stairs, the silenced shot ricocheting off the parquet floor a few inches behind John who dived behind the massive free-standing fireplace. He popped up immediately and fired two shots toward the head of the stairs, then ducked back down, three silenced shots smacking into the metal exhaust hood and chimney above the hearth.

Tonia came racing up the corridor from the back door. John motioned frantically for her to stop. She spotted him at the last possible moment and skidded to a halt. He pointed up toward the head of the stairs. She nodded her understanding.

The hotel was silent except for the crackling of the fire and the wind in the flue. To the right a big woman lay on her back in a pool of blood just within the bar. To the left the one with the green parka from the Tiergarten lay up against the registration counter, his head at an odd angle, his eyes open. There was a lot of blood splashed against the wall and message slots behind the counter.

John eased around to the left side of the fireplace and peered around the edge of the hearth. The stairs ended in a corridor on the second floor. The lights were out. He couldn't see a thing in the darkness.

"Father!" he shouted.

Two more silenced shots were fired from above, one whining off the hearth stones, the second ricocheting off the floor as John ducked back the opposite way and snapped off one shot through the open fireplace.

Tonia had moved to the end of the staircase. She suddenly reached up over the banister and fired four shots in rapid succession.

Someone cried out. An instant later two shots from an unsilenced pistol that sounded like a .38 to John came from above, and the same man as before screamed, this time the sound almost inhuman. Two more shots were fired from the opposite side of the corridor and a figure moving fast appeared at the balcony railing just above the registration desk. Before John had a chance to react, a man dressed in a nylon jacket and fur hat leaped over the railing. He hit the counter badly, his left leg breaking with a loud pop, and he flipped over, crashing to the floor, his forehead bouncing off the tile with a sickening crunch, blood splattering everywhere.

John jumped up from behind the fireplace, his pistol at arm's length in both hands, but Kochetkov didn't move. His eyes were open, staring toward his right hand in which he still held his gun. John cautiously approached the body and kicked the gun away; only then did he step back releasing the breath he had been holding.

"John?" his father called from above.

John turned around. "It's okay now, Fa—" he started to say, when he realized that Tonia was pointing her gun at him. "Shit," he said, measuring the distance between them, trying to estimate his chances.

"Don't," she said. "I am an expert shot."

"Now what?"

"Drop your gun," she said.

He hesitated.

"Now," she ordered. "Or I will kill you."

He eased the hammer back on his Beretta and let it fall to the

347

floor. He still had the policeman's gun in his jacket pocket. There was still a chance.

"Uncle?" she called out.

"Here," Chernov called down.

Mahoney appeared at the head of the stairs, his gun in his right hand, and started down. He stopped short when he realized the situation in the lobby, and started to raise his gun. Chernov came out of the gloom behind him, bringing up his gun.

"Put it down, Wallace," he said.

Mahoney started to turn.

"No, Father!" John shouted. "Do as he says."

Mahoney hesitated.

"Don't make me shoot you," Chernov said. "There is still much for you and me to accomplish."

Still Mahoney hesitated. John could see the indecision on his father's face, and he understood what the old man was going through. But there was nothing to be done. None of them would come out of this unscathed. It wasn't possible, and finally after these five terrible years, he wasn't at all sure if he cared any longer. *Ashes to ashes, dust to dust.* The words from the funeral came back to him. Sometimes at night, trying to sleep, he would relive everything that had happened over and over again in a mad spiral of thoughts and impressions and feelings that at times threatened to drive him completely insane. Perhaps he had been waiting for this moment from the very beginning. Perhaps now he would finally find the peace he had been so desperately searching for. Perhaps they both would.

"Do what he says, Father," John called up. "There's nothing left. It's over."

Mahoney sagged. He let the pistol drop from his hand to the carpeted step behind him, then started down, his left hand trailing tiredly on the banister, Chernov moving cautiously directly behind him.

"Are you all right, Uncle?" Tonia asked in Russian.

"What are you doing here, little one?" Chernov replied harshly.

"Stopping you before it's too late." Tonia spat. "There is a helicopter down the hill by the lake. We will use it to go across the border. I'm glad that I'm not too late."

"But you are, Tonia," Chernov said. "I told him everything. He will stop the madness."

"We will kill them both. No one will know."

"I forbid it!" Chernov roared.

Tonia was taken aback by the intensity in his voice. She looked uncertainly from John to him. "We mustn't. They're calling you a traitor."

"Only the military. I have friends. You'll see."

"No," she said.

"There is more happening than you realize, little one. So much more. Put down your weapon and back away. Go to the helicopter. I will join you in a minute."

"No!" she screamed.

Chernov turned slightly and aimed his pistol at his niece. "Leave while you can, little one. Before it is too late, you must trust me."

Her eyes had gone wide.

John casually put his hand in his coat pocket, his fingers curling around the grip of the cop's pistol. But Chernov noticed the movement out of the corner of his eye.

"If you have a gun in your pocket and you mean to pull it out now, I would advise against it," Chernov said.

John froze.

"You must trust me, Tonia," Chernov said to his niece. "Go to the helicopter now."

For a long time she stood there, her gun hand shaking, her lips moving but no sounds coming out.

"We will convince them that what I have done is correct," Chernov said. "Together we will make them understand."

Finally she lowered her pistol and stepped back. Chernov diverted his aim to John. "Now, please remove the weapon from your pocket and drop it to the floor."

John did as he was told. He looked at Tonia but he could read nothing from her expression.

She turned on her heel suddenly and stalked across the lobby. When she was gone, Chernov sagged a little and turned to Mahoney.

"The traitor in your service is Sylvan Bindrich," he said. "I have been his control officer since 1948. His name is my second gift to you."

John rocked back on his heels, the blow almost physical. It was all over now. There wasn't even the slightest chance that any of it would work out. He was almost glad, and yet he was deeply frightened.

"All these years," his father was saying.

"You could never win against me, because I always knew your next move. Sometimes even before you made it."

"Why?"

"You will have to ask Sylvan that. It wasn't money. Ideology? Insanity? I don't know, though there were the superficial answers in the beginning. Habit, perhaps, in the end."

"You both used me against each other."

"At times," Chernov admitted. "We had our quarrels like lovers. What agent and his runner don't? We taught each other lessons, sometimes." Chernov smiled wanly. "But you were the best, Wallace. The very best. Even with the advantage that I had, you very nearly won."

"What have you told him?" John asked, his voice stronger than he felt.

Chernov glanced at him, an odd, almost uncertain expression on his face. "Your father will tell you."

"I want to know now," John insisted, the faintest glimmer of hope at the back of his head. They would pay. He had to make sure the killers were made to pay. No matter what it took. He couldn't give that up.

"Never mind, John," his father said.

"We can't let them escape!" John blurted.

"I'm afraid you don't have much choice in the matter," Chernov said before Mahoney could speak. He motioned with his gun toward the back corridor. "Step aside."

"Goddamnit!" John swore.

Chernov cocked his pistol. "If I must kill you I will. Believe me."

Mahoney took his son's arm and pulled him toward the corridor. "Just go. I'll take care of everything from this end."

"I never killed your wife, Wallace. I swear to you."

Mahoney nodded. "Go."

John allowed himself to be led away, but his brain was seething. There had to be a way out for him. There had to be. Somehow. Flames and sparks were dancing up from a night sky in his head. He could hear his wife and children screaming. All these years he had blocked out that noise from that night. But now he could hear them, screaming, crying for help that he could not give them. Darrel Switt had killed them. Robert McBundy had given the order. The CIA had killed his wife and babies! He had the proof!

Behind him Chernov picked up both guns, pocketed them, then turned and hurried across the lobby and out into the snowstorm. John tried to pull away, his vision blurred, his heart racing, his stomach pounding.

"Let me go!" he shrieked.

350

"John!" Mahoney shouted, his voice barely penetrating the haze.

"Traitor!" John screamed after Chernov. "Traitor!" he screamed again, and he shoved his father aside. The popping and crackling noises in his ears were driving him crazy. The screams were coming louder now.

He cleared the end of the staircase and headed in a dead run around the fireplace. At the last moment he realized that Kochet-kov wasn't dead. The Russian had somehow managed to reach his gun. He was raising it. John tried to sidestep, but he lost his footing on the parquet floor wet with snow that they had tracked in, and he slipped. A tremendous hammerblow slammed into his chest, shoving him even farther off-balance, and he was falling faster and faster, the floor coming up to meet his head, darkness rapidly closing in all around him. "Elizabeth!" he cried the moment before he died.

Mahoney watched his son fall forever, it seemed. Kochetkov slumped over dead, his grip slackening on the gun, his face relaxing into a slight grin at all the carnage he had caused in such an incredibly short time. He had not been shot once. The fall had killed him. For a long time Mahoney stood rooted to his spot, unable to move or even to dredge up the will to try. How long had he known or at least suspected that all was not right with his son? Months? Years? Certainly the last time he had seen him six months ago he'd known something wasn't right. He'd wanted to suggest psychological counseling. The job got to everyone, some sooner than later. He had put it down to fatigue, though in his heart of hearts he had had a feeling that it was more than that. Just as he had often wondered about Bindrich. So, in the end, Mahoney thought, he had been a complete fool: the biggest fool of all, guilty of pride, of ambition, guilty of allowing the feeling of guilt itself to dominate his life. And now he had truly lost everything that mattered to him. His wife, his grandchildren and their mother, and both of his sons. There were no Mahoneys left on this earth. It was the end of a line. Not a dynasty, there had never been that, but there had been a family there for a while. Flawed and not strong, but a family nonetheless.

Finally he walked across the lobby to John's body. He knelt down beside his son and touched his still-warm cheek. It had not been the CIA who had killed Elizabeth and the babies, of course, though Switt had planted the bomb and McBundy had given the order. Nor had it been the KGB's fault. Or the network's. Only

Chernov. He'd been guilty of all this. It had been his hand all these years that had caused so much damage, so much death, so much destruction. Chernov had been mad, but brilliant, and only now near the end of his life had he tried to make amends. Even then he had tried to keep John as his ace in the hole, though even John had probably not suspected that Chernov was Bindrich's control officer as well as his. Who had Chernov planned for John's runner? Tonia Trusov? They would have made a good team. He shuddered.

Chernov had won again. Even in stopping the madness of nuclear war over China, and uncovering his agent in the CIA, he had still won.

Minutes or hours later, Mahoney had no real recollection of the passage of time, he heard the helicopter rise up from the lakeside. He got up slowly and walked outside. The snow was falling hard, but he could hear the sounds of the machine's rotors clearly on the strong wind. Something was wrong. The engines seemed to be choking and sputtering as if they weren't getting enough fuel, or air.

The helicopter appeared out of the snow, moving low and fast, but at an odd angle. He could just make out two figures in the machine before it climbed nose-up a hundred yards away, turned over on its back, and then dipped sharply into the trees on the hill. For a long second the helicopter had simply disappeared from view, but then a tremendous fireball rose from the woods, and the sound of the explosion came to him and he sagged.

It was over. Truly over now. Time to go home.

Farley Carlisle's insides were churning. This was the second dead body he had seen in less than two hours. Sylvan Bindrich, blood trickling from where he had shot himself in the head, sat slumped on the floor at the end of one of the file stacks in the basement archives section. One of Duff's people had found him like that during the building search.

"Why?" someone was asking.

"I don't know," Carlisle mumbled, though he'd asked himself that very question. Remorse over an operation gone bad? He'd been friends with Wallace Mahoney for forty years. Was there a connection? It didn't seem possible. He'd pinned all his hopes. . . .

Someone came running down the corridor. Carlisle turned as one of Hayes's people from Operations skidded around the corner, out of breath.

"Thank God I've found you, sir," he gasped.

"What's happened now?" Carlisle asked, alarmed. What in God's name was coming next?

"It's the director, he wants you in his office immediately. Mr. Mahoney telephoned. He's on the line right now, from West Berlin. Something about the Soviet hydrogen bomb test and the Chinese."

Tom Clancy's

#1 NEW YORK TIMES BESTSELLERS

___ **THE HUNT FOR RED OCTOBER**   0-425-08383-7/$4.95
"The Perfect Yarn."—President Ronald Reagan
"A fine thriller... flawless authenticity, frighteningly
genuine."—*The Wall Street Journal*

___ **RED STORM RISING**   0-425-10107-X/$4.95
"Brilliant...staccato suspense."—*Newsweek*
"Exciting...fast and furious."—*USA Today*

___ **PATRIOT GAMES**   0-425-10972-0/$4.95
"Elegant...A novel that crackles."—*New York Times*
"Marvelously tense...He is a master of the genre he seems to
have created."—*Publishers Weekly*

THE CARDINAL OF THE KREMLIN
(On sale August 1989)
"The best of the Jack Ryan series!"—*New York Times*
"Fast and fascinating!"—*Chicago Tribune*